W9-BXM-758

WILLOWWOOD

Also by Mollie Hardwick

BEAUTY'S DAUGHTER
CHARLIE IS MY DARLING
LOVERS MEETING

WILLOWWOOD

A Novel by
MOLLIE HARDWICK

ST. MARTIN'S PRESS, NEW YORK

Copyright © 1980 by Mollie Hardwick
All rights reserved. For information, write:
St. Martin's Press, Inc. 175 Fifth Ave., New York, N.Y. 10010
Manufactured in the United States of America

Library of Congress Cataloging in Publication Data

Hardwick, Mollie.
  Willowwood.

  I. Title.
PZ4.H266Wi 1980   [PR6058.A6732]   823'.914 80-14637
ISBN 0-312-88207-6

Alas! the bitter banks in Willowwood . . .
D. G. Rossetti

In dreams we'll take the field again,
In dreams the willow wield again,
And see the red ball spinning in the sun –
Ah, memory will play again
Many and many a day again
The game that's done, the game that's never done.
Herbert Farjeon

AUTHOR'S NOTE

My warmest thanks are due to Mr Joe Lister, Secretary of the Yorkshire County Cricket Club, for his invaluable help and information about the Club's early history, and to Mrs Herbert Farjeon for permission to quote from the poem *Willow The King*.

WILLOWWOOD

Young Lilian de Wentworth, after
years as an invalid, is just about
to accept a timid clergyman's proposal, when a virile undergardener
comes into her life.

PRELUDE: SPRING, 1861

The pony galloped joyously across the moor, scattering frightened black-faced sheep in its headlong career, its hooves hardly seeming to touch the springy turf. The girl on its back laughed exultantly, her head thrown back and her long red hair streaming in the wind, her strong small hands in perfect control of her mount. It was a blue and gold day, one of those rare days of spring that turn Yorkshire into a vast paradise for gods to play in. Elder and hawthorn were in full bloom, their bushes loaded with blossoms of cream, white and brilliant pink, the moors lying ahead were great carpets of green and gold, the hills beyond them reaching into the clouds.

Down in the valley, far behind the pony and its rider, the grey bulk of a rambling Tudor house looked down across gardens to a small one, turreted in the fashionable Gothic style. The girl had glanced back several times while the houses were still in sight to make sure that censorious eyes were not watching, for she had been forbidden to ride out alone on Beauty, the pony she had trained herself in defiance of her uncle's wishes. There were plenty of grooms to do that sort of thing, he had pointed out; she was not proposing to set up in business as a horse-coper, was she? Her mother lamented that the child would rather ride than read, as she should be doing. It was most unfeminine to be always striding about in that mannish habit and whistling, a dreadful skill learned from stable-boys.

The pony leaped a little stream rippling over stones, sending up points of light where the sun-rays caught it. They were on a downward slope, another meadow ahead where sheep and lambs grazed, still unalarmed by the approach of the thudding hooves. There was an iron gate in the fencing wall of piled stones; the rider saw that it was firmly latched. Too much trouble to get down and open it, spoiling the lovely speed of their progress. 'Over, Beauty!' she cried, with a touch of her boot to the pony's side. It speeded up,

9

soared over the wall, and caught a hind hoof on one of the loose stones on top of it, coming down with a crash on the other side, its rider sailing over its head to land some yards away.

After a moment the pony struggled to its feet. But the girl lay motionless where she had fallen, the chestnut of her hair spread like a fan on the short-cropped grass.

BOOK ONE

The Moated Grange

There's a new foot on the floor, my friend,
And a new face at the door, my friend:
   A new face at the door.
                   Alfred Tennyson

CHAPTER ONE

Lilian Adeline de Wentworth brushed impatiently at a bee which hovered persistently round her, perhaps attracted by the blue of her muslin dress. If the stupid thing mistook her for a flower it might as well go and sample the real ones in the garden. A well-aimed thwack with her book sent it buzzing angrily into the sunshine through the wide-open window.

Lilian sighed and touched her brow with her handkerchief, damped with eau-de-cologne. She was so dreadfully hot, lying on her wicker couch in the small conservatory that had been built out from her bedroom, so that she might enjoy as much fresh air and sunlight as possible. The doctor, a progressive man, had suggested this, as being the best tonic for a young lady unable to take exercise, and had got his way, in spite of Mamma's protests that poor Lilian was too delicate for such exposure. Sometimes Lilian liked the conservatory, from which she could see the road, carriages and riders passing, and people moving in the gardens of Scarbrick Hall, which adjoined the Dower House where she and her family lived; and, to the east, the high hills of Scardale and the little town of Fellgate in the valley. Sometimes, as on this torrid afternoon, she hated it and the sickly overpowering scent of the hothouse plants surrounding her. It would be nice to ring for someone to carry her into the cool dark bedroom.

Once it had seemed humiliating to be carried everywhere, but she was used to it now. For seven of her twenty years she had not walked; ever since the day she had gone over the head of her pony, and the doctors had said her back was broken. It could not have been, or she would have died, they said later, when she came out of black unconsciousness into a world of pain and laudanum. The pain had grown less over the years, until it became an almost disregarded ache, her constant companion.

But she was so weak, her long slender legs powerless to carry her.

She raised the hem of her skirt and surveyed her ankles. Yes, they were still elegant and shapely. But sometimes she feared that her waist was thickening, her figure spreading with endless inactivity, lying like a log, day and night, she who had been able to run like the wind and gallop her pony until it tired.

They had not shot the pony, though Mamma had wanted it done. Lilian had pleaded for it, because she said it was all her own fault. She had only herself to blame, which made things no easier to bear. Suddenly irritated by her own thoughts, she shook herself, as crossly as she had brushed away the bee. What was the use in brooding on it all? In the Hall gardens a game of croquet was going on: Sir Lewis had house-guests. She had heard her brother and sister go out: they must have been invited. She watched, trying to make out the faces of the players, but could only see their bright clothes, the summer dresses of the girls, the white straw hats of the young men.

She was startled by a voice beside her. Maggie Royds, the elderly maid, was saying, 'Mr Augustus is downstairs. I told him you were havin' a rest.'

'Oh. Well, I'm too hot to sleep. Tell him to come up, Maggie.'

The prospect of the Reverend Augustus Hambleden's company was not exciting, but perhaps a little more so than staring at unknown people enjoying themselves. The only son of Sir Lewis, and heir to Scarbrick Hall, he had disappointed his father by taking Holy Orders, and was now ordained as curate of an industrial parish on the outskirts of the nearest big town, Leeds. It was Sir Lewis's hope that the lad would get all that pious rubbish out of his system and come home in due course to manage the estate; also that he would come to see the sense of settling down with some strong capable young woman instead of mooning around his cousin by marriage, for what use would a helpless cripple be as mistress of the Hall and one of the richest estates in Yorkshire?

Lilian was well aware that Sir Lewis disapproved of his son's attentions to her, in spite of his gruff kindness when he called. He had given Mamma and the Dower House nine years ago when Papa, Colonel de Wentworth, had died of the fever he had brought home from India, after the suppression of the terrible Mutiny in 1858. The Dower House was rambling and shabby, Tudor bricks smothered in ivy and Virginia creeper, dark, low-beamed rooms cheerless to live in. Yet they had so much to thank Sir Lewis for, including presents of game and produce from his kitchen gardens. But it was more than Lilian could resist to do a little flirting with a young man who so obviously worshipped her. She saw few men besides her brother Arthur and his friends, hearty youths who seemed a trifle frightened of her. Augustus was different.

She fluttered her eyelashes and arranged herself in a becomingly languid pose as Maggie ushered him in, a short, stocky figure in clerical black. The town-pallor of his cheeks took on a flush; his kindly, earnest eyes behind the pince-nez beamed respectful adoration. And indeed she made a charming picture lying there, like a blossom fallen from a tree, he thought, the full skirts of her pale blue dress of spotted muslin almost hiding the couch she lay on, the tiny frill of net that edged the high bodice less white than the long, slender neck it touched, the full sleeves pointing the delicacy of her hands.

And then her hair! He recalled guiltily that St Paul had regarded women's hair as something peculiarly sinful, and indeed it would be exceedingly difficult to preach with such a head of hair in a front pew. It was a rich red-gold, like ripe chestnuts or autumn leaves before they fall, and the fashionable chignon crowning her head was no false creation built up over a 'rat' of wool to pad it out, as worn by so many ladies, but all her own. So much hair she had that from where the chignon ended, at the tender nape of her neck, a cluster of long curls hung, bewitchingly draped forward over one shoulder.

'Well, Gussie,' she said (and how he wished her voice held the thrilling warmth he longed to hear in it), 'it's kind of you to call, especially on such a fearfully hot day.'

'Oh, a pleasure, dear Lilian. And they were urging me to play croquet, so I thought . . .'

'You thought you'd come and cheer the poor invalid. No, don't look so cast down, you goose, you know I always tease. Sit down, do, and take off those ridiculous tight gloves – I don't know how you can bear them. Will you bring us some tea, Maggie?'

Perched on a small cane chair, nervously twisting the gloves into a ball before depositing them in his round clerical hat, he said, 'I don't like to hear you call yourself an invalid. It seems so . . . so inappropriate.'

'You think I look too well? Bonny? Blooming?'

'Of course not. You are rather pale today, dear. I hope you have not had a turn for the worse.'

She laughed sharply. 'I'm neither worse nor better. I never am. Sometimes the pain almost goes away, when Mamma allows me a glass of port after dinner, and I bribe Arthur to pour me another one. There, now you're shocked. Don't be alarmed, I haven't taken to drink – yet. Now tell me, how are your parish affairs?'

Augustus heaved a small sigh. 'I mustn't complain. The work is demanding, I must admit, but I'm grateful to God that He has given me the opportunity to till a very rough field. A parish like this, now, would be no test of a man.'

'I haven't noticed the Reverend Worsley looking particularly tested, I must say. He's as fat as one of his own prize pigs and rides to hounds every week of the season.'

'Precisely what I mean. My father's tenants attend church regularly, as do all the folk hereabouts. Now the mill-people at Mardsley need a very great deal of persuasion even to enter St Bede's. As for having their children christened – well, they might as well be outright heathens.'

'And does the same apply to getting themselves married?'

Augustus blushed. He would not dream of polluting his cousin's pure ears with tales of the sinful things that went on in the grimy back-to-back houses of his parish, or such terrible incidents as the night he had been called from bed to the family of a young girl who had been dragged from the filthy waters of the River Aire, horribly mutilated. Recalling it, his face grew sad, full of the despair he sometimes felt, and Lilian was suddenly sorry for him and ashamed of her teasing. She put out a hand to him and let him hold it in his grateful clasp, hot and sweating though that was.

'Oh, Lilian,' he said, 'how well you understand. What an angel you are to me!'

It was thus that Mrs de Wentworth found them as she hurried in. She had been disturbed to hear from Maggie that Mr Augustus was upstairs and Lilian unchaperoned. Not that such a noble and virtuous young man could be suspected, for one moment, of improper behaviour, but etiquette was etiquette, and the very fact that Lilian's Bower, as her mother liked to call it, adjoined a bedroom, was quite enough reason for insisting on propriety.

16

She was pleased to see the clasped hands and Lilian looking, for once, amiable. She greeted Augustus warmly, even bestowing an auntly kiss on his brow, before settling herself comfortably for a chat. There was no need for the boy to hurry away; here in the country nobody bothered too much about the prescribed length of an afternoon call.

Florence de Wentworth resembled her daughter not at all, except in the small-boned elegance of her figure. Lilian had inherited her father's auburn hair and green eyes, like aquamarines: what a handsome man he had been! Florence's dark hair, just greying, was still youthfully chignoned, even though a tiny lace cap adorned it, and her brown eyes were large and mournful in a face prematurely lined by sorrow and anxiety. She had been young and impressionable when Lord Byron and Percy Shelley had still been fresh in people's minds, and had grown up intensely romantic, in an age which was turning away from romance in favour of such things as Steam, Science, the Improvement of the Poor, and the excellence of virtuous family life as exemplified by the young Queen Victoria and Prince Albert.

Fortunately for Florence's romance-starved heart, she had been introduced during a Scottish holiday to a large, solemn, impressive young man called Alfred Tennyson. He was a poet, the first she had met. One day he would be made Poet Laureate. Flattered by her awed admiration, he had presented her with two volumes of his poems, which proved to be full of the stuff of her dreams; lovely maidens, usually in distressed circumstances, gallant knights, sweet ineffable sorrows and fairy spells. She was still bemused by them when she married Hugh de Wentworth, whose name had the ring of a Tennysonian hero's. But Hugh was nothing of the kind, being a conventional, no-nonsense Yorkshireman. He scoffed loud and long at the names she gave their first-born son and daughter. The boy was Arthur Bedivere, called so from Tennyson's vision of the dying King Arthur, and the girl was Eleänore, namesake of a particularly unearthly lady in a very long lyrical poem.

Needless to say, both grew up as hearty, red-cheeked and loud-voiced as even their father could have wished. Arthur (who would much have preferred to be called something sensible like George) grumbled at being sent up to Cambridge after spending his school-days excelling at sports and bullying boys he considered to be

17

namby-pamby, while Eleänore rechristened herself Nelly at an early age and devoted all her days to hoydenish pursuits. It was a dark day for Florence when she heard of Nelly attending a cock-fight in her brother's clothes.

Undeterred, when a second daughter was born, Florence, ill and weak after her confinement, pleaded that she be named Lilian Adeline, after two of her favourite Tennysonian maidens. Hugh, who had hoped for plain Victoria, could do nothing but agree, but was delighted to watch the baby grow up into a healthy, handsome girl. He did not live to know of the accident which turned her into the frail creature of her mother's dreams.

At least their young relative, Augustus, was everything poor Florence admired. He was talking now of the difficulties of his calling now that there was so much public outcry against Ritualism, the extreme High Church movement then in fashion.

'You would hardly think my parishioners could have heard of such a thing,' Augustus was saying. 'Few of them can even read, goodness knows. Yet I have only to go out wearing this very small cross on my watch-chain and I hear whispers that I've gone over to Rome and will soon be introducing Confessions and the Mass.'

' "High cockalorum",' murmured Lilian.

Her mother's eyebrows rose. '*What* did you say, dearest?'

'Only something I read in *Punch*. It went something like, "Harum scarum, Bishop Sarum . . ." '

Florence held up a hand prohibitively. 'I'm sure Augustus has no wish to hear such rubbish. These humorous journals are becoming far too irreverent. Now tell me, dear boy, what is life like for you in Mardsley, apart from your pastoral work?'

'Well, I'm still lodging at the vicarage, and I must confess not altogether comfortably. The family is so large that I occupy a very small attic room, on the same floor as the servants, and it *is* rather cramped. I . . . if I may mention such a thing, I find it very difficult to keep as clean as I would wish.' He spared them mention of the fleas, lice and bugs he met with in his daily round and all too often found accompanying him back to his lodgings. 'You won't tell my father of this, Aunt, will you. He becomes so, er, agitated at any mention of such drawbacks, though I have assured him many times that I count them nothing besides the privilege of doing the work I love. Besides,' he beamed at them, 'I think it not too early to hint

18

to you that I have the vicar's word that he is shortly going to speak to the Bishop for me. About a living of my own, that is.'

'Oh, I'm so glad, Gussie!' Lilian cried. But Florence's face was radiant. A certain dream of hers might well be coming true.

'How splendid, Augustus, and how gratifying, when you are still so young. Have you any idea where it will be?'

'Some way from Mardsley, on the other side of Leeds, if our hopes are fulfilled. The incumbent is very old and anxious to retire. Naturally, I would dislike very much profiting from another's weakness, but I understand he has a daughter in comfortable circumstances with whom he wishes to live. And the place is *so* pleasant,' Augustus added wistfully. 'It is in the Headingley direction, almost in the country, and yet with many of the same problems as those in Mardsley. A good churchman enjoys the challenge of a flock who truly need his help.'

' "All they like sheep . . .",' Lilian said reflectively. Augustus looked at her doubtfully. He was never quite sure how serious she was. But now, surely, she was only quoting the Scriptures.

They talked further of the happiness of his prospects, and of how Sir Lewis must be reconciled in time to a clergyman son who could be seen to be successful. 'You might even,' Florence said raptly, 'become a bishop. Or Archbishop of York! Yes, I can see it, Augustus. Imagine, a relative of ours living at Bishopthorpe, Lilian – in a palace!'

Augustus sighed. 'A little too much to hope for, I fear. And now I really must go. The Leeds train leaves Fellgate in less than an hour, and it is extremely hot even for walking downhill.' He rose, donned his gloves, and bashfully produced from his coat a small volume bound in green and gold. 'I, er, thought you would perhaps enjoy this.' His eyes were on Lilian, but it was Florence who embraced and kissed him after reading the title.

'*The Princess, and other Poems, by Alfred Tennyson.* Oh, Augustus, what a kind, thoughtful boy you are, how truly delightful.'

'Oh, well,' replied Augustus airily, 'I knew you would like it, Aunt, and I thought Lilian might, too.' His face turned an even deeper pink. 'I . . . I marked one or two passages you might find meaningful.'

Before he left them Florence kissed him again, at the spot where his rather thin hair receded on each side of the centre parting known jocularly as the Curate's Lane. But Lilian gave him a long appraising look and a cool handshake.

On the hilly road down towards the station he found himself humming a silly chant of his college days of which Lilian's *Punch* lampoon had reminded him. 'O how bella my puella, I'll kiss secula seculorum, If I've luck, sir, she's my Uxor, O dies benedictorum!'

It seemed oddly appropriate.

'I told you, Mamma,' Lilian said furiously. 'He has Intentions, and this is his silly, spoony way of expressing them. *I* know Gussie.'

'Pray, my dear, don't use that ugly slang – it sounds like Arthur and is not at all nice on a young lady's lips. What is it you've found?'

Lilian pointed to a marked passage at the end of *The Princess*. 'That.' She read it aloud, with ridicule.

> "I waste my heart in sighs; let be. My bride,
> My wife, my life. O we will walk this world
> Yok'd in all exercise of noble end,
> And so thro' those dark gates across the wild
> That no man knows. Indeed I love thee: come,
> Yield thyself up: my hopes and thine are one;
> Accomplish thou my manhood and thyself –
> Lay thy sweet hands in mine and trust to me."

'There. You see? He hasn't even the courage to come out with it himself.'

Florence subsided into her chair and passed her hand wearily across her brow. 'I think the verse is very beautiful, and a charming way of expressing feelings which Augustus is perhaps too bashful to put into words. Oh, Lilian, he loves you so deeply, and he needs a wife so much. More than ever, if this living is granted to him. Can't you understand?'

'Oh, very clearly. He wants a woman to take on half the parish work, as these poor d . . . creatures the clergy wives do. And what sort of use would I be to him, chained to this couch and my bed, hardly able to lift a finger?'

'That is not quite true,' Florence returned with a show of spirit. 'Only your back and your limbs – legs – are weak. You could do –

well, church embroideries, cassocks and altar-cloths and things, and write letters – clergymen have so much correspondence, you know – and give advice to female parishioners. And besides that, think of the comfort your company would be to Augustus, poor lonely man – and of the love and care he would give you!'

'Don't you think he might give me something besides, Mamma? It's well known that vicars' wives have more babies than anyone else. How do you suggest I produce them – like this?' She gestured towards her helpless legs. 'And how many am I to endure before my strength gives out? The usual baker's dozen, or is it vicar's dozen?'

Florence turned away and stared blindly over the gardens.

'How can you be so very coarse? What am I to say to you, Lilian? Even your mother can hardly discuss such matters. I can only suggest that . . . that Augustus would be considerate and kind . . . that he would not inflict . . . I am sure you know what I mean. Oh, this is very difficult for me. And I would beg you to remember that he will be very rich when Lewis dies, though we mustn't think of that, with only two sisters to share the legacy. He would be able to take care of my poor girl when I am gone . . .' She began to weep softly, dabbing her eyes with a tiny handkerchief more lace than linen. Downstairs a door banged, and loud voices were heard shouting cheerfully to each other.

'There!' Lilian said crossly. 'Now Arthur and Nelly are back, from the croquet-game, I expect, and I shall have to hear all the tiresome details. I *won't* be bothered with them and I *won't* be made deaf with all that shouting. Go and tell them my head aches very badly and they are to be quiet.'

'Oh, my darling!' Florence moved to her, maddeningly forgiving and cherishing. 'Does your head indeed ache? Would you like some . . .'

'Yes, it does, and I ache all over and my back is ready to break in two. No, I don't want any medicine, only to be left alone.' She turned on her side, hunching her shoulders, her back towards Florence. Keeping very still, she heard the quiet sobs recommence, and her mother go softly out, through the bedroom on tiptoe, so as not to disturb her further.

'What a rotter I am,' Lilian said aloud. 'What a perfect bounder. I could kill myself. Why don't I? I'd be better dead, after all.' The

21

binding of the Tennyson poems winked up at her in a shaft of sunlight. She picked it up and hurled it through the open casement, its pages flying through the air like a shot pigeon's feathers until it landed on the garden path.

Remorse overcame her, confused in her emotions as she was. The book was costly, and Gussie was very poor. From the flower-bed on the far side of the lawn a gardener was wheeling a barrow full of uprooted plants. She saw that it was not old Howard, who had looked after the garden for years, but someone younger.

'You!' she called, her voice sharp and clear in the still air. 'Pick up that book.'

The man stopped and looked up, pushing his cap a little back from his brown forehead – not, she noticed with annoyance, raising it as Howard would have done. It seemed a long time before he spoke, and his words astonished her.

'What did tha say?'

'Are you deaf? I said, pick up my book. And then take it round to the kitchen door and tell them to send someone up with it.'

He stood surveying her, hands on hips. Then he said, or rather shouted, 'I'll do nowt o' t' sort. Come down and get it thisen.'

'*Oh!*' Lilian was speechless with rage for a moment, before she managed to get out 'How dare you be so insolent! I'll have you dismissed.'

'That tha won't. I work for Sir Lewis, not thee – whoever tha might be.'

'I am Miss Lilian de Wentworth,' she said in her iciest tones, 'and Sir Lewis is my relative. Perhaps you have not been informed that I am a helpless invalid, unable to walk – or that servants don't usually question orders.'

Staring haughtily down at him, she felt herself being considered, appraised, judged, perhaps, by this inferior, disagreeable man, and was all the more offended by his arrogant air. His features and expression were invisible against the strong sun, but the poise of his body, relaxed and irritatingly graceful, was eloquent enough. He was young, possibly no older than Arthur. Perhaps he was one of these would-be revolutionaries who followed the doctrines of the German reformer, what was his name? Something like Angels – who was stirring up so much trouble among the workers. How could Sir Lewis have allowed such a person to serve on his staff?

The gardener spoke at last, very mildly for a dangerous revolutionary.

'I'm sorry tha'rt badly. Tha should ha' said. I'll tek it round for thee.' He picked up the book and walked away without a backward look, leaving her fuming and very much inclined to cry from a mixture of temper and humiliation, and the knowledge that she had been rude to him first. Her soldier father had impressed on her, as though she were a boy, that a good officer didn't insult his men. 'They serve Her Majesty just as their generals do. Remember that, and don't let me hear you speak so to Maggie again.'

She had forgotten that lesson; how unbearable she must have sounded. And yet how dare the man have answered her so?

Her back had not been aching when she had told Florence it was. Now the familiar racking, nervous pain took hold of her, spreading from shoulders to hips and down to her knees. When Nelly burst in with the returned book, large and hearty in her sweat-stained white frock, dark hair straggling down over healthily flushed cheeks, Lilian lay ashen-white, fists clenched and tears trickling from under tight-closed lids.

'Law!' said Nelly inelegantly, and, running to the door, shouted, 'Artie! fetch Mamma.'

CHAPTER TWO

Dr Stansfield, driving his dog-cart up the twisting stony lane to the Dower House, hoped that his summons had been a false alarm. Miss Lilian seemed to him one of those flowers, blighted in the spring, which linger on indefinitely through the seasons. Her family were not rich, he knew, merely pensioners of Sir Lewis; but Sir Lewis was the Squire, and they his kin, not to be despised as patients. Through the years they had brought him a fair harvest in fees, the mother for her heavy colds and fainting attacks, the elder daughter and son for bruises, sprains and cuts sustained in the hunt and other sports. It was only a pity that Colonel de Wentworth had died before they came to the Dower House; but his end had been swift and beyond the help of physicians.

The doctor was all the more daunted to find his young patient in pain almost amounting to spasms, unable to speak to him clearly, feverish (though that might be partly due to the general heat) and in a poor nervous state. He glanced with disapproval at the conservatory. The windows were closed now, shutting in the hot air. He did not care for the look of the patient's bedroom. Used to his own daughters' fondness for blues and pinks, with plenty of chiffon bows and pretty nonsense, he found its uniform creams and greys depressing, very unsuitable for a young lady not quite twenty, and the furniture heavy and old-fashioned. Perhaps the decoration was rather her mother's choice than her own.

Discreetly, through her lawn nightgown, he prodded her spine and shoulders, hot and flinching beneath his touch. He straightened up.

'A high degree of sensitivity, soreness, ma'am. I can't tell if any further harm has been done to the backbone. There seems to be a high temperature.'

Florence moved Lilian so that she lay on her back, but instantly an arm came up to shield her eyes, and she turned her face against the pillow.

24

'You see?' her mother said. 'I can get nothing from her. Something has happened to disturb her – she is almost as she was when the . . . the accident happened.'

'A disturbance in the mind, perhaps? Some family trouble?'

'No. No. Only . . . A gentleman wishes to offer for her hand. I think it has caused her some heart-searching. Oh, Doctor, he is such a good young man! It would be the salvation of her to marry him. He has such prospects in the Church, you see – in time I might even be able to live with them, these country vicarages are so very commodious.'

Her large eyes glowed at him in the twilight of the room, her tiny clawlike hands were clasped. A man experienced among the hardy folk of the Dales, he wondered how she had ever come to live in these parts, how married an ordinary man, and a soldier at that, how borne three children? If ever there was a die-away London sort, he saw one before him.

He cleared his throat. 'Have you thought, ma'am, of sending Miss Lilian down to Fellgate Wells House? They do miracles there with rheumatic cases. Hydropathy, Turkish baths, alternate cold and heat, all the newest treatments and every possible convenience. The place is like a superior hotel. I can recommend it, indeed.'

'Oh. I had heard . . . It sounds very strenuous. She can barely move, you know. Two of our maids carry her everywhere.'

'There are plenty of nurses and assistants to move her.'

'But . . . I like to nurse her myself, Doctor.'

Unable to restrain himself, he barked, 'Miss Lilian is not a doll, but a young woman. She needs professional care, ma'am, unless you want her to end her days here – and very soon. I suggest you think seriously.'

He saw the tears rise in Florence's eyes, and hardened his soul against them. Gently touching Lilian's shoulder, he asked, 'Did you hear what we were talking about, Miss Lilian?'

Something like a 'Yes' came from the pillow.

'And what do you feel?'

The arm came down from where it had lain across her brow. 'I'll try,' she murmured. 'If you say . . . So sad here, so sad . . .'

'My darling!' Florence flung herself upon the prostrate girl, to be unceremoniously hauled off by Stansfield.

'Don't smother her, ma'am, she needs all the air she can get.

25

To start with I'll open these windows. Make her eat and drink something, and I'll drive down by the Wells House and speak to Mr Lucy myself. There should be no trouble about getting her in.'

Nor was there. By the following evening Lilian was established in a private room in the south wing of the Wells House, an imposing essay in the Scottish Baronial style, all turrets and red brick faced with flints, set against the tree-clad fells that hid Lilian's home from her, with a view extending over the miles of Riding Moor, now green with young heather against purple skies. It was very quiet. Down in the gardens a fountain plashed, an elegant Gothic affair shedding drops of pure mountain water into a marble basin, in memory of the German scientist who had discovered the water-cure. Somewhere, in the warren of rooms downstairs, patients and their guests were taking tea, gossiping, playing parlour-games, or listening to a lecture on 'The Way to Better Health'.

Lilian smiled. There was a strange relief in being away from the place where she had been struck down, had been for years her mother's broken doll, an embarrassment to her sister and brother and their friends. They had tried teasing her with the bits of poetry Mamma had labelled her with: 'Airy, fairy Lilian', 'Faintly smiling Adeline', and such rubbish. It *was* rubbish, and they knew it, and she knew it. When she had been as they were (and how like a tombstone it sounded) she would have had a dog or a horse shot in pity if it were as helpless as she, even though it had been her dear pony.

She had left Gussie's green and gold volume behind for her mother to enjoy. But a poem from another volume had stayed in her mind, or just arisen in it, in the quiet of this place; something about a lady called Mariana in one of Shakespeare's plays, those boring pieces from which she had been made to learn wedges by her governesses. Who Mariana was, or what was the matter with her, Lilian had no idea. Only Mamma's friend Mr Tennyson had written a song about her, alone and sighing in a moated grange.

> "She only said 'My life is dreary,
>   He cometh not,' she said;
> She said 'I am aweary, aweary,
>   I would that I were dead!'"

26

There was a lot more of it, all seeming to have something to do with herself. Yes, she was aweary, aweary of aches and dullness, sympathy and the pity in the eyes of stronger girls. Yet why, she wondered, gazing up at the lights from the garden lamps reflected on her ceiling, should she feel with Mariana the absence of somebody unknown?

'He cometh not, she said.' Who? Gussie, the only man ever likely to want to marry her? Perhaps she had been so disturbed in this last few days because she had sent him away with something like mockery, when he had humbly offered her the queenship of that visionary vicarage. 'The place is *so* pleasant . . .' She began to imagine it, the hallway, the downstairs room she would have for her own, the lighted church at Christmas that she would see from her window, Gussie in a cassock hurrying off to early service . . .

The shadows of the room closed round her, and she slept.

The two weeks that followed were something quite new in her experience. Strong arms carried her from one treatment to another, only setting her down for rest-periods.

Sipping from the mid-morning tumbler in the sitting-room where she and other female patients assembled between treatments, she heard the water commended.

'We always drink coffee at home at this time. But Mr Lucy says it is dreadfully bad for the liver and to be avoided at all costs. I shall insist on water being served in future.'

'But my dear, this is Spa water, full of potassium and iron and all kinds of things so good for one. They say it can be bought in bottles to take home.'

'Then I shall certainly buy some. Don't you think my colour has improved, Daisy? I was positively yellow when I arrived.'

'Yes, dear, you've become quite a milkmaid. And I'm sure I've lost whole inches round the waist with the wet-sheet treatment.'

An invalid chair was procured for Lilian, in which she was pushed out every morning, after being given a warm bath, to sit under the trees in the garden. Sometimes she would watch the more active patients contesting in the bowling-alley, or playing gentle croquet, or strolling in the grounds. It amused her to put them into categories. There were the Stouts, manufacturers' wives from

27

Leeds and Bradford, portly and puffing from heavy meat-eating and pounds of creamy Yorkshire pudding. The Leans were tall bony ladies, often spinsters, with red tips to their noses and sallow complexions; they, Lilian noticed, tended to sit or stroll very near to where the gentlemen patients congregated, and then drop their handkerchieves or fans with great regularity. 'There's many a good match been made at a Hydro,' she was told, though she saw no evidence of it.

Then there were the Belles, young ladies who had nothing wrong with them at all and merely came to beautify themselves, gossip and flirt, to the great irritation of the Leans. Some of them tried to make friends with Lilian, pitying her isolation in her favourite corner under the beech-tree, but there was so little to talk about. She had no interest in deriding the old ladies who still wore spoon-bonnets ('like something out of the Ark, my dear') or discussing the advantages of the charming new crinolette over the old-fashioned crinoline, *so* enormous and uncomfortable.

'I've never worn crinolines,' Lilian said. 'When one has to lie or sit every moment of one's time it's hardly convenient to wear a great padded cage.'

The pretty Arabella looked abashed. 'Of course not. I beg your pardon.' After a moment she put up her parasol and strolled away. She had intended to compliment the invalid girl on her beautiful chignon and ask if it were real or just a very good match, but there was no point in talking to someone who only answered rudely and obviously preferred to be left alone.

Florence, visiting, was worried that the more severe medical treatments had been withdrawn. 'I said they would be too much for you. Already you may have been injured by them. Oh, if only Dr Stansfield had not given such foolish advice!'

'I'm no worse, Mamma. It was only that some of the treatments distressed me and made me more nervous. Now that I am put to sit here all day I'm really not in much pain. You can have no idea how much pleasanter it is to be in the open air than lying on my couch.'

Florence was thoughtful. 'Yes, I think you have a little more colour, dearest – but you must be careful not to let the sun touch your face. It *is* expensive to keep you here, though. Three and a half guineas a week, and even the first consultation cost a guinea. I don't like to ask Lewis ...'

'Then let me come home – why not? Millie can give me a warm bath every morning, as they do here.'

Florence patted her hand. 'Oh, I would rather do that myself, my darling. I miss my baby girl so much.'

Lilian said nothing. It had been rather pleasant to be handled and waited on by strong impersonal attendants, after Mamma's cosseting.

'But the chair,' Florence went on. 'We have no such thing at home for you.'

'I expect they'd lend one, or hire it. They seem to have dozens.'

The director was only too pleased to hire a bath-chair out for a shilling a week, and a shade relieved to see the last of an excessively fragile patient who took up so much of the nurses' time. The chair was loaded on to a farm-cart and Lilian carefully lifted into a cab hired from Fellgate Station, and as carefully driven along the hilly road back to the Dower House.

Her reception at home was cordial. Nelly was pleased to work off her enormous energy in pushing Lilian's chair much too fast round and round the garden, while Arthur affected to find his sister the picture of rude health. 'Well, and how's Airy-Fairy? Blooming belle of the ball, you look. Don't I just wish I could take myself off to the Wells House and have a romp with some of those handsome girls Mamma told me about! Think I look a bit pale? Needing a bit o' wateropathy, or whatever they call it?'

'I think you look exactly the same great hulking ox you always did,' Lilian snapped. 'All you need is exercise, lounging about the house all day.'

'Well, it's the Long Vac, ain't it? What's a fellow to do for four whole months, when there ain't any shooting till the Twelfth and the hounds not out till after I've gone back to college? Bored, that's what I am, bored.' He lit his third cigar of the day and hastily put it out as his mother was heard approaching with Augustus.

Lilian was not reproved for her bluntness to her brother, or Arthur for the still-burning cigar, so anxious was Augustus to see Lilian.

'M-my dear.' She was wearing a wrapper of very pale pink, which she knew to be becoming. Augustus's eyes were glued to it, and to her face. 'How charming you look.'

'I know. Quite a colour. So they all say.'

'Oh, no. That is, just a faint tinge.' He was staring at her nose, its ivory whiteness touched with a few pale golden freckles, filtered through the beech-tree leaves. 'I can see you are much stronger.'

'Can you? Then you see more than I do. Never mind me, tell me how you've been getting on, Gussie.'

'Oh. Well, old Mr Morison of the living near Headingley has asked the Bishop to accept his resignation. I can't expect it to come my way, as a matter of course, and I hope I have more meekness than to do so. But I did preach the Sunday before last, when Mr Dodds was indisposed with a heavy summer cold and sneezing too much to speak, and I'm told the congregation were very gratified.' He looked down at the shiny knees of his trousers; Lilian guessed they were worn down with prayer, and was touched, knowing so many of the prayers had been for her. There would be no more Wells Houses once she was married to Gussie; she would be a respected clergy wife, with the Fats and the Leans and the Belles coming to her for counsel. What counsel was she fit to give? Be guided by Mr Banting, and eat less – or don't, and eat more – or settle on one of those flash young men you're always tormenting . . . What did it matter? She threw Augustus a thrilling smile, and settled down to listen to his account of his parish experiences, including an invitation to Bradford for the ceremony of presentation to the eminent public benefactor Titus Salt of a splendid silver soup tureen. Gussie was really rather sweet, in his simple way, and could be brought to heel a good deal more easily than Mamma; besides, he was the best she could expect. None of the men at the Wells House had so much as looked her way, except for some of the older ones, with wandering eyes and damp lips.

Arthur burst in to the drawing-room, where they were all assembled by an unnecessary fire, Lilian enthroned on a horsehair-padded sofa, wrapped in rugs.

'I say, here's a thing, now,' he announced. 'Uncle Lewis has got up a cricket match tomorrow in the Long Meadow. Just a few swells he's got staying and some men from the town – Shaw from the Red Lion and Birtles the tobacconist have promised – and one or two from the estate. And yours truly's to open the bowling, how about that?' He mimed the hurling of a ball which would have shattered his mother's chandelier and the mirror over the fireplace, had it been a real one.

Nelly gave a theatrical yawn. 'Oh, cricket. Gallons of beer and no tea and ices, and the men all yapping to each other about long-stops and short slips and extra points, and such nonsense. I wish Uncle Lewis would stick to croquet so that we girls could have a chance. What's the fun in sitting about watching men chasing a little ball and falling over each other?'

'You may think it no fun,' Arthur retorted, 'but you needn't come if you don't like it. I'll be glad of a change, I can tell you.' He picked up a small cushion and swiped it across the room, causing his mother to give a nervous scream. 'You go and play croquet if you want to. I daresay Lil will back you up. Or would you like to watch the fellows instead, Fairy, now you've got your push-chair?'

'Yes, I should,' Lilian said. 'And I hope Augustus can stay to watch.'

Augustus's face was a study in mingled disapproval and disappointment. The prospect of a day at the side of his beloved, even watching cricket, which he had suffered from enough at school, was a dream of pleasure, but it could only be a dream.

'I'm afraid . . . Sunday would be impossible. We have three services, and I shall probably have to take one of them, with the Vicar's cold still bad. Nor do I really think a clergyman should be seen attending . . .'

Arthur launched into a hideous nasal bray in imitation of a clergyman intoning with a bad cold, and was stopped instantly by his mother.

'Arthur! I will not have religion mocked in this house. As for cricket matches, I'm not at all sure about any of you attending. Tomorrow is the Sabbath, after all. I wonder Lewis hadn't thought of that.'

'Don't worry, he has, Mamma,' said Arthur. 'But he don't care, provided the tenants go to morning service. Nothing to say they can't do what they like after that, is there? Nor us, neither,' he added inelegantly.

Florence subsided. Arthur was very exhausting to argue with, and in any case she only put up a token resistance to Sunday sports.

31

The Lord's Day Observance Society was a very Low Church move-ment. She would quite have enjoyed the Ritualism Augustus so much deplored, with its delicious-smelling incense and Latin prayers and thrilling confessionals. Suddenly she was very tired of her children, even Lilian, who was letting the departing Augustus linger over her hand, and smiling in the most encouraging way.

'I say, Lilian,' murmured the doting curate, his mouth very near the rosemary-scented chignon, 'you *have* got jolly hair.'

'Have I, Gus? Thank you. You won't mind if I have it cropped, will you? I'm thinking of following Mrs Amelia Bloomer's example, though it *is* a little out of date. One gets so tired of wearing long skirts all the time, and short hair does seem to go with trousers, doesn't it?' She watched, with naughty attention, the growing shock, disbelief, and self-reassurance on Augustus's face.

'You're teasing, of course. Sometimes I think you are still quite a child, dearest Lilian.'

She shrugged away from him, averting her cheek from the proffered kiss. Yes, Augustus, she thought, I *am* a child, a stupid creature not able to walk and with nothing to talk about, waiting to be dressed and undressed by Mamma and having my pretty hair praised after somebody else has put it up for me. I hate my hair, I hate it, hate it. She gave the long tress that hung over her shoulder a savage tweak. Arthur saw her, and by some unusual ray of sensi-tivity guessed something of her feelings. 'Never mind, old girl,' he said, clapping her painfully on the shoulder. 'Carrots is in season, don't you know? Red wigs all the rage in London, they say. Cheer up, never say die, for a-cricketing we will go.'

'I can hardly wait,' she said with heavy sarcasm.

A golden August afternoon lit the Long Meadow, that nearest thing to a flat stretch of ground on Scarbrick Hall land. It lay beneath gently rising slopes where sheep grazed and bracken was beginning to turn bronze. Scarbrick Woods stretched away to the west, almost to Riding Moor; pheasant, grouse and woodcock soared serene in a lapis lazuli sky, unaware that in a few days the guns would be out. The meadow had been well cropped down by sheep, and Sir Lewis's gardeners had scythed it as flat as they could, but even so tussocks and knots of couch-grass presented hazards to a running man. The players cared nothing for that; the game was what mattered, the old, great game of England.

They were not, of course, of the despised race of professionals, men who were paid for playing cricket. Such persons were increasingly to be found here in Yorkshire, where ambition rose above class, and Players aspired to do better at the game than the Gentlemen who had taught them, in the days when a squire would make up his own team from the servants in his house.

Sir Lewis had moved on from those days. With his usual energy he had assembled a team of gentlemanly amateurs from among his own friends and those of his two daughters, Elsie and Louisa, one married to 'brass' in Sheffield and the other to a Manchester alderman. The opposing eleven came from Fellgate and thereabouts: tradesmen, cab-drivers, gamekeepers, stable-lads, anyone who could swing a bat or bowl a decent ball. They were gathered round the hut that passed for a pavilion, a motley crew in garments of all colours and materials, their working clothes – for they could not afford to spoil their best ones.

The Hall team presented a more uniform spectacle in neat white flannels, scarves tied round their waists, straw hats or caps on their heads to keep the sun off, one gentleman splendid in a solar topee. Sir Lewis, a mighty figure, grey moustache and beard bristling with energy, had lost the toss, and was leading his side in to field. His large, leonine head was crowned with a striped cap of many colours. His late wife had complained that his cricketing friends saw more of him than she did, though it was only a token complaint, for he was an exhausting man to live with.

Lilian, too, felt awed at the sight of him striding to a position in the field where he could inflict most harm on the other side. She shrank further back into her chair, which at her request had been pushed some distance away from where the other ladies were sitting. Both Elsie and Louisa had brought their children, five in all, and Louisa was very obviously expecting again, in an elaborate robe heavily trimmed with ribbons and bows which were supposed to disguise her shape. Lilian hoped that if she married Gussie she would not have to see too much of her sisters-in-law and their noisy offspring.

She was hot and uncomfortable in her best summer dress, fashionably striped in blue and rose-colour. Flies buzzed round her, interested in the presence of humans in this meadow where Sir Lewis's sheep usually grazed. Irritably she whisked them away with her gloves. Undeterred they came back, and she pulled forward the veil which hung from the back of her hat, so that it covered both the hat and her face. Perhaps that would keep the wretched things away.

Presently she closed her eyes, lulled by the incomprehensible cries from the field. 'No – yes.' 'Get 'im, Billy!' 'That'll be four, that will.' ''Owzat?' Again and again came the thud of bat against ball. She had seen the blacksmith's son go in to bat, and hoped his muscle-corded arms would not send the ball in her direction.

A shout of triumph from the field. Lilian opened her eyes to see the blacksmith's son departing, a short, square, dejected figure. The next batsman crossed him on his way to the wicket. She surveyed him idly, wondering who he was, for he looked a good deal more presentable than the rest of his team. He wore flannel trousers and white shoes, like the Hall players; a brilliantly white shirt was unbuttoned at the neck, contrasting with his brown throat, and the rolled-up sleeves showed equally brown arms. She speculated idly that he might be a gentleman's gentleman who had come with the house-guests, since he was nobody she recognised from the village or the town. But he looked too healthy for that, not at all like somebody who spent his time brushing his master's clothes and ironing dress-shirts. Well, it was very unimportant, just something to occupy her mind. She shut her eyes again and drowsed, to be wakened by the clanging of a handbell and the noisy departure of Elsie, Louisa and their brood, together with the other watchers who had joined them.

The reason was obvious. Sir Lewis's butler and several maids were bringing refreshments on to the field, trays laden with teapots, cups, lemonade and sandwiches. Behind them came two more maids bearing a large metal pail between them. 'Ices! There's ices!' the children were shrieking, falling over themselves and each other in their hurry to get to the picnic-spot where the players and spectators were eagerly gathered. Nobody had noticed that Lilian was still in her place; nobody had thought of refreshments for her. She sighed; an ice would have been very pleasant. She raised her veil; perhaps it was making her invisible.

But someone had noticed her, and was coming towards her. It was the young batsman with the impressive flannels; she recognised the slender figure and a certain air of elegance about him. His swift

34

strides brought him to her side in a moment across that wide field.

She looked up into the bluest eyes she had ever seen; or perhaps they seemed bluer against the sun-brown of his face. Crisp dark hair, damp with exercise, curled into his shirt-collar. He wore neither whiskers nor moustache to hide a full, shapely mouth and determined jaw. Lilian experienced a curious feeling, as though she had been dealt a blow over the heart.

They seemed to stare at each other for a long time, yet it was only a moment before he said, 'I thought tha might like summat fetching.' She recognised the voice, though she had only heard it once before, when he had refused to retrieve her book from the garden. So it was the insolent young man with the wheelbarrow, and now she would have a chance to reprove him properly. Instead she said meekly, 'Yes, please. How kind of you.'

'What, then? Tea or lemonade, or one o' them ices?'

'An ice would be delightful. But I think you'll find the children have had them all.'

'They'd better not have,' replied her rescuer, and strode off again. He was lost to sight in the crowd, then reappeared and returned with astonishing speed, carrying a silver bowl filled with ice-cream, and two silver spoons.

'You got some!' Lilian exclaimed. 'How clever of you!'

'Oh, there's ways,' said he calmly. 'Tha won't mind if I take some misen? I'm fair heated, I can tell thee.'

'Of course not, please do, as much as you want – you've brought far more than I can eat.' She handed him one of the spoons, and felt a mad impulse to say, 'Won't you spoon with me?' the joke that came out regularly at every picnic where men and girls foregathered. In spite of herself she laughed, and he, disposed gracefully on the grass beside her, looked up with a smile that quite transformed his expression, which was normally slightly grim; at least when he was batting, thought Lilian, realising that she must have watched him for longer and more closely than she thought.

They shared the ice-cream in silence. Lilian spoke first, full of curiosity about him. 'You play cricket very well.'

'Should do. I've been at it all mi life.'

'Oh.'

'You like watchin', then. Know summat about it?'

35

'Oh yes, quite a lot, from my brother, you know,' Lilian lied, quite unaware why she did so, except that she had no wish to appear an ignoramus before him. He began to talk about the match, in terms which baffled her. She nodded at what she hoped were the right moments, wearing a look of rapt attention, and was rewarded when he said, 'There's not many young women knows owt about t'game. It's a change to meet one as does.'

Lilian was trying to think of a suitable reply which would not give her away when the picnic gathering broke up and the players began to drift back into the field. Her companion rose, briskly collecting the empty bowl and spoons.

'I'm off now, then,' he said, giving a brief nod which she took to be his form of farewell. A few yards from her, as though he felt her wistful eyes following him, he turned and called over his shoulder, 'I'll be back.'

Watching him at the wicket, thinking over the strange encounter and stranger conversation, she realised that he had talked to her exactly as if they were social equals. Yorkshire servants were sturdy and independent in character, not given to thinking of themselves as menials, but even gruff old Maggie, who had brought Lilian up, would hardly have spoken to her with such complete disregard of class. It was very odd; and somehow agreeable. He had not mentioned her disability, either, or made her feel that she was in any way different from other girls.

A tempting short ball came his way, and he hooked it largely and rashly, straight into Arthur's hands, a clean catch. A joyful cry went up from the men of the House, and the batsman, apparently unruffled, turned and walked back to the pavilion. His successors had brief and undistinguished lives. In half an hour the match was over. The ladies around Lilian began to rustle to their feet, collecting children and possessions.

'Dear child,' Louisa said patronisingly as she rolled statuesquely past Lilian's chair, 'how quiet you've been! I declare we never noticed you. Did anyone fetch you tea, or anything?'

Lilian smiled. 'Oh, yes, thank you. I was well looked after.'

Arthur was the next to enquire after her welfare. Glowering and red-faced, he asked, 'What were you doing, talking to that fellow? I saw you, never think I didn't. I'm surprised at you, Lil, I really am.'

'What was I doing? Well, what a funny question. Talking to him, I suppose – and eating the ice-cream he kindly brought me, the one I didn't notice *you* bringing me. It was very nice, and a kind thought on his part.'

'Oh, well,' Arthur muttered, 'imagined you'd be looked after, your own fault if you weren't. But hark to me, I don't like to see my sister hob-nobbing with all and sundry.'

Lilian looked up innocently. 'Then you needn't take notice, need you. In any case, who was "all and sundry"?'

'Don't know the fellow's name, how should I? Ask Uncle if you're so interested.'

'Thank you, I will.' She was all impatience for him to go away. Obligingly he did so, leaving her twisting her handkerchief, waiting, waiting. It seemed she was invisible today, as person after person passed her; she might have been a tree, a feature of the landscape. Only one person remembered where she was and came back, dark against the sunset sky. He had a jacket on now, giving him even more the look of one of the gentlemen.

'Right,' he said. 'Want a hand?'

'A hand?'

'Well, a push then.' He indicated the chair. 'Back home, unless you're goin' up to t'Hall?'

'Thank you. No, I'm not. But if you're invited back, please don't mind me.'

'Oh, there's some kind o' do on, supper or summat. There'll be plenty left.'

She temporised. 'I – my brother was supposed to have taken me home . . .'

'If your brother's who I think he is, that was fieldin' at midwicket, he's tekking a bottle of ale wi' some o' the lads. I'd forget him if I was you. Come on.'

Being pushed by him was quite different from Arthur's impatient and clumsy propelling. He seemed to know the surface and curvature of every path, to calculate exactly the weight and poise of the chair, as though he pushed helpless invalids about for a living. All the way he said not a word, nor did she. She was aware of the violet and rose tints of the sky, the sleepy song of a blackbird, the fact that her hands were still sticky from the ice-cream, though she could have wiped them with the eau-de-cologne she carried.

But they had held the shared bowl, and she cherished that touch of him by proxy. She seemed enclosed in a coloured prism, where she felt no pain, nor irritation, nor anything but a strange expectancy.

At the balcony door of the Dower House he paused. 'This is where you go in.'

'Yes. How did you know?'

'I've watched you, times. Goodneet.'

Boldly she reached out and caught his sleeve. 'Tell me your name!'

'Jack Ellershaw.'

'And you're gardener to Sir Lewis?'

'When Howard's off wi' rheumatics, like he is now.' His face was quite impassive; he was giving nothing, only the information she asked. On an impulse, she pulled off her hat and ran her hands through her hair, so that the ruffled chignon spilt its strands over her shoulders, a red glory in the sunset, and held it spread with her hands as though offering merchandise. For a moment, only a moment, she saw wonder and hunger in his face, before it reverted to its normal imperturbable expression. Then he turned and began to walk swiftly away.

'You'll come back?' she called after him. But he made no answer.

In the parlour someone carrying a lamp was unbolting the french door; Mamma, with a face like Judgment Day.

CHAPTER THREE

The inquisition went on until almost midnight. Florence was in the state of mind of a mother who beats her child which has just escaped the hooves of a runaway horse.

'You read too many romances, Mamma,' Lilian said wearily. 'There was no abduction about it. I simply waited for Arthur to bring me home, or send someone else to do so, and nobody came, so I accepted this young man's offer.'

'You foolish, irresponsible girl! Didn't you think for a moment of what might have happened to you – alone, at night, with a strange man?' Florence shuddered with real chill.

'No, I didn't. Perhaps I haven't as much imagination as you. I merely thought that sitting under a tree all night, watching the bats catching insects and getting a severe chill on the lungs, was not perhaps the pleasantest of prospects. And the young man seemed perfectly respectable and well-intentioned.'

'Who was he? Did he not even give a name?'

'No.' Lilian reflected in passing that she was becoming quite an accomplished liar. 'Uncle Lewis recruits all kinds of people for his matches. He might have come from . . . Huddersfield, for all I know. What does it matter?'

'I shall find out. Arthur will know.'

'I should like to go to bed now, Mamma. I'm very tired.' That, at least, was true. For once her mother was not sympathetic.

'You shall go to bed when Arthur has told me this person's name, and not before. You deserve some small punishment for putting me into such a state. Wasn't I completely devastated, Nelly?'

'Oh, yes, Mamma.' Nelly, who had stayed at home rather than yawn her head off, as she said, at boring cricket, was annoyed now that she seemed to have missed some excitement. 'I really thought you'd have one of your turns.'

'I have a very, very bad headache, as it is. Find my vinaigrette for me. We will all sit up for Arthur's return.'

But Arthur's return was between two stalwart friends, who were none too sober themselves, knocking and ringing at the front door most alarmingly.

'Sorry, ma'am,' said one of them to the horrified Florence, 'he ain't up to much, as you can see. Shall we put him to bed for you?'

Arthur, pale green of complexion, swayed on their arms, trying to smile and speak and succeeding in doing neither.

' 'S all right, ma . . . goo' fellows. Bit . . . tired.' He hiccupped.

' 'F I were you, ma'am,' said the less drunk of the friends, 'I'd let us take him up before, er . . .' He indicated the handsome, though worn, Brussels carpet in the hall.

'Wait! I want to speak to him! Arthur, you must listen to me!'

But Arthur was beyond listening, only too thankful to be dragged upstairs like a sack of potatoes. Florence stood at the foot of the stairs, impotently raging. Nelly had come out to see what the commotion was, and stood laughing in the doorway. Florence turned on her.

'And what you find so amusing I don't know, miss. Go up after them and demand that Arthur tells you the man's name.'

Nelly snorted. 'Catch me, Mamma. I'm not going near the disgusting creature. Let his friends put him to bed, and welcome. In any case, why should he know who pushed Lil home, if he wasn't there to see? You'd best go up to the Hall and ask Uncle tomorrow.'

This seemed so sensible that Florence went back into the parlour. The sight of Lilian put her anger out of her mind temporarily, for her daughter lay prone on the couch, as white as her namesake flower, her eyes shut. She was utterly exhausted, partly from physical tiredness and partly from relief. Arthur had told her at the match that he didn't know the name of the 'fellow' who had so presumptuously fed her with ice-cream, but he might have found out since. What a mercy he had come home in that state! Somehow it was very important to her that Jack Ellershaw's kindly action should not be the cause of his dismissal from Sir Lewis's employment. If he were dismissed, it would be her fault for letting him do anything so rash. (Not that she had thought it rash at the time.) And why should a man have to suffer for doing a chivalrous action? Mamma was always going on about the knights of King Arthur's

Round Table, who sounded odiously priggish, but Lilian was sure any of them would have pushed an invalid damsel home rather than let her languish all night on the edge of a cricket field. That is, if they played cricket; perhaps it hadn't been invented and they only played war-games like tilting . . .

'Lilian, speak to me!' Florence cried. 'Oh, Nelly, she's swooned.'

'No, she ain't, Mamma, she's asleep.' Nelly pulled the bell, its clangour sounding faintly from the kitchen. 'Millie's sure to be up, we can manage her between us.'

Arthur, when he awoke, very early next morning, was in that distressing state in which drink has drawn a heavy black curtain between a man and his memories. An invisible butcher's cleaver was chopping relentlessly away at his skull, his mouth felt like an Arabian desert at midday, and his digestion was in turmoil. A mixture of Sir Lewis's home-brewed ale, gin punch, and a few glasses of claret had done its work. From his mother's questions he turned his head away.

'Don't know anything, I tell you. Don't remember. Oh, do go away, Mamma. I'm ill, in case you can't see for yourself.'

Florence, trotting relentlessly up to the Hall, was daunted to find her cousin in a similar state, except that Sir Lewis was made of sterner stuff than Arthur. He was occupied with his bailiff, discussing the week's estate matters, when she arrived, and in no very good temper.

'Well, what is it, Florence? I'm busy, can't ye see? Can't it wait?' A sudden twinge went through his head; he winced, reaching for the glass of seltzer at his side.

'No, it can't.' She recited the events of the night before and sat back awaiting his horrified reaction. It did not come.

'Well? What of it? One of my chaps had the decency to get the lass home – more than your son did. No, I *don't* know who it was. D'ye think I watch 'em like a nursemaid? Great grown chaps can look after theirselves, and so can Lilian, I daresay, a sight better than you think she can, for all she's such a poor wisket of a thing. She's got spirit, if you ask me, and you're a fool, Florence.' He took out a huge watch and consulted it, frowning. 'I've no more time to waste.'

So the whole alarm died down. Florence admitted to herself, if to nobody else, that she had acted impulsively and that no harm

41

was done. Only Nelly looked askance at her sister, aware of a far-away look and a changed quality about her. Nelly thought there was a young man in question, and having no young man of her own at the time decided to amuse herself by finding out who it was and what had happened.

To all questions, hints and guesses Lilian remained impervious. She was not going to give Jack away, that was certain. When Nelly said she'd changed, she agreed, inwardly. It had all been so slight, so unimportant, and yet she felt that something new and marvellous had come into her life. Somehow she felt healthier, more normal, or as though she *could* be healthier, if she tried. She began to make small efforts: to sit up straight instead of reclining, though it made her back ache, to stretch her arms up above her head, like a cat, flexing them, trying to strengthen her soft muscles. She thought back to the days when she had been as much of a tomboy as Nelly, climbing over the fells like a young goat, in search of the first primroses and rock daffodils. And riding, demurely side-saddle when adults were watching, daringly astride when they weren't, in defiance of their delicate hints that something quite unspeakably awful might happen to her if she did.

Well, whatever it was (and she had a good deal better idea now than then) it could not have been so awful as lying here, on the wicker couch in her conservatory, day after fine day, waiting, until the sunshine seemed to mock her. She longed to have again that day in the cricket-field: went over and over in her mind how he had looked, what he had said. If only he would come back . . .

But he did not come.

In fact, Jack Ellershaw had made up his mind not to return to the Dower House. Faint rumours had reached him of the storm that had followed his taking Lilian home. The bailiff had been all ears in the next room during Florence's interview with Sir Lewis, and had passed it on to somebody else, who in turn passed it down the line until it reached Jack.

Of course it had been daft of him to go off with the young lady like that, without getting somebody to go with them – a chaperon, these people called it. Very nasty minds, some of 'em had, Jack thought. He hoped he was above such things, but since others weren't he must give them no more chance to make trouble for him or for Miss Lilian, poor lass.

It was not that he didn't think about her. Though he was too preoccupied with other matters in his life to bother with women at this stage of it, he had as much of an eye for a pretty girl as any other chap; and this girl was the prettiest he had ever seen. Not just the hair, and the face, but there was something about her . . . It was not even her helpless state, enough to make any man sorry for her. That should have repelled him. Jack worshipped the physical perfection he cultivated in himself. He had turned away in the streets of Leeds from diseased and deformed beggars, the bandy-legged rickety poor folk, the old soldiers who had lost their legs and propelled themselves horribly in little carts.

Not usually given to self-analysis, he asked himself: if she'd a hump-back would I ha' liked her as much? He visualised the hump-back, and then Lilian's face, the frank way her eyes had met his, her lovely long throat and pretty figure: and decided that he would have liked her as much.

And she liked him, he knew, though he was not familiar with the ways of ladies. They had not come his way much. Neither of Sir Lewis's daughters had ever given him so much as the time of day when they walked in the gardens, though they might condescend to nod to Old Howard, who had been there when they were children, or enquire after his rheumatism. And Old Howard – so old that he still wore knee-breeches and a top-hat for work, as his father and his father's father had done – answered them no more politely than if he had been speaking to people of his own kind. Jack admired that. When one was not long turned twenty there was a lot to be learned from the old. Old Howard's example had been before him when the young lady at the Dower House had addressed him so rudely. She had not been offended by his answering in kind: he even felt that it had impressed her. In her life she'd probably had a deal too much soft talk and wanted a change.

Yet they would never be equal in Society's eyes, he and she, never in this world. It was a pity, for when Jack took a wife he wanted just such a straight-talking, easy-mannered young woman, with a good head on her – someone better than the giggling gormless girls of his own village, with nought but lads in their minds and not caring which way they got a wedding ring. But Jack was a realist. It was not his way to entertain dreams of princesses with

43

hair as bright as October leaves or factory fires by night. He had one set ambition, one road to tread; best tread it alone.

He went to Old Howard and told him a tale of how he was troubled about the kitchen gardens. He suspected them of being riddled with some kind of pest or fungus – might he be taken off other jobs to give more time to them? It was only a half-truth, but it would do well enough to keep him away from the Dower House.

It was unfortunate that Florence, of all people, chose to send up to Sir Lewis for someone to clear the lawns. The extreme heat had caused the trees and hedges to shed their leaves out of season, littering the grass and making the view from the drawing-room very untidy. Sir Lewis passed on the request to Old Howard, who deputed Jack for the job.

Lilian's chair had been put in a corner of the garden from which it could not be seen from any window. In her present state of suspense she felt that her mother's constant, obsessive watch over her would drive her to make some wild silly remark that would at the very least hurt Florence's feelings, and at the worst give away her own preoccupation.

The hot sunshine had given way to grey skies, pressing the air down until it seemed like a solid dimension, hardly breathable. Lilian's hair stuck to her forehead and her clothes to her skin. She wondered how people who could move about were able to bear it at all. She was trying to embroider a panel of woolwork fruit and flowers for a firescreen that she and Nelly were giving Florence for a birthday present. It was supposed to be a secret, wrapped up hastily whenever Florence approached, but of course was nothing of the kind, in a family like theirs. Lilian finished off the red bloom on an apple which had taken days to work, and pricked her finger, drawing blood. She was not really good at embroidery, she knew, but Mamma liked to think of her as an enchanted Lady of Shalott, weaving a magic web with colours gay, shut off from the world in her island bower.

The gate in the hedge clicked, and he was there, a broom of twigs in one hand, a basket skip in the other. Seeing her, he stopped dead. Her embroidery slipped from her fingers to lie unregarded on the dry grass.

'Well,' she said brightly, at last, 'I thought we were never to see you again, Jack Ellershaw.'

'I'd other things to do.' He put the skip down and mechanically began to sweep up leaves.

'Oh.' The conversation was getting them nowhere. He was not going to talk to her, after all this time of waiting for him. He would move away from her across the garden, and go, and she would never have the chance of talking with him again. I love you, could you love me? she wanted to say and must not.

'I wondered,' she said desperately, 'what you meant, the other day, when you said that you'd been playing cricket all your life. Are you not a gardener, then?'

To her relief, he paused. 'Not when I can help it. Only because I must.'

'Were you brought up to it?'

'Nay. I were bred to coal-minin'.'

'Oh. But there is none round here, surely?'

'No. Near Doncaster's where I come from.'

'Then why did you not make it your living?'

Jack surveyed her as a father might a foolishly prattling child. 'You young ladies from down south don't know much, do you. I didn't go down t'pit because mi feyther nigh got his death in it. Forty years is the life of a miner, did they ever tell you that? – if he's lucky. Coal-dust chokes 'em if they're not killed in an explosion, like the Oaks Colliery one last year. Dad was lucky. His lungs wasn't quite etten away, only part, and Mam nursed him back.'

Lilian's face was horror-struck. 'But how dreadful. And how did you all live then – for I suppose you depended on his wages?'

'Aye, we did that,' Jack said dryly. 'Mam got a bit of a market garden together, and we made do wi' sellin' stuff from it. There was only them and me to keep – t'others were dead, three of 'em, and Mam wouldn't see me go down the mine, though I could ha' even though I was but a little lad. So I grew up to make this mi trade.' He gestured with the broom.

'And where does cricket come in?'

Jack regarded her with pitying disbelief. 'I thought you knew about such things.'

'Oh, I do,' she said hastily, 'I mean, about the game, from my brother, as I told you, but not about . . . well . . .'

45

'Professional cricket,' Jack supplied. Slowly, as to one of limited understanding, he explained how cricket had once been a game for the gentry only, but had now come to be a game for all, in which high and low met together, and men from any walk in life could make a good living from it. Here, in the north, men played it with passion and concentration, every little lad hoping one day to belong to a professional club and play against the giants of the south, Marylebone Cricket Club, Kent, Surrey.

'There's been a Yorkshire Cricket Club these last four year. Soon as I know I'm good enough I'm goin' to ask to be given a try.'

'And when will that be?'

'When I think fit.'

There seemed to be no more to say, but Lilian suddenly found the right words. 'I'm *not* a young lady from down south, you know. I was born five miles from here.'

His look brightened. 'I'd never ha' thought it. You don't talk like us.'

'I do – if you listen carefully. Has tha got cloth ears, lad?'

This daring, if unskilled, imitation of his dialect actually made him laugh, and Lilian blushed.

'Nay, I haven't, and tha's a proper caution, lass.'

Holding his eyes, so that he would not go away, Lilian began to talk rapidly, not caring what she said, only wanting to make him understand her and keep him by her side.

'I'm so glad you spoke to me last Sunday. It was very kind of you. No, I don't quite mean that, because as a rule people are much *too* kind to me. Now you haven't once asked me how long I've been like this, on my back, and whether it hurts.'

'No, I've not. I wouldn't want to be asked it if I was t'same.'

They were talking, yet saying nothing significant, and neither wanted the talk to end. A flutter of a skirt round the corner of the house told Lilian that Maggie was coming out with her mid-morning milk. 'You'd better move away,' she said hastily. 'It wouldn't do for them to think I was wasting your time. Will you – will you finish that sweeping today?'

'Nay,' Jack replied solemnly. 'I'll mek a long job of it.' His smile was beautiful, perfect teeth in a gipsy-brown face.

At supper that evening Lilian chattered so animatedly that

46

Florence began to be anxious. She half-turned from the table to inspect her.

'Be careful to chew your food properly. It is not like you to eat so fast.'

'Or so much,' put in Nelly.

'Is there any reason why I shouldn't?' Lilian demanded. 'I'm very fond of mushroom pie.'

'Too much food is not good for you,' said Florence, gently pushing the dish that held it out of Lilian's sight, but not out of Augustus's. Dining with his cousins was a treat in more ways than one. His eyes glistened as Nelly helped him to more, enquiring as she did so, 'What do they give you at that vicarage of yours – church mouse stew?'

At Lilian's laugh Florence looked round again. 'You have a very high colour, dearest. Are you sure you haven't a fever?'

'Of course not, Mamma. I feel very well.'

Nelly glanced round, about to be purposely, mischievously in-discreet. '*I* think,' she said, 'I think our Lilian's spoony.'

In the silence that followed, Lilian's excited colour became a suffusing blush that spread from brow to throat. She put her hands to her cheeks, then dropped them, hoping they would cool off themselves, but still the blush burned. Three pairs of eyes regarded her with varying expressions, Florence's startled and shocked, Nelly's mocking, Gus's baffled. If only it were possible to get up and run out of the room: but she was trapped. With a high, affected laugh, she said, 'Don't talk such stuff, Nelly. We don't *all* have men on their minds like you. And before Augustus, too – I'm surprised at you.'

Augustus looked down at his plate, embarrassed but with a faint ray of hope shining somewhere in his soul. Could what Nelly had said be true of Lilian – and about *him*? Who else was there, after all?

Florence laid down her knife and fork with a clatter as sharp as her voice. 'If no one has anything more sensible to say I suggest we should all keep silence until we have finished our meal.'

Like Augustus, Florence had felt a leap of hope at Nelly's words. Perhaps her ice-maiden was melting at last, her heart softening towards poor Augustus. But another feeling, a vague apprehension,

47

troubled her. There was something very strange about her beloved daughter these days.

Arthur was surprised, coming home from a day on the moors with the guns, to be sent for by Lilian, who seldom requested his company, and even more surprised to be asked to supply some information about the game of cricket.

'What d'you want to know for?' he demanded. 'You looked dozy enough in the Long Meadow t'other week.'

'I'm amazed you noticed . . . no, Arthur dear, I don't mean to quarrel – for once. It's because of that, really, that match – I found it so dull and it seemed to me that I might gain a new interest if I learned something about the game. I have so few interests, you know,' she added, pathetically, opening her eyes wide. Arthur was not impressed by this, but reasonably flattered to be asked to air his knowledge. Thumbs hooked in waistcoat, he held forth about the tactics of setting the field so that each man be in the most advantageous place to catch a careless ball from the enemy batsman, the wiles to be used by the batsman to combat the fielders, the importance of the wicket-keeper, the batsman's various skills, and the difference between slow and fast bowlers.

Frowning with concentration, Lilian took it all down in a notebook. Little though she understood it, she would work it out somehow. Then she made Arthur draw up a rough plan of a field set for a slow bowler, and another for a fast one.

'Oh, devil take it,' he said, scribbling, 'don't ask me any more questions, Lil, for I can't see what use all this stuff can be to a girl, and it makes one confoundedly dry gabbing on so much.'

'I won't bother you any more,' she said meekly. 'Thank you so much. And Artie – don't tell Mamma and Nelly, will you. You know how Nelly teases, and Mamma will say it's bad for me to exert my mind.'

'All right, I won't say a word. Fancy you taking to sport. Rum creatures, females . . .'

Jack came to the Dower House almost every day, half-angry with himself at giving in to its lure. He was surprised to find Lilian turning the talk to cricket, and airing theories which he was pretty sure she had not held when they first met. Indeed, her knowledge seemed to have improved phenomenally, even though she did sound a little like a copy-book as she reeled off technical terms. It took him some time to realise that she had, in fact, been learning all this by heart for his benefit – for his sake; and he was amused and touched. Nobody had ever taken such trouble for him before.

He let her chat airily on before interrupting, straight-faced.

'So, if you was me playin' a ball pitched on the inside of leg, how'd you tackle it?'

Lilian looked startled. 'Leg? Oh. That's the side away from . . . no, I mean the same side as the bat. Or is that called "on"? Oh dear. It's either "off" or "on", I know that.'

Jack shook his head slowly. 'Tha'll ha' to do better than that. Come on, now, tell me, who's been teaching thee? I warrant none of this was in thi head when tha boasted at t'match about knowin' all about cricket.'

'I didn't then, but I do now, Jack, oh, I do! It was very difficult at first, like the game with flamingoes in *Alice in Wonderland*, but I can see it now very clearly. It's a beautiful pattern, isn't it, the eleven men in the field and the two batsmen who have to outwit them. It's like a sort of dance.'

'Tha's a very, very clever lass,' he said. 'Maybe now tha'd like to give me a lecture on flamingoes, for I know nowt about 'em, or this Alice neither, no more than tha did last week about cricket, and tha might as well own up.'

'I do own up,' she said meekly, putting her hands together like a child. 'It was Arthur – I made him explain to me, though he got rather out of temper. I thought I ought to know, to keep up with you. And if you really want to learn about flamingoes, they're a sort of pink bird with very long necks and wings. You can find them in the Cape Verde Islands, should you be going there, and Alice used one as a croquet-mallet.'

Jack laughed as she had never seen him laugh. It came into his mind that he knew very little about women.

Because Florence and Nelly were invited to a weekend house-party, for which they left on Friday, and Arthur to shoot on the estate of a friend of the Prince of Wales, Lilian and Jack were free to see each other when and where they liked.

'Maggie won't think it odd if I'm seen talking to you, and Millie's too stupid to notice,' Lilian told him. 'You could even tell Maggie you'll carry me downstairs for once, as Arthur's away. What fun it will be!'

49

So next morning he was shown up to her room, and for the first time saw how she lived. To him the heavy furnishings with their drab colours were grand, daunting, and seemed to put her at a great distance from him, even now when for the first time she was in his arms, melting with delicious weakness to find herself there, being carried to the garden under the watchful eye of Maggie, who thought it quite odd that Miss Lilian should have invited in this strange gardener with his swarthy good looks and uppish manner.

To Jack she seemed pitifully light, and warm and soft and sweetly-scented. Her hands were clasped round his neck as though that was where they rightly belonged, and her bright head lay comfortably on his shoulder. He was sorry to set her down in the bath-chair, sorry and glad and confused, all at the same time.

In their three days of freedom they grew as close as though the days had been years, yet no word of love was said between them. Both knew that nothing could come of it; both hoped, secretly, that something might, by a miracle.

It was Monday, their last day, and time to go in, and light drops of rain were falling, pattering among the leaves.

'Come on,' Jack said. 'By, I wish tha were stronger.'

'You must be my strength. I'd like that.'

'It's not enough. Hast ever tried to stand?'

'Oh no. It hurts even sitting upright without a prop for my back.'

Jack surveyed her speculatively. 'Let's see, shall we. I don't want to hurt thee . . .'

'I don't mind.' But she set her lips tight as he gently raised her and put her on her feet, holding her close to him, his arms supporting her tightly.

'It didn't hurt! Oh, Jack it didn't! Don't put me down yet!'

They were very near to kissing, her eyes and her lips invited him, her body responding to his. Nelly, just returned, watching avidly from an upstairs window, saw what looked like a prolonged embrace. With the speed of light she flew downstairs, then slowed down and sauntered out through the french doors.

'Well, well! Won't you introduce me to your beau?' she said with malice. Lilian went very pale. Jack set her down in the bath-chair and arranged her shawl round her shoulders before saying

50

coolly, 'No need for introductions, miss. I'm Sir Lewis's under-gardener.'

'I am hurt, Lilian,' Florence said; her eyes were still brimming with tears, though the conflict seemed to Lilian to have been raging for days. 'Very hurt and very bewildered. All so unlike you, to engage in a vulgar intrigue – and there's no use in saying it was only a friendship, for how could such a thing exist with a common man? I thought there was some change in you – I saw it. Didn't I say so, Nelly?'

'We all saw it, Ma. We said there was something jolly queer about Lil. Didn't we, Artie?'

'Leave me out of it,' Arthur said gruffly, guilty about his own instruction of his sister in the Rules of Cricket. So this was the reason, the sly cat. He went out, slamming the door on the three women.

Lilian heard the voices go on and on, her mother sighing, complaining, scolding, Nelly putting in little goads to keep the pace up: sometimes her own voice, interrupting with a protest that was instantly silenced. Nothing she said seemed to make sense to them. She memorised the pattern on a needleworked antimacassar on a chair: roses, violets, nameless foliage and a butterfly. The rain of the morning had come on heavily and now was lashing against the windows. She was glad, it suited her mood. She knew they would separate her from Jack for ever.

It did not surprise her to hear her mother declaring that for the present she would be kept to her room. 'The conservatory door will be closed, of course. We can't risk another repetition of your little adventure – if it was no worse than that. And the bath-chair shall be put away.'

'You always wanted me to be the Princess in the Tower, didn't you, Mamma?' Lilian said wearily. 'Now you are to have your wish and I hope it makes you very happy.'

CHAPTER FOUR

The room at Scarbrick Hall which was known as the Study may have been a study, in the days of Sir Lewis's forefathers, for its walls were lined with calf-bound volumes of *The Gentleman's Magazine*, the *Annual Review*, journals of country sports, the works of eminent divines, all thick with dust, untouched for many years. The huge desk which Chippendale himself had made for a Hambleden ancestor was invisible under a mass of papers, the whole room untidy, littered with guns, fishing-rods, cricket-bats and headgear of various descriptions. A strong scent of cigar-smoke hung on the air. Sir Lewis sat at his desk, puffing irritably at a fine Havana.

'I don't pretend to understand it, Ellershaw,' he said, between puffs. 'Women's matters mean nought to me, never did. But what am I to do but send for you, when my fool of a cousin comes rushing up here all of a lather to tell me some tale I can't make out about you and young Lilian? Don't understand it, don't believe a word of it, with the girl a helpless cripple, poor creature. You see though, don't you, that I've got to do summat about it, or she'll spread the word all over seven parishes?'

'Aye, I do,' Jack replied impassively, staring straight before him at a portrait in oils of a hard-featured squire in a stiff grey wig.

'Can't very well keep you on here, in the circumstances. Old Howard's past being bothered with women's clatter, and I'd not put it beyond Flo to go shrieking at him. I'd hoped to see you take over head gardener's job when Howard retires. Can't do that now, but there's my girl Elsie down in Sheffield crying out for someone to look after their acres of fancy gardens. Could you do that, d'you think?'

'I could, but I won't. Thank you all t'same. I've other plans.'

'Oh? May I ask what?'

'I'd rather not count any chickens till they're hatched.'

'I see. Very wise. You'll . . . be all right, though?' Sir Lewis was not given to human attachments, much preferring dogs, horses and sporting gear, but he confessed to himself a certain liking and respect for this straight, no-nonsense young man, a splendid bat with a style one didn't see often, and a very tidy fast bowler. What a contrast to wretched, girlish Augustus, and how he wished that the fairies the country folk talked of had changed the two over in their cradles.

'Oh, I'll be reet.'

Sir Lewis cleared his throat. 'Well. I knew it had to be done, so I got Edmundson to make up your wages. Two weeks.' From a desk drawer he removed a packet and handed it over. Jack knew by the feel of it that more than two weeks' money was there. Now his mother would not have to go short of what he sent her regularly.

'Thank you,' he said, 'sir.' And, with a brief nod, was gone.

Sir Lewis stubbed out his Havana and cursed, long, fluently, and in language much used in cock-fighting circles and the prize-ring. He cursed all women, and most particularly his cousin Florence, her great rampole of an elder daughter and that poor dieaway creature the younger one who had caused all this upset. He wished with all his heart that he had begotten nothing but boys, manlier boys than Gus, who would by now have been men enough to have begotten boys of their own. Then, seizing a gun from a corner, he flung it at a dangerous angle over his shoulder and strode out to work off his feelings on rooks and jackdaws.

In the drawing-room of Scarbrick Hall Florence was telling the story, with tearful embellishments, to Sir Lewis's sister Frederica, while that lady reclined gracefully with her feet up on a footstool, eating sweets, a splash of rich colour in that gloomy masculine room. She was tall and handsome and almost fifty, though she would be officially forty-five for the next ten years at least. Her hair would have been as white as her brother's had she not applied a discreet brown tint to it once a fortnight, and her naturally high complexion was heightened by pearl powder and the addition of black pencilling to her already fashionably thick eyebrows. Like Florence, she was a widow; her stockbroker husband Timothy had left her well off. Her gown, of fashionable London cut, was a striking shade of purple, the skirt caught up in loops above a storm-grey underskirt, both obviously of the best silk. Round her neck was a string of pearls which would have paid the wages of Florence's servants for some years, and her rather large hands were covered with rings. Florence's children called her Aunt Freddy, and in the view of Arthur and Nelly she was a regular jolly fellow.

She heard out Florence's tale of woe in silence, making the right sounds at appropriate moments. Her comments, when they came, were forthright.

'Have a fondant. The pink ones are delicious, though no doubt very bad for the teeth. Now, Florence, I must say I find all this very queer. I really can't believe little Lilian's been . . . well, naughty, with this hobbledehoy.'

'Oh, no, no!' Florence protested. 'My Lilian has always been an angel of purity. I should know, having been at her side night and day since her accident.'

'I daresay you have, dear, but that's not to say you know her like a book. One never does know anybody like a book. What I mean is that I'm sure this adventure of hers has been because she's a very lonely girl.'

'Lonely! with me, and her brother and sister?'

'Quite so – a very happy family, I'm sure. But, my dear Flo, the child has no friends of her own, has she? I know Arthur and Nelly have plenty, but they're not her sort at all – out of *quite* a different stable.'

'Well . . . They lead very active lives.'

'Exactly! and she don't. So when she finds a good-natured lad to push her round and talk to her, it's not surprising if she makes eyes at him now and then. She has very pretty eyes, much prettier than your Nelly's, if I may say so. Take it from me, this was just an innocent frolic, and frankly, dear, I wouldn't put it past Nelly to be telling an out-and-out story about what she saw from the window.'

Florence bridled. 'Nelly is a very truthful girl.'

'H'm. What does Lilian herself say about it?'

'Some very unlikely story – that she asked this person to help her to stand on her feet.'

'There you are, then.'

'But Frederica, that alone shows how foolish and irresponsible the whole affair was! Everybody accepts that Lilian is a helpless invalid. It might have done her untold harm to be lifted and pulled about like that. Lucky for him that he hasn't her death on his conscience.'

'I do think you exaggerate things.'

'Think so if you please,' Florence said with a shrug. 'I'm Lilian's mother and should know best.'

There was a pause. Frederica would dearly have loved to let fly at her cousin with a few home-truths, the first being that she was behaving like a dying duck in a thunderstorm and the second that Lilian was unlucky to have been born into a family of thoroughly stupid people. Frederica had no daughter, only a son, Digby, who had entered the Guards and was hardly ever at home, naturally. She knew what loneliness was, too well. She would have loved a daughter to gossip with, go shopping with, dress in charming clothes, and bring out in Society with a series of dazzling parties. But there was no use in telling Florence how fortunate she was, and how differently she ought to behave. Florence was set in her ways, though younger than Frederica herself.

'Well,' she said. 'And what will you do now – with Lilian, I mean? Keep her away from this dangerous character, what's-his-name?'

'Oh, that is all taken care of. I believe Lewis is dismissing him at this moment. Lilian, of course, is confined to her room, and I shall not allow her to go out until I hear from her that she is truly sorry for her behaviour, and will never do such a thing again.'

A violent expletive, picked up from her soldier son, rose to Frederica's lips. She amended it to 'Upon my soul. Why don't you have her clapped into Fellgate Gaol, while you're about it? Or send her over the Pennines to Lancaster? I believe they've some delightfully quaint leg-irons and manacles there, left over from the old days, in the Castle dungeons. Now, don't make such a face at me, Flo. I know you think I'm talking out of turn and ought to keep out of other people's family business. But you *did* tell me about it, and in a way ask my help, I suppose.'

'No, I didn't,' Florence said sullenly. 'I merely thought you ought to know.'

'So I should jolly well think!' Frederica jumped up and stood imposingly over the limp Florence. 'I'm as much a relative of yours as Lewis is, and we all know *he* has precious little interest in female matters. When you came into this room I was just thinking to myself how awfully boring the country is, and how I wished I'd never left London for a visit because my people are cleaning the house from top to bottom, and how dismal it is to be in a place full of stags' heads and stuffed birds, poor things. But now I feel *much* better, because I have something to do with myself.'

Florence quailed from what was coming. 'And that is . . . ?'

'To take Lilian out of your clutches. Oh yes, clutches, my dear, for you're the very picture of an old hen with her claws round her chickens, sitting on 'em at the same time. Well, if Nature didn't push the chickens out of the nest, they'd smother, and so will Lilian if you're not careful. That child needs friends, cheerful company, a change of scene, all that sort of thing. I shall take her back with me to London and see she gets them.'

'She is not strong enough! The journey would kill her!'

'Not at all. I've plenty of money, I'll see to it that she travels in as much comfort as the Queen. As the Queen would, that is, if she ever did travel instead of staying cooped up at Windsor in a black shawl. Now come, Flo, say you think it a capital idea! And it will be a rest and a change for you, you know, after all this nursing.'

'But who *is* to nurse Lilian, in London?' Florence quavered. 'Except for myself only her maid Millie has ever looked after her. There's so much to be done – lifting, washing, everything the child can't do for herself . . .'

'Then let Millie come with her,' returned Frederica briskly.

'Millie is . . . not very bright. A good servant, but – '

'I don't care if she's feeble-minded. I've plenty of servants of my own to keep an eye on her. Think of what I can give Lilian, Flo. A handsome house in Chelsea, right on the Embankment looking over the river – so much to see without even going out – and people to wait on her hand and foot, and the fun of London . . . Why, she can have a little Season all to herself, conducted from her couch. And then, I have so many interesting friends.' No point in explaining to Florence what kind of interest lay in them for her, or how Lilian's looks fitted in with their image. The child would be a success, that was all that mattered.

'Young *men?*' asked Florence suspiciously.

'Well, naturally, some of them are men – I don't run a convent.'

'Nothing must come between Lilian and Augustus. They are

56

practically engaged. It's the most suitable match she can hope to make. When they are married I shall live with them, and everything will be almost as it always has been.'

Frederica bit back her views on her nephew Augustus. She considered him a dreary, canting, duffer, Lewis's Bad Luck, and no fit husband for any woman who wasn't as dreary as he. Aloud, she said, 'Augustus may visit Lilian in London – if his duties will let him.'

Florence brightened. 'That would be something. He can then tell me exactly how Lilian is getting on.'

As much as I let him see, Frederica thought.

When Florence left the Hall, convinced by Frederica's rapid arguments, yet feeling she had somehow been browbeaten into submission, she passed without noticing it the silver tray on the great oak chest that stood in the hallway. It held visiting-cards and letters for the post or to be delivered by hand. There were very few; Sir Lewis was not fond of letter-writing. In the tray lay one envelope, unstamped, addressed in large stumbling print to Miss de Wentworth. A few hours later one of the servants saw it, and took it down to the Dower House.

Nelly received it, aware it was meant for her sister. Slowly, savouringly, she ripped it open and read. The writing was that of one who only wrote or read painfully, though in a firm hand.

'Miss de Wentworth I hope you will not mind me writing. I am sorry for all the trouble I have brot on you. I cant any longer stay at the hall. I am going to Sheffield to try my Luck for Yorks, like I told you. I think I deserve good Fortune. I think of you. Take care and . . .' (here came a blot and some crossing-out). 'I will be back believe it . . . Yours truly Jack Ellershaw.'

Nelly read the note again and again. The wretch, daring to write to a lady of good family, particularly after the scandal he'd caused. And too ignorant to know that *she* was addressed as Miss de Wentworth, her sister as Miss Lilian. Trouble, indeed. Just for a moment pity rose in her for the situation she knew in her heart to be the truth, but she killed it. The gardener's boy was handsome and attractive, a sight more so than the beefy or pimpled youths

57

in her circle. If he had been bent on a flirtation with a lady above his station it should have been with her, not with sickly Lil. Not for a moment did Nelly believe that what had been between them had been wrong. Even the embrace, now that Lilian had given her explanation of it, she knew to have been innocent.

But she screwed the note up into a tight ball and flung it into the heart of the fire. Lilian would never read it now.

The stuffiness of the room pressed on Lilian like a blanket. Nobody had been to see her for a long time, not even Millie. Perhaps Mamma had given orders that she was to be left to starve. It was not hunger that troubled her so much as feeling unclean, her face and hands dirty, her hair greasy, her nightdress the one she had been changed into last week. Not, she thought with bitter humour, altogether like the Lady of Shalott. All very well, weaving away at her magic web, seeing shadows of the world in her mirror, very snug and comfortable so long as she didn't look down towards Camelot, and saw him in the mirror, Sir Lancelot of the Lake.

'His broad and clear brow in sunlight glow'd,
On burnished hooves his war-horse trode;
From underneath his helmet flowed
His coal-black curls as on he rode.
As he rode down to Camelot.'

Jack's dark curls were in her mind's eye, his voice, his laugh in her memory. They had talked so little, and yet every word came back to her. Jack talking about cricketers of the old times, John Nyren, May, Brooker, and Quiddington, Silver Billy Beldham. Jack remembering his father washing in a tin tub before the fire, after coming up from the pit, and the small boy he was, wondering how long it took to grow so tall and handsome – only he had some other, dialect word for it. The same small boy huddling close to his mother, in the raw air at the pit-head, as broken men were brought up, one by one, after a terrible explosion, and each one they thought would be his father; but then they saw him, walking towards them, alive and whole.

Jack laying down the right way to train a puppy. Jack kneeling to tend to a failing plant in the Dower House garden, which seemed to come alive and blossom in his hands. The same brown hands, as long and delicate as an artist's for all their strength, fastening a brooch at Lilian's neck that had come undone, with a touch as light as a butterfly. Jack pausing on the way through the house to look at her father's books, unread now, with a look that she could interpret because she knew him so well already: a look that said I can't read you yet, but one day I will. Jack, strong as a horse, gentle as a woman, proud as a hawk.

Lilian reached out to her bedside table and drew towards her the old, yellowed photograph of her father in his colonel's uniform. Upright and cheerful, with bristling moustachios, he looked back at her, the daughter who had meant more to him than either of the other children. She had been so young when he died, and before that he had been away for two years and more, in India. Then he had come home, and they had all gone to a great celebration in Leeds. The city had been like fairyland, humdrum Briggate blazing with lights, transparencies and gas-lamps in every shop-window in Albion Street, Boar Lane, and Park Row, and banners everywhere. But Papa had not joined in the cheering, saying that it was impossible for a man to rejoice for anything to do with the Mutiny, when he had seen how terribly the women and children had been murdered. Then he had pulled his young daughter close to his side, and wrapped his cloak round her shoulders.

For the first time she knew to the full how much she missed him. Something of him had come back to her with Jack, though the two men were so different and Jack not much older than she was. Now she had neither of them.

But he wouldn't desert her; she knew that. He was not one to be driven away with hard words. He would find a way of coming back to her.

For days Lilian hoped. Somehow he would get a message to her. Perhaps he had tried already, and Millie had been too stupid to understand. One day when the girl brought her meal she tried to ask in a roundabout way whether anybody had been enquiring for her, but Millie only gaped and shook her head. Every evening Florence came to her room with the same question.

'Tell me, dearest, have you come to acknowledge the wickedness of your behaviour?'

Lilian stared back, stony-eyed. 'No, Mamma. There was no wickedness about it. I've told you.'

Five times the question was asked and answered. On the sixth evening Lilian broke out, 'I suppose you think if you let me escape I'll run off with Jack? An elopement in a bath-chair – what a novelty.'

Florence smiled a thin smile. 'Oh, there's no danger of that, dear. The young man has left the district. I suppose that shows *some* sense of decency.'

Lilian's world crumbled. Of course he would not stay in a place where such a commotion had been made about him, and so unjustly. He could get work anywhere, after all. And he had never said anything to her that might mean what people called Intentions. How could he? The whole thing had been a crazy illusion on her part. Perhaps her mind was failing, as well as her body.

She refused her supper, and all her meals the next day, and the morning after, turning her back on Florence and the maids. At last, frightened by her weakness and extreme pallor, Florence raised the siege she had laid to her daughter's will.

'Now, dearest, look at me, for I have a delightful surprise for you. Your Aunt Frederica has invited you for a visit to her home in London.'

The words meant nothing to Lilian at first. Sitting on her bed, gently stroking her wild unbrushed hair, her mother explained quietly the offer Frederica had made, omitting to mention that it had been accepted a week ago; Lilian had not deserved to be set free too quickly. The special carriage on the train, the servants, the house by the Thames, were all produced as though Florence herself had thought of them.

'I shall miss my baby dreadfully, of course, but it is all for her good. And Augustus will visit you and bring me news. The Chelsea house is being cleaned and redecorated; it will be ready next week to receive you, your aunt says.'

Lilian struggled to understand, almost too enfeebled to think. 'Aunt Freddy . . . Did she write? How did she come to ask . . .'

'She is staying at the Hall for a week or two,' said Florence rapidly. 'Houses are so very uncomfortable with the decorators in, it seemed best for her to come north, though country life is not really . . .'

'Then why hasn't she been to see me?' Lilian demanded. She read the answer in her mother's face. Frederica had been told she was too ill to be visited, of course, when all the time she had been a prisoner. At that moment she knew that she would never feel the same towards her mother. Something in the relationship had died, just as something in Lilian's heart had died when she heard of Jack's desertion. Florence was watching her anxiously.

'Now we're not to have any more silliness, are we. And I can tell Aunt Frederica that you thank her very much for her kind invitation and will be glad to take advantage of it. You *will* go, dear, won't you? I was very doubtful at first, but I feel sure it's the best thing for you.'

'Oh, I'll go.' Lilian's voice was coldly matter-of-fact. Florence was disappointed that no tender emotional scene had been played.

'And you *will* eat again, dearest?'

'I might as well.'

'What do you fancy most? Some nice little delicacy? Uncle Lewis has kindly sent us a brace of woodcock. We had one roast yesterday, and the other to be eaten cold today, with a stuffing. Wouldn't that be a treat?'

'I don't care at all, Mamma,' Lilian shrugged. 'Bread and butter will do just as well.'

By the day of departure she had gained some of the weight and colour lost in her fast. Carefully they dressed her in her best, a dress of pale golden-brown over an under-petticoat of quilted calico, in case the weather turned cold in London, a neat jupe jacket fitting the waist and flaring out over the hips, a little round hat of cream straw tilted forward from the piled-up chignon.

Frederica flung her arms round the occupant of the bath-chair.

'My dear girl! How smart you look. I feel quite put in the shade.' She had no need to, being a vision to stop the traffic in a majestic ensemble of light and dark reds, her tiny fashionable bonnet crowned with a whole stuffed bird. She stood impatiently by while Lilian was damply embraced by Florence, in floods of tears in case she had not done the right thing or would miss her daughter to a painful degree. Lilian endured the embrace stoically, and the peck on the cheek bestowed by Nelly, a dutiful gesture which was all Nelly could bring herself to make. She had long ago forgotten her brief compunction at tearing up the gardener's note. After all, nothing could have come of it. And she was bitterly jealous of Lilian, being carried off in state to London – just what she would have liked herself, with a chance to show off and dazzle the men, something Lil could hardly do in her state of health. Life was very unfair – or Aunt Freddy was. Arthur was fortunately absent: he had no particular fond farewell to bid Lilian, and Augustus, who had, was engaged in assisting at a series of funerals, including one of the Mardsley murder victim, which was expected to be attended by enthusiastic crowds.

The train from Fellgate to Leeds had only seventeen miles to travel. Lilian, occupying a large part of the first-class carriage in her chair, watched the familiar landscape glide by, Yorkshire in autumn's green and gold, hills not too high as to be awesome sweeping down to valleys where grey stone cottages and farmsteads basked in the bright sun, rough roads, perilous ancient stone bridges over sparkling becks, tiny squat churches like old grey cats. What if I should never come back? she thought. Will they bring me home to be buried?

In the meantime she was very much alive. She had not travelled by train for many years. It was irresistibly exciting to be conveyed along at such speed, to feel the rhythm of the wheels in one's blood, to see so many new faces at every station, and especially to watch the countryside beginning to merge with town as the train approached the western borders of Leeds. Now black mill chimneys reared up, sending out clouds of smoke denser than the high clouds overhead, and the Aire was a much dirtier river than it had been, and a bewildering number of roofs crowded in on one's gaze.

At Leeds Northern Station, the terminus of the branch line, Lilian, her luggage, her aunt's luggage, Millie and her aunt's personal maid, were efficiently removed from the train to cabs which conveyed them to the Wellington Station, a much grander one than the Northern. The bustle and confusion on the platform made Lilian's head ring. Nervously she caught her aunt's sleeve.

'We shall never get through all these people to the London train.'

'Oh, yes, we shall. Keep calm, child.'

She was right, of course. In a sort of triumphal procession, one porter pushing Lilian's chair and two more carrying the baggage, they were conducted to a fine large smoke-breathing dragon with MIDLAND RAILWAY inscribed in gold on its green coat. Inside it a luxurious apartment awaited them, all plush and walnut, quite like a drawing-room. A table was laid for luncheon, with silver cutlery and wine-glasses. At the end an open door showed a glimpse of a smaller room, with a little bed in it, the chintz cover turned down. ready for the sleeper.

'I thought you might fancy a rest on the long journey, my dear, after your illness,' said Frederica. 'We shall take luncheon first, and then you can sleep, or not, as you please.'

Lilian was looking round her in amazement. 'But can *anyone* travel like this, Aunt Freddy?'

'Well, hardly, or the railways would be out of business. No, this is the carriage the Earl uses when the House is in session and he has to travel up to town. He had it shunted on to the train when I told him about you – such an obliging old fellow. Won't you take a little sherry? It's very dry – possibly you'd prefer a sweeter one, gels often do.'

'Yes, I mean no,' Lilian said mechanically. Her mind was a muddle of images and questions. Who was the Earl, and why should he oblige Aunt Freddy? How did Aunt afford to travel in such luxury? And what, if this was merely a railway train, would London be like?

CHAPTER FIVE

Jack sauntered out of Victoria Station, Sheffield, as though he had not a care in the world and was merely out for a day's enjoyment; though Sheffield, city of steel, was hardly the place for that. Smoke from countless factory chimneys lay heavy on the air and painted a black patina on the buildings, mingling with the peculiar aroma of railways and the reek from the Gas Works. The narrow streets were crowded and noisy, too narrow for the vehicles and pedestrians that choked them. There was nothing about Sheffield to suggest that it was the headquarters of Yorkshire cricket.

He had arrived too early; there were almost two hours to kill before his ten o'clock appointment. The civic centre of the town lay before him, offering free and improving entertainment to any visitor less preoccupied than Jack. He paused at a tailor's shop-window, appearing to study a suit advertised as being the very latest style, 27/6d, but actually surveying his own reflection. He flattered himself that he looked neat, clean and presentable in his best suit of rough woollen weave, its darkness enlivened by a grey flannel high-buttoned waistcoat. His immaculately white shirt was topped by a black silk neckcloth, the gift of his mother who knew her son's taste for elegant wear; and on his head a velveteen cap was tilted at an angle. He debated whether to straighten it in case it looked too rakish, but decided against it. Better to look like a sporting chap than a grocer. On the whole, he was fairly pleased with his appearance; he hoped They would be.

In the square flanked by the Town Hall and the Corn Exchange was the Market Hall. He knew it well and always enjoyed its varied pleasures. It had the rich smell of all covered markets, a blend of butter and cheese, raw meat and sawdust and soap, with a whiff of the fish caught yesterday at Hull. At the clothes-stalls

64

women haggled over garments made from the good wool of the sheep that had been Yorkshire's living for so many centuries: petticoats, drawers, stockings, skirts and the bright shawls which most working women wore instead of bonnets. Children howled, pointing to the toy displays – hand-carved wooden lambs fleeced with real wool, Dutch dolls with black shiny painted hair and jointed limbs, cups and balls on a string for the popular game of trap-ball, and beautifully made miniature cricket-bats, produced by such masters as Sykes Holroyd of Horbury and the Wainwright brothers of Leeds. Jack had owned one before he was knee-high to his father; it would be an unusual boy that didn't, where he came from.

Because he had very few shillings in his pocket, reserved for necessities, he ignored some of the goods he would have liked to buy – fine neckcloths, a pair of almost-new boots that might have fitted him, from the display of second-hand clothing. Only when he had been round the market twice did he allow himself a tin of good tobacco to be shared with his father, and a piece of almond soap for his mother, whose hands suffered from so much gardening. At a stall of fancy goods he paused, surveying ladies' handkerchieves, pretty with flower-embroidery, small, almost transparent, some worked with forget-me-nots, some with daisies, others scattered with tiny rosebuds. One in particular took his eye. He would dearly have loved to buy it for Lilian, it reminded him of her so much, and he knew she would like it, though he had only the vaguest idea of what her tastes were. He told himself not to be so soft. There was no reason to suppose she would welcome a gift from him, after the trouble his innocent attempt to help her had caused. And it might be a long time before he saw her again . . .

He summoned the stall-holder. 'Missis.'

'Aye?'

'How much?'

'Sixpence to thee.'

'It's a lot.'

'I said, to thee. Ninepence to others. I can see it's for thy sweetheart, so I'll let it go cheap.'

'By, missis, tha'rt sharp.' He handed over the sixpence and took the tiny scrap of cloth, folded into a paper wrapping.

The time nagged at him. He wished, as he often did, that he owned a watch, but there were plenty of stern-faced official clocks stationed on public buildings to remind laggards of time's passing. One of them clanged, drawing his attention to the hour of nine o'clock. He left the temptations of the Market, and walked southwards down Haymarket and Norfolk Street. The Free Library was open; he entered the silent Reading Room, and, among others with nothing else to do, scanned the morning paper. He could read perfectly well, though not as fast as he wished, a fault he intended to remedy one day. He would learn to read books, all the books in the Dower House, books that would make him as clever as he was strong. And bring him closer to Lilian, a voice said, but he hushed it. There were other things on his mind this morning.

Norfolk Street, South Street. Better be early than late. He knew every step of the way from the many times he had walked it to matches. The washy blue of the sky, peering through a smoke haze, dissolved into light rain. When he retraced his steps later that morning it might be raining stair-rods, fit to soak his best clothes. Would he care by then what it was doing? too depressed, too elated? made, or destroyed? The most fateful moment of his life was coming for him.

When, far too early, he stood before the door of the Adelphi Hotel, he felt that his heart was beating in his throat, the throbbing of it to be seen by all. But the scattering of regulars sitting quietly in the public bar seemed to notice nothing, not even his presence. He approached the barman.

'Mr Ellison's expecting me. Cricket Club Committee.'

The man looked up from rinsing glasses. 'Oh, aye? You want door round t'side. But they'll not be there yet, not for another half-hour.'

'Oh.' Jack wandered to a corner where he hoped he would be inconspicuous, and sat down. Now Time, which had raced in the town, slowed down to an intolerable crawl. He felt that he could barely live through the next thirty minutes, yet somehow he must keep calm and sane, however much he knew himself to be rather less so than a cat on hot bricks. Wistfully he eyed the casks above the bar, with their inviting taps. How tempting it was to go and order a glass of ale – only a half-pint – to steady him and give him a bit of Dutch courage. And go before Them smelling like a brewery? He turned his back on temptation and studied the walls: framed posters advertising prize-fights, a large portrait of the Queen at her most forbidding, somebody's race-horse photographed with a grinning jockey. His eye was caught by a framed newspaper cutting, yellowing under glass, with the name of a London journal above it, and the date 1861.

'Yorkshire, you are wanted, that is, the leading men and cricketers of Yorkshire are wanted, to bestir themselves, beat up the wealth, rank and influential men of their shire, and establish a County Cricket Club. Good cricket grounds you have already in various parts of the county. Cricketers are ready at hand of that metal and ability that even under the present disorganised – or rather, NO – state of things, were found an eleven that could beat Surrey.'

Then followed an impressive list of players' names.

'It is our opinion that if Yorkshiremen would but establish on a proper basis a County club, they would in a year or two be enabled to bring such an eleven into the field as would make Yorkshire a cricketing county second to none in England . . .'

The clock over the bar, set five minutes fast, crawled round towards ten o'clock. The barman peered out over the frosted glass of the window.

'Mr Wostinholm's carriage is out yon,' he informed Jack. 'They'll likely all be there bi now.'

'Thanks.' Cold and hot by turns, he left the Public and re-entered the inn by the side door round the corner, reading over the door the gold letters on black that said 'H. Sampson, licensed to sell Wines, Ales, Spirits and Tobacco'. Harry Sampson, the great little man who had played cricket in the days of top hats and single-wicket contests, and still liked his game. He would be up there, waiting, a member of the Committee.

At the top of the oilcloth-covered stairs a half-glassed door had the notice COMMITTEE ROOM pinned on it. Jack knocked, heard a summons within, and entered.

The room was long and barely-furnished with stacked wooden chairs, a piano, rows of hat-pegs, a corner bar. The Adelphi did a roaring trade in wedding receptions, funeral parties, and gatherings of Oddfellows and Freemasons. This morning a number of tables had been put together to form one long table, at which sat, like a jury, twelve men. They were all men of Sheffield, all of good repute and substance, all players or ex-players of cricket. Jack, taking the chair offered to him on the opposite side of the table, tried to look thoroughly comfortable and at ease, as his gaze rested on some faces familiar to him from matches at Bramall Lane Ground, Sheffield, on the field or in the pavilion. There was Harry Sampson himself, foursquare, sturdy, inclining to a fatness owing something to his own ales, mutton-chop-whiskered in the old style. J. B. Wostinholm, the Club Secretary, every inch a Yorkshire gentleman in his fine silk-faced coat and dashing bow-tie, heavily bearded like a sea-captain. His piercing eyes surveyed Jack keenly, as they would survey any man bold enough to offer himself for the Eleven.

In front of him was a large, virgin blotting-pad and a pewter ink-well holding an imposing pen that seemed to be made of steel, as, in Sheffield, it might well be, together with a sheaf of writing-paper. Jack wondered if it would take all that to record his qualifications. The man next to Wostinholm, in a chair with arms and a high back, addressed Jack after what seemed an hour-long silence.

'Well, Mr Ellershaw, I expect you know most of us by sight?'

'Aye, Mr Ellison.' Ellison and Ellershaw: they sounded like a comic duo, but there was nothing comic about the appearance of the Club's President and Treasurer. His fine domed head was the head of a thinker, his features grand and severe, with a hint of kindliness around the mouth framed by a thick round beard lightly touched with grey. He looked a little as Jack imagined God might. His suiting was of the costliest tweed, his waistcoat enlivened by a gold watch-chain and fob.

'Now, then,' he said, 'you've applied to join the Cricket Club, I understand?'

Jack agreed that he had.

'And you've played for Fellgate Eleven? Can I have the papers, Mr Wostinholm?' He took and perused Jack's laborious record of his amateur career, read carefully the newspaper cuttings mentioning his name, raised his eyebrows as he read out to the Committee some impressive batting and bowling figures. There were nods and murmurs of approval. A dark-haired young man whom Jack recognised as Roger Iddison, Captain of the present team, asked him, 'Do you think you're up to professional standard? You're on the young side, seems to me.'

'I'm nobbut two years younger than you, Mr Iddison.'

The Captain flushed faintly, then laughed. 'My mistake.'

'We can do with some young blood, in my opinion,' Ellison said mildly. 'A lot of us go on after we're past it.'

'Here, here!' Harry Sampson exclaimed. 'Art gettin' at me?'

'Nay, Harry, no need to be touchy. Your reputation's safe enough. Age cannot wither thee, nor Custom stale. Mr Ellershaw, I see here you've a good record both for batting and bowling. Do you consider yourself an all-rounder?'

'Aye,' said Jack, leaning back in his chair, feeling his breath returning to normal with the trend of the conversation. 'I reckon I can tackle either, and I'm noan so slow in t'field. I've taken a many catches at slip, and I'm pretty good at long stop when ball's heading for four runs.'

'That were my place, long stop,' commented Harry Sampson.

Wostinholm scribbled something on the paper before him and asked, 'How do you feel about standing up to shooters?'

'I'm not frightened of 'em. I've had plenty bowled at me, and never had mi head knocked off yet.'

'What are your feelings about South Country clubs?' Roger Iddison asked. Jack, thinking quickly, remembered that Iddison had been a leader of revolt two or three years before, refusing to form a Northern Eleven in a North v. South match, and thereby intensifying the rivalry which had until then only smouldered.

'I don't allow myself feelings,' he answered. 'If a chap plays professional cricket it's his job to play when he's asked, no matter who it's against.'

This was exactly the ruling made by the Committee itself at the time of the famous dispute; as Jack well knew. The two senior members nodded at each other, eyes were collected round the table. Then Ellison cleared his throat. 'We seem to be pretty well agreed on your merits, young man. There's just one thing more—

can you support yourself during the winter when there's no play? We've had some sad cases in the past over men who gave up regular employment in the summer.'

'I shan't be in t'workhouse, sir.' He had not meant to say sir, but it slipped out. 'I work on my father's market-garden and on other farmers' land when they need somebody.' He mentioned Sir Lewis, and a few reputable land-owners in the Barnswood area. Wostinholm scribbled; there were more satisfied nods. The Yorkshire Club disliked having members forced to apply for parish relief. To Jack's surprise and pleasure, he was told to report at the Manchester ground in a week's time for one of the late fixtures of the season, against Lancashire. Then Wostinholm handed over to him some money, carefully counted.

'That should take care of your travel to Manchester and back. The match-pay will be three pounds.'

Even Jack could not control his delight at such generosity. The smile which broke through his reserve brought an answering one to Ellison's face. He rose, as did Wostinholm, and both shook hands with their new player across the table.

'Goodbye. Good luck to you, Mr Ellershaw.'

Outside in the street Jack felt like a disembodied creature, transported with happiness. His feet hardly seemed to touch the grimy pavement as he returned to the main door of the hotel, entered, and bought himself a glass of the strongest ale. It was a poor heart that never rejoiced. Then he walked down Bramall Lane to the fine cricket ground he knew so well as a spectator. The gates were shut; he stood, looking up at the ten-foot wall that surrounded it, imagining himself inside, one of the privileged, a professional player at the beginning of his career.

For he was going to be a name in the history of cricket; he knew it.

'So it's a hero's welcome home.' Amos Ellershaw clapped his son on the shoulder as powerfully as he could, being so much shorter than Jack's six-foot height. Amos had never been tall, and was bowed now as were so many who had been coal-miners, and partly crippled with the rheumatism the mines bred. His hair was prematurely white and his face marked with many lines of pain, but his smile was warm and beautiful; Amos, people said, was a deal more cheerful than many folk who'd less to complain of.

'Well done, lad,' Jack's mother said. The opposite of her husband, she was tall and strong, toughened by the hard work she did in the market garden; a fine figure of a woman still, ample bosom and broad hips set off by the neat print frock which she had made herself, as she made all her clothes and her menfolk's shirts. Her greying hair was tightly scraped back in the style worn by Queen Victoria, her eyes, once as blue as Jack's, faded with time but still bright, missing nothing. Usually she was not to be seen without the pinafore that covered her from neck to knee, to protect her dress from the wear and tear of her work, but tonight it was laid aside in Jack's honour. She had said little to him yet, her pride hidden by a mask of conventional reticence. But inwardly she glowed with it: she knew as much about cricket as a man.

Jack stretched luxuriously in the best chair, a high-backed upright with arms, and re-filled his pipe. It was good to be home, in front of a bright fire made with coal from the local seam and apple-wood from a dead tree his mother had chopped down, sending out fragrant smoke, his feet on the fender. Stainbeck Cottages was, in fact, one dwelling, though it had once been three. The old buildings had been knocked into one by a previous tenant. For many young couples it would have been too large, but Mary Ellershaw maintained that folk should live as well as they could and not like pigs in a sty, all thrutched up together. When she and Amos had moved into it they had had three young children and expected to have several more, a good big family for a good big place. But the children died within days of each other from a fever. Then Jack was born, a strong child who survived the hazards of life without difficulty. Mary's next pregnancy was well advanced when a neighbour came rushing in to tell her there had been a colliery disaster and Amos was somewhere down there. He was one of the fortunate ones, as it turned out, but the shock brought on a miscarriage; and after that there were no more babies. So here were the Ellershaws, only three of them, in a five-roomed house of sturdy grey stone, like peas in a drum, Mary sometimes said. But it was the way she liked it, plenty of room to breathe.

The low-ceilinged parlour was flag-floored, scattered with

bright coloured rag rugs made by Amos and Mary in the long evenings of winter. Some of the simple furniture was Amos's own work. He had a skill in carpentry which came in useful after illness kept him out of the mine, bringing in some much-needed money. But the focal point of the room, the family show-piece, was a great oak press, two-storeyed, three cupboards at the bottom and two at the top, ingeniously carved with oak-leaves and acorns by some long-dead hand. It had belonged to Mary's mother, once in service at Burton Castle, given to her by a housekeeper there who had been given it as a retirement present by the then Countess. So the Ellershaw home was graced by a piece which had come from a Castle, and great respect was theirs on its account. Their mantelpiece also gave them great satisfaction, bearing at each end a coloured china figure, one of the Queen as a young woman, one of the late Prince Consort with black moustaches and red and blue tartan trousers, and in the middle a bust of John Wesley preaching. On the wall above hung a likeness of Jack as a boy, with cricket bat, done on a piece of wood by a travelling signboard artist. The parents thought it beautiful, but Jack said it was very good of the bat.

'Eh,' his father exclaimed, not for the first time, 'I can scarce believe it. Our Jack in t'County side. It does credit to thee, lad, it does that.'

'Oh, it were nowt,' Jack answered modestly. 'I had mi doubts when I went in, though. They were a reet dowly lot.'

'They would be. They've not got onto t'committee wi' bein' all smiles.'

'It's t'brass I can't believe,' Mary said. 'Three pound. Three pound for a first match.'

'Why don't you come and watch at Manchester? You'll not put me off my stroke.' Amos shook his head.

'Nay, it's too far. Costs too much. And I'm takin' nowt out o' that money o' thine.' He had caught his son's gaze resting on the coins provided for travel.

'I shan't need all this for Manchester,' Jack said with elaborate casualness. 'I'll use a bit of it to go to Fellgate.' He was not looking at his mother. 'I've got to go back to the Hall, Sir Lewis's place, where I were working. To see someone. I'll come straight back.'

'Oh? Who's that?'

72

After an audible pause, Jack said, 'Someone I promised I'd get summat in Sheffield for. They're expecting me.'

His mother regarded him long and hard. She knew her son, so like her in many ways. It was unusual for him to be anything less than direct to the point of bluntness, and now he was being evasive, pretending, taking his pipe out of his mouth, looking at it critically and tamping down the tobacco as though it were the most solemn procedure in the world. Men and their pipes, thought Mary, they're like bairns wi' toys, particularly when they've got summat to hide. But she asked no more; if he was not willing to tell her, she was not going to waste words asking. They were a stubborn pair, mother and son.

In bed that night Amos asked her: 'Dost think he's bound to see a lass?'

'That's his business,' Mary snapped. 'He's old enough to look after hissen.'

The garden of the Dower House looked very neglected, as though nobody had touched it since he had been sent away with hard words. He went to the servants' door and knocked boldly. The elderly maid, Maggie, answered, tossing her head at the sight of him. But at least she did not shut the door in his face.

'Well? What do *you* want?'

'Can I see Miss Lilian? Just for a minute. I've summat for her.'

Maggie tilted her square, bristly chin higher. 'That you can't.'

'Well, will you give it to her, missis?' He held out a very small brown paper package tied, man-fashion, clumsily with string. Maggie surveyed it as though he had offered her a worm.

'No, I won't,' she answered roundly, 'and for the very good reason that Miss Lilian's not at 'ome. She's gone to London, if you must know, not that it's any business of yours, and I'm surprised you've got the presumptuousness to show your face at our door at all.' She was gratified by his cast-down look. So much for cheeky whippersnappers.

He knew he was beaten, but before turning to go he asked, 'How is she?'

'She's grand,' Maggie said. 'Never been better, and enjoyin' herself like a two-year-old. Now take yourself off.'

He walked, slowly for him, along the garden path and through the familiar gate that led to Sir Lewis's grounds. He had been a fool to come. There was neither rhyme nor reason in the wasted journey, for what if she had been at home? She might have been no more welcoming than the servant, and she had never answered the note he had left for her. She could have written a line to him through Sir Lewis, if she had cared anything about him at all. He was hot with shame at thought of the foolery he had committed, his self-deceit, his humiliation at the hands of Maggie.

He took out the small parcel from his pocket, minded to throw it into the hedge. Then, on an impulse, he unwrapped it and looked at the tiny handkerchief he had bought in Sheffield. A little square of fine cotton patterned with lilies of the valley. It was too pretty to throw away, and he had been brought up to waste nothing. It would do just as well for his mother.

CHAPTER SIX

'Dear Mamma,' Lilian began, after several false starts to her first letter home. The little table beside her was loaded with stationery, best quality cream paper embossed with Aunt Freddy's Cheyne Row, Chelsea, address, long envelopes to match, wax, a seal and a small scented candle to heat the wax, a gold inkstand – could it be real gold? – inlaid with bright blue chasing, and a gold fountain-pen in the shape of a long thin bird in flight, its beak the nib. There was every inducement to write letters, yet Lilian found it curiously difficult.

Perhaps it was that she was still tired, a week after travelling south. The journey, luxurious as it was, had been long and wearying, and Aunt Freddy tended to fuss in quite a different way from Mamma. And since arriving at Cheyne Row everything had been so strange that Lilian would like to have gone to sleep for several days, long enough to clear her brain and let her confused senses recover.

But duty must be done. 'Dear Mamma,' she began. 'You will be glad to know I am quite recovered from my travels. I cannot tell you what a wonderful train brought us to London. It was not at all like the one on which we all travelled to Leeds for the Celebrations.

'Aunt Freddy's house is in a very fashionable part of London, just by the river and quite near the Houses of Parliament. I have not been taken out yet to see the sights, as Aunt thinks I should rest more first, though I am quite well in myself. I am reading a *History of Chelsea* which is most interesting. The great writer Thomas Carlyle lives a few doors away from this house. I should like to see him when I go out. They say he is very old and rather fierce.

'I don't know how to describe Aunt Freddy's home, because I have never seen anything like it before, except that it is very artistic and unusual. It is all done in what I suppose is the modern style, not at all like the Dower House or even the Hall.

'Tell Nelly nobody hunts or even rides here and they don't seem to play games, she would not enjoy it at all, so she needn't envy me any more.' Lilian looked at the last words, then put a thick line through them. There was no satisfaction in being rude to her sister at a distance.

'The change is doing me good already,' she went on. 'Aunt and the servants are very kind and there is more food than I can eat. My Cousin Digby has called, he is at present with the Guards at Windsor where the Queen is in residence. I should like to stay here as long as Aunt will have me, if you do not miss me too much.'

She finished off the letter and sealed it. Some of it was true, some not. Impossible to explain to Mamma which was which, for she hardly knew herself. The *History of Chelsea* told her nothing of the real Chelsea which was all around her, strange and distracting after her home. When they had carried her in she had caught a glimpse of the old red-brick houses of Queen Anne's time, built in terraces, the way only poor people lived in the north, and of the River Thames, wide and grey, with small craft scuttling about on it and tall chimneys on the far bank.

Now she could see nothing of the Row or the busy bridge beyond. Her bedroom was on the ground floor of the house; through the windows she could see only the top halves of the houses opposite. What Chelsea meant to her was chiefly noise. Barrel-organs, those scourges of London, which came on the streets at breakfast-time and stayed until evening, grinding out their popular tunes, the same ones over and over again, 'Jessie's Dream' and 'Home Sweet Home' and 'I Dreamt that I dwelt in Marble Halls', until the rhythms and phrases went on and on, maddeningly, in one's head. Behind them a low continuous roar of traffic from the bridge filtered through to the Row, and the clatter of nearer traffic, tradesmen's carts and private vehicles. The calls of street-hawkers quite frightened Lilian at first, so loud and aggressive that they sounded like battle-cries, except for the sad, twilight call of the muffin-man with his melancholy clanging bell. Then there were the dog-fights. London dogs seemed to be of a low and warlike class, not only engaging in fearful fights on

76

the pavement but drawing their owners into the contest to exchange loud words, some of which Lilian had not heard before. When the dogs, the organ-grinders and the hawkers went home, and traffic sounds died down, the pianos started up in neighbouring houses, sending out tinkling music sometimes charming and accomplished, more often stumbling and incapable, accompanied by the warblings of the player's family and friends.

And when they were all, it was to be hoped, in bed, the cats would begin a night-long ceremony of courtship and rivalry. From back garden and backyard wall they sent out their terrible eldritch screams and snarls, sometimes subsiding into low mutters long enough to allow one to sink towards sleep, then breaking out again in shocking cacophony. The night-peace of the Dower House, the calling of owls and the rustle of wind in the trees, seemed in Lilian's memory something she would never recapture even when she went home, so hag-ridden was she by broken nights.

Yet the days were interesting, there was no doubt of that. As soon as Aunt Freddy considered her sufficiently rested after her arrival she was put into her bath-chair and wheeled all over the ground floor of the house.

'We don't want to keep you like a parrot in a cage with a cloth over it, do we. Come and get the feeling of the place.'

The feeling of the place was a feeling of grandeur, wealth, luxury and a strangeness which utterly baffled Lilian. It was not like any house she had seen before. Ordinary tables and chairs did not exist in it, nor ordinary walls and ceilings. Perhaps it was furnished in imitation of an Eastern palace, though Lilian had no very clear idea what that would look like.

Impossible to take in the whole, there was so much of it, so many patterns and designs. On the walls, strange flowers that never grew in mortal gardens vied with bright birds stealing fruit or fluttering among tropical branches, and into them were set painted panels portraying long, languid ladies with crowns or wimples on their heads, young knights and kings in robes and armour, all noble and unearthly in their looks. The furniture was hand-made and individually designed, no two pieces the same, very plain, very upright, and on the whole spiky and uncomfortable, Lilian thought. It made her back ache to contemplate sitting on

77

one of the rush-backed chairs, or on the narrow settle with its flower-painted canopy.

There were more paintings on cupboards and doors, scenes of chivalric life, of wooing and scorning and death, quite beautiful if a little disturbing to the mind. Faces, faces everywhere, angels and saints in the stained glass of windows and landing-lights, bordered with scraps of Latin inscribed on banners, and lines of poetry. Even a piano was painted all over with scenes from a legend. Lilian wondered if anyone had ever dared to sit down at it and sing one of the vulgar songs Arthur was so fond of, 'Champagne Charlie', for instance. Probably not, especially under that ceiling papered in silver-gilt, on which faintly haloed heads could be seen in changes of light.

'Well? How do you like it?' Frederica asked, when they had finished touring the rooms.

'It's very . . . very pretty,' Lilian said politely. 'Are there many houses like this, Aunt?'

'Oh, I shouldn't think so. Topsy did it up specially for me, and no one has quite his touch.'

'Topsy?' It sounded a frivolous name for the creator of these solemn splendours.

'William Morris. Absolutely the coming man in design. Surely you've heard of him?'

'I haven't heard about anyone or anything,' Lilian said, a trifle sharply. 'Living where we do, it's rather hard to be fashionable.'

Frederica patted her hand. 'Of course. Well, you shall meet them soon. One forgets what a little provincial you are.' She surveyed her niece critically. 'And I must say you look it. Hair is simply not worn like that any more. It should be down, like this.' She gave Lilian's head light tweaks and tugs, removing some hairpins so that the heavy tresses fell down in an untidy straggle. 'No wonder you have headaches, with all that weight piled up on top. And your dress! Well, it might do for croquet, very well, I daresay.'

'I don't play croquet.'

'No, poor thing, of course not. But all the more reason for not looking as though you do. Never mind, I'll get someone to see to it all.'

Lilian began to say that she was quite contented with her dresses as they were, that her mother had spent a lot of their scarce money on having them made up, and that in such changed surroundings she would prefer not to be too much changed herself. But there was no getting a word in. The very next morning a small, pale woman who hardly spoke (perhaps fortunately, since she generally had her mouth full of pins) spent two wearisome hours crawling on her knees round Lilian's couch, measuring bosom, waist, length of arm and leg. Frederica inspected the results with interest.

'Very thin, child. But that's fashionable. And good long legs to show off draperies. Yes, a very nice model on the whole, don't you think so, Miss Hake?'

A murmur through pins affirmed this, as Miss Hake draped a piece of filmy cloth across Lilian's hips and secured it, sticking one of the pins painfully into her flesh.

'What's the use of draperies,' Lilian asked, 'when I have to lie about all the time?'

'Oh, my dear, they're *in*, don't you understand? And besides . . .' Ignoring Miss Hake, Frederica took Lilian's hand affectionately and held it for a moment. 'You won't deny me the pleasure of looking after you and giving you pretty things, will you? I lead a very boring life here, you know, plenty of company but nobody of my own except Digby, and one can hardly count *him*. Even as a little boy he was always in fights and never looked a credit to me. Believe me, I'm truly glad to have you here and I want so much to do my best for you.'

'You're very kind, Aunt Freddy,' was all Lilian could reasonably say. Thereafter she put up patiently with endless fittings, tuckings and pinnings, and the rapid delivery of one after another gown made in a vaguely Grecian style, very loose and flowing.

'Very nice,' Frederica pronounced when half-a-dozen were finished. 'Now we can get rid of those objects that would be suitable only to a vicar's extremely prim daughter. I'm sure we can find some nice charity to take them.'

Lilian saw her old gowns being contemptuously gathered up by Frederica's maid. 'Oh, no, if you please! Do leave them. When I go home again I'm sure I shall want them for – for everyday. And Mamma would be hurt.' She was fond of the humble spotted and striped frocks in which she had once felt quite smart. She

79

ordered Millie to stow them away in a wardrobe painted with scenes from one of the Canterbury Tales.

Only a week had passed, for poor Miss Hake had sat up half the night stitching the new gowns, only thankful that her patron didn't fancy complicated patterns and the heavy embroideries that had ruined Miss Hake's mother's eyesight and that of many another sempstress. And Mrs Stevens-Clyne paid very well. It was a pleasure to sew for her; or at least as much of a pleasure as anything was for Miss Hake.

'Now, Lilian, I think it's high time you Came Out,' Frederica announced briskly, appearing at Lilian's bedside as she was finishing her breakfast.

'Came out where, Aunt?'

'Don't be obtuse, dear. I told Florence you were to have a kind of Little Season here all to yourself, and so you shall. Now you look fit to be seen you must receive company.'

'But — I've been here such a little time . . . I haven't seen anything yet, London itself, I mean.'

Frederica beamed. 'That's it, of course, of course you must see London. The brougham shall be brought round this afternoon. You and I will take a nice, gentle drive somewhere: up to the Park, perhaps, round the Serpentine and then tea at Gunter's. Oh, but that will hardly do for you, will it. Very well, something shall be sent out to you. And you must have my green mantle with the astrakhan fur, now the weather has turned so chilly.' She clapped her hands like a girl. 'What a lark! Why didn't I think about it before? Oh, and there's a letter for you.'

The letter was from Florence, in reply to Lilian's. Her beautiful, small, old-fashioned writing with its f's for s's informed her daughter that she was sadly missed, life had not been the same without her. The house was very quiet, Arthur having gone back to Cambridge and Nelly to stay at Harrogate with some cousins. She, Florence, had been up to the Hall for a very pleasant little dinner-party . . .

It was true, the house had not been the same without Lilian: it had been much more agreeable. Florence did not miss her baby half as much as she had thought she would, and she certainly did not miss the many tasks she had done for the invalid, though she had prided herself on her maternal tenderness as she carried them out. She wondered, just a shade maliciously, whether Lilian was finding Millie's hands incompetent and clumsy, compared with Mamma's.

Pleasant, too, to think that Millie's wages were no longer being paid out of Sir Lewis's allowance to the family. With the removal of that expense, and what Lilian cost to keep, there was really quite a nice little balance in the cash-box. Perhaps she would go down to that clever dressmaker in Fellgate to have a new dress run up, and buy a new bonnet at the same time: it was so long since she had had anything for herself, with two girls to dress. The new clothes would do for the small parties which would be held that winter in various houses round about, agreeable little affairs with cards, tea and gossip. She could mention airily the London mansion where Lilian was staying – 'very artistic and unusual', the child wrote. That probably meant good oil-paintings (perhaps a portrait of Frederica by some fashionable artist), rich curtains and carpets, a whole room in tartan, possibly, that odd fabric made popular by the Queen. There would be a striped awning over the front steps to protect ladies from the rigours of weather on their way to their carriages, perhaps a butler and a footman or two in powder. Florence's imagination ran riot. These glories would make delightful conversation over the tables. She could begin practising at once, on the servants. It would be nice to impress Maggie, who was not easy to impress.

Maggie had, unbidden, told her about the visit of that impudent scoundrel, the gardener, and his scandalous request.

' "Give 'er this", indeed! Who knows what nasty thing it might be? Well, she's away, I told him, beyond the reach of such as you, and you needn't bother calling again, that's what I said. And off he goes like a kicked dog,' said Maggie with relish, repeating the tale next time with even more embroideries.

Florence was not quite reassured. She took the opportunity of dropping a note of polite thanks for the dinner-party to see Sir Lewis personally and enquire what had happened to the gardener.

Sir Lewis was taciturn. 'Gone back where he came from.'

'And where is that? A good distance, I hope?'

'How should I know?' (But he did.) 'Sheffield or Bradford or

81

Sowerby Bridge, it's no business of mine.' Or of yours, his tone implied. With that Florence had to be satisfied.

The object of her anxiety was at that moment engaged in lifting turnips in the top field, high above Stainbeck Cottages. It would have been back-breaking work to one less strong than he. Heavy rain had made the ground a mess of sticky clay, clinging to the roots so that they had to be torn out of the earth. Jack could only move slowly along the field, for at each step his boots sank into the clay as though he walked on a quicksand. Since his return home he had forbidden his mother to do the roughest work. He found it neither hard nor tedious, and when their own land was fallow he intended to offer himself for casual labour at a nearby farm where they were always glad of extra hands, now the Paddies had gone home to Ireland. The more he worked, the fitter he would be next season.

He had acquitted himself well enough in the Manchester match, though not as well as his high standards demanded. When his next chance came, he would show them . . .

He straightened up and looked round him. The country was dying into late autumn, trees almost leafless, the beech hedge two fields away a blaze of copper. Overhead, in a leaden sky, rooks wheeled, cawing, on the lookout for anything eatable he might turn up with his spade. On the edge of the copse that bordered the small-holding an old woman bent as a twig herself was gathering firewood. By rights he ought to have gone down and turned her away, for there were only orchard trees on the Ellershaws' land, and it was generally understood that they had first call on the branches that fell in the copse; but he let her stay, for, poor soul, she was worse off than they were.

The air was damp and sweet, curling Jack's hair into tendrils, cooling his face pleasantly. He thought of the winter to come, and the spring that would bring him the way of life he wanted. There had been something else he had wanted, until events had shown him how impossible and unsuitable it was. She was happy now, clearly, and better off without him. He picked up a small stunted turnip, weighed it in his hand, and hurled it towards a stake fence. Two stakes fell backwards at its deadly impact. Jack laughed. 'Clean bowled the bugger,' he said.

Almost two hundred miles away to the south, Lilian roused uneasily from the rest she always took after luncheon by doctor's orders. Her mind caught at the skirts of a vanishing dream, but it was gone. It had been disturbing, distressing. She had tried to call on someone to help her, but the name had gone from her memory, in the dream, leaving her to face alone whatever had menaced her.

She touched her cheeks, and found them wet with tears.

BOOK TWO

The Blessèd Damozel

Dear dead women, with such hair, too . . .
Robert Browning

CHAPTER SEVEN

The door of Lilian's room banged behind Frederica's impatient exit, leaving Lilian to the mercies of Crowfoot, her aunt's maid. 'That Millie of yours is completely incompetent,' Frederica had said. 'When I was a girl in Yorkshire we should have called her cack-handed. She may be all very well peeling onions and potatoes and that sort of thing, but only a real lady's maid can dress hair properly.'

'Millie always used to wash my hair and put up my chignon nicely,' Lilian defended. 'She isn't used to this new style – and I'm not sure I like it, Aunt.'

'You must learn to adjust. Crowfoot is most adept. Now we have only an hour before the guests arrive, and I want everything ready.'

Crowfoot, a large, silent woman with strong hands, began to tug at Lilian's tresses with a comb, causing her keen agony.

'Ow! Don't! Why can't you just brush it?'

' 'Cause it's to be frizzed, miss. All the young ladies has theirs frizzed now.' Lilian held her head as far away as she could from the painful wrenching, trying to hold the roots with her fingers so that only the ends of her hair, not the whole scalp, felt the pull. Crowfoot worked steadily away to the accompaniment of her own tuneless humming, like a bee gifted with a perpetual sting, until the thing was done to her satisfaction.

'I can't stand this every day,' Lilian said despairingly. 'You must tell my aunt, Crowfoot. It's no fault of yours, I'm sure, but it makes my head ache dreadfully, and I'm sure it looks horrid.' Indeed, it did, as reflected in the mirror Crowfoot held up – a puffed-out corona making her face appear unnaturally thin and sharp. When the maid left her she lay with her hands to her aching brows, feeling the old surge of resentment rise at being treated like a doll, to be dressed at its owner's whim. At least

Mamma had never tortured her like this. If she rang the bell and said she felt ill perhaps she could escape the evening dinner-party, the occasion which was to introduce her to Aunt Freddy's friends and start off her Little Season. She was thinking herself into a state of fever when a knock at the door startled her into a normal un-feverish 'Come in.'

But her tone was welcoming as she greeted the visitor. 'Cousin Digby!'

Digby Stevens-Clyne was a very large young man indeed. Six feet four in height, he had square broad shoulders, a poker-straight back, a boxer's narrow waist and hips. They, as much as his crisp moustache and luxuriant brown whiskers, proclaimed him the guardsman he was, though now he wore immaculate evening dress. He was his mother's son in his high complexion and forthright manner, and in a sort of eager liveliness of eye, but his unexpectedly gentle voice and warm smile were all his own. He and Lilian had met on the day of her arrival in Cheyne Row, when she had been too tired to do more than be aware of him as a friendly, welcoming presence, before being carried to her room, and he had called several times since.

'I thought I'd look in on you, Cousin,' he said, 'that is, if it's no bother to you.'

'Indeed, no – I'm very glad to see you. Do sit down.'

He lowered himself into a ridiculously small chair. 'I hear Mamma's giving one of her celebrated parties tonight.'

'Yes. Will you be there?'

'Lord, no. Not my sort of jollification at all. Mamma did suggest I attend, but I'm afraid I invented a previous engagement. I shall run down to Henley and spend the weekend with a pal of mine there, just to make it look convincing.'

'Do you know anything about them, all these people, artists or whatever they are?'

'Well,' Digby looked at the ceiling for inspiration. 'I've met some of 'em, yes, at tea-parties and such, but no oftener than I can help.'

'Why? Are they horrid?'

Digby laughed. 'I don't know that I'd go that far. A bit odd, perhaps, as you'd expect of artists. One's got a barking sort of manner, like a dog, or a sergeant-major – bushy-haired chap with a beard Mamma calls Topsy. Otherwise they're a mild enough lot. Don't ask me about the sort of pictures they paint, I only know the ones in this house, and I don't care for 'em. May be my bad taste, of course.'

Lilian looked alarmed. 'Oh dear! I don't understand all these paintings, on the furniture and everywhere one looks. I did ask Aunt Freddy to explain them, but she seemed a little vague about what they actually meant – or perhaps she thought I would not be able to take it in.'

Digby leaned forward confidentially. 'Tell you what I think – that Mamma don't understand 'em any more than we do. She's an intelligent woman, mind you, ought to have gone to Harrow instead of me. She's a great one for taking up things, is my mater, fashions and fads and such. Before this it was hospital work. She fancied herself as a sort of Miss Nightingale, but that didn't last long. Too unpleasant. She's always got to have an interest, bless her.'

'Yes. I envy her rather, Digby. I wish I'd had an interest, all this time I've been – like this.'

'Rotten luck. I say, Lilian, don't worry yourself about these people. They may think me every sort of chucklehead, but they'll take to you instanter because you're a jolly pretty girl. You needn't say a word if you don't want to.'

'Thank you. But Digby – now do be quite frank – do you like the way Aunt has had my hair done?'

Digby looked embarrassed. 'Not for me to say, old girl. No eye for ladies' matters.'

She pursued him relentlessly. 'That means you don't. Nor this dress which Aunt had specially made?'

'Well . . . it's the style they all go in for, I suppose. Not very keen on it myself, though it's better than a crinoline, I suppose – anything would be.'

'I don't like it at all. Especially this shade of green. It's just like pond-weed. Ugh! But you won't say anything to Aunt, will you? She's been so kind and generous to me and I wouldn't want her feelings hurt. Which shows how much good London has done me, because I've really quite a waspish temper.' But Digby was looking at her not at all as one looks at a wasp.

He thought the green of the dress-material quite sickly, and

89

the hair-style frizzed out with fire-tongs very ugly, but they made
no difference at all to his opinion of his cousin as being a Little
Duck. It was the highest accolade he or his friends could award
to a young lady, bestowed as it was for prettiness, charm, and
that indefinable Something which makes a girl attractive. At first
sight of his cousin he had been moved by her invalidism, and a
little repelled; then, knowing her better, he forgot her weakness
and admired her spirit and the charming body clothing it. Only
the healthiest young ladies had so far made any impact on Digby's
emotions, but he was taken by her, in her unbecoming finery with a
beguiling twinkle in her jewel-bright eyes. It even struck him
that he might go so far as to call her a Regular Sport, something
a Little Duck could seldom hope to be. But the clock in the hall
was chiming, and he had a train to catch. He said goodbye to his
cousin, and with a gesture quite foreign to him lifted her thin
hand and kissed it. She looked after him wistfully, regretting that
he could not be by her side during the evening to come.

The guests were ushered into the drawing-room, announced
with toneless majesty by hired footmen in powder and knee-
breeches. Mediaeval-styled lamps shed a soft glow on the plain
draped robes of the women, all cut in the fashion Lilian was
wearing, and most of drab colours, sludge-greens, snuff-browns,
muddy greys. In contrast the men seemed like tropical birds in
their rich velveteens of red and emerald, with silk cravats at their
necks. Beards and long tightly-waved hair predominated. The
women's faces wore a studied pensiveness; they might have been
a family of sisters. As Lilian was presented to them she took in
few names, all her attention absorbed by the strangeness of these
people so different from the country society she knew. Even
Frederica, whose evening it was, looked out of place among them
with her high colour and fashionable air: like a racehorse among
gazelles. What had Digby said: 'She's a great one for taking up
things.' That the things, in this case, were the Pre-Raphaelites, a
band of brothers formed by idealists, Lilian did not yet know.
Rebels against convention, against the Royal Academy's domination
of art and the sentimentality of Victorian painting, escapists to the
Middle Ages as they saw them: these were the New Romantics,
now a trifle middle-aged and weary, yet still a cult.

A man was bending over Lilian, holding her hand longer than

politeness decreed and searching her eyes with his own dark heavy-lidded ones, made the more startling by the ring of white surrounding the iris. He was perhaps in his forties, short and stocky, with an unbecoming square-cut beard and thinning brown locks. Lilian could think of nothing to say to him except 'Good evening.'

'Have you come from the grave?' he asked. His voice was soft, with an accent hard to define; was it slightly foreign, or Cockney? He was like no one Lilian had ever encountered before. She struggled with a desire to answer 'No, from just north of Leeds.' But the gentleman, whoever he was, would clearly not think that funny. Slowly he loosed her hand, and left her, with a long backward look.

She threw an appealing, summoning glance at Frederica, who left the group she was chatting to and came to her side, obviously impatient.

'Who was that man – the one who was talking to me? There, in the brown suit.'

'That? Rossetti, of course.'

'I'm sorry to appear ignorant, Aunt, but who is he? I know nobody here.'

'No, dear child, of course you don't. He is Dante Gabriel Rossetti. One of the founders of the P.R.B. – and I suppose you don't know what that is, either; the Pre-Raphaelite Brotherhood. One of our greatest painters. Did he speak to you? What did he say?'

'He asked me if I'd come from the grave.'

'Oh.' Frederica studied her. 'I wonder why? Perhaps you reminded him of his wife, poor Lizzie. Yes, now I come to think of it, you're not at all unlike, though she was fairer.'

'Did you know her, Aunt?'

'No,' Frederica answered shortly. 'One has seen a great many portraits. Look, there's Topsy. William Morris,' and she pointed to a thickset bearded man with wild hair and a loud barking voice. 'The lady next to him is his wife, Jane. Oh, such a romantic tangle. Jane and Topsy, Jane and Gabriel, Topsy and Georgina Burne-Jones . . .' Frederica heaved the satisfied sigh of someone involved with other people's affairs without being responsible for them.

'Don't you think her looks remarkable? Topsy's prime model, you know, and Gabriel's, of course.'

Lilian would never forget her first sight of Jane Morris. Tall and thin, standing in an attitude as gracefully posed as a statue's, she was all the ladies in the mediaeval paintings scattered about the house, all the brooding angels and princesses of legend. Her robe of purple set off the paleness of her long, fine-boned face, with its dark, deepset, melancholy eyes under thick dark brows, her mouth, extraordinarily full-lipped and pouting, long, projecting pointed chin and long neck. Was she truly beautiful? Possibly not, but there was something beyond beauty in her looks that kept the eyes riveted to her. Lilian noticed that Jane's dark hair was piled into great masses on each side of her face, frizzed out by comb and curling-tongs as her own had been. Beside Jane, every other woman in the room looked commonplace.

Suddenly, to her surprise and alarm, she saw that Jane was looking in her direction. Worse, she was moving majestically towards the couch. Lilian feared that her staring had seemed rude.

Jane lowered her tall self in one graceful sinuous movement into the chair nearest Lilian, who was too awestruck to speak. Then she said, with the stricken look of a Tragic Muse, 'I do hope the food will be decent, don't you? We haven't had any today, because Top threw his dinner out of the window and Cook went on strike.'

'Oh,' said Lilian. 'How . . . how unfortunate.'

'Yes, it was. He said it was bloody awful and we weren't to eat ours in case it poisoned us. The children have been very cross ever since, I thought Jenny would go into a convulsion. She has terrible fits. Have you any children? Oh no, I suppose you're too young.'

'I'm not married. I . . . I'm an invalid.'

'Ah yes, Freddy did say something. How lucky you are.' Jane sighed profoundly. 'I wish *I* could lie on a couch all day. I have the most dreadful back, always a pain just *here*, but Top says it's all imagination.'

'I'm so sorry, Mrs Morris.'

A beautiful, infinitely sad smile lit the legendary face. 'Thank you, dear, and please call me Janey, I'm sure we shall like each other. You don't come from round London, do you?'

'No, from Yorkshire.'

'I thought you sounded different. Ned there comes from Birmingham, and I come from Oxford.' Her pleasant, rather flat voice was distinctly countrified; Lilian afterwards learned that she was the daughter of a stablekeeper. 'I see,' Janey went on, 'you're going to be a Stunner.'

'A Stunner?'

'Don't you know what that is? It's a slang word Top and Gabriel and all of them have for women and men they admire. I'm a Stunner, Lizzie was a Stunner, now you're going to be one. They'll be painting you soon, mark my words. How clever of you to dress like that, and do your hair like mine.'

'It was not really my idea, but Aunt Freddy's. I . . .' She had been going to say something disparaging about the style, but that would be to disparage Janey's appearance too, and she could not hurt someone she liked so much at first sight. There was something oddly vulnerable about Janey, too, so sensational in appearance yet so commonplace in conversation. Lilian sensed a real unhappiness about her that was nothing to do with legendary woes.

At that moment the dinner-gong sounded. 'Good,' said Janey, 'I'm starving, aren't you? Oh, but . . .' For the first time she took in Lilian's immobility.

'I shall have my meal here, on a tray. Don't worry about me, Mrs M – Janey. I don't mind at all.'

'I wish I could have mine with you. What a nice talk we could have had.' For a second a long, white, too-thin hand rested on hers, then Janey rejoined the others, who were moving in pairs towards the door.

The company returned after dinner in lively spirits, Morris's loud voice and staccato laugh dominating the buzz of conversation, and the musical tones of Rossetti, talking excitedly and waving his hands. Tea was served, the inevitable postscript to a meal; during this social interlude all the ladies in turn came up to Lilian and talked politely with her. But there was no opportunity for a 'nice talk' with Jane, who was being monopolised by Rossetti, while Morris appeared to be flirting with gentle little Georgina Burne-Jones. At last Frederica clapped her hands.

'Quiet, everybody! Topsy is going to read his poems to us.'

'Nonsense,' Morris growled, 'you've heard 'em all.'

'But we want to hear them again, of course we do. Come now, which will you give us?'

'All right then, but I'll read one of Gabriel's first.'

There were demands for this and that title, until Morris held up his hand and announced, 'It'll have to be a short one, then, for I've a devilish cold.' Frederica produced a bound volume and gave it to him. He flipped through the pages and began, the others clustered round him, like people carefully arranged for a painting. Rossetti was sprawled on the floor, his head propped up on his hand, his eyes sometimes resting on Janey, sometimes slewing round towards Lilian herself, with a look of – what? fascination, repugnance, fear? Janey contriving to recline languidly in a painfully upright chair, the sad-faced woman who had been pointed out to Lilian as Rossetti's sister, Christina, gazing into the middle distance, fingering the cross she wore, two Madox-Brown girls close together like birds on a wintry bough, a dark man with a sketchbook, also glancing now and then at Lilian.

Perhaps because she had drunk no wine and was in a nervous state, Lilian was acutely, abnormally conscious of tensions in the room. A three-way pull between Janey, Morris, and Rossetti, something powerful, unidentifiable: desire, sorrow, pain, jealousy? There was something wistful in Georgie Burne-Jones's look towards Morris, then towards her husband, as though she pitied both. But the strongest tension lay between the dark woman in the chair, the man lying at her feet, and the poet reading his works.

Caught up in these feelings, Lilian hardly noticed what he read in his abrupt, harsh delivery, not like a poet at all; yet at last the words came through to her:

> O ye, all ye that walk in Willowwood,
>   That walk with hollow faces burning white;
> What fathom-depth of soul-struck widowhood,
>   What long, what longer hours, one lifelong night,
> Ere ye again, who so in vain have wooed
>   Your last hope lost, who so in vain invite
> Your lips to that their unforgotten food,
>   Ere ye, ere ye again shall see the light!
> Alas! the bitter banks in Willowwood,

With tear-splurge wan, with blood-wort burning red;
Alas! if ever such a pillow could
　　Steep deep the soul in sleep till she were dead –
Better all life forget her than this thing,
　　That Willowwood should hold her wandering!

What awful rubbish, Lilian thought. Worse than Mamma's dreary princesses, enough to give one nightmares. Wandering in Willowwood, unable to get out, fighting the branches, falling into the water – because where there are willows there's always water – ugh. I wish something interesting and cheerful would happen.

The door opened to admit a stiff-backed hired footman.

'Mr Leoline Bevis,' he announced.

CHAPTER EIGHT

He came into the room like a breeze stirring those rapt, spell-bound people into life. A young man, perhaps twenty-five, neither tall nor short, smooth-complexioned, fresh-cheeked as a girl, shining-fair hair with the neatest of beards, dressed like the others yet more expensively than his seniors, in black velvet jacket and light grey pegtops, a pink cravat sporting a tiepin which winked and flashed back prismatic colours to the lamps. He smiled round on the company like one who knows himself welcome.

Frederica swam forward to embrace him. 'My dear boy! What a surprise. We thought you were in Italy.'

'I was, dearest Freddy, until most un-Italian floods of rain drove me out. You never saw a wetter place than Venice once the sun leaves it.' He went from one to another of the company, obviously known to all, receiving a painfully hearty slap on the back from Morris, who had closed his book and was now blowing his nose with stentorian vigour. Janey granted the newcomer the faintest of smiles as he kissed her limp hand, then the hands of the other ladies, and finally, to Lilian's astonishment, Rossetti's hand. Nobody seemed to think this at all odd; perhaps it was an accepted act of homage. Frederica led Bevis up to Lilian's couch.

'My dear, this is an old friend of mine, or rather a young one. This poor girl has had nobody but us antiques to talk to, Leoline, ever since she came to stay with me. Now you're here you must cheer her up as you know very well how to.'

Lilian's hand was raised and kissed, as the others' had been. His lips were warm and dry, and not at all unpleasant against her skin. When he lifted his head, still keeping her fingers in his, his look had the same intentness Rossetti's had held, a sort of searching curiosity and urgency in it: as if, she thought, I were some ancient object that had just been unveiled and might crumble into dust before they could get a good look at me. Then she wondered

96

why such a horrid simile should have occurred to her. As though drawing life-blood from his arrival, the party became animated again, though it was almost midnight. Lilian hoped, without much assurance, that Leoline Bevis would come and rescue her from her isolation. As though her thought had reached him, he turned, standing as he was with Burne-Jones in the farthest corner of the room, smiled at her, and was at her side.

So tired she was that afterwards she could not remember what they talked about; mere commonplaces perhaps. His manner was light and easy; he seemed not to notice how little she knew about her aunt's friends. But she was so tired.

'I think I must ask Aunt to let me leave,' she said. 'Would you be kind enough to speak to her for me?'

'Of course I will,' (poor child, said his eyes warmly). 'But look, Mrs Morris is going to sing.' Janey had drifted to the painted piano and was seated at it, graceful there as everywhere, playing simple, minor chords to which she presently added her voice. Her singing was soft, breathy, utterly natural, the singing of a farm-girl binding sheaves, or a peasant mother rocking her baby; and her song was an old ballad of a youth who walked out one May morning, and met a fair maid searching for her father's strayed lambs, and won her heart. Lilian had never heard it before, yet it touched her strangely, so that some of the words went through and through her head. ' "I'd rather rest on a true love's breast Than any other where . . . For I am thine and thou art mine. No man shall uncomfort thee . . ." '

Morris's face was a study in pain. Lilian looked away from him and said hurriedly to Leoline: 'Mrs Morris is very accomplished.'

He nodded. 'Topsy has created her in his image.'

She lay in bed that night unable to sleep for the scenes spinning before her shut eyes, the voices and faces, until they merged into a wild dream, in which Morris was hacking out of stone a vividly-coloured statue of herself. Then the sculptor became someone who was neither Rossetti nor Leoline, but a blend of both; and then a root of ivy sprang from the ground to twine round her ankles and creep up and up her body while she tried to fight it off, reaching her throat at last, and she knew that her throat was long and slender like Janey's, and that the ivy would be slow in strangling her.

97

It was a blessed relief to wake, damp with sweat, and fumble for the matches and candle beside her, so that she could ring the bell for Millie.

'Eeeh, miss, what's t'matter?' The maid was yawning and bleary-eyed, unused to dawn summonses.

'I don't think I'm very well, Millie. Perhaps you'd bring me a warm drink.'

As Millie passed the long wardrobe-mirror on her way out Lilian saw her own reflection propped up on pillows, but turned away from it, for fear of the face she might see there.

It was late morning when she next woke, bemused but refreshed. As she drank her fourth cup of tea Frederica sailed in, flourishing an envelope.

'What an amazing conquest you made of Leoline last night!' she said. 'This note came round by hand before I was even awake, saying all sorts of kind things about the party and asking whether he may take you for a gentle drive today. I never knew anything so sudden, I must say.'

'*I* made a conquest of him? I hardly said a word!' Lilian protested. 'What with being unused to company, and all those . . . remarkable people I was quite stupefied. As to driving out with him, I don't know him, Aunt. Had you not better tell me who he is?'

Frederica plumped herself down on the end of the bed. 'What a cautious little northerner you are. Leoline is one of the most charming young men in my circle. As to who he is, I believe he was up at Oxford when the Brotherhood were painting their famous murals for the University Union. When they came back to London he came with them, a sort of disciple, I suppose one would call him. He paints a little, writes poetry, all that sort of thing.'

'What does he live on?'

Frederica shrugged. 'Private means, I suppose. One never asks about such things. He has a set of rooms in Tite Street – I went to a very amusing party there last winter.'

'Is he married?'

Frederica twinkled. 'Aha! No need to blush, my chicken, it's a very wise question. No, he has no wife, they all marry late, these artists, but he simply adores women. You'll find him the most delightful escort.' She looked sharply at her inert niece, lying back on the pillows with her frizzed hair loose about her, very pale of face. 'You weren't thinking of refusing, were you?'

'I *am* a little tired, Aunt. I've been moved about so much lately. Don't you think it might be wiser for me to rest?' Her back was aching already at the thought of being lifted from bed, washed and dressed by the skilful but hard-handed Crowfoot, carried out like a sack of coals and hoisted into the terrifyingly high brougham, to be jolted through the streets. Only the fear of seeming ungrateful to her aunt made her agree.

'That's a dear girl. You wait and see, it will do you all the good in the world.'

She was weary when Leoline called for her, soon after luncheon, already regretting having said she would drive with him. He kissed her hand, taking in her paleness and the dark circles round her eyes, and she knew instantly that her feelings had been communicated to him, and that he understood them perfectly. As the butler and Crowfoot carried her out of the hall into the street, Leoline was beside her, contriving to steady her so that they did not jerk her going down the steps. And there, waiting, was not the brougham she disliked, but a carriage low-built and covered by a collapsible hood, into which she could be lifted painlessly: or was it Leoline's presence and tactful help that made it seem painless? When they were seated he placed a fur rug over her, tucking it in expertly, then slipped a cushion into the small of her back, just where the ache and the stress were.

'Oh!' She was delighted. 'That's so much more comfortable. Is this your carriage?'

Leoline shook his head, smiling. 'Alas, I don't run to one. Merely a victoria from a livery stable. Ladies find it much more agreeable than most vehicles. I hope it's not too redolent of horse.'

'Oh no, I love horses and the smell of them. I used to ride a lot . . . my uncle keeps a fine stable. Do you ride?'

'Not much. I'm a town fellow, like Gabriel. To tell the truth, I'm not overfond of their teeth and back-legs.'

'It's all a matter of how you approach them. When you feed them you must always hold your palm out flat, like that, and you never walk about behind them unless they know what you're up to and have complete confidence in you.' She chattered on about horses, Leoline watching her animated face with an indulgent smile, occasionally putting in an intelligent word. She decided that he was the most understanding person she had ever met, and that driving with him was a good deal pleasanter than with Aunt Freddy, well-meaning as Aunt was. The breeze was fresh on her face, the river lively with craft as they drove along past the grounds of the Royal Hospital, where a few old pensioners, like scattered scarlet poppies, sat gamely taking the wintry sunshine. Leoline told her of the founding of the Hospital, the legend that Nell Gwyn had persuaded King Charles to give it to his old soldiers. Then, neatly turning the horses (which he seemed to control very well in spite of his avowed dislike of them) he steered inland, into Church Street, talking of the wits and celebrities who had lived there, of Sir Thomas More, buried in the Old Church without his head. 'His daughter Margaret had it taken down from the spike above London Bridge, and laid in a family vault in Canterbury. It's there still, a skull in a sort of cage.'

Lilian shuddered. 'What horrible things people used to do to each other. I don't like to think of them.'

Leoline glanced sideways at her. 'You were not stuffed full of historical horrors as a child, surely?'

'Oh no, Mamma wouldn't have permitted it. My governesses stuck to dates and kings and things – not that they meant much to me.' She remembered fine mornings in the schoolroom, a buzz of flies round the shut window, the drone of a governess's voice competing with them, herself stealing wistful glances out towards the sunny garden and her pony grazing up in the Hall paddock. Weariness and sadness touched her, a vague longing for something she had never had, or had held perhaps for too brief a moment, and she was suddenly sick of London, and cold, and her back was aching again.

As though the brow beneath the little tilted bonnet were transparent, Leoline turned the victoria towards the perfect place to restore flagging spirits. It was a modest old house, much like its neighbours, with only the sign HOTEL below its first-floor windows to indicate that it was any different from them. Outside it Leoline stopped the victoria, beckoned to some urchins, playing in the gutter, to hold the horses for the munificent sum of sixpence, tucked Lilian even more firmly into her seat and disappeared into the hotel.

A few minutes later he emerged followed by a respectable-looking maid in cap and streamers, bearing a neat tray of tea, steaming hot in a silver-plate teapot, and a plate of freshly-toasted muffins dripping with butter. Resuming his seat beside Lilian, he deftly poured tea, and severed the muffins with a knife so that they could be eaten tidily, having laid a crisp napkin across Lilian's lap. She ate heartily, pinker in the face now, and turned to him grate-fully, mopping the butter from her lips.

'How did you know that was just what I needed, Mr Bevis?'

'I think I have some perception of feelings. When a young lady's face is blue with cold and her charming mouth turns down at the corners, the most insensitive man knows that what she needs is tea.'

Both laughed, then Leoline turned on her a curious, intent, searching look, recalling the pity that shone from the stained-glass eyes of his fellow-artists' church windows, the eyes of St Johns and tortured Christs. 'Women are such tender things,' he said softly, 'so infinitely fragile. Man's privilege is to cherish them before they fade.'

She thought he was going to take her face in his hands, but he only touched lightly the fur on her high collar. Part of her disowned the pity and understanding, wanting to show by better spirits how much good he had done her. It was almost irritating to be treated as her mother had treated her, like a helpless baby. And yet – he was a man, clearly conscious of what beauty she had, charmed by her, sympathetic to her. Even Gus had never enveloped her in such tender concern.

And over what, good sense asked her? Tea and muffins. What a romantic nonsense the conversation was becoming. She wiped her hands on the napkin, glancing up at the sky. 'I think it will rain soon. Should we not be going back?'

He paid off the swarming urchins, throwing single pennies to them, amused at the sparrow-fight that ensued. On the drive back to Cheyne Row they were silent, Leoline apparently lost in thought. As they reached the door of her aunt's house she said, touching the arm that lightly held the reins, 'Thank you, Mr Bevis. It was a most enjoyable drive.'

Unexpectedly he answered, 'How well you have been brought up. Do you think you could forget your schooling enough to call me Leoline? In our world we don't deal in Misters and Misses.

101

Can we not call each other by our own names, frankly and honestly?'

'Well . . .' She was taken aback. 'It isn't usual. But I suppose in London things are different. Mrs Morris asked me the same thing. Very well; but perhaps not when Aunt is listening.'

He laughed, a schoolboy's laugh. 'Don't you know I call her Freddy? She would be the first to approve of it.'

Lilian was still a little doubtful. 'Why were you called Leoline? It's a very odd name, isn't it?'

'My mother was devoted to the poems of Tennyson. I suppose I was lucky it was no worse: in fact I rather like it, don't you?'

'How very extraordinary! So was mine. That was how I came to be called Lilian Adeline – ugh. And no, I don't like it, at least I don't think so. I don't like any poetry. Mr Morris's last night made my flesh creep. If I mustn't call you Mr Bevis I shall call you Leo. My Uncle Lewis had a very nice retriever called Leo – it will remind me of him.'

'Thank you,' he said gravely, whether in pleasure or mockery she was not sure.

For a week after that he neither called nor wrote. Then, on a wet dark Monday morning, a messenger-boy arrived with a bouquet for her, a great sheaf of white, waxen flowers on long stiff stems, giving out an overpoweringly sweet scent. At first sight she thought them artificial, then, pinching a petal between her fingers, found it moistly cool. Tied to the ribbon surrounding the bouquet was a florist's card, inscribed *Liliae Liliarum*, which she had just enough Latin to translate *To the Lily of Lilies*.

'I thought lilies were little things with white bells that come in May,' she said to Frederica.

'Those are common lilies of the valley. These are arum lilies – sometimes called Madonna lilies. Haven't you seen them before? Nonsense, of course you have. Look, the angel in that window is holding one. What a pretty compliment – and how expensive, at this time of the year. I'll get Crowfoot to find a vase for them.'

The lilies were duly placed in a tall vase of Frederica's favourite blue and white porcelain, and placed on a corner table so that Lilian could see them from her bed. Their beauty and perfection constantly drew her eyes, but by evening she rang the bell that summoned the maid.

102

'Would you please take the flowers out, Crowfoot? Their scent is lovely, but it makes me feel rather faint, and I don't think I could sleep with them in the room.'

Crowfoot obeyed. In the maids' room she said to the house-parlourmaid, 'Funny sort of present to send a sick lady, if you ask me.'

'What is?'

'Funeral flowers.'

'They aren't, are they? Coo, yes, there was some on the coffin when they took us in to see Aunt Maud, I remember now. Well, I don't s'pose these artists think of 'em like that.'

While the lilies slowly wilted in their exile, their recipient lay watching the rain, listening to the galoshed feet of passers-by slopping through the mud, and longed for a cheerful sound, even one of the hated barrel-organ tunes, to reach her ears. Nobody called in such weather. A letter arrived from Mamma which was so dull that Lilian almost tore it up. Then she relented, admitting to herself that the dullest thing about this dull time was that Leoline did not call to see her. Perhaps she had been rude or abrupt on that drive, and had offended in some way. She was not clever with men, it seemed. Well, if he took offence at something too slight for her to recall, he was not worth fretting for. Yet, like poetry or hate it, the moan of Tennyson's Mariana came back to her, with some meaning now.

'She only said "My life is dreary,
"He cometh not," she said . . .'

Miserably she was aware that Frederica was getting a little bored with her. It had been one thing to bring home a pretty niece with an interesting complaint and present her to distinguished friends; it was quite another to put up with the niece housebound and short-tempered, and nobody calling because the weather was so dreadful. That, at least, was what Frederica hoped was the reason. Lilian was beginning to discover that her aunt was not, after all, a member of that enchanted circle of Bohemians. Asked for a book about art, she was unable to produce one, only some works by John Ruskin which she kept about the house because everybody revered

Ruskin and it looked good to have them. Frederica's own taste ran to such fashionable magazines as *The Lady's Realm*.

So the great party-night had been something Frederica had worked for, a rare social triumph. The knights, ladies, angels of the painted furniture and ceilings remained, impassive, frozen in glass or wood; but their creators and inspirers neither called nor issued invitations. Perhaps Leoline, too, had only been a passing visitor. Lilian lost interest in her food. Her hair need no longer be painfully frizzed, since there was nobody to see it; that was one good thing.

Digby's breezy arrival made a change in the tedious routine of waking, eating and sleeping. Huge, cheerful, highly-coloured like some visiting god descending to a captive nymph, he sat at ease beside her, smoking a cigar, by her permission. It made the room smell of something beside the faint, sickly lavender fragrance that usually pervaded it.

'Splendid to see you, old girl. But I say, ain't Mamma feeding you properly? You look precious peaked to me.'

'I'm quite well, thank you, Digby.'

'Don't look it, then.' She could see that he was genuinely concerned, and felt a surge of the affection she had once – ah, only a few short weeks ago! – felt for him. Listening to his lively talk about Court life she smiled mechanically and made occasional comments as he described the new vitality of the Queen, emerging at last like a vigorous butterfly from the chrysalis of her widowhood. 'Disraeli's done it, if you ask me. Kissed hands as Prime Minister and took over where poor Albert left off – just between these four walls.'

'Digby!' Even Frederica was shocked.

'Oh, nothing like that, Mamma. It's just that for a Jew, he's got the real Irish gift for the blarney – calls her the Fairy Queen and all sorts of fancy names. So that's bucked the old girl up no end . . .'

'The Queen is only in her forties,' said his mother with asperity. She was almost exactly the same age.

'Yes, well, only a manner of speaking. So we're back in town for her to hold a few Courts at the Palace – takes most of the trade away from poor Princess Alix at St James's, but I don't suppose H.M. cares about *that* much, with Bertie still kept out of the limelight. He can't or won't leave the girls alone, that's the trouble, but then H.M. won't give him any official job to do – can't blame the man.'

'And what about you, Digby?' Frederica asked. 'No charming debutante captured your heart yet? It's time you gave me a daughter-in-law, you know.'

'I suppose I will one day, Mamma.' His cigar had gone out. He re-lit it, moodily for him.

Yes, Lilian thought, a daughter-in-law to take my place, when I've been sent home. She could only see herself through his eyes, a poor creature, perceiving nothing of the trouble in them for her, the Little Duck who had somehow swum up the wrong channel and was now in uncomfortably deep waters. In spite of her invalidism he had hoped she might be happy, the first time he had seen her in his mother's drawing-room, so helpless yet so pretty, so jolly pretty . . .

He felt now that he was boring her, and on a lame excuse left them. Back to the Palace and a routine life, Her Majesty as imperious and incalculable as ever, Bertie, Prince of Wales providing plenty of scandal for the smoke-room, lovely deaf Danish Princess Alix earning everyone's admiration, little actresses offering themselves in exchange for champagne suppers and desirable nests in St John's Wood to those who could afford 'em. If only he could have done something for Cousin Lil! But there was nothing anyone could do.

Nothing, until the day the front-door bell pealed through the house and Millie came running in to her.

'Miss, it's 'im! Mr Whatsisname.'

Leoline came into the room sweeping off his broad-brimmed soft hat. He was at her side, kissing her hand with the soft warm kiss she remembered. On a silly, pettish impulse she withdrew it and turned away from him, hunching a shoulder.

'Lilian, Maid Lilian. Don't reject me. I would have come before, believe me, but . . .'

'Why didn't you?'

'Family troubles. Too complicated to explain. I knew you would understand. I came as soon as I could. Poor child, have you been ailing?' He had turned her face towards him, eagerly scanning its paleness, the hollow cheeks, the lank uncurled hair, the look of helplessness. Like a lover or a father, he stroked her forehead with gentle rhythmic strokes, soothing away her pettishness, putting her once more at peace after weeks of unrest.

'Don't fret any more, little dove. Your true knight has come to set you free.'

It was an empty, artificial speech, an echo of her mother's favourite poems. A child could have seen through it, and through his design in tempting her with courtship, then staying away to whet her appetite for it. But she was weak, longing for comfort, and she turned to him in gratitude, unsuspecting.

CHAPTER NINE

The sun was shining with a benevolent wintry lustre on the grey river, dappling it with points of light, making golden pools on the damp pavement; on Lilian, warm-wrapped in furs, being pushed in her invalid chair by Leoline, very dashing in his wide-awake hat and swirling cloak. Behind followed Millie, an unwilling chaperone commanded by Frederica. They were on their way to Tudor House, Cheyne Walk, for, Leo told her, Rossetti was absent, in the country.

'In Scotland, to be exact. With poor Janey at some German spa being cured of lumbago (of all unromantic complaints), what else is the poor fellow to do?'

'Why?' Lilian asked. 'Is he painting her?'

'Painting her? Always. And living and breathing her. Gabriel is an Italian, he must always have a burning passion to warm him.'

'Oh. Doesn't Mr Morris mind?'

He laughed. 'Old Topsy? If he does, he's not the fellow to let anyone see it. He writes a few more stanzas of his *Earthly Paradise*, designs a new wallpaper, or carves the perfect chair, and keeps his thoughts to himself, which is more than Gabriel does, with his every brush-stroke a sonnet to Janey.'

'I thought her rather ordinary. Nice, but ordinary, though of course very striking to look at.'

'All divinities are ordinary, sweet Lilian. It is we who breathe heavenly fire into them. *You* are ordinary, until I make you immortal.'

Before Lilian could enquire how she was to be immortalised they were at the gate of No. 16 Cheyne Walk. It was a large imposing house of Queen Anne's time, bow windows built out from its red brick frontage. The paintwork was peeling, unpruned creepers pulling at the bricks and straggling up towards the roof. Weeds grew between the flags of the small courtyard, the front

107

door stood carelessly open in what Lilian thought a very dangerous way, with gangs of thieves haunting the streets of London, but Leoline said so many people came and went that there was no point in locking the door. 'Gabriel keeps his money loose in a drawer, hundreds of pounds, sometimes, but no one would think of stealing a penny.'

He propelled the bath-chair into the hall, so dark that one had to blink and stare hard in order to see anything at all, the only illumination coming from the dirty fanlight over the front door. Equally dark corridors led off it towards the back of the house. Lilian thought it very gloomy, and not improved by an overpoweringly strong smell which was neither damp nor dust. She sniffed, then put her handkerchief to her nose.

'What on earth is it – that stench?'

'That? Oh, some of Gabriel's menagerie, I daresay. One doesn't notice it when one spends so much time here.'

One did notice it, very much, when one had only just come in, Lilian thought. Millie, too, sniffed disgustedly.

'I don't like it 'ere, miss. I niver could abide stinks. Can I go for a bit of a walk?'

'Aunt did say you were to stay with me . . .' Lilian began, but Leoline said, 'Go out in the garden, Millie. You can find something there to amuse you, I daresay. That side gate is open.' Lilian was relieved when Leoline opened the door on the right hand side of the hall and pushed her in, for the air was distinctly clearer. The room was panelled, book-filled, festooned with drawings, untidy but reasonably normal.

'One of the sitting-rooms,' Leoline said. 'Treffry Dunn has it at the moment. There are always people staying here – Swinburne, sometimes, and Gabriel's brother, and a very rum cove called Howell, and . . . all sorts and conditions. I have a little studio here myself.'

Leoline sounded vague, as though his mind were on something else. They left the sitting room, crossed the hall, and moved down one of the dark corridors to emerge into a large, brilliantly lit room which was obviously a studio. Canvases in dozens were propped against the walls and on easels, lay-figures draped and undraped stood or lay about, a model's throne of gilt wood was backed by a rich velvet curtain. A paint-stained smock hung on a hook. The

108

pleasant smell of oil-paint filled the air, mingled with cigarette-smoke, but it was combated by another, either worse than the odour in the hall or an intensified version of it. Lilian motioned Leoline to stop the chair.

'Leo, there's something *awful* here. Do have a look for it. Someone must have left some food about and it's gone bad. I really don't think I can bear to stay in here unless you take it out.'

He patted her shoulder tenderly. 'All divinities have delicate noses. Of course it shall be removed if it offends my lady.' He searched the tables, the spaces where the propped canvasses leaned away from the walls, the alcoves beneath the short staircase that led to a gallery, but found nothing. Lilian had been propelling her chair, which she could do with some difficulty, round the room. She stopped it and pointed.

'There.' In a corner stood a canework sofa, loosely covered with blankets.

'That's Gabriel's place for taking a rest when he paints all day,' Leoline said. 'There's nothing on it – look.' He pulled the blankets away.

'Well, look under it, then.'

Leoline bent down. 'Phew, you're right,' he said. The object he dragged out was large and limp, a mass of tarnished feathers that had been white. It was a peacock, and it had been dead a long time.

Lilian suppressed a scream with the back of her hand. 'Take it away! Oh, get rid of it, quickly!' But Leoline was standing, hands on hips, surveying the corpse with thoughtful interest: perhaps he visualised the inclusion of it in a painting. Lilian shrieked at him.

'Take it out *at once*!'

He seemed to come to himself with a start. 'Of course, of course.' He pulled the unsavoury object by its feet towards a door which led to the garden, and on returning left the door open. 'I do apologise,' he said to Lilian, who had succeeded in finding her smelling-salts in her reticule and was vigorously inhaling them. 'You see, Gabriel has a passion for creatures, animals, the more exotic the better. He has an affinity with them and they with him, but he sometimes forgets how many he has or where they are – hence that unfortunate bird. He mostly keeps them in cages, and his man goes round and feeds them every day, so I trust we shall find no more.'

'I trust not,' said Lilian's muffled voice. 'I think I would like to leave now, if you please.'

'Oh, but you must see the studio first. It's a tremendous privilege to have a private view of Rossetti's works, finished and unfinished.'

Two faces looked out from the canvasses. Janey Morris, dark, sultry, a Queen of Sorrows: Janey as The Lady of Shallot, crazed by enchantments, Janey as Queen Guenevere, gazing at the richly-ordered bed where she had lain with Lancelot, Janey as La Pia de' Tolomei, languishing in prison, Janey as Proserpine, the pomegranate half-way to her bee-stung lips, the great brooding eyes full of foreknowledge of her dark fate. And in every touch of light and shade, as Leoline had said, the painter's obsessive, worshipping passion.

The other face had the sensuous lips, massed hair, and thick column of neck which to Rossetti were symbols of ideal beauty. But the hair was bright gold, the colour of ripened corn, the complexion fair, the expression worldly, with a very slight look of calculation ('how much is he paying me for this?') about the mouth, and instead of the classic simplicity of Janey's costumes this woman was bedizened with rich brocades, jewels, peacock-feathers, pearl combs, everything, Lilian reflected, but pans and kettles. Yet she was very beautiful; Rossetti must love her, too.

Leoline answered the unspoken question. 'Fanny Cornforth. Gabriel's housekeeper for years.'

Lilian was about to remark that 16 Cheyne Walk was not much of an advertisement for Miss Cornforth's domestic talents when it occurred to her that in this unconventional society the word 'housekeeper' might have a double meaning, so she said nothing. Leoline pointed to another portrait of Fanny. '*The Kissed Mouth* – one of Gabriel's favourites. She seldom sits for him now; a shade over-ripe. But she still keeps him amused. The Elephant, he calls her, and she calls him the Rhinoceros. With Gabriel, amusement counts for much.'

'But Janey isn't amusing – is she?'

'Janey is his mystical love, his ideal.'

Lilian was unable to take her eyes from a head-and-shoulders painting of Janey, looking full-face from the canvas, her hands parting a thick screen of leaves as though trying to force her way out of a prison, her hair pulled back to the nape of her neck to keep it out of the way of the clutching branches, on her face an expression that seemed part dazed enchantment, part desperation.

'That?' Leoline said. 'An image from one of his own sonnets.

"Better all life forget her than this thing
That Willowwood should hold her wandering!" '

Lilian shuddered. 'It frightens me.'

'Come. We'll find a warmer place.' He looked back at the picture, as though reluctant to leave it.

The mournful eyes of Janey followed them from the studio.

A flurry of footsteps: Millie, flying in from the garden, her bonnet on the back of her head. 'Oh, miss, there's a gret bull out yon roarin' at me, and it's getten its chain half o' t'ground!'

'A bull? You're imagining things, Millie.'

'No, she isn't,' Leoline said. 'I'm afraid Gabriel does keep a bull in the garden, but he doesn't look after it very well. I'll give it some fodder.' He went out, to a shed, Lilian could see through a small uncleaned window, emerging with an armful of something which he took down to the end of the long, tree-hung garden, where a whitish form could be seen kicking and prancing.

'It's etten all t'grass away,' Millie said. 'Bulls want pasturin' i' fields, not scranny little patches like yon, poor thing.'

'I don't suppose there are any fields in Chelsea, Millie. And I don't think Mr Rossetti knows much about keeping animals.' Out of the corner of her eye she perceived on a low table in the corridor a large cage in which creatures were moving. As Leoline returned, shutting the door to the garden, the light caught what looked like scales.

'Are those snakes in there?' she asked him directly, aware that if he said yes she and Millie would have to leave at once, for the country girl had a mortal fear even of harmless slow-worms.

'Snakes? No, of course not. That is, he did have two, but they weren't a success, I believe. Those are armadillos. I don't think they're quite warm enough.'

'Neither is Millie, I fear. Is there a room with a fire anywhere?'

'There's one in my studio. But I think Millie would be better off in the kitchen. The cook always has the range alight, whether Gabriel's at home or not. Down the stairs at the end, Millie, and mind the turn, it's rather dark.'

Lilian was cold herself, even shivering, partly with a sort of

111

nervous apprehension that was exciting enough to make her want to stay in this strange house. No harm could come to her, surely, with Leo, so gentle and protective towards her. Whatever was in his studio – and she felt something was there important to her – she wanted to see it.

Unlike Rossetti's studio, huge and open-planned, made in the place of the old staircase of the house, Leoline's was a small, high-ceilinged room at the back, once, perhaps, part of the servants' domain, with double doors, one of oak, one backed with green baize. As he had promised, a fire burnt in the grate. He lit an oil lamp, producing a welcome golden glow. Lilian thankfully loosened the collar of her wrap, letting the warmth touch her throat. Leoline saw, and taking her hands in his, peeled off her gloves.

'They'll only keep your hands cold. Come nearer the fire – there.' She held out her blue numbed hands, rubbing them until the feeling began to come back to them. Leoline was at a cupboard, getting out what she hoped were teacups, but he turned to say, 'What we need is a glass of good red wine. I always keep a bottle in the hearth this weather – heresy, the purists say, but the heat brings out the warm sun of Italy lurking in the depths.' Lilian would very much have preferred a pot of Aunt Freddy's Lapsang Souchong, but he was already pouring for both of them. The wine was almost hot from its long session on the fender, and went down very agreeably, she had to admit to herself, besides producing an entertaining feeling of extreme wickedness. Two glasses were gone before she was aware of having drunk one.

'If they could see me now at Scarbrick,' she said with a giggle. 'We only have wine at Christmas, and then it's because Uncle Lewis kindly sends it. I shall be going back to Aunt Freddy quite drunk, at this rate.'

He said something in what she took to be Italian, laughing; then 'Wine is part of an artist's existence, as you'll find when you come to live with me.'

'I'm coming to live with you, am I?' It sounded no more fantastic than anything else that had happened in the last hour. Perhaps it was a proposal. He did not answer, but produced from his pocket a box containing six long, dark cigarettes.

'These are part of it, too. Won't you try one?'

112

She surveyed them doubtfully. 'I smelt them in Mr Rossetti's studio. I don't think I should. Though Aunt does, now and then. It's considered a very *fast* thing to do, isn't it?'

He lit one with a live coal from the fire, puffed at it, producing a little cloud of blue smoke, then put it to her lips. The gesture was ritualistic, a kiss by proxy. She felt her cheeks flush as she drew in the smoke, coughed, and gave it back to him.

'Ugh! No, it's too strong.' He nodded.

'All in good time.' He was drawing the heavy curtains, shutting out the gloomy, darkening afternoon. Then he turned up the lamp, bending over it like an acolyte at the altar; then, still with an air of priesthood, held it up and moved slowly from one portrait to another, where they hung low on the walls, the blue vapour from his cigarette drifting before them, incense. Lilian knew that this was why she had been brought to the house, not to see the smouldering beauty of Janey Morris or the opulent charms of Fanny Cornforth, but the face that looked out from portrait after portrait. Sometimes she was Shakespeare's Viola or Sylvia, Ophelia, floating flower-strewn in the brook, Dante's Beatrice, the Immortal Beloved, refusing him her kiss in a procession. A pale face, oval-shaped, set on a long slender neck, eyes of a light blue-green, red-gold hair. A haunting face, with a look to it suggesting that the full, calm lips could tell a strange story. Lilian stared and stared, half-recognising the face, aware that Leoline was watching her keenly.

'Well?' he asked. She shook her head.

'I don't know . . . should I know her?'

He took a mirror down from the wall and put it on a table beside her. Then, gently, he undid the strings of her small fur-trimmed bonnet, took it off, and began to pull out the tortoiseshell pins that held up her hair, ignoring her startled protest and the hand she put up to stop him. When it was all down, loose about her shoulders, he placed the lamp on the table and held the mirror up before her. And her own face, but for its youth and a detail or two, was the face of the woman in the portraits.

Seeing her realisation, he nodded, satisfied. 'You, ma donna. And also Elizabeth Siddal, wife to Rossetti.'

'The Stunner,' she said. ' "Lizzie was a Stunner." '

'Where did you learn that?'

'From Janey.'

He raised the lamp to illuminate a life-size painting that filled the end wall. Elizabeth Siddal sat, green-robed, by a sundial, relaxed, her face tilted upwards, the eyes shut, lips half-opened, dreaming. A glimmering misty landscape of Florence made a halo round her head, and a halo crowned the crimson dove which flew down to place a white poppy in her open hands.

'She's dead,' Lilian said.

'Yes. It was painted after her death. *Beata Beatrix*, The Blesséd Damozel, receiving the white flower of death and chastity.'

Leoline was standing hehind her, his hands on her shoulders.

'Of course I remember now. Aunt Freddy told me. I never thought any more of it.'

'But Freddy never knew her. I did.' She had not heard such emotion before in the voice that normally held a smile.

'Has she been dead long?'

'Seven years. And was dying, long before that.' It occurred to Lilian that Leoline must be older than he looked, or must have moved in Rossetti's circle at a very early age. But Aunt had said he had been at Oxford when he first met the Brotherhood. She would like to have glanced at his face, to see whether it was indeed perfectly unlined, smooth as a girl's, but he remained behind her chair, his fingers still pressing into her shoulders.

'She was dying,' he said, 'when they lived at Chatham Place, by Blackfriars Bridge. The house was very old, leaning out over the river, with a balcony where he made her sit for him, sometimes for hours, in all weathers. The timbers of the house were rotting, sending a smell of decay through all the rooms, and the river poured its vapours out to poison those who breathed them in. The river is a sewer, you know, choked with London's filth.'

'Please, Leo ... I don't want to hear about it.' But he went relentlessly on.

'Lizzie lived there with Gabriel for nine years. He married her two years before the end, because he thought it might save her life. She grew more and more beautiful, as the flush of disease came up in her cheeks, more and more like a spirit walking on the earth. She hardly spoke, because her voice was common compared with Gabriel's, and she was proud both for herself and him. One of his friends had found her serving in a milliner's shop – her father was a cutler in the Kent Road. But Gabriel breathed his genius into her

114

and made her into a poet and a painter. Her poor little poems and her poor little paintings! She tried so hard to be worthy of him, but it made neither of them any happier. There was always Janey, from the Oxford days, though there was nothing in it then. And then there was Fanny – she knew about Fanny from the start. Janey, too.'

He was telling the story in a strange, pedantic way, as though it had been rehearsed to the last syllable, and recited many times. Lilian was acutely disturbed by it, longing to be away from the sound of his voice and the mask of sadness on the face of Beata Beatrix. But she was held as though by a spell; even if her legs had not been helpless she could not have moved.

'She had a baby, still-born. Long after it had been buried she would sit rocking the empty cradle and singing a little tune to it. Then one night Gabriel went out for a few hours, leaving her going to bed. When he returned she was unconscious, with an empty laudanum-bottle at her side, and a little note pinned to her nightgown. It said, "My life is so miserable I wish for no more of it."

'She looked so lovely in death that Gabriel tried to kiss her awake, and when she lay unmoving he sent for the doctor to bring her out of her trance. When at last he realised the truth he put his new book of poems, still in manuscript, in the coffin with her, between her cheek and her glorious hair. Then they took her up to Highgate Cemetery and buried her on a hilly slope, under a tree. Seven years ago.'

In the silence that fell, Lilian said, 'You must have loved her very much.'

'Loved her? I worshipped her. To me she was Love itself.'

'And you hated Mr . . . Gabriel?'

'Hated? How could I hate him, poor soul? Only I envied him, because he had her.'

The fingers that had bitten into her shoulders moved down along her arms, across her breast, touching and clinging, rousing sensations in her that were very disturbing. She wanted to pull away from them, and at the same time to hold them to her and give in to their demands, her wine-warmed blood rising to them. There was a sort of sweetness in being touched where she had never been touched before; she was pleasantly dazed in the light that shone around Beata Beatrix's head, ready to yield to she knew not what.

115

A voice broke in on her half-dream, the strident voice of Millie. 'Miss! it's past four. Oughtn't we be gettin' back?'

The hands were suddenly withdrawn, Leoline opening the door for Millie (had he turned the key before, as he unlocked it now?).

'Yes, of course, Millie. Good gracious! How time passes.'

The fire was low in the grate, almost burnt out, but the lamplight showed her Leoline's face, calm and smiling and boyishly unlined, though a part of her brain had been doing sums and had come up with the fact that it was sixteen years since Lizzie Siddal had gone to live with Gabriel Rossetti in the rotting house by Blackfriars Bridge. Sixteen years; Leo would have been a child then, or a boy at most. Surely he had only known Lizzie for part of those years, in his very young, impressionable days. Yet, as they left the picture-lined room, and the dark corridors and gloomy hall, where horrid traces of the dead white peacock still lingered, she felt oddly proud and flattered that Leo had seen his dead lady's likeness in her face. Now that her hair was up again and her bonnet on, she could hardly remember why she had been frightened in the studio. After all, though strangely told, it had only been a sad story of a sick woman and an artist who had selfishly used her for his art. Leo must have told it many times to chill people's blood. Suddenly conscious of something that had puzzled her, she asked him, 'Does Mr Rossetti mind you having all those portraits of his wife?'

'Hardly, since I painted them myself. Oh, from his originals, and others – the Ophelia is Millais. I'm little more than a copyist, though not a bad one. Believe me, I'm perfectly satisfied with copies.'

I am one of his copies, she thought, the living model of Lizzie Siddal. Well, there are worse things to be, I suppose.

A chill wind blew from the river, where lights had sprung up here and there on the south bank, and chimneys and masts were ghostly dark shapes. The mephitic river-smell was there, though only faintly on this wintry air. Lilian imagined it at its worst in summer, drifting up to the girl on the balcony at Blackfriars, poisoning her lungs and long, lovely throat, tingeing her face with the greenish pallor of the last portrait, the Beata.

'Oh, it's cold!' she said. 'Do hurry.'

He leant over her, his breath warm on her cheek, murmuring.

'Love! thou art leading me from wintry cold.
Lady! thou leadest me to summer clime.'
'I do wish you would *not* quote poetry at me, Leo. I've told you,
I don't like it, and I shall not come out with you again if you go
on in such a way.' But she knew that she would.

CHAPTER TEN

'The Reverend Augustus Hambleden, madam,' announced the parlourmaid.

Frederica looked up in astonishment from the letter she had been writing.

'Augustus! Good heavens, what a surprise. What are you doing up from Yorkshire?'

'I'm sorry to drop in on you without notice, Aunt Frederica. I was ... I thought I would spend a few days in London, and besides, I ...'

'Well, well, sit down. Do get rid of your hat and umbrella – not in here, dear boy. They should be left in the hall when so *very* wet.' She was not overwhelmingly pleased to see her nephew; Lewis might have given her some warning of his visit, but then Lewis never wrote letters except to *The Times*, and those invariably abusive. However, one could hardly tell a relative one was not at home when the maid had already admitted him. Resignedly she put her correspondence away, preparing for a boring hour with the young man who looked so uncomfortable in the angular Morris chair, his feet planted awkwardly.

Augustus was feeling every bit as awkward as he looked. It had taken some courage to follow up his irresistible impulse to visit London and see Lilian again. He had always been a little overawed by his Aunt Frederica, even at the Hall, and in her own surroundings she was positively frightening. He had not dared, so far, to look carefully at the décor of the room, merely taking in that it was wild and fantastic and utterly unlike the setting he had imagined from Aunt Florence's rhapsodic description of the house where Lilian lived. But for all its shockingly bright colours and the images painted everywhere (could Aunt Frederica have gone over to Rome?) it was the house that held Lilian, his jewel.

Manfully he made conversation, helped out by Frederica, an

118

expert in small talk. They discussed the dreadful weather, the Queen's extraordinary burst into authorship with her *Journal of Our Life in the Highlands*, the sensational Mr Disraeli. Augustus, encouraged, had it on the tip of his tongue to enlighten his aunt about the recent Irish Church Disestablishment Act, as being the news item that interested him most; but his guardian angel whispered to him that she might not share his feelings. All the time, as they talked, he looked furtively for signs of Lilian's presence, listened for the sound of her voice in another room.

Frederica rang for afternoon tea. 'Well,' she said brightly, 'and what news from Scarbrick? How is Lewis?'

'Oh, pretty well, I think. That is, he had a severe attack of gout last time I called on him.'

'I'm not surprised, the amount of port and sherry he drinks, and the tempers he flies into. And your Aunt Florence?'

Augustus brightened. They were getting round to the subject of Lilian.

'She seems very cheerful. Gets about a good deal, I believe. Papa lets her have the pony-trap since he got the new gig. Er . . . does she write to Lilian frequently?'

'I really couldn't say,' Frederica's tone was indifferent. 'I'm not the sort of guardian who scrutinises my charge's post.'

'No, of course not, Aunt, I never supposed it. I only wondered . . . how *is* Lilian?' There, now he had got the question out; but what instinct made him fear the answer?

'Well – that is, as well as can be expected. The change of scene has certainly improved her spirits, and she has made new friends, which is always a good thing. I feel that the greatest part of life is Society, don't you? But no, I suppose you don't, with your spiritual concerns. What news of your future parish?'

'Oh, the best, indeed yes. But – ' he choked on a cake-crumb, washed it down with a draught of tea, put down the cup which was trembling noisily in his saucer, and asked, an equal tremble in his voice: 'May I see Lilian?'

Frederica was perfectly aware of Augustus's aspirations to his cousin, and quite determined not to encourage them, but since he had come some hundreds of miles, she could hardly forbid him Lilian's presence.

'Well, she is engaged at the moment, but I daresay she might

119

spare you a few minutes.' She rang, and when the maid appeared, said, 'Tell Miss Lilian her cousin the Reverend Augustus has called, and hopes she can receive him briefly.' To Augustus she said, when the maid had gone, 'Lilian is having a sitting at the moment.' He looked completely blank. 'She is sitting for a portrait,' Frederica explained patiently, 'to an artist. I mix a good deal in artistic circles, and Lilian has been given the kindest reception by my friends. Naturally, being both interesting and pretty, and with a fashionable style in looks. I am so pleased for her.'

Augustus's knowledge of art was about the same as his grasp of the mathematical equations of electro-magnetic induction, recently discovered to the benefit of Science. It consisted of a vague awareness of the gloomy ancestral oil-paintings that hung darkly on his father's walls, an equally vague idea that in Paris a colony of artists led very shocking lives, drinking poisonous liquors and painting from nude female models, and a memory of having seen in the *Illustrated London News* reproductions of modern paintings hung in the Royal Academy Exhibitions. With thumping heart and damp palms he was shown into Lilian's room.

Nothing had prepared him for the sight he saw. Lilian lay on a flat couch, draped in purple. Her dress – if it was a dress – was a robe of saffron yellow that clung to and outlined her limbs and form; her hair was down, as Augustus had never seen it – such a quantity of it! her arms crossed on her breast, holding a cluster of flowers; and her face was calm, like a face sculpted in stone, her eyes closed. Augustus hardly noticed the young man in the smock who sat at an easel sketching her, for his first alarmed impression was that she was too ill to move.

Then she opened her eyes, and with a pleasant smile said, 'Hello, Gus. Give me another cushion, Leo, I can't lie flat like this and talk at the same time.' The cushion provided, and her head solicitously propped up by the artist, she said, 'Well, how surprising to see you. What are you doing in London?'

'I called,' said poor Augustus, 'to see you.'

'How very kind. Oh, I must introduce you – Mr Leoline Bevis, who is painting me – my cousin Augustus from Yorkshire.'

The men exchanged unenthusiastic glances and murmured words of greeting.

'And what's the news from home? Mamma doesn't want me back, I hope!'

'I don't think so – that is, I don't know. I . . . how are you, Lilian? Not worse, I hope? You look somewhat thinner.'

'I'm perfectly well – it's these clothes. Don't you think me very elegant?' Her smile teased him. 'But I suppose to you I look odd. Leoline is painting me as – what is it, Leo?'

'Beatrice on her bier receiving the kiss of the Angel of Love,' Leoline said in a tone implying that an infant in arms would have recognised the subject.

'I don't see the angel,' Augustus said.

'Oh, Leo is to pose for that himself. He draws from his reflection in the long mirror there. Look, you can see the figure in the drawing.'

Augustus made no move to inspect the drawing, or Leoline to offer it. There was unspoken resentment between them, though Leoline's bearing was as calm and urbane as usual, a faint smile playing above his blond beard, as though such intrusions were things to be borne gracefully. Augustus wished intensely that he would go. He sensed that Lilian was not happy, yet was stopped by something from expressing it. By what? It was beyond him. He only knew for certain that he was desperately ill at ease, longing to talk to Lilian as they had once talked. In the awkward silence he asked, 'Why are you making a drawing, Mr Bevis? I thought my cousin said this was to be a painting.'

'So it is. But the hours of sitting which I would ask of a model would be too much for Miss de Wentworth's strength. We have agreed to the preliminary work being done here, the final touches at my studio.'

Within limits it was true. More accurately, Millie's story of the bull in the garden and her exclusion from the Cheyne Walk studio had come to Frederica's ears from the scandalised Crowfoot, who was privately prepared to believe anything of her mistress's artistic friends. Frederica was more easily shocked than she appeared. The admired, lionised young artist was all very well as a party pet, and a tribute to her niece's charms, but that he should take liberties with the girl's reputation was intolerable. Frederica had never cared for the introduction of the oafish Millie into her household. Obviously she was quite untrustworthy, and Lilian incapable of taking care of herself. Of course, nothing would have *happened*; Leoline would never have taken advantage of a poor invalid. Nevertheless, Frederica had dictated that any paintings were to be done as far as possible by means of drawings made where she could inspect artist and model at frequent intervals. Leoline's pleas that he had never worked in such a way were ignored. As to whether Lilian was glad, or sorry, or indifferent, about the arrangement Frederica simply could not tell, the girl was so odd in her manner.

Determined to make the most of the few minutes he had, Augustus decided to pretend that no third party was present. There were things he must say.

'Did you enjoy *The Princess*?'

'What?'

'The book I gave you. Tennyson's poems.'

'Oh, that. Yes, how kind of you.'

He thought of the marked passage, the lines that had said all he would have said himself, and despaired, but there was more that must be said.

'You remember what I told you about the living. The living my vicar told me might possibly come my way. Well, he has heard from the bishop, and the incumbent is to retire within six months. After that it will be mine. I shall be vicar of Armsforth.'

Her face was a blank, as though he were talking of foreign places and people. It was left to Leoline to give her a cue, saying, 'I must congratulate you.'

'Thank you.'

Lilian smiled. 'I'm so pleased, and Mamma will be too, but of course she must know already. It was kind of you to come and tell me.'

And so, in less than a minute, Augustus's house of cards collapsed around him. The roomy vicarage, the pleasant view up through a gap in the hills from the back windows, towards the ancient church from the front, the sweet air after the grime of Mardsley, the voices of his own ring of bells for Matins and Evensong; all meaningless now. And, sadder still, the vision of Lilian by his fireside, and, by some miracle of God's mercy, a child in the sunny room he had wistfully marked out for a nursery.

He rose, stiffly bowing to both of them.

'Goodbye, Lilian. Mr Bevis.'

As though she were suddenly sorry, she held out a hand to him. He touched it lightly, feeling the coldness of the fingers.

'Remember me to Mamma and Uncle,' she said.

'I will.'

He shut the door carefully and returned to the hall. His hat and umbrella lay on a chair where he had left them. Etiquette dictated that he return to the drawing-room, or at least summon a maid to make his farewells to Mrs Stevens-Clyne. But he knew that neither his aunt nor anyone else in that house cared how correctly he behaved or what he did. Fumblingly he opened the heavy front door and let himself out, walking with his head bent and his umbrella furled, so that people in the street stared curiously at him, for it was raining hard. An insistent feeling nagged at his mind; the certainty that he had been in the presence of something evil, and that his beautiful cousin had been part of it. He made his way to Chelsea Old Church, and remained kneeling in the More Chapel for over an hour.

'You could have sent him away sooner,' Leoline said.

'How could I? He is my cousin, after all, and . . . very fond of me. Don't be cross, Leo. It doesn't signify at all.'

'I'm not cross, as you call it. Merely annoyed that we have all these interruptions when working like this is so damnably slow at the best.'

'Well, it can't be helped. Aunt won't have it otherwise.'

He glanced at her over the top of his sketching-pad. 'But *you* would like to sit at the studio?'

'Yes. That is – I think so. Yes, I would, very much. Only I hope there are no more peacocks, or anything like that.'

'Don't be afraid. Gabriel's man has taken care of everything. So you'll come next week?'

'If you'll be ready by then.'

'We must work now.' He moved to her side, pulled away the cushion so that her head lay flat, and spread out her hair. As he folded her hands together his fingers closed over them, then slid along her arms to her shoulders and down the length of her body, making her shiver convulsively, lingering to cause her delicious agony, then suddenly lifting.

'No, no,' she said, and 'please . . .'

He shut her eyelids, his fingertips resting on them lightly.

'One day,' he said, 'they'll lay pennies on them to keep them shut, your crystal eyes. They were on Lizzie's, the night she died; but I took them off and laid gold pieces on instead. The others were not worthy.'

'Leo, don't, don't frighten me!'

'What is frightening about death, the death of the beautiful? And the money is only Charon's toll, you know, paid to him for ferrying us across the Styx.'

A very perturbed Florence sat reading her nephew's letter over and over. It seemed preposterous, sitting in her quiet little parlour overlooking the snowy garden, that even in far-off London such things could occur. Her fragile, innocent child posing as an artist's model! The words conjured up the same unspeakable picture in her mind as in Augustus's; abandoned females totally without clothes leering at lascivious bearded painters. The sitting had taken place in Frederica's house, certainly, but as Augustus had given her no description of the circumstances she could only imagine the worst. Frederica was a worldly, sophisticated woman, everyone knew that, but how could even she permit such things? She sat down at her writing-desk.

When the protesting, exclamation-mark filled letter arrived on Frederica's breakfast tray it met with a chilly reception. She had faint doubts, it was true, about the sort of attentions Leoline was paying to Lilian; she would much have preferred a straightforward courtship, with a portrait, if any, in the sort of conventionally pensive pose Janey so often assumed – a corpse on a bier was something rather outré even for Gabriel himself. It worried her, too, that Lilian was becoming strange in her manner. She seemed to be losing strength, too, inclined to lie in bed later and later, disinclined to get dressed or be taken out, only to sit at the window waiting for Leoline. She ate very little : but that was perhaps understandable since she had no exercise or fresh air.

Still, it was outrageous of Florence to suggest that she, Frederica, was allowing the girl to be debauched, to put it as strongly as that. The letter which went speeding back to Yorkshire was tart.

'My young friend Leoline Bevis is certainly paying his attentions to Lilian, but I take the deepest offence, as I am sure he would, to your implication that she is in any way behaving immodestly. The "sittings" to which Augustus refers are conducted entirely under my supervision and in the most irreproachable conditions. I think you would find Lilian much improved in mind and taste, and if you'll take my opinion for what it is, Florence, she would be a good deal better off with Mr Bevis than with that ninny of a clergyman. Unless you insist on removing her I shall do nothing to break the connection.'

By the same post a note went off to Leoline giving permission for as many sittings as he wished to take place at the studio, provided Lilian's health could stand it; and, of course, provided she were suitably chaperoned.

Leoline received the news joyfully. An extra large fire was built in the studio, warm blankets laid on the couch where Lilian was to lie. Millie, sternly warned by Florence to remain in the studio all the time Miss Lilian was there, had a comfortable basket chair by the fire. Lying prone, saffron-robed, her head on a purple cushion fringed with gold, Lilian idly watched Leoline mixing his colours.

'How odd to be here, being painted myself.' She looked up at the many faces of Lizzie, dreaming on the walls. 'To think you will make me look like her.'

'You will be so like, my darling, that even Gabriel will not know the difference.'

'Won't he?' said a voice from the doorway.

'Gabriel! I'd no idea you were back.' Leoline went to shake him by the hand. Lilian, smiling stiffly at him from her awkward position, thought he looked older and more dissipated than he had done in her aunt's house. He seemed fatter, shabbier, his frayed coat unflatteringly fastened with one button at the neck, the thin dark curling hair, growing round a spreading bald patch, seeming not to have been brushed for some time. Above all she noticed the eyes, that must have once been very fine but now were inflamed and staring. The stare seemed interminable. Lilian began to fidget under it, wishing he would go away.

'She's like – too like,' he said at last.

125

'Not for me, Gabriel.'

'Oh, you've got your wish, I've no doubt.' The laugh was bitter. 'Why do you look so infernally well, Bevis?'

'I am happy. I am doing what I want to do.'

'And you feed on it, like the worms . . . I saw the bird again this morning.'

'What bird?'

'I told you,' impatiently. 'The chaffinch that came down and crouched at my feet. I picked it up, but it wouldn't fly. First in Scotland, now here. I know it's Lizzie's spirit, come to absolve me.'

'You're still determined to have it done, then?'

'Yes. A letter has gone off to the Home Secretary. Perhaps when it's done I shall be free, at peace. But I can't face it, Bevis – I can't go myself! Not that, though I long . . . I long so much to see her again . . .'

Leoline went over and put an arm round Rossetti's shoulders. 'You must not go, it would be the worst thing you could do. I'll go myself, I promise.'

'And you won't . . . won't recoil . . . ?'

'No. I promise you that, too.'

'Of course. I know you, or I ought to by now. You always envied me.'

Lilian fancied, through her half shut lids, that Leo gave his master a warning glance. She no longer wanted to hear what was being said. The next moment – or had some time passed? – a hand was on her shoulder, then stroking her brow.

'Leo?'

'Yes. Are you awake?'

'Yes. What was he saying?'

Leo was kneeling at her side, speaking softly into her ear, pushing aside the hair so that she missed nothing.

'I told you he buried his new volume of poems in her coffin. Now he needs them. So – he must have them back. There's an order for exhumation.'

She struggled to wake, to look at him, make some kind of horrified protest, but her limbs would not obey her. She heard him laugh softly, saying, ' "Your nerves are all shut up in alabaster, And you a statue, Lady." Have you been taking the medicine?'

'Yes.'

126

She had taken it every night, sometimes at mid-day, the colour-less, oily stuff from a bottle with which Leo had supplied her, warning her to keep it out of her aunt's sight. It would bring her sleep, he said, banish the fantastic and sometimes horrifying dreams which visited her, particularly in the early morning, when she seemed to be tormented by real, physical demons, sharing her bed.

Sometimes the visions were not unpleasant. She seemed to drift among picture-people: Rossetti's paintings, her aunt's decorations, come alive. Rueful kings and queens, forlorn, long-necked maidens, angels with lutes and psalteries, love-struck Dantes, pale Beatrices. They were gentle, courteous creatures, seeming to talk in wordless murmurs and to sing softly to their pleasant instruments, and they moved glidingly, like spirits. Sometimes they smiled faintly at her and stretched out their hands, as though inviting her to join them. 'But I am one of you already!' she would cry, not knowing if they heard her or not, for they never responded, only melted away into a backcloth of towers and tapestries and colours.

Her sleep grew shorter and her wakings earlier, wakings of mournful thought, self-reproach, harkings-back to the accident and sudden frenetic illusions that Beauty, her pony, had been shot and she had had to watch. After that came a time when her body was taken over by a force which might be Leoline himself, or a devil in his shape; sweet, sickly, painfully passionate dreams from which she roused hardly believing that it was she who had dreamed them, or that her seemingly untouched body had not suffered them. She longed and longed (who had just been talking of longing?) yet shuddered away from what the longing meant.

Perhaps it was on the next day, or another. By now she felt physically ill. She was lying on the studio bier, very sleepy from the doze she had fallen into after whatever they had managed to make her eat for luncheon, and feeling curiously unwell, some-times shivering, sometimes burning hot. There was no sign of Millie in the chair by the fire: she managed to ask why.

'Gabriel has a new rabbit, a white one with dark eyes. Cook is keeping it warm downstairs, and Millie is with her. She's fond of rabbits, did you know? Are you listening, Lilian? You must obey me and listen, you know. "Prythee weep, May Lilian, if prayers will not hush thee, like a rose-leaf I will crush thee, Fairy Lilian." '

She tried to stop him, to say that her brother Arthur used to tease her with the silly rhyme, but either the words would not come out or she could not hear herself say them. It was like one of her mad dreams, when a bewitchment threatened her and she tried to get out the names of God and His Son and could not speak them, for her mouth was useless, as flaccid as cotton-wool, and her throat sore. Then she felt a cool hand on her forehead, and a drink at her lips, and came back to consciousness.

'I want you to listen,' Leo was saying. 'Are you awake?' His arm was round her shoulders, her head comfortably propped up. The smell of oil-paint and cigarettes was strong in the room; she even fancied that he waved a cigarette to and fro under her nostrils, making her cough.

'Listen, now. You'll never hear anything so strange or wonderful. Are you listening? Good. Last night I went up to Highgate Cemetery up on the northern heights, above London. You can see the church from some points in the City, a tall pointed spire. We found the grave easily, on the western slope of White Eagle Hill. Just a small party of us, myself and Howell and Henry Tebbs the proctor, Dr Llewellyn Williams, and the grave-diggers. First they lit a fire, for the night was very dark, only a reddish glow from London in the sky.

'When it blazed up the men began to dig. Not very far down. There was one coffin under hers, old Gabriele Rossetti the blind poet, Gabriel's father. The men lifted the coffin, her coffin, on ropes, quite easily. There was a strong smell of earth and it was very cold. The doctor and I shared a flask of brandy. Then the coffin was laid on the ground, near the fire, and the men prised open the lid. We all drew nearer, the proctor reluctantly, I think. There she lay, with dank draperies round her, padding out the corners of the coffin. They were green with furry mould, and the mould was on her robe, too. Gabriel had forbidden them to put her into a shroud. And the coffin, Lilian, the coffin was full of red-gold hair. It grows, you know, after death. Hers had grown until it covered her; her lovely hair, as bright as ever.'

He picked up a handful of Lilian's tresses, ran them through his fingers and kissed them, then with a palette-knife roughly severed one of them, hurting her.

'We could only see her by the firelight glow, but she seemed

128

perfect, still woman-shaped. Then the flames flickered on her face, the face between the wings of lovely hair, and I saw the hollows that used to be her eyes and cheeks, and teeth where her lips had been. You can see them there in the *Beata*, above the sweet sharp chin. (And *that* was still there, still firm, not fallen as I feared.) And next to the bone of her cheek was the little grey-bound book with the red-edged leaves, the book he wanted. They lifted it out very carefully, but a strand of the hair came away with it. They let me keep it, see.'

He held it up, glittering in the firelight, tied with a black ribbon, then kissed it as he had Lilian's hair.

'Mr Tebbs then testified as to the nature of the book, to comply with some law about the removal of papers from a grave, and Dr Williams wrapped the book so that it could be taken away and disinfected.

'I longed to kiss her, Lilian, as I had longed to kiss her dead face so many years before, and I would have done it, even as she was, but they kept me back.' He folded the lock of hair carefully, then laid it on a shelf under the *Beata*, beside a bowl of white flowers.

'So it will have to be you, won't it, Lilian? you that I kiss and embrace in death.' She must have nodded or made some sign, for he sounded satisfied. 'And you shall tell me all the secrets of the dead, of the lilies and the black swans, and whether spirits can desire and feel. I have seen the Blesséd Damozel but she could tell me nothing, so I must learn from you.' Then she felt his lips on hers, but her mouth was too numb to respond. The pressure grew more painful, and his arms were pinning her down. She made a desperate effort to free herself, and fainted.

CHAPTER ELEVEN

When Lilian came to herself she was back in her bed at Cheyne Row. Firelight flickered cheerfully on the ceiling, a stone hot-water bottle wrapped in flannel was at her feet. By the fireside sat Crowfoot, knitting by the light of a lamp turned well down.

'Crowfoot?'

The maid rose and came to the bedside, her sharp face for once concerned and sympathetic.

'Miss Lilian, you're awake. Well, that's a mercy. We thought you was never coming round.'

'Why . . . am I ill? What happened?'

'That we don't know, miss. Millie came running from Mr Bevis's studio yelling and crying, saying you'd been took bad, but we could get no sense out of her about what the matter was. Your aunt sent a carriage round and between us we got you home. Mr Bevis was in a rare taking, I can tell you. He was downstairs till a few minutes ago. It seems Millie went down to Mr Rossetti's kitchen to see some rabbit or other, the stupid girl, and when she came up again you was unconscious.'

Aunt Freddy was in the room now, though Lilian had not heard her enter, her face as troubled as Crowfoot's.

'Lilian, my dear girl. What has happened? We've all been quite frantic.'

'I . . . don't know, Aunt. But I feel very poorly.'

'Leoline said you were lying very comfortably, talking to him as he painted, then suddenly collapsed in a swoon. He could think of nothing that might have caused it. Can you remember anything?'

She could remember nothing, only a vague sense of shock and horror and the onset of a terrible coldness, as though her blood had turned to ice. She was just as cold now, in spite of the warm room and the warm bed.

'Cold, so cold,' she said. Her teeth began to chatter. They

130

renewed the water in the stone bottle, wrapped her in shawls, piled more blankets on her, but still the fearful cold continued, followed by sharp cramps and sickness, and a terrible thirst. She was in the grip of cholera, the disease bred by the foetid Thames. The chill gave way to fever and delirium, in which the same dreams came again and again, like magic-lantern images repeated. She was in a wood, bare-footed and thinly clad, trying to reach a clearing at at the other end, where daylight could just be seen; but the branches writhed and twisted round her, sometimes letting her go only to spring up again in front of her, barring her way. Then she would walk free for a few paces, and stumble into a stream of icy water, clambering out of it soaked and bruised, her flesh already bleeding from the scratches the branches had made; and the daylight was as far off as ever. Those who watched beside her heard her mutter, 'Don't, don't, don't!' when the dream changed to a worse one, a lid coming down over her and hammers driving nails through it, shutting her into dank darkness that went on for ever until a fire flared up to burn out the sides of the box she lay in, and faces looked in at her from above.

At other times scenes would come into her mind which refused to form themselves properly, as though some influence stood between them and her. She was in a garden, or a field; there was someone with her dressed in white, and a warm deep voice speaking, and sometimes she was on her feet again, as she had been as a child, but held and sustained by a strong arm. Always the face of Leoline would come up, just as she was about to remember who was holding her, and then the whole vision was blotted out by a horrible vivid viewing, over and over again, of Lizzie's coffin, just as he had described it to her, but a thousand times worse in the exaggeration of fever.

Frederica's family doctor had seen cholera patients die in large numbers. He knew there was little that could be done beyond the administration of fluids, other than water. So Lilian was constantly fed with the juice of pressed oranges and lemons, barley water, thinned ice-cream and buttermilk, while mustard plasters were applied to her tortured body. A nurse had been called in, hard-faced but clean and efficient. Between her ministrations, and Lilian's youth, the disease dwindled and died, and the patient lived. Then came the luxury of freedom from pain and fever and thirst, the comfort of Cook's beef tea and steaming coffee, and the limpness of utter relaxation. Yet she grew no stronger.

There was no worsening of the spinal condition, the doctor declared – 'though of course that would be impossible to detect, unless we doctors could photograph bones through flesh'. He laughed heartily at this ludicrous thought. Nursing and cheerful company were the best prescriptions now. He would not recommend sedatives, for all contained opium, a drug dangerously suppressive to the body fluids.

Frederica passed all this information to Leoline, who had been a constant caller. 'Now you must be very composed in your manner, Leo. Quiet cheerful company, the doctor said. No planning any more paintings, just calm ordinary chat.'

He smiled. 'You may trust me.' He smiled, too, at Lilian, a tender pitying smile as he took her hand and kissed it, ignoring the slight start of revulsion she gave at his touch. 'You're very ill, poor child. Only I can do you any good.'

'But the doctor said – I am getting better.'

'What does a stupid old man like that know? All he can do is mutter parrot-phrases and collect his fee. No, my dear, I've seen cases like yours before. Don't you remember what I told you about Chatham Place, and the vapours from the river that poisoned Lizzie? Why, he wouldn't even allow you your draught.' He produced a small, unlabelled medicine-bottle from his pocket. Lilian turned her head away.

'That stuff. I don't want it. I don't like it.'

'But you must sleep, darling, so that I can talk to you in your dreams. Now, just a spoonful. Then we'll hide the bottle here, behind the books, where they won't find it, and when it's done I'll bring you some more.' The dose unwillingly taken, he sat beside her bed and chatted lightly, amusingly, about Gabriel's latest pet, a wombat, and the armadillos that had escaped and got into neighbouring houses, with terrifying results to timid servants. His manner was just as usual; she would have responded to it if only she could have forgotten the horrible tale he had told her, and the things he had said about death – pennies on her eyelids, the fee to Charon.

There was something else, too, a nagging half-realised fear. When he got up to leave he bent over her, a hand on either side

132

of her body, not kissing her quite, but with his lips very close to hers.

'Beatrice on her bier,' he said. 'Mine.'

She lay and shivered, after he had gone. What had happened at the studio? When she fainted, had he possessed her body, enjoying the unconsciousness that mimicked death? She thought she remembered something – a physical discomfort she had never experienced before : but its memory was blotted out by illness. She felt a violent revulsion from him now, and a great fear, yet his power over her was no less. The chloral began to filter into her veins, and every day he administered another dose which she longed to refuse, but her voice would not obey her when she tried to call someone.

He sat by her bedside, avidly watching her.

'Will you promise to play it with me, Lilian?'

'Play . . . what?'

'The Game of Love and Death. The game that ends when I feel you growing cold beneath me, your parted lips chilling, your arms falling from their clasp round my neck. And the colder you grow the more I shall love you.'

'But I shall be dead.'

'Yes. You know you must die, don't you, Lilian. Die, to be mine.'

'I know.'

'I kiss your lock of hair every night. Your soul is in it, and your body. I shall always keep it, even when you are like Lizzie, and it will bring you back to me.' The voice went on, saying things that horrified her to hear, but she was too strongly dominated by him to stop her ears or call for help. Even when she had gone his influence ruled her. It should have been so easy to speak to Aunt Freddy – to anyone; but who would believe her? Least of all her mother, who had rushed up to London to be with her. Arguments went on between Florence and Frederica.

'But I *must* take her home. She would never have been in this state if you had not insisted on bringing her here. I told you she was too frail for such a change.'

'Florence, you know perfectly well the doctor has said she must not be moved on any account. Besides, can you give her the nursing care I can? Be reasonable. She has everything here an invalid can possibly need.'

Then Florence would begin to cry. 'I'm going to lose her, I know it. All very well for him to say she's not consumptive – I know better. Don't we see her getting weaker every day? My poor child, my baby...'

Nelly and Arthur came, reluctantly because both hated illness, and sat by her bedside making hearty, encouraging remarks. Arthur gave her an extremely dull account of a game of Rugby football in which he had distinguished himself, and Nelly revealed that the eldest son of a rich manufacturer from Keighley had joined the local Hunt, and was showing signs of interest in her. Otherwise, they could think of little to say to the thin, white-faced sister who no longer made sharp remarks and sarcastic jokes. After another stormy scene Florence left with the children.

Gus's visits were the most painful. He came hampered by the burden of his railway fare, but ever-hopeful, ever-anxious, always exhorting her to pray with him, which she could not do, lying with her gaze on the window while he knelt by her bedside.

'Let me bring you the Sacrament. Aunt tells me you have not been taking it.'

'No, Gus. It would do no good.'

'Why, Lilian? Is it as I suspect; are you in the power of something infernal?'

'How should I know? At any rate, I don't feel ready to take it. Leave me alone, do.' Then, in pity for his pleading face, 'Gus, I know you love me dearly. I always knew it, but I used to tease you dreadfully. I'm sorry, now. Just go away and forget about me, and marry some nice girl who will make a good wife to you – I never should have done.'

'Are you in a state of Grace, Lilian? Oh dear, my vicar would think that a very Roman question. But I know what I mean to express by it.'

'So do I, dear Gus, and the answer is no.'

Of the Pre-Raphaelite band only Janey Morris came to visit Lilian. Statuesquely beautiful, her presence in the bedside chair seemed to fill the room, as she absent-mindedly ate the invalid's grapes with a languid grace which made the commonplace action a work of art.

'I wish we could take you to Kelmscott,' she said. 'Did Gabriel tell you about it?'

'No. I hardly know him – Mr Rossetti. I have only been to his house twice.'

'Of course. That was when you got this tiresome fever, and I must say I'm not surprised. So damp, right on the river. Damp is really quite an enemy of our family; Topsy thinks me soft for going on about it, but he has dreadful gout himself sometimes, and our little girls are so much better away from London. Now Kelmscott is quite dry, though it stands among the water-meadows : at least I *think* it's dry, the Elizabethans built very soundly, Topsy says. He is madly in love with it. Of course he belongs to the Middle Ages, not to today at all. *I* think he's an Old Soul, as the Spiritualists call it, one of the monks who used to spend their time illuminating Books of Hours. Gabriel doesn't care for Kelmscott so much.' She stared, beautifully, into the distance. 'He's a born Cockney, of course, not a country person like Topsy. We *were* all to have lived at Kelmscott all the time, weaving tapestries and painting; but I don't think it will do, somehow ... Gabriel sleeps very late into the morning but Topsy gets up at dawn, and goes round opening all the windows Gabriel prefers to keep shut; and he thinks Gabriel's brother William a bloody fool and doesn't care for his friends in general. Oh, dear.'

'Are *you* happy at Kelmscott, Janey?'

Janey turned the wonderful eyes on her. 'I? Well, happier than in London. I am really a martyr to illness at our house in Queen Square, but Gabriel and I walk for miles in the country. Yes, I believe I *am* happier at Kelmscott – when Gabriel's there.'

Oh dear, indeed, thought Lilian. What a tangle these poor people are in, for all their cleverness; and how will it all end?

Janey returned to Kelmscott, and no more of Frederica's friends called. Only Leoline came every day. Frederica left them alone together now, for what danger could even the most attractive young man be to such a sick girl? It was generally accepted that he was her suitor, utterly devoted, ready to marry her on her deathbed, if need be. Lilian knew only too well that it was true. He kept her supplied with chloral so that she accepted dully the melancholy it induced, and the terrible weakness of body, and Leoline's presence, the spiritual vampire draining her life. She was too feeble now to be taken out, her blood too thin to face the still wintry weather,

135

too apathetic to notice the coming of Spring, the tapping of young green leaves against her window, the shrilling of fledgling birds.

It was late April when Digby came home from attending a three-months course at the School of Musketry, held at Shorncliffe Camp on the south coast of Kent. He had made one or two excursions to London without visiting his mother. An encounter with Leoline, just before the beginning of the training course, had caused a violent quarrel. Of all Frederica's friends he disliked Leoline the most.

'Why d'you let that stuffed dummy hang about Lilian's bedroom?' he enquired angrily after Leoline had left the house in dudgeon. 'If she hadn't gone to his rotten studio in the first place she wouldn't be the way she is now.'

'You have no right to say that. Nobody was ever more devoted than he is to her. And I don't like my friends insulted in my own house.'

'Friends! Funny friends you have, I must say, Mamma. I've some information for you. I was talking to one of 'em at some party of yours, baldish chap with a face like a bloodhound, called Smith or Jones or something . . .'

'Ned Burne-Jones, I suppose. Go on,' said Frederica icily.

'Well, this Jones said that Bevis had been hanging round them all for the best part of fifteen years. So I'd very much like to know how he manages to look just down from Eton, with a complexion like a baby's bottom and a beard I'll bet wouldn't grow any longer if he was marooned on a desert island.'

'Leoline has a very youthful appearance, certainly. I've never troubled to enquire his age. What on earth has it to do with anything, least of all Lilian?'

'Because the feller's not natural, that's what, and I don't want him playing about with my cousin. You know what they say about touching pitch. All right, I can't stop him, it's your house. But until I know the place is clear of him, you can say goodbye to me, Mamma.'

Frederica's rare, cold notes to Digby had mentioned that Lilian was no better, but nothing prepared him for the shock of seeing her when at last he came home.

'Good God,' he said. 'Good God, Good God. What in hell have they done to you?'

136

She gave him a wan smile, her eyes scarcely focussed on him. 'Don't swear so, Digby. I'm very weak, that's all.'

'So I see. What do the doctors say? Are they bleeding you, or some old-fashioned rubbish of that sort?'

'No. It's just that I . . . I can't eat. And I sleep very poorly, with dreadful dreams. I can't talk much, I'm afraid. Don't go, just sit with me. It's nice to see a different face.'

When he at last went downstairs he sought out his mother.

'That feller still calling?'

'If you mean Mr Bevis, yes. He visits Lilian every day. Poor child, she has nobody else to cheer her up. I suppose you grudge her that?'

'I don't grudge her anything,' Digby said in a tone his fellow-officers would have recognised as dangerous. 'I merely tell you this, Mamma; next time I meet him in this house I shall kick him downstairs. And if Lilian wants cheering up, I'll do it. When did she go out last?'

'Out? In her condition? You must be mad.' Mother and son confronted each other with steely eyes.

'Oh no, I'm not mad,' Digby said softly. 'Nor is she. If anyone's mad in this quarter of town it's you, Mamma. You do happen to have noticed that it's like summer outside, while that girl lies in a room like a bloody field-hospital? I'm just pointing it out to you, that's all.'

Frederica rose and left the room, her robe sweeping behind her like a queen's train. She wished her only son at least a thousand miles away, and his soldier-servant, Jim Stokes, with him; preferably on an island with no means of return. But obnoxious as Digby was, there was nothing he could do other than create an unpleasant atmosphere. She sent a note round to Leoline hinting that it might be better if he did not call again until after her son had left. There, as far as she was concerned, the distasteful incident ended. She was losing interest, just a little, in the Bohemian circle, and Leoline had lost some of his charm for her since it became obvious that her niece, not herself, was the object of his interest. But he was quite harmless : it was ridiculous of Digby to make such a fuss.

Digby, however, had studied tactics among other military matters. He knew that his mother took luncheon and tea with an

137

elderly friend in Kensington on Saturdays. A few casual enquiries from Stokes in the kitchen confirmed that she would do as usual on the coming Saturday. Stokes's black whiskers and broad chest-measurements captivated the female domestics so much that if he had enquired where their mistress kept her jewels they would probably have told him and led him to the key. At a quarter to twelve on Saturday, both men watched the brougham departing, with Frederica in it.

'Right,' said Digby. 'Fetch a cab and stand by.'

Stokes saluted. 'Sah.'

Lilian lay staring blankly at the sunny window as her cousin entered her room, Millie behind him.

'Well, my dear,' he said cheerfully, rubbing his hands, 'it's a lovely day. Come on, we're going to get you ready to go out.'

'Out? But . . . Digby, I never go out. I can't, I'm too weak. Surely Aunt has told you. Please don't be silly. You're joking, aren't you?'

'Never more serious in my life, cousin. All right, Millie, you know what to do. I'll give you fifteen minutes – by the clock, mind you, not ladies' time.'

At first Lilian protested weakly, but Millie had been well instructed and well paid. She washed her mistress, dressed her fully as she lay on top of the counterpane, brushed and put up her hair. Then she opened the door and called, 'Ready, sir.'

'That's my girl.' Digby surveyed her with pride. 'Get her bonnet and jacket, Millie.' They were fetched and put on her. The effect of the chloral was wearing off, as Leoline had not supplied her with any during the week of his absence, but she was still sufficiently confused by it to do what she was ordered to do without struggling. Digby swept her up in his arms and carried her downstairs as though she had weighed no more than an infant. Outside a hired cab was waiting. With Stokes's assistance, while Millie kept watch in the hall for the possible appearance of other servants, Digby lifted her in and settled himself massively beside her. To the driver, who had viewed the proceedings with interest, he barked, 'Lord's Cricket Ground.'

Lilian gasped. 'Cricket?'

'What else, on a fine day? Besides, you follow it, don't you? I'm sure you told me so once. Myself, I'm a shootin' and boxin' man, but we've played quite a lot down at Hythe. Though it's a bit early in the season. Now you sit back and enjoy yourself. You'd like to see Yorkshire play M.C.C. and Ground Staff, I know. We'll get there just in time for the luncheon interval.'

From the cab Digby carried her into a dream. A dream in which once again the sun shone warmly on her, and as if the trees that made Lord's appear like a rural ground were studded with emeralds. The grass in the field behind the spectators' stands was young green, too, untrodden yet by many feet, and people in bright clothes wandered about like angels in a Rossetti painting. Miraculously, Digby had provided a bath-chair for her; she sank into it gratefully, tired from the cab-journey, watching Stokes lay a large white tablecloth on the grass and unpack a hamper of crockery, food and bottles. Where had the hamper come from? Possibly from the boot of the cab. Lilian decided not to bother her dazed mind with any more questions. One doesn't ask questions.

A cab stopped at a nearby entrance gate. From it emerged a sensationally pretty girl with golden ringlets and a great deal of lilac ribbon decking her fashionable shepherdess dress. She and Digby ran towards each other, and she was lost in his huge embrace.

'Penny, my darling. Come and meet my cousin Lilian. Lil, this is Penelope Crozier. We, er, met in Hythe.'

'At a ball,' Penelope explained. They were both faintly pink and an almost visible glow of rapture surrounded them. 'So you got away!' Penelope exclaimed, giving Lilian an impulsive kiss. 'I *knew* Digby would do it. How do you feel now, you poor dear?'

Before Lilian could answer, Digby interrupted. 'She'll feel a lot better for a glass of bubbly, if you'll do the honours, Stokes.' In Stokes's hands a green bottle and its cork parted with a tremendous pop; a bubbling fountain of golden wine filled four glasses.

'Champagne!' Lilian breathed. 'It is, isn't it, Digby?'

'What else, for such an occasion?'

'I only had it once at the Hall. It's lovely.' Several times in the last half-hour she had thought she would faint, but now all fear of that had left her. Digby, looking at her, felt a glowing pride in his achievement. It would have been too bad if she had died on his hands or even gone into a coma; but he had betted on her native spirit pulling her through the small ordeal he had arranged for her, and the bet had come off.

It was a picnic none of them would ever forget, even the impassive Stokes. Digby and Penelope lounged on the grass while Stokes waited on Lilian in her chair; there was even a little collapsible table for her to put down her glass and plate. And she, who had only pecked at food for months, found herself eating tiny sandwiches of delicate pink ham, others of wafer-thin cucumber, neat bread rolls with a finger of new asparagus in each one, mousse of salmon from a cut-glass dish, all washed down with the champagne which rivalled the blossom-scented air of St John's Wood in exhilaration. Penelope, who ate a great deal in the daintiest possible way, yet never seemed to stop talking, told her how she and Digby had met because he had stepped on the hem of her dress and torn it while passing her on the dance-floor with another partner, and how he had asked her for the supper-dance, and there was salmon mousse *then* which would always seem to her a particularly romantic food, and of course they couldn't get married yet because she was only nineteen, but when they did Lilian must certainly be a bridesmaid. And Lilian told Penelope how she herself was a soldier's daughter, and how Papa had been a little, just a little, like Digby.

'Then he must have been *very* handsome, quite a love!' declared Penelope, clasping her pretty buttery hands, for she had been so unladylike as to remove her gloves. A bell clanged three times, from inside the ground. People began to stream into the stands, men and boys and women, all in holiday dress, chattering excitedly.

'Come on, you girls, play's going to begin,' Digby said. The remains of the picnic were consigned to the hamper by Stokes, who then took charge of Lilian's chair. Led by Digby, they moved off to Henderson's Nursery End, where, in a gap between two stands, the chair was positioned next to a bench on which Penelope and Digby seated themselves, Stokes remaining as on sentry duty behind the chair. Digby explained that M.C.C. had played their first innings that morning, and Yorkshire would be batting throughout the afternoon.

The dark-clad, bowler-hatted umpires had taken up their stance as the fielding side came out of the pavilion, eleven men in neat white flannels. Only then did a memory of another game come back to Lilian: a rough field and a motley assortment of players. The miasmas swirling round her in the past months had wiped out any recollection of why she had been sent to London in the first place. But surely there had been something, a country match, a momentous day . . .

Then she saw him, the taller of the two men coming out to bat at a dignified stroll. Dark curls touched his shirt-collar as they had that first time, neat side-burns fringing his brown cheeks gave him a maturer look. She knew that the eyes narrowed against the sun were the bluest of blue, and that the hands swinging the bat in a practice-stroke were as beautiful as they were strong. For a second a black mist hid him from her sight as shock hit her like a towering wave. She gripped the arms of her chair until her knuckles stood out white, willing herself not to faint.

Digby, without looking directly at her, saw the sudden ashen paleness of her face followed by a tide of crimson.

'The fair boy's rather sweet,' Penelope reflected, studying her scorecard. 'Very fine moustaches. But the dark one's nice, too. J. Ellershaw.'

Lilian turned to Digby, who met her gaze squarely. 'You know,' she said.

'Yes.'

'How?' They were talking very quietly, unheard by Stokes or Penelope.

'Slipped down to Uncle Lewis's for a weekend party. Heard the whole story, with variations. Thought there might be something in it. For you, that is. (Oh, beautiful stroke, sir. Might make a two. Yes, it has.) Knowing a few fellers in the cricketing world, made enquiries and found out where he was. Lil – did I do right?'

'Yes, oh yes!' A tremulous smile lit her face for him, though she could hardly look away from the graceful figure who had once again sent the ball flying with an elegant square-cut.

Digby heaved a deep sigh of relief. 'Want me to do anything about it – him, that is?'

Lilian did not answer at once. The sight of Jack had brought back in a rush of feeling the brief time they had had together and all that it had meant to her. How could she have forgotten? Yet the memory had been with her all the time, hidden and buried deep, not only because of Leoline but because she had not wanted to dwell on the thought that Jack had abandoned her. She felt hot with shame at the recollection of the physical feelings Leoline had aroused in her, before revulsion set in. It was Jack who had awakened them; Jack whose touch and glance had lit the fire of life in her body, whose beauty and strength had taken her heart. Now she blamed herself, not him, for the gulf that had opened between them. He had never said a word of love to her: why should he, when everything seemed against them?

And now that she saw him again she longed for him more than ever. But – that he should see her in such a state of wan emaciation, the shadow of the girl he had held in his arms at their last meeting in the Dower House garden! Would he even recognise her, much less find her attractive?

Digby was watching her. 'Shall I ask him to come over?'

'Could you . . . send him a note, perhaps?' she half-whispered. 'Just to say I'm here, and should like to . . . to wish him well?'

Digby nodded. 'I'll send it with Stokes. Don't know when he'll be free, mind. The way he's playing he might be there all day. Oh, well stopped, sir,' as the fielder nearest them returned a ball with lightning agility, almost shattering Jack's wicket before he had reached the crease. 'I daren't keep you out too long or Mamma will raise the devil.'

Lilian was immediately miserable. Not to speak to him now would kill her, she thought. It was dreadful to hope he would be out soon, but that was what she must hope.

'What are you two whispering about?' Penny asked.

'Nothing for little girls,' said Digby. 'You watch the cricket and don't distract that man on the boundary. He hasn't come here to flirt.

'It's a nasty rough pitch, no mistake. No telling what the ball's going to do. I hear Yorkshire went at M.C.C. like a regiment of artillery this morning, bowled them all over the place. Even the mighty Grace got a royal battering, though you wouldn't think anything could damage *him*.' He indicated an enormous young man with a black beard like an accumulation of birds' nests, crouching at point with huge hands covetously outspread for a possible catch, a fearsome glower on his features.

'Who on earth is that?' Lilian asked. 'He looks more like a pirate than a cricketer.'

'As a matter of fact, he's a medical student, though I don't know why he bothers when he can play cricket like a man inspired. The

Gloucestershire Terror, they call him up here. Got more boundaries under his belt than ten ordinary fellows. Know what they say about him in Gloucestershire? "He dab 'em but seldom, but when he dab 'em he do dab 'em for four." Pity you aren't seeing him bat.'

'Yes,' said Lilian, who had hardly heard a word he said, and was too intent on watching Jack, trying to photograph him on her mind, to care about anything else.

'Emmett got him out for a measly ten this morning, though. Iddison caught him – he *will* hook 'em, you know. In fact, Yorkshire got them all out for 66.'

'Is that a lot?' Penny asked.

'No, it isn't, my love. Especially not on their home ground. I say, our friend's batting very stylishly, even if he isn't making many runs.'

'What *should* he be doing?' Penny enquired.

'Well, playing just about the way he is. An opener shouldn't throw away his wicket just to cut a dash. Probably treating the bowler a bit cautiously, too, with a rotten pitch like this. Shaw's fairly hurling 'em down . . . oh, I say!' Both the girls exclaimed as a ball smacked down in front of Jack and bounced up at him, hitting him violently on the shoulder. He recoiled, rubbed his shoulder, smiling ruefully, then picked up his bat as though nothing had happened.

'Oh, dear!' Penny squeaked. 'Do you suppose he's really hurt, Digby, and trying not to show it? How brave!'

'Seems all right. Might find he's cracked a bone afterwards. Hope not, though.'

'Do they ever get killed?'

'It's been known, when a chap's been hit on the head.' Lilian had gone very pale. Digby applied a gentle pinch to Penny's arm, and, when she turned a wondering face to him, shook his head slightly and touched a finger to his lips. He saw that she understood she was to say no more. They watched as Jack faced up to the next ball, another fearful delivery. This time he ducked sooner, expecting it, so that it soared over his head and raced away towards the Grand Stand, chased by a fielder. Jack and his opposite partner, John Thewlis, ran two.

'He'll have to watch his man,' Digby said. 'Any minute now he's going to . . . blast and damn it, sorry ladies. Shouldn't have played

143

that one. Just the way Grace went.' The ball had flown into a pair of eager hands, whose owner measured his length in a successful attempt to hang on to it.

'Oh, poor man,' Penelope cried. 'Is he hurt?'

'Not he.' And indeed the man was back on his feet, a broad grin on his face, watching Ellershaw's leisured stroll back to the Pavilion for a mere sixteen runs. A wave of relief swept over Lilian.

The next wickets fell cheaply; Joe Rowbotham, clean bowled by Grace, E. B. Rawlinson gone to a brilliant diving catch, the great George Freeman, 'prince of bowlers', a victim of Wootton for only one run. Still Thewlis stayed there, a patient Casabianca, collecting discreet runs here and there, to be joined at Number Six by Roger Iddison, Yorkshire's captain, to whom Penny took an immediate strong fancy.

'Oh, Digby, isn't he *sweet*. Such a nice stern expression and lovely whiskers. Can't you invite him round to have tea with us?'

'No, I can't, you goose. Wouldn't be etiquette at all.'

'Won't he *get* any tea?'

'Of course he will, with the others, in twenty minutes or so. And I hope it chokes him, if you go on making eyes at the fellow like that. We'll have our tea under the trees – Stokes has another hamper in the carriage.'

'Oh, hooray, I'm starving.'

Under Lilian's nervous, intent gaze, Digby tore a page from his notebook, scribbled on it, folded it and gave it to Stokes, with a murmured direction. Stokes disappeared in the direction of the Pavilion, returning some minutes later. Digby was satisfied with the message he brought.

When teatime came Thewlis and Iddison were still there, urged by the more vocal in the crowd to get on with it or else get out. Back in the pleasant spot where they had taken luncheon, Stokes unpacked an elegant tea, fit for a lady's At Home. Lilian could eat almost nothing. There seemed to be a knot constricting her throat, and her cup trembled in her hand when she tried to drink. Digby watched her apprehensively, hoping she was not on the verge of collapse. When everyone else had had enough tea and the umpires were coming out on the field he tucked Penny's arm firmly through his own.

144

'Come on. We're going back to our seat. Lilian's staying here.'

'Oh, why can't she come with us?'

'You'll see, all in good time, Miss Inquisitive. Come on now, and feast your eyes once again on Iddison's whiskers.' As he led her away she glanced back anxiously at the lonely figure of Lilian, reclining in her chair in the shade of a pink may-tree.

And there Jack found her.

CHAPTER TWELVE

He was too used to controlling his expression to let her see the shock that went through him at the sight of her. He had never expected to see her again; and now, like this. If there were such a thing as a pretty skeleton, he reflected, that was how she looked, all bones, hollowed eyes, and hair, that glorious hair weighing down her head with its coppery wealth. For an infinity they looked at each other, yet in the field beyond the Nursery Stand only one ball had been bowled.

'Well,' he said. 'Well, I never. Where did *you* spring from?'

'From a sick-bed. Except that I would hardly call it springing.'

'Aye, it were a daft question. A chap as called himself your cousin sent me a note that you'd been ill.'

'He is my cousin, and I have been very ill. They say I'm dying.'

Without answering, he looked placidly round their corner of the field, noticed a substantial log which was propping up a roller, and carried it effortlessly to her side, disposing himself gracefully upon it.

'Been standing up long enough out there.'

'Yes, we were watching. You played beautifully.'

'Beautifully? I made a right . . .' He abandoned what he had been going to say. 'I should never ha' got out to a ball like yon.'

'No, indeed,' she agreed gravely.

'You've remembered all the cricket stuff you learned up, then?' There was a suspicion of a grin on Jack's lips. Lilian flushed.

'No. But it will come back, I know. If . . .'

'If you live long enough, is that it? Aye? I thought so. Well, let's have it, what's the trouble? What are you dying of?'

The matter-of-fact approach startled Lilian. 'I don't know.'

'That's a queer sort of do. Haven't they told you?'

'Only that it was some kind of disease which gets worse and

worse, until the patient has no more strength left. I'm so weak, you see. This is the first time I've been out for months.'

'Then you will be weak, won't you? Is it your back that's bad?'

'No . . . at least I don't think so.'

Jack picked up her hand and held it, not so much in a lover-like manner as that of a butcher testing a piece of meat. The muscles were soft, the fore-arm wasted, but Jack had seen many men who were dying, mates of his father's, and their touch had not seemed like Lilian's, nor had her face the deadly whiteness of theirs, and the look of death.

'Have you got a cough?'

'No. Why are you asking me all those questions?'

'Because I reckon there's summat wrong about all this. I reckon someone's not been straight wi' you, and you're not being straight wi' me. Hadn't you better tell me about it?'

Lilian hesitated. 'I . . . I only wanted to see you to say goodbye. I don't think I should tell you things that might – concern other people. Besides, there's hardly time. The others will be back soon.' She glanced towards the spectators' stand.

'Not if they've any sense. Game's in a very interesting state. We're only thirteen short of their first innings total. Come on, now, I reckon me and you know each other pretty well, whatever some folks might think.'

She had grown used to obeying, and she began to talk.

Penelope paused in eating an ice-cream. 'But,' she said, 'how can a batsman be out leg-before-wicket, as you call it? I mean, *both* his legs are before the wicket, if he's standing there.'

Digby sighed. 'I thought you'd played cricket with your sisters, darling, and knew all about it.'

'Oh, we did play but I'm sure I never heard of a rule like that. Oh. Perhaps it was because of our skirts. I mean, nobody could tell which was leg and which was skirt, could they – so that must be it.' She returned to her ice-cream. Digby eyed her with fond indulgence. He disliked intelligent women, having met all too many in his mother's drawing-room. He felt that he was going to be very happy with Penny. He only hoped, however, that she would not ask him to explain the niceties of fielding positions, for

147

he felt that the stern bewhiskered old gentleman sitting next to her might find it just the least bit irritating.

The halting story was finished. Lilian had begun to shake during the telling of it; Jack took her hand and gripped it tight.

'Now, now, steady on. Nowt to get upset about.'

But he was himself upset. He knew nothing of artists and poets and their ways, but he did know that he had just heard an account of a deliberately planned murder, told by the victim. He had read enough newspapers and heard enough low talk to know that the human race was capable of some very nasty divergencies from the normal. The man she called Leo was quite evidently one of them. He blamed Lilian's aunt and her doctor and everyone else involved for not seeing it with their own eyes and doing something about it; but the only villain in the case was Leo Bevis, and if Jack could at that moment have got his hands round Leo's white neck he would unquestionably have wrung it like a chicken's. For besides the attempted slow killing of Lilian by suggestion, it was clear to him that there had been a rape as well, though she was unaware of it, he felt sure. He would never tell her that he knew.

'This medicine he gave you to take,' he said, 'what was it like?'

'Oh . . . rather oily. No colour. It was to make me sleep. Only the dreams were so bad it would have been almost better to be awake. And I think it may have been that that made me feel sick so often – because I haven't had any for a week, and I ate some luncheon today, and enjoyed it too. It was beautiful, little sandwiches,' she added wistfully.

The language going through Jack's mind would have shocked stronger ears than Lilian's. He quelled it. 'So if it hadn't been for this cousin turning up, and this . . . this devil staying away, you'd not be here now? I see. Well, I'm glad and thankful he did, and I'll tell him so when he gets back.'

She caught at his hand. 'You won't go away? Oh, Jack, don't leave me. I think I must have been very foolish and very . . . weak, and I shouldn't have told you. But please don't leave me.' For the first time since her illness she began to cry like a woman in distress, no longer the easy trickling tears of illness. Jack let her cry until the worst of her stress was spent, then dried her cheeks with a large, immaculately clean handkerchief.

148

'Blow thi nose. That's better.' Very tenderly and reassuringly he kissed her mouth. 'I won't leave thee. Where's this cousin, then?'

She pointed. 'Over there.'

'Right, come on. I ought to be back in Pavilion, but I'd like a word with him first.'

Digby and Jack liked each other from the first handshake. Digby had already summed the cricketer up on the evidence of his eyes and what he had learned at Scarbrick, and Jack, sublimely indifferent to social distinctions, was impressed by Digby's soldierly bearing and frank, amiable face. Penelope was all eyes and dimples at her introduction to the handsome young man and the revelation of his romantic connection with Lilian, which was very obvious from her bright, changed face and the adoring looks she gave him.

'I've go a lot to thank you for,' Jack said. His only concession to obvious gentry was to moderate his dialect slightly. 'Seems to me you got Lilian out of as mucky a hole as she's ever likely to be in.'

'I'm glad it came off – it might not have done. Bit of a gamble, I suppose. She looks better already for a bit of cheery conversation.' And a bit of love-making too, Digby guessed. Penelope, drawing her own conclusions, squeaked with excitement.

'Oh, are we to congratulate you? How deliciously exciting! Digby, you sly person, you never said. Oh, I do think it the most romantic thing *ever*.'

Deeply embarrassed for Jack, Lilian and himself, Digby said, 'Penny, Penny, be quiet, if you please. Just keep Lilian company for a minute while I have a word with Mr Ellershaw.' The fierce-whiskered old gentleman got up and left, disgusted at the prospect of having not merely one but two females chattering next to him.

A few yards away, out of earshot, Jack said, 'She's got to get away from that place, Captain. I know it's your ma's house but it makes no difference.'

'Lilian's told you something – and it's bad?'

'Bad as can be. If she stays there I'll not answer for it. There's a plot going on. It'll be the death of her if she's not moved. Her aunt can't or won't stop it, nor the doctor, neither.'

'Something to do with Bevis?'

149

'Aye. He's poisonin' her, and there's a bit of fairground trickery in it as well, cat-and-mouse stuff, I reckon.'

'I thought so. Damn the fellow. I've been as firm as I can, but I suppose he'll worm his way back somehow. Do you suppose, if I talked to Mamma, she'd see sense?'

'She'd not believe you,' Jack said flatly. 'Women never do. The chap's a pet of hers. She wouldn't understand it, for a start – *I* don't, not wholly. You can't look after Lilian yourself, can you?'

'Gord lord, no. Now I've finished my course at Shorncliffe, it's back to Windsor for me – and there'd be a scandal, anyway. She could go home to her mother, I suppose, but I know Aunt Florence, she's a tartar. You'd never see Lilian again.'

'Right. Then I'll take her. If you'll help me. I'll need some help.'

Digby was shocked. 'You mean you're going to elope with her?'

Jack grinned. 'Not quite like that. I'm going to take her to my mam's and we'll see how she gets on there. It'll be all above-board, never you worry.'

Digby shook his hand. Then they talked of ways and means. Jack would be in London until Monday evening, when he would return to Yorkshire after the close of play. He was staying at a lodging-house near King's Cross, the best he could afford, though a long way down in comfort and cleanliness from Yorkshire standards. He would be there the whole of Sunday, not budging out until he got a message from Digby, to whom it was left to plan the escape operation. An alarming thought struck Digby.

'Suppose Lilian jibs – won't go with you?'

'She'll go if I say so,' returned Jack calmly.

A furious Frederica awaited the return of the cousins to Cheyne Row. On her face was the look Digby associated with 'wiggings' in his childhood, and a major wigging was impending now. She was not alone; on the sofa, smoking a cigarette, sat Leoline. Digby entered alone.

'So you've condescended to come back.' His mother's voice was ice itself. 'And what have you to say for yourself? I really look forward to hearing your explanation.'

Digby seated himself comfortably and lit a cigar. Smoking was not normally permitted in the drawing-room, but if that fellow had lit up, so would he.

'Explanation? None needed, Mamma. It being an exceptionally fine day, I took Lilian for an outing.' They had agreed to say nothing about the cricket match; it might lead Frederica into connecting one thing with another.

'An outing? Where?'

Digby blew a smoke-ring. 'Oh, just into the country. Hertfordshire way, very pretty out there, gardens and things. Brought you some asparagus back.' True, he had, bought from a shop in St John's Wood High Street. Leoline was saying nothing, his eyes going from mother to son and back again, as if waiting for the first lie or the first statement that would advantage him. Frederica was getting more and more angry. Digby had always been able to do this to her, remaining maddeningly cool even when threatened with a beating. She launched into a tirade. How had he dared to drag a sick, probably dying, young woman from her bed of pain, on some crack-brained excursion that might have killed her then and there?

'Well, it didn't, and she don't look any worse for it – better, I'd say. A bit tired, that's all. So am I, come to that.' He yawned realistically.

'We shall see when the doctor comes. And another thing: do you realise, you stupid boy, that you may have compromised Lilian's reputation by taking her out unchaperoned? You might at least have taken a maid, yet both Crowfoot and Millie say they know nothing about the business. I suspect Millie knows more than she says, however. I shall make her tell me, never fear. Lilian's cousin you may be, but not a close one, and in any case it was highly improper . . .'

Digby yawned again. 'Nothing improper about it. A young lady friend went along for company.' His mother stiffened in outrage.

'*What* young lady friend? You mean some ballet-girl? I suppose that's the sort of female you associate with.'

'Only now and then, Mamma, and I don't see that they're any worse than your artist-model friends. No, it was Penny Crozier. You might have heard of her father – Brigadier-General Sir Rufus Crozier. She's staying with Lady Ponsonby – Henry Ponsonby's wife, you know. He was one of the Prince Consort's equerries.'

Frederica was dumbfounded. She knew nothing of her son's private life. But he seemed to have trumped all her aces in this scene. It was Leoline, speaking up for the first time, who rescued her.

'I think my permission might have been asked before Miss de Wentworth was taken on this very rash expedition.'

Digby surveyed him very slowly from shining head to neat boots, then let his eyes travel upwards again until they rested somewhere about the other's cravat. Then he said, in tones implying that a beetle had spoken, 'You? Who are you?'

'You know perfectly well who I am, sir.'

'Not in relation to my cousin.'

'Very well. Lilian is my fiancée. We are engaged to be married.'

'Curious. I didn't notice any ring.'

'Unofficially. In view of her health. Isn't that so, Frederica?'

'Yes, of course,' Frederica answered hurriedly, afraid of witnessing a mortal struggle on her bearskin hearthrug. 'I must see how she is.'

When she had gone neither man spoke. Digby lay back contemplating the ceiling as though its painted scenes were of enthralling interest to him, puffing occasionally at his cigar. Leoline was troubled. He did not believe for a moment in the story of Miss Crozier and her chaperonage. It was all a tale to distract Frederica from her son's designs on Lilian – for such, Leoline was convinced, was the case. Why had the brute threatened him so fiercely a week ago? Why had he come back to live at his mother's house at the first opportunity? Somehow Lilian must have been persuaded to go on that idiotic outing; had she taken a fancy to the fellow? It was all very disturbing.

Frederica returned. 'Lilian is quite exhausted and very flushed. I thought her too ill to be questioned. You see what you've done, Digby.' Digby said nothing. Lilian had been excited coming back in the cab, and if she was flushed it was with the rediscovery of Jack. Besides, they'd shared a half-bottle of the champagne which had not been drunk at lunchtime . . .

'And what's more,' his mother continued, 'she had been *drinking*. You know the doctor permits no wine. I am very bitterly disappointed in you, Digby.'

'I'll go and have a word with her,' Leoline volunteered eagerly. 'She always responds well to me.'

'No, thank you, Leo. Nobody is to go near her except Crowfoot, and her door will be kept locked.'

Oh blazes, that's done it, thought Digby.

A long, long, Sunday wound its course from the moment Stokes brought his shaving-water to the last glimpse of the May moon in the waters of the Thames, as he walked the Chelsea streets wondering what to do. As though she knew he was up to something, Frederica kept a dragon's watch on Lilian's door, either she or Crowfoot unlocking it whenever necessary. Digby raged quietly, aware of the prisoner within hoping for news of release. He thought of going to church, of calling on Penelope, of taking a boat to Richmond, anything but lounge about his mother's house. In the end he did nothing, only studied Crowfoot's movements. She was regular in her habits. First her mistress's costuming and hairdressing, then church – the eleven o'clock, as she was above such matters as the preparation of luncheon and had no need to rise for Early Service. Then luncheon itself, taken in state downstairs with the other staff, herself, the favoured lady's maid, getting the best bits of meat. After that came Lilian's own luncheon, taken in on a tray, followed by the disappearance of Crowfoot, presumably upstairs for a nap. Looking furtively about him like a wanted criminal, Digby made his way down the uncarpeted steps to the basement. If anyone caught him he had a story ready about a new supply of matches being wanted upstairs.

His luck was in. Only Millie was in the room grander houses would have called the servants' hall, crouched dismally by the fire darning stockings. She looked up sharply as he appeared, fear in her face.

'It's all right, Millie. Where is everybody?'

'It's their afternoon off. All but me. Missis says I'm to stop in, 'cause of . . .' She sniffed.

'What, Millie?'

'*You* know, Captain. Yesterday. Getting Miss Lilian dressed, an' then sayin' I knew nowt about it. Missis says she's thinkin' of turnin' me off.' She drew a stocking across her eyes. 'What am I goin' to do then? I've got nowt but a few shillin', an' I hate

153

London. I hate it, hate it. I'll chuck misen in t'river, that's what I'll do.'

'Oh, come, don't be silly.' He patted her heaving shoulder. 'I'll see you're all right – get you back home, if that's what you want. There's just two more things I have to ask you to do. Don't look so frightened, it's nothing wicked. The first is to get this note on to one of Miss Lilian's meal-trays, hidden, somehow. And the second is to get me the key of her door, tomorrow, after tea. Get it so that Crowfoot won't miss it for an hour or two. Can you do that?'

She was wide-eyed with fear. 'How'd I get it off 'er?'

'Well, I don't suppose she keeps it round her neck, does she?'

'No – on a bunch. Missis's jewel-box, and summat of her own, and one or two little 'uns.'

'And where do they usually live – hang – whatever they do?'

'On a 'ook by t'fire.' She pointed to the hook itself, on the wall by the old-fashioned grate, beside a warming-shelf for linen where the cat spent most of its days. Digby gazed at it longingly, for it bore the keys at that moment. If only it were not Sunday, if only he knew a handy locksmith or even a well-disposed burglar . . .

'How often are they there?' he asked. Millie shrugged.

'Dunno. She's in bed now. She'll tak' 'em to Miss Lilian's room when she gets 'er tea, then they go back on t'hook, till she taks 'em upstairs at bedtime.'

'And when does Miss Lilian get her tea?'

'Five o'clock, mostly.'

'Right, then. When the keys go back on the hook tomorrow, you take off the one for Miss Lilian's room and bring it to me. Don't ask me how – I'm sure you can do it. Just see it's done, some-how. And if there's any trouble I'll look after you myself.' He turned and ran upstairs before any arguments, or worse, tears, could be produced against him.

Strolling by the river, late that evening, his cigar a dim red star in the shadows, he wondered if he were mad, if the whole exercise had been a sort of crazy Charge of the Light Brigade in which everyone might come to a bad end to no purpose. What if Lilian were really at the point of death, and were to expire during her escape? There would be a fearful scandal which would get to the newspapers. He might be cashiered, even though it was not a military matter. Her Majesty would certainly take a poor view if it came to her ears, for all that her views were remarkably democratic. And, thinking of democracy, was it right to commit a young lady of de Wentworth blood to the arms of Jack Ellershaw? Ellershaw was a good sort of chap by any standards, but by no standards was he her social equal. Of course they were attracted to each other, two good-looking young people. Would it last, when she found herself in Jack's world with no way back to her own? Would his people welcome a helpless invalid with what they would no doubt term fancy ways?

Digby leant over the rail of the embankment, the river washing gently below him. He decided that he was on the whole a stupid sort of fellow, and that darling Penny would be well advised to take up with somebody else. Then he threw the butt of his cigar into the moon-silvered waters, went home, and wrote a note which Stokes immediately conveyed to a lodging-house in Somers Town, behind the Great Northern Railway terminus.

Lilian surveyed her room with amusement. Once again she was in prison, and for the same reason. It was just a little silly of her aunt to incarcerate so firmly a person who could not even set foot on the floor. She had heard the key turned on the outside of the door. There was no chance of anyone outside the house noticing her, even if she were to make distress signals, since from her bed she could only see the attic windows of the houses opposite, from which the servants were hardly likely to be watching out for drama on the other side of the street. The lace curtains draped across her own windows effectively prevented anyone looking in, even if they were impertinent enough to cross the front strip of garden. And even if the door had been wide open and the window bared to the public gaze, she could hardly have stirred a finger to escape.

Utter physical lassitude possessed her. After weeks of illness and inertia the outing, with all its excitements, had left her body weak and aching with exhaustion. It would have been bliss to have lain back in that soft bed, yielding herself up to relaxation, tended and comforted by gentle hands as she had been for so long. Rest, rest and sleep beckoned; but she must give way to neither. Her brain seemed on fire, her mind racing, pictures and sounds from the previous afternoon going through it like projections from a magic lantern. All night she had slept only fitfully, half-dreaming, then waking to wander down paths of feverish thought. Yet when Millie had brought her breakfast she had eaten it ravenously.

She was glad it was Sunday, the street-hawkers and their cries silent. Many streets away a wandering evangelist was playing a dismal hymn on a trombone. At six o'clock the church bells would begin; how many hours till then?

There was a book on the bedside table, a novel she had listlessly taken up two days earlier, read for a little, then put aside. She picked it up and tried to read, but the print blurred into nonsense and she let the book slip to the coverlet, giving herself over to recollection. The moment when she had first seen him at the match; the recognition, and the return of her drug-blurred memory. Fool, fool, to have let herself be duped into forgetfulness of one who had come into her life like dawn after a long and dreary night! Yet she had thought he had tired of her, forgotten her, since he had never tried to reach her after the awful scene with Nelly and Mamma. But he must have remembered, after all : must care something for her, to have said what he did.

'Goodbye,' she had said forlornly, in the silence that fell between them, hoping that he might kiss her again, as he had done out of kindness when she had blurted out her sorry story. Or at least take her hand; she longed so much to touch him, to feel the electric response of her skin to his. It would be a kind of death to see him walk away from her, and she had just come back to life. 'It was very nice to see you again,' she added politely.

'Aye. Well, I'll round for you Monday, latish.'

'You . . . *what* did you say?'

'Didn't the Captain tell you? I'm taking you back wi' me.'

Of all the extraordinary events of the day, this conversation was the most strange and dreamlike. Jack took pity on her, and launched into what was for him a long speech.

'Your cousin and me thinks it's best for you to get away from yon house and yon chap you were telling me about, seeing your auntie won't do owt about it. He can't look after you, and I can. There's plenty of room at our house for you, and my mam and dad won't mind if it's for a friend of mine.'

'But . . . Oh, Jack, I can't take in what you're saying. How can I travel as far as that, even if . . .'

156

'You got here all right, didn't you?'

'Yes, but . . . I've been very ill. I might have a relapse.'

'You won't. You look ten times better nor what you did when I saw you earlier, and it's never just the cricket, not after the exhibition our lads made of 'emselves, ninety-one when we should ha' been all of a hundred and fifty. It's the change and the company, and the good fresh air. We've plenty o' that in Yorkshire, too.'

'Yes.' To her longing for Jack's company was added a longing to be at home, among moors and mountains, under wide skies, away from the miasma of Chelsea and the stuffy sickroom. What a risk to take; what a wild gamble, and yet, what a prize might lie at the end of the perilous journey.

Jack searched her eyes. 'Don't you trust me, Lilian?'

'You know I do. I'd trust you anywhere, with anything.'

'All right, then. Trust me with thisen.'

She put her hand into his, letting it linger in that strong warm clasp; it was thus that Digby found them when he returned.

And now, in the long slow Sunday hours, it was Lilian's task to appear absolutely calm. They had agreed that Millie was to be told nothing. It was unfair to involve her, and she was not bright enough to be made a fellow-plotter. All she need do was to dress Lilian on Monday morning, having been told that her mistress felt strong enough to sit up a little; Frederica might object, but would hardly go to the length of undressing her again. Lilian tried to feel compunction for deceiving her aunt, but could feel none. What had once been kindness had become something else, which had turned Lilian into a pawn in a social game.

Time passed with weary slowness. Because it was impossible to read, Lilian began to recite anything she could remember; snatches of Tennyson (though that recalled the old life, her mother cherishing her as a pining princess), verses from *Alice in Wonderland*, nonsensical enough to suit her present condition.

'For I'm sure,' she told herself, 'Alice was never in quite such an odd situation as this. "You are old, Father William",' she went on aloud,

> ' ". . . the young man said,
> 'And your hair has become very white;
> And yet you incessantly stand on your head —

157

Do you think, at your age, it is right?'

'In my youth,' Father William replied to his son,
'I feared it might injure the brain;
But now I am perfectly sure I have none – ' " '

The key turned in the lock. Frederica entered the room.

'Why are you talking to yourself, Lilian?' she demanded. 'Are you feverish again?'

'Not at all, Aunt. I was just reciting.'

'It sounded very silly stuff to me.'

'What do you think I should be reciting? Hymns? The works of Mr Morris?'

'You're very impertinent. I don't think it a very suitable return for weeks of nursing.'

'If your friend Mr Bevis hadn't taken me to a very *un*suitable place I should not have needed nursing at all.'

Frederica stood at the foot of the bed, her face set in angry lines.

'You have been a very great disappointment to me. I shall be glad to be rid of you.' She turned and went out, turning the key noisily on the outside. Lilian gazed after her, making an unladylike grimace.

'You will be, Aunt, sooner than you think. Oh, please God, you will be.'

If Digby's Sunday was stress-laden, Jack's was far worse. For the entire day, from an early waking, he hung round the grimy lodging-house, where many tenants lurked behind many doors. His own room was fairly unsavoury, and the window refused to open, a considerable trial to one who loved fresh air. There was nothing to do but read old newspapers and a copy of *All the Year Round* which lay on a dusty shelf in his room. He would have liked to go to Lord's and practise in the nets, or get exercise by walking the streets. He could do neither, in case a message came and he was out.

As he sat on the edge of his hard narrow bed, staring at cobwebs and the holes in a rough mat, some of the doubts that beset Digby went through his own mind. Yet, unlike Digby, he was strengthened by something he did not understand, that was neither quixotry nor anger at a woman's plight. There had only been one thing he wanted in his life so far: to be accepted as a top-class professional cricketer and earn a decent living by it, enough to support his

158

parents and himself. Now he had another aim, to own as his wife a girl who could do nothing to help him or them, a girl out of his class. Why it should be so he had no idea, but he lived by instinct and his instinct told him that he must do the thing which seemed, on the face of it, a piece of madness.

The door-knocker sounded a smart tattoo, followed by brisk footsteps mounting the rickety stairs two at a time. Trooper Stokes, that unlikely messenger of Cupid, had brought news, and it was good.

He was glad to be occupied in playing throughout Monday. M.C.C.'s second innings on Saturday had resulted in a total of 161, Grace scoring a fine 66 in the teeth of determined and accurate bowling, on a pitch as bumpy as Saturday's, balls flying like bullets about his ribs, shoulders, head and legs, while he stood there rock-like, taking the blows without a wince. It was a wonder, Jack reflected, that he had not been maimed or even killed by one of them. As it was, he must have hardly a square inch of unbruised flesh on that immense body. Jack himself had done pretty well with the ball, taking three wickets for ten runs; yet Yorkshire had won only by a wicket and 28 runs, which Iddison had considered not good enough. Jack was uncomfortably conscious that he had lost his concentration for once, the adventure of the coming evening weighing on his mind. At 21 he had hit his wicket in drawing his bat back for a handsome drive; it was not the way a man would choose to be out.

The green omnibus which carried him southwards seemed to have the oldest horses in the business in its shafts, the traffic congestion at Regent Circus and Charing Cross was worse than anything he could have imagined, even in London. The self-control he had exercised all day became nervous tension. Constantly, when not being jostled by other passengers or moving his cricket-bag out of the way of their feet, he studied the map of Chelsea Digby had sent him. He must get off the omnibus at the beginning of Westminster Bridge and turn westwards, following the river. Some minutes' walk at a good pace should bring him to Cheyne Row.

On that fraught ride the sights of London left him unmoved. Nelson's Column and the Monument, towering over lesser buildings, invited his attention in vain; the Tudor Gothic immensities

159

of Barry's Houses of Parliament were merely a landmark, showing him where the Bridge began and where he must get off. In a minute he would be on his feet, no longer at the mercy of the crawling green monster.

The pace of his journey to Cheyne Row was fast enough to have brought cries of 'Stop thief!' after him. He took a last glance at his instructions.

'Go round the side of the house and ring the tradesmen's bell about 7 p.m. I will see to it that Stokes answers. He will bring you straight to me. Good luck.'

And I'm going to need it, Jack thought grimly. The brass bell marked 'Tradesmen' sounded like the Last Trump as it pealed through the kitchen. To his intense relief it was indeed Stokes who answered the door.

'About the rifle, was it?' the Trooper said without a flicker of expression. 'Captain's expecting you in the smoking-room, if you'll step this way.'

The cook, reading a servants' magazine by the fire, never raised her head as they passed. Mr Stokes had mentioned casually, taking care that as many people as possible heard, that his master was expecting a man who had a gun for sale. They saw Crowfoot's back, pressing a frilled apron with a goffering-iron, a delicate business which occupied all her attention. Then they were through the green baize door, hurrying towards the small smoking-room off the back of the hall. Digby was pacing, tiger-like, inside.

'Thank God you've come! Mamma's still dining. I said I'd a touch of the colic – left the table after the soup. Come on, we've no time to spare.'

Quick and light-footed, they sped along the hall to the door off a small corridor at the end, Stokes hovering near the dining-room with an excuse should the mistress emerge. She liked to linger over her meal when she dined alone.

Digby turned the key. 'All right to come in?'

Lilian lay on the bed, her eyes blazing stars of anticipation, her breath coming fast. She was fully dressed as far as the top layer, one of Miss Hake's loose artistic robes in an unbecoming shade of sludge brown, but her hair streamed about her shoulders. Wildly

160

she said 'Oh, I'm so glad to see you, but look at my hair! Millie can't do it and Aunt wouldn't let Crowfoot come in – and I haven't any boots on! What are we to do?'

'Find some,' said the practical Jack. 'Where are they kept? Right.' One by one he took the slender feet (cold, though their owner's cheeks were burning) and got them into delicate kid boots, Lilian too agitated to enjoy his gentle touch. He struggled with the twelve tiny buttons apiece, then gave up. 'You've no need to walk, any road. Have you got a cloak or jacket or summat?'

'In the wardrobe. The green one will do. And a bonnet. Oh, what a muddle I feel! My hair – what *shall* I do?'

'My dear girl, it looks charming,' Digby reassured her. 'Nothing unusual about a young lady's hair left loose these days. It makes you look rather young, that's all.'

'About ten,' Jack said, 'just about right to get me taken up for cradle-snatching. Are you fit, then, because it's time we were off?'

'My bag! The reticule and the bigger one – I got Millie to pack some things in it with a story about going home soon. That's the one. Oh, dear!'

'Calm down,' Jack said, and swept her up in his arms, holding her close for a second. Against his shoulder she said 'Am I too heavy?'

'Heavy as a bunch of flowers. Right, Captain.' He was out of the room, Digby behind him with the bag. There was no sign of life in the hall; the dining-room door was still shut.

'Stokes ought to have got a cab by now,' Digby said. He glanced through the window of the porch. 'Yes, by Jove he has. Come on, hurry.'

Single-handed Jack got Lilian into the waiting cab, while Digby threw the cricket-bag and Lilian's portmanteau after him. They were all breathless, flushed, triumphant so far.

'Well, that seems to be the lot,' Digby gasped. 'Good luck, both of you, and get word to me somehow.'

'I don't know . . .' Jack began. He wanted to say how deeply grateful he was, to express complicated thoughts that had only just come to the surface of his mind. But there was no time, and he was a man of few words. He held out his hand, and Digby took it. 'Thanks,' Jack said, and Lilian blew him a kiss.

'Digby, you *are* a sport, and make no mistake. We'll make it up to you someday.'

The cab rattled off, its driver with a guinea of Digby's in his pocket. It would not be his fault if he failed to reach King's Cross station in time for the last train to the North.

Discovery, when it came, was noisy and prolonged. Packing in his dressing-room, Stokes helping him, Digby heard his mother's shriek as she found Lilian's door open and the prisoner gone. Then came cries, running footsteps, banged doors, a whistle blown in the street for a policeman.

'I say, we're in for it, Stokes,' he murmured.

'Yessir. Never say die, sir.'

Frederica burst into the room like a hurricane. 'Lilian's gone, vanished! She's been abducted, her clothes are gone too. Digby, what are we to *do*? How can you stand there so calm? Didn't you hear the noise?'

'Thought something must be up – some little domestic fracas. Sit down, Mamma. All right, Stokes.' He was left alone with Frederica, on whose face a dreadful realisation was beginning to dawn.

'Yes, Mamma, look no further, it was my doing. Just listen to me, don't talk. I know you meant to do your best for Lilian by bringing her here, but she got into bad company; your Mr Bevis, if you want to know. You must have noticed how very much worse she'd grown, with him influencing her.'

'It was not Leo! He adored her – what harm could he have done her? This is some kind of plot!'

'So I'm informed, but not against Mr Bevis, who's been doing his best to poison her. I should have him looked into, if I were you.'

'You've always resented my friends, because you don't under-stand them, you great ignorant lump! What have you done with Lilian? Where is she?'

'Gone, where you won't find her, with a man who'll look after her better than you could, or Mr Bevis, or any of us. An old flame, you might say. She needs very special looking-after, you know, Mamma, and I can't think of anyone who'd do it better, truly.'

'I'll have her brought back! There's a policeman downstairs now.'

'Brought back from where? Paris, Boulogne, the Irish packet, the mews round the corner?' Frederica advanced on him, her hand raised to strike. Gently he pushed it down. 'I don't fight with women, Mamma. Just take my word, Lilian's safe.'

She shook him then, as she had not shaken him since he was a small boy, fury and agitation lending her strength, gasping out incoherent words of rage. He let her, knowing that she must express herself somehow, guilty that he had brought this trouble on his mother, and filled with fresh doubts that he had done the right thing. He had intended to spend the night at an hotel; now he realised that it would be cowardly. He must stay and face the recriminations, deal with the policeman downstairs, turn away endless questions, write to Sir Lewis and Lilian's mother. There was no criminal charge they could bring against him, or even against Jack, if by bad luck the fugitives were caught, as Lilian was turned twenty-one. He would face up to it all as though it were enemy fire; on the whole he would rather have preferred that, for at least then he would have known that right was on his side.

But, right or wrong, nothing now would bring Lilian back to Cheyne Row.

BOOK THREE

The Weald and the Willow

And o'er the hills, and far away
Beyond their utmost purple rim,
Beyond the night, across the day,
Through all the world she followed him.
Alfred Tennyson

CHAPTER THIRTEEN

Jack admitted to no doubts as they journeyed in the cab that was taking them to the Great Northern Railway Terminus at King's Cross. His only way of telling the time was by the church clocks they passed on their way, but he was confident of reaching the train comfortably before it left for Leeds. Just as any captain sums up the wicket and the weather before the start of play, he had worked out the distance from Chelsea to the railway-station by questioning a cab-driver, the night before inspected at King's Cross the furthest distance he would have to carry Lilian to the train, learned the fare for the train-journey (his match-fee would pay for both nicely), and bought the tickets.

Lilian had no such confidence, once the excitement of escape had died down. Suppose someone had seen them from a window and was now in another cab, following them? Suppose Digby yielded under his mother's pressure and gave their destination away? Then there was Millie. Somebody was sure to connect her with the plot. If only she could ask Jack for reassurance! But common sense told her he knew no more than she did of probable events at Cheyne Row.

They sat in silence, Jack conscious of the warmth of her arm against his and the perfume she used, which fought a losing battle against the hackney's reek of horses, straw, stale cigar-smoke and ineffable memories of other passengers. There was nothing particular he had to say, so he said nothing, concentrating his thoughts on the match he would be playing in the following week. Lilian glanced at his serene profile, not daring to interrupt whatever profound things were going through his head, wishing he were not so silent. Suddenly he said, 'King's Cross any minute now.' Sure enough, the cab was passing the massive building-pile that was soon to be St Pancras Station, and the approach to the station she remembered was in sight.

The cab stopped in the forecourt. Jack got down, lifted Lilian out with ease, then stood, suddenly nonplussed, with her reclining in his arms, the luggage at their feet. The driver, in spite of Digby's guinea, made no effort to get down from the box and help, but cracked his whip and moved away to a waiting group of passengers, leaving Jack standing, supporting Lilian. In all his calculations he had not worked out that he could not possibly carry both her and their two bags to the train.

Thus precariously balanced Lilian felt extremely uncomfortable and foolish. Jack's arms were strong and sure, but even her light weight might be too much for him if she moved at all, and she had no fancy for measuring her length on the ground.

'Well, are we to stand here all night?' she demanded. 'People are looking.'

'They'll look at owt.' He was gazing round, working out the possibilities, which included the snatching of their luggage. He had not reckoned on having to pay a porter, but no Cockney thief was going to make off with his precious bat and flannels, and a porter was approaching pushing an empty luggage-trolley.

'Hey!' Jack called. 'Give us a lift, will you?'

The man stared first at them, then at their two pieces of luggage, before he noticed that the young female seemed unable to stand and appeared distressed.

'Want a hand, missis?' he asked ingratiatingly. 'Not feeling too clever, ain't she, sir?'

'If you think I'm drunk . . .' Lilian began furiously, but Jack broke in. 'She's been ill, can't walk. If you'll give us the loan of yon thing I'll shove it to the train.' Commandeering the trolley before the porter could object, he deftly placed Lilian on it.

'But Jack, I can't . . .'

'Oh yes, tha can. It's that or miss train. This lad'll bring the bags.'

The lad, who was all of fifty, followed somewhat dazedly as the northerner unconcernedly steered his lady along the forecourt to the barrier, where a grinning ticket-collector took their tickets, on to the platform at which the train was already waiting, and stopped outside an empty third-class compartment. At the gleam of a shilling the porter willingly assisted in the transference of Lilian and the bags to the carriage, under the amused stares of other boarding passengers, settling her along the length of a seat. Fairly convinced that both of them were mad, he accepted his tip graciously. It was seldom that he got more than fourpence except from the gentry.

Lilian glared across the carriage. '*Well!* a nice spectacle you made of me, didn't you. What must people have thought? Surely you could have arranged for something rather more dignified . . .'

Jack leaned back, folding his arms. 'Oh, aye? What, for instance?'

There was really no answer, for she had not the least idea. It occurred to her for the first time that Jack was no Digby, and had no money for hired invalid-chairs or champagne picnics, or any of the comforts she had been used to. She remembered, with longing, the up-journey with Aunt Freddy: the luxurious saloon, the little sleeping cabin, the delicious luncheon and obsequious service. And from that, to come down to being pushed on a luggage-trolley to a compartment which had Third Class stamped on its every feature, not only on the door. The upholstery was hardly more than a piece of rough carpeting material tacked on to bare boards, highly uncomfortable to lie on, even with her reticule packed behind her head. There was an all-pervading smell of smuts and steam; if one touched the seat or its backing, dust came out. Frankly filthy and degrading.

Another realisation came to her with a shock. There was no means of leaving the compartment during the journey. On Aunt Freddy's train there had been an up-to-date convenience. Wild thoughts went through her head. Suppose she . . . suppose it were necessary to . . . The full horror of the situation overwhelmed her. Now she realised the awful impropriety of travelling without a maid. It was no mere convention that a lady did not travel alone, and for an invalid lady female companionship was essential. Even had Jack been her brother, it would have been awkward enough, but to be accompanied by a stranger . . . A stranger.

Her change of colour and wild glance at the doors told Jack her feelings as clearly as though she had spoken.

'Don't fret,' he said. 'I know it seems a bit shut in, but there's stops on the way. I'll see thee looked after, lass.'

Alarmed as she was, she gave him a grateful smile. He was very tactful and very kind, and somehow it was less embarrassing to travel with him than with a gentleman of her own class.

A whistle shrilled, a green flag fluttered, and the train began to move. The advertisements, bright-coloured lettering on sheets of tin, slid past: FRY'S PURE COCOA, ROWLAND'S MACASSAR OIL, LIPTON'S TEAS, RIDGE'S CHEMICAL FOOD, DR COLLIS BROWNE'S ORIGINAL CHLORODYNE (ACCEPT NO SUBSTITUTE). Sidings, engine-sheds, trucks, appeared and were past, the northern suburbs of London already coming into sight. It was the same prospect Lilian had seen in reverse on her arrival, how many months ago; now she was going back, not to her comfortable, familiar home, but to an unknown place to live among people she had never even met, in Heaven knew what conditions. A lump of misery formed in her throat. She very much wanted to cry, but told herself sternly that it was all her own fault, brought on herself by rashness, and crying would do no good at all.

Besides, it would trouble Jack, and she did not want to do that.

Dusk came on, then the dark, as they rushed through lighted towns and villages, through long tracts of open country, into stations which clanged and clattered with brief life, then were gone. Jack had watched her anxiously for signs of distress, ready to alert the guard and hold the train up if she must alight, but she slept, her head turned a little to one side on its lumpy pillow, the long lashes unflickering on her cheek. He saw, approving, that they were not damp. She had not allowed herself a tear, and only that one flash of temper at King's Cross, when he had reluctantly had to make a spectacle of her. It was all of a piece: she was good stuff. He promised her silently to make up for it all.

He slept himself in time, forgetting his hunger and the discomfort of the seat, lulled by the rhythm of the wheels, and became conscious with a shock to find that the train was in a large station, pausing to have mail-bags loaded. To his relief he saw BAWTRY on the name-board. They were one station away from Doncaster, where they must get off, and he would need plenty of time for that operation. Gently he touched Lilian's cheek. Her eyes flew open, bewildered. 'Where . . . ?'

'Nearly there. Just a bit further. I'd try to sit up now, if I were thee. Here, I'll give thee a hand.'

170

She winced and grimaced. 'Oh! I'm so stiff. I can't.' But she did, with much help from him. When the train drew in to Doncaster he left her propped in a corner while he leapt out and beckoned a porter – the only porter, it seemed, a bent old man who was of little use beyond taking charge of the two pieces of luggage and holding the carriage door open for Jack as he lifted Lilian out. A few more passengers left the train, glancing curiously at the pair. The porter, who had been hoping for prosperous passengers to direct to an hotel and escort them on their way, was disappointed to find himself lumbered, as he thought of it, with such unpromising customers.

'Yo'd best go in t'waitin' room, if young woman can't walk,' he grumbled, toiling after them the few steps across the platform. The waiting-room was cheerless, bare of any furniture but a plain deal table and benches round the walls. Jack looked critically at the empty grate. 'Haven't you got a fire, then?'

The porter snorted. 'I' May?'

'Makes no difference, May or January, this time o' night it's cold.'

'Theer's other places tha can go if tha doesn't like this 'un.'

'Where, for instance?' asked Lilian. The same question was in Jack's mind. Mentally he kicked himself for not having thought of it before. It was half-past eleven at night. There was no possibility of reaching Barnswood before morning, when he would be able to hire some sort of transport in the town. The porter, following his thoughts wth grim satisfaction, said, 'They'll not have thee in a hotel, wi'out a proper portmanteau or summat.' His fishy gaze took in Jack's lack of an overcoat, his workmanlike cap, and Lilian's eccentric style of dress, the effect of which was not helped by her hair flowing about her shoulders. Jack could see that he thought her no better than she should be, at the least.

'This lady's not strong,' he said, keeping his temper. 'Can't you find owt better for her till morning?' He knew Doncaster well enough to be aware that to apply at the Angel and Royal Hotel, or even the Turf Tavern patronised by racing folk, would be to invite a snub and a slammed door. The porter turned and hobbled away without replying. They looked after him gloomily.

'I know he thinks I'm drunk,' Lilian said. 'Everyone seems to, today. Tonight, that is. Oh dear, Jack, what are we going to do? I'm so cold, and stiff, and uncomfortable – I can't spend the night

171

in this wretched hole.' It did not occur to her that Jack, for all his strength, was also cold, stiff, and uncomfortable. He wondered despondently whether she thought of him seriously at all or whether she were merely using him as an escape-route. After all, she had gone off to London that time as gay as a lark, from all accounts, never answering his letter or trying to get in touch with him. The whole enterprise, in the dim flickering of the waiting-room gas-lamp, seemed a dreadful mistake. He stole a look at her. Her bonnet was over one eye, her hair wild, her gloves filthy from the train, her face grimy, but she still managed to look superior to any young woman he had so far set eyes on. She surveyed him in turn. His hair was tousled, his shirt-collar rumpled, his face blacked as though he had after all chosen a life down the pit. Lilian began to laugh, and laughed and laughed. When she could speak, she said, 'Your f-face! If you could see it!'

'Aye, well, what about yours? Talk about a poppy-show! For two pins I'd tak' thee to yon mirror!' Then he began to laugh too, and it was thus, holding on to each other helplessly, that the station-master found them. His porter had knocked on the station-house door with the news that two suspicious characters were lurking in the waiting-room. Correctly dressed in full daytime wear, complete with top hat, he waited patiently in the doorway until these obviously eccentric young persons had calmed down. Then he coughed politely. Politeness would do no harm, even if they were raving mad.

'Mr Buck tells me you're in some sort of trouble, sir, ma'am.'

Lilian mopped her eyes, adding more streaks to her dirty cheeks. Still gasping with laughter, she began to explain their predicament. 'It is so late at night and we have nowhere to go. I am unable to walk, which makes it so much more difficult. I'm afraid we look very strange, but we had to leave London in ... in a hurry, with no time to collect any more luggage. If you could just suggest something, sir, we would be so grateful ...'

The station-master was impressed with her educated voice and gracious manner. The case was not as Mr Buck had suspected; but then Mr Buck had a suspicious mind at the best of times. He saw from the way the girl was lying along the bench that she was indeed disabled. A friendly man who liked his station to maintain a good name, he said that he and his wife were still up, late as it was, for he always saw the last train of the night out of the station before retiring. 'I'm sure my good lady would provide shelter for the night if you'd like to come with me, Mr and Mrs . . . ?'

'No,' Lilian said, as Jack looked baffled. 'I am Miss Lilian de Wentworth, and this is Mr Ellershaw.'

'I see,' said the station-master, who didn't; hoping that no scandalous complications would set in, he led Jack, carrying Lilian, to a neat cottage at the end of the platform, built on to the rest of the station. The room he led them into was glowing with warmth, a good fire in the grate and a cheerful lamp on the table, at which was sitting a stout little woman neatly gowned and shawled but topped with an enormous frilled nightcap.

'Mrs Thorp, my dear,' said her husband, 'I've brought you two young people to look after. The young lady's not best suited to sleep in our waiting-room. We can find her a bed, can't we, and the young man another somewhere?'

Mrs Thorp could not have been more delighted. The life of a busy station was always throwing up some agreeable excitement for a woman who liked getting mixed up in other people's affairs, and here was a very promising case. She saw that they were too exhausted to entertain her with a long explanation, and lost no time in having Lilian conveyed into the back parlour, where a comfortable wide sofa would serve her as a bed. Then the men were firmly shut out as Mrs Thorp devoted herself to a limp but grateful guest, while Jack smoked a pipe by the fire at Mr Thorp's invitation, took a glass of ale, and conversed about cricket with a knowledge which earned his host's rapt admiration, as well as reassuring him as to the young man's character. Then he was led up the stairs to the small bedroom the Thorps' son had occupied before leaving home to get married.

So ended the day of their flight. Mercifully for the travellers, they had fallen into the hands of kindly people. Jack knew all too well how different their fate might have been.

The pony-trap Jack had hired carried them at a brisk trot through country lanes melodious with bird-song, between hedges full of wild flowers. Lilian was securely strapped to her seat in case of lurches, but completely in possession of herself again after Mrs Thorp's careful dressing of her. Once a lady's maid, the station-master's wife thoroughly enjoyed attending to the details of a young lady's toilette and brushing out the beautiful hair, even though the dress was very odd, London-fashion, she supposed. In vain she tried to get out of Lilian what she was sure were romantic secrets about herself and the young man, but nothing was forthcoming, only that they were travelling to visit relatives. Wistfully she waved them off.

'Well, now we've time to talk,' Lilian said.

'That's right.'

'For instance – what are your parents going to say to me?'

' "Come in" – I hope, anyway.'

'Don't be silly, Jack. I mean, are they expecting me?'

'O' course. I wrote.' On Sunday he had penned a short, difficult letter trying to tell them that he was bringing a friend home, a young lady friend, who had had a bad time of it in London and wanted a bit of country air. She'd summat wrong with her back and couldn't walk, but would be no trouble. Finally, searching for words and crossing many out, he put that he hoped they'd understand.

The lane brought them to an open land of low hills and meadows, the dark austere shapes of pit-heads against the sky breaking the soft contours on which sheep cropped, grey-coloured as the cottages and small farmsteads. Coal was here, but agriculture, too, apple- and pear-trees rich with blossom in small gardens, linen pegged out to bleach in the May sun.

'We're not far off now. In front of yon hill, by the wood,' Jack pointed. Lilian watched the low grey building draw nearer, saw the neat coloured patches of vegetables in front of it, the orchard at the side, a woman's figure in a lilac dress and a long white pinafore moving about with a basket on her arm. The pony slowed to a walk at a word from Jack, taking them up the slanting path that led to Stainbeck Cottages.

Jack's mother came down to meet them. She stood at the swing gate which shut the market-garden off from marauding animals, one hand shading her eyes, making sure it was indeed them. Then she opened the gate, moving with a grace Lilian recognised as being like Jack's, and waited, watching the trap go by her, up to the front door. Jack hitched the reins, picked Lilian up, climbed down with her in his arms. It seemed that she was always there nowadays.

174

'Well, Mam,' he said, carrying his burden through the door and setting her down in a chair. Mary Ellershaw bestowed the sketch of a kiss on his cheek, without having to reach up to do so. 'Well, Jack. You got here, then.'

Lilian felt an awful impulse to giggle coming upon her. She had suffered from it badly as a child, though it had faded in later years. Jack was the very pattern of a gallant knight, a young hero quite after Mamma's Galahad style, bearing home a lady rescued from nameless horrors to his castle, and what was his reception? 'You got here, then.' It could only happen in Yorkshire. She composed her face to greet the tall handsome woman who was surveying her, assessing her. 'Mrs Ellershaw,' she said.

Mary was not easily disconcerted, but for once she found it difficult to collect her thoughts. Jack was not a great letter-writer. His confused note had conveyed to her a picture of a servant-girl ('young lady' was a gentlemanly euphemism, of course) with some malformation, a hunch-back, perhaps, or one of those sad cases to be seen in the big towns. She was not at all prepared for the young person propped up in her best high-backed chair, thin, pale, a bit funnily-dressed, but quite clearly a lady born, both in voice and looks, and with no hideous deformity in sight. Well, Jack had always been different from other folk; it was only like him to pick a different sort of lass.

'This is Miss Lilian de Wentworth, Mam,' he said. 'She's been ill. We've known each other a long time now, from when I worked at Sir Lewis's.'

'I'm Sir Lewis's cousin,' Lilian said. 'Or sort of cousin. Jack was very kind to me in those days, and when we met again in London we thought . . . we thought it would be a good idea to come here.'

Mary nodded slowly. Lilian loosened the strings of her bonnet; the sunlight from the small window blazed up in her hair, making a Burne-Jones angel of her. Mary saw the look in Jack's eyes as they rested on the angel.

'We'll have some tea, shall us. I expect you could do wi' a cup, Miss . . .'

'Lilian, please.'

'Lilian.' There were no arguments about etiquette in this family. 'Good thing I baked yesterday. I've some date cake, almond fingers, butter curds – and there's dough for pikelets warmin' by t'fire.'

175

Amos entered, a bent figure, leather-aproned, a basket of newly-picked gooseberries on his arm. Introduced to Lilian, he expressed no surprise at her presence, appearance, or anything else, but merely shook hands heartily with her and hoped she was keeping well. Jack's letter might have been a model of clarity and the situation perfectly normal. As they all ate Mary's cakes and drank the strong good tea with milk in it from a neighbouring farm, he explained that picking goosegogs was finicking work, but he did it because it saved him bending too far. 'Mi back's none so clever.'

'Nor is mine, Mr Ellershaw,' Lilian assured him.

'Aye, Jack did mention it. Well, young bones can mend, mine can't. We've all got our troubles.' But he smiled so brightly that there was no self-pity in the remark. 'Them's fine goosegogs, Mother. I expect your crops is a long way ahead of ours, Miss Lilian, being so far south?'

'Oh, but I'm not from the south. I'm from Fellgate.'

'Fellgate, eh? Not all that far, then. And you're a Wentworth. Anything to them at the House?' Lilian knew of the mansion near Rotherham where the Earl of Fitzwilliam lived in state, surrounded by the paintings of Old Masters and relics of his ancestor, Charles the First's Black Tom Strafford, who had died on the scaffold betrayed by his king. She shook her head. 'Only a very long way back. According to Mamma there was a brother who went over to Ireland just before the Civil Wars calling himself de Wentworth, and we're descended from him. But we wouldn't be received at Wentworth House, I feel sure.'

Mary had been listening keenly. 'You've a mother, then, at Fellgate?'

Lilian realised she had given away more than she had meant to. 'Yes. Well, near there.'

'Then don't you think you'd best let her know where you are? Likely she'll be worryin' her head off if you came away from London in some sort o' pickle, and wi' only our Jack for company? We don't want a hue and cry after you.'

Lilian glanced helplessly at Jack. 'It's . . . difficult.'

'There's things you don't know yet, Mam,' he said, 'and I'd sooner not talk about 'em. It's too nice a day. Let's say that if she'd not be received at Wentworth House, she wouldn't be at home,

176

neither – or it'd be wrong sort of reception. Isn't that how it stands, Lilian?'

'Before I went to London,' Lilian said, 'I was shut up in my room and allowed to see nobody, for something Mamma thought I'd done wrong. Then I was taken to London, and . . . everything went wrong again. If it hadn't been for Jack, and somebody else, I'd have been in dreadful trouble. It's very hard to explain.' She felt she would never be able to tell these good clear-eyed people about Leo Bevis.

'Then we'll leave it at that,' Mary said briskly. 'Come on, Dad, shift the pots. I've got to get back to t'young cabbages, seein' waggon'll be here first thing tomorrow. I'll want a hand, our Jack, if you've got one to spare.'

Jack paused beside Lilian when his parents had left the room. Gently he stroked her cheek from temple to chin.

'Well done, love,' he said.

Her eyes challenged his. 'You never said that before.'

'Said what?'

'Love.'

But he only smiled, and went out into the garden.

CHAPTER FOURTEEN

Whatever Lilian had expected of life at Stainbeck, she soon discovered that it was not going to be an idyll. In childhood she had been into many such cottages, the homes of Sir Lewis's tenants, but nothing had prepared her for the stark quality of the life that was lived in them. Nobody seemed to have a moment to sit down except at mealtimes. Nobody read, or engaged in social chatter. The vegetable gardens occupied the Ellershaw family from morning to night, while Mary cooked, brewed, baked and sewed when she was not helping her men. Every day a Mrs Mossop arrived in a rickety cart drawn by an equally rickety old horse to do the rough cleaning, and once a week took away the family washing to her own cottage. A timid sparrow of a woman, she seemed afraid of Mary, who referred to her off-handedly as a poor thing as needed the brass, being left a widow with no skill at owt but scrubbing. She was allowed to do nothing for Lilian, who was left to the tender mercies of Mary.

It was quite clear that her presence was resented. To Mary she was a useless encumbrance. Such attendance as Mary gave her was perfunctory and graceless, filling her with embarrassment at having to accept such unwilling service. The room allotted to her was at the back of the house, looking on to a yard and used partly as a store-room. It was barely furnished and far from cheerful, and the turn-up bed she occupied was hard and lumpy. She missed the capable hands of Millie, and even those of Crowfoot, when it came to putting up her own hair and washing in a basin of cold water.

Yet Mary was not deliberately unkind or neglectful. Jack had put this feckless creature in her care, and care for her she would. Whether Lilian liked it or not, she was relentlessly dosed with a pick-me-up mixture, which fortunately was palatable, a compound of honey, sage and rum from a bottle kept strictly as medicine. As an extra remedy nettle porridge appeared for supper, a pleasant dish made from young spring nettles boiled and chopped, thickened with oatmeal and butter, and seasoned with pepper. It had to be eaten with oatcakes to do real good, said Mary.

'Likely you'll have a bad chest, being so thin, nowt but a bag of bones,' she said. 'Long Life Emulsion's best for that, and it's easy made.'

'No, no,' Lilian said hastily. 'My chest is perfectly healthy. I only look like this because I had an illness in London. Please don't trouble.'

She asked Jack, when he came in to see her in the evening, '*Do* I look like a bag of bones? Your mother says so.'

He surveyed her. 'I wouldn't say that, no. I'd say you've filled out nicely, got a bit of colour in your cheeks. More like the lass I remember.'

'Thank you. I'm relieved to hear it. I've only been here four days – your mother's medicine must be very effective.'

'Oh, aye. So is being two hundred miles from yon house.'

'Yes, I know. You were quite right to do what you did. Even though . . .'

'Even though the living's a bit rough, like Mam's tongue?'

She flushed. 'I wasn't going to say that. I'm sure I'm a dreadful nuisance to her. It's only that – I've been spoiled, I suppose, with servants and things, all my life, and I'm not quite used to doing without. But – oh, Jack, I'm so bored!'

Jack looked thoughtful. 'Bored . . . Now that's not a word we use much, in our family. But I can see as it might come about with you. I'd like to be with you a bit more, only there's more jobs than there's time.' He sat down on the end of the bed, then looked apologetically down at his working clothes and earth-grimed hands. 'I'm not fit to be near a young lady, not without smartening up a bit, but it's a case of where there's muck there's money.'

'I understand all about that. And I don't mind muck. Or anything . . .' Come nearer, her eyes pleaded, touch me, kiss me, show me you haven't brought me here just out of pity! But he made no moved towards her, only watched her face with a thoughtful grave look.

'If you're bored,' he said, 'why not ask Mam to give you some jobs? There's plenty you could do, like slicing up beans and such . . . things that take time up for her.'

179

'What a good idea,' Lilian said brightly. 'I'll ask her tomorrow morning.' But when he had gone she turned over and wept into her pillow, because he had said no word of love to her, and perhaps never would.

The party-walls of the house were of stone, through which no words could be overheard unless they were shouted. In the parlour Mary and Jack confronted each other, Amos nervously looking on, fearing a domestic battle.

'Lilian's fretting,' Jack said. Mary snorted.

'Fretting, her? After all the waiting on, hand and foot, she gets from me? That's a good 'un.'

'You'd need waiting on if you couldn't walk. She's not enough to do. I've told her to ask you to let her lend a hand, make herself useful as far as she can.'

'And how far's that, lying there like a lump? If you ask me, yon wench was born lazy.'

'Mother, Mother!' intervened Amos, seeing a familiar glint in his son's eyes, and an equally steely one in his wife's.

'Don't you Mother me. It's time our Jack heard a few straight words about the way he's treated us, lumbering us wi' some fancy lady he picked up in London and wants to keep for a pet, at least that's the way it looks to me...'

'Then it looks the way it's not, Mam!' Jack flashed back. 'Lilian's no fancy lady of mine, nor anyone else's. She's as honest a maid as you were when you married Dad, and as bonny and brave as ever I saw. I can take women or leave 'em – aye, and I've taken a few in mi time, as a man ought if he's a man at all – but I'll not be leaving this one, I tell you straight. I've said nowt to her yet, and I'll thank you to do the same. If she's a bother, then I'm sorry, but I brought her up here for two reasons. The first was that she was like to die if I didn't. The second was that I wanted her to see me the way I am.'

'I don't know what you're getting at, lad.'

'Just this. It's all very well for a lass to get soft on a chap all dressed up in cricket togs like the King o' the May, knocking t'ball all over t'shop and getting clapped for it. That's loving wi' the eyes. But loving wi' the heart, which is the sort as matters, that comes of seeing a chap as he is, in his own place, all hours of the day, in and out of temper, clean or mucky, that's the test of proper

180

love. Or whatever they call it,' Jack added, suddenly embarrassed by his own utterance of a word which had probably never been uttered in that house before, other than as a casual form of address. A silence fell. Mary, who had been belligerently facing Jack, subsided into a chair.

'So it's like that,' she said heavily. 'I see.'

Amos spoke up for the first time, as troubled in his mind as Mary.

'What use will she be to thee, lad, even if she comes to fall in with our ways? She'll never be able to do a hand's turn in the gardens, or drive a cart . . .'

'Or rear thy bairns,' Mary put in, looking hard at her son.

'Let's not worry about my bairns till they're born, eh?' he returned. 'I may get a quiver-full or I may get none. It's Lilian we're talking about now. All I'm saying is give her and me time, Mam, and have a bit of a gossip wi' her now and then. She'll be glad of a kind word – you've made it pretty clear to her what you feel about her. Do you know what they say down south about Yorkshire hospitality? that's it's the best in the world. Don't give us a bad name, Mam!'

Mary tossed her head, just a little ashamed of herself, saying, 'Get on with you. And there's summat else. We're not to have t'constable round after her, are we? I don't know what you two were up to in London, but I hope it were nowt on t'wrong side of t'law.'

The same fear had crossed Jack's mind more than once, of a threat to his parents and to his own career. But Digby had promised him that when Frederica's inevitable wrath died down a little he would make some sort of explanation to her, and tell her that Lilian would write when she felt able. Digby, Jack was sure, would somehow prevent his mother from making any dramatic dash northwards with an escort of detective police. 'Put that out of thy head, Mam,' he said.

The next day he left to play in a three-day match. Amos saw the downcast look on Lilian's face, as she watched Jack through the open door of her room, tenderly packing his bag of gear; much more tender than his leave-taking of her was his handling of his precious bat and leg-guards. And Amos was sorry for the lonely girl who was trying not to cry over the dish of strawberries Mary had given her to de-stalk. He was lonely himself, in his way. He thought often of the baby daughter who had died so many years ago, and lay in the churchyard of Barnswood village; Jane would have been twenty-four now, a bright face about the house, company for him and Mary, or married with youngsters of her own, other bright faces, voices to call him Grandad. Mary was a woman made to be the mother of sons. Amos was immensely proud of Jack, deeply fond of him, but he would so much have loved a daughter . . .

One evening, some days later after Jack's departure, when Mary was up to her elbows in brewing, he wandered into Lilian's room. She was idly fingering her way through *Pilgrim's Progress*, looking at the illustrations. Amos had looked at them himself in his time and found them wanting in entertainment value; indeed, depressing to the spirits.

'Nowt much to look at, have you, lass?' he ventured.

She sighed and smiled. 'Not much, Mr Ellershaw. I'm afraid I'm more used to magazines.'

'There, now. I thought tha'd ha' been a great one for book-learnin'.'

'Not a bit of it. I used to like riding, things like that.'

'Cricket?' He was watching her closely, noticing the flush that came up in her cheeks.

'Yes, especially cricket. That's where I met Jack, at a village match. And then, this last time, at Lord's.'

'Lord's, eh? I've allus wanted to see Lord's. It's a grand owd ground, Lord's is. Is it all they say?'

'Oh, it's beautiful, like a country ground, with trees all round, and a pretty church and nice little villas, and a big, handsome pavilion. You can get tea and ice-creams, and I daresay a proper luncheon – but we took ours, in a picnic-basket. It was lovely . . .'

Amos knew what had made it lovely. By and by he would let her talk about Jack, and tell her the sort of things about his boy she would want to know. But it was too soon. He picked up *Pilgrim's Progress*.

'What d'you reckon to this, then?'

'I suppose it's very good – very worthy, that is. But I find it most dreadfully dull – that silly man, trudging through all those awful places, the Slough of Despond and things, when he might just as well have moved out of the City of Destruction and lived in a tent, or somewhere.'

'Aye. Or he might ha' got up a cricket eleven,' Amos said meditatively, pleased to hear her laugh.

'Yes, I'm sure J – anyone sensible would have done so, instead of making himself so extremely uncomfortable. Don't you think so, Mr Ellershaw?'

He was sitting by her side, hands on knees, smiling his beautiful smile which drew children to him. 'I think tha's a hard nut to crack, young lady, that's what I think. Didst never get told any stories when tha were a bairn?'

Lilian thought. 'Stories? No, I don't believe I did. Mamma read me a lot of poems about King Arthur and his knights, but I used to mix him up with King William, who died before I was born, and imagined him with a head like a pineapple and organ-stop eyes. So I suppose he never seemed quite as romantic to me as he did to Mamma. Besides, my brother's called Arthur and the most unromantic person you ever met.'

Amos leaned forward, his face alight with mysterious promise. 'I'll tell thee a tale about King Arthur I'll bet tha's never heard afore.'

She clasped her hands. 'Oh! please, do!'

'Then sit back, and listen like the good bairn thou art. Once upon a time – and it were a long time ago – there lived a man i' Richmond. Tha knows Richmond town, up i' Swaledale? Well, this chap's name were Potter Thompson, and he were a reet ne'er-do-well. He were a cobbler by trade, but that idle he'd lost all his customers. His wife ne'er let up on scoldin' him, and one neet he were that sick and tired of it he went out for a walk, wi' a notion in his head to drown hisself. But River Swale looked cowd, so he passed it by and daundered about t'Castle rock. And there, in t'cliff side, he saw an openin', as it might ha' been the mouth of a cave. And he went in, to see what were there.'

'Go on!'

'He walked, and he walked, and he walked; and though it were darkish outside, there shone a light i' the tunnel as came from nowhere, and got brighter as he went. All of a sudden, he turned a corner. And there were the light, a great lantern hangin' from an owd cresset up in the high roof of a cavern the size of Leeds

Town Hall. And under the lantern – there were a stone table. And on the table – there were a great owd sword and a great owd horn, all worked wi' gowd and ivory. And on t'floor there lay knights in armour, owd plate and chain armour, wi' helmets on their heads, and on the head of t'biggest 'un there were a crown of gowd, and by his side there lay the bonniest lady any mortal ever set eyes on, let alone Potter Thompson, in a long red dress wi' white fur at her neck, and long gowd plaits wi' a little crown atop, all ashine wi' jewels. And the whole boilin' of 'em were fast asleep.'

'King Arthur and Queen Guinevere!'

'Aye, Jennifer, common folk called her. And Potter Thompson stood like a stuck pig, lookin' at 'em, for he knew King Arthur and his knights waited for the hour when England would call 'em to help in her hour of need. He were a poor sort o' thing, but summat got into him then, and he stepped up and laid hands on sword and horn, and lifted 'em. And one big knight shifted a bit, then raised hisself on his elbow. And Potter Thompson, he were feared out o' his wits, and he dropped sword and horn and ran like a scared rabbit, back the way he'd come. And behind him there sounded a voice, loud and mockin', and it said –

> "Potter, Potter Thompson!
> If thou hadst either drawn
> The sword, or blown the horn,
> Thou'dst been t'luckiest man
> That ever yet was born."

'So, he lost his fortune because his heart failed him. Think on, young Lilian.'

' "Think on",' she said in a passable echo of his accent. 'Aye, I will.'

Amos told her many tales after that, as eager to talk as she to listen. He had not talked so much since Jack was a little boy, and he was a born story-teller. His tales were all of the mysterious and the uncanny. There were the evil doings of Mother Shipton, the Witch of Knaresborough, who in return for selling her soul to the Devil was able to prophesy modern happenings, though she lived as far back as the Wars of the Roses: railways, iron-clad steam-ships, the Crystal Palace, the Crimean War.

184

'But it were in Ilkley a chap called William Butterfield saw summat even stranger nor Potter Thompson did. He were on his way to open t'door of the bath-house by the wells when he noticed the birds singin' fit to bust their feathers off. He thowt little of it, till he come to turn bath-house key: and it wouldn't turn, but spun round and round as though it were bewitched. Then he forced t'door with his shoulder, did William, and what dost think he saw inside? Why, a whole lot of people swimmin' and playin' in t'water, all dressed in green and none of 'em longer nor my arm. Well, William felt he'd like to have a word wi' 'em, not having seen owt like 'em before; but he could think of nowt sensible, so he shouted out, "Hello there!" And at that they took fright and scampered off, squeakin' and jabberin' in a language he didn't know, and he never in his life again saw one o' them People.'

'Why do you call them people, instead of fairies?' Lilian asked. Amos put a finger to his lips.

'Hush! It doesn't do to name 'em. Tha may call 'em the People, or the Other People, or the Folk, or what tha likes, but not *that*.'

Mary was standing in the doorway, hands on hips. 'What a load of rubbish, Amos Ellershaw! I never heard the like of it. I'm surprised at thee.'

'But he believes in it,' Lilian said earnestly. 'I can tell he does – don't you?'

He nodded gravely. 'Doesn't do not to believe.'

Mary sniffed. 'Next time I see one of them little green people I'll believe, too. I'll believe I've etten summat as didn't agree wi' me.'

Since coming back to Stainbeck Lilian had slept deeply, the refreshing sleep chloral had never brought. The place was so quiet at night, only the occasional cries of owls and their small prey, the sough of wind through the orchard trees, the baa of a sheep in a distant field. But on this night she woke with a start, wide awake in a second with her heart thudding.

The night was moonless. Only a faint square lighter than the rest of the room showed where the window was. She was conscious of a presence in the room – nothing to fear if it were Mary or Amos stolen downstairs to make sure all was well with her after so much weird tale-telling. The thought had barely flashed through her mind before she knew that it was neither of them. She shut

185

her eyes and pulled the sheet round her face. Then the voice spoke.

'Lilian? Can you hear me? Then look. Uncover your eyes and look.'

In spite of every instinct she did so. Against the darkness was Leoline's face, illuminated by some invisible lamp, shining, almost phosphorescent, red lips and pink skin, butter-yellow hair and beard, like a perfect balloon in the shape of a head.

'Lilian? You can't move, can you.' It was true. Her limbs seemed to be tied to the bed by invisible cords. Just a movement of her arm would have found candle and matches on the bedside table, but the arm lay paralysed beside her.

'Listen to me, Lilian. I hold you as fast as if I lay upon your body, pinning you down. Do you remember when I did that, Lilian?'

Her lips tried to form 'No', but were powerless to move.

'Shall I tell you how I hold you so fast, Lilian? Have you forgotten the lock of hair I cut from your head, that day? It lies beside Lizzie's, the red tress that came away from her skull when they took the poems. And another lock, Lilian, that you never saw. Because of the hair I have power over the women who wore it, and so I found you out, Lilian, though I don't know where you lie tonight. My spirit has sought yours at the hour when you are alone and defenceless, and you must answer it.' There was a pause, in which the face seemed to grow in size and intensify in brightness. 'Tell me where you are, Lilian.'

She knew that her lips could form no words, but that her thoughts would tell him what he needed, and she fought to control them pushing the name of the cottages and the village out of her mind, trying to keep it a blank, but certain things would not be suppressed.

'Yorkshire,' said the voice, complacent. 'And a house of grey stone. Not enough, Lilian, not enough.' Then, coaxing, 'You promised to play the Game of Love and Death. Now keep your promise and tell me. Where are you?'

Two things kept her from telling. The knowledge that he was not physically in the room, and the necessity for focussing on something that was not the place where she was. Her mind obeyed her. Like the turning of a page the picture came before her eyes of herself and Jack, under the may tree at Lord's. She tried to blot him

186

out so that Leoline should not see him, only herself in her invalid chair, and the tree.

'That's wrong.' The tone was irritable. 'I said now, at this moment, at night. What are you showing me?'

Jack, she thought, Jack, help me, but would not visualise his face. After a moment of struggle she knew that the evil thing was beaten, unless she weakened. She heard the voice beginning to chant. 'I conjure you, go to her, Melchidael, Baresches, Zazel, Firiel, Malcha, and all those who are with thee! I conjure you . . .'

Then she fainted, and her mind slipped from his power.

In the morning everything was blessedly normal. Mary came in with breakfast and a copy of last week's *Yorkshire Post*, dropped in by a neighbour. When she drew the curtains soft morning light filled the room, from grey skies in which the sun was just beginning to gleam.

'I'm told there's summat in this about Women's Rights,' Mary said, briskly holding the paper. 'Marched to Parlyment, a crowd of 'em did, shoutin' for the Vote. As if we'd not enough to do!'

Lilian smiled, answered, drank a cup of hot strong tea, propped up with the extra pillow Mary put behind her back. But for a heavy drained feeling, she might have passed an ordinary night with a bad dream somewhere in the middle of it. She tried to settle into the comfortable everyday world, the clatter from the kitchen, Amos's hammer ringing in the workshop, the song of birds. The nightmare would fade and go away, as nightmares do if left alone.

Yet this one hung obstinately in the air around her. In her mind's eye she saw vividly the frighteningly real face and heard the insinuating voice. Leoline had not been in the room physically; that was impossible. If he had been only the figment of a dream, why should she have dreamed his words in such detail? Whose was the third lock of hair which she had not seen? Whose names were those he had recited? None she had ever heard. She could only remember the sound of them, a sort of Biblical sound. They were certainly not the names of angels or archangels. Could they be devils?

The memory came to her that Augustus had called when she was ill and offered her Communion, and she had refused it. What was it he had said? 'Why, Lilian? Is it as I suspect, are you in the power of something infernal?'

187

Of course it was ridiculous to believe in such things. Yet . . . Amos's tales of mystery, told with such conviction, had prepared her mind for anything strange to happen. Perhaps Potter Thompson had indeed seen King Arthur and his knights – perhaps William Butterfield really had disturbed the Other People bathing. If such legends had lasted for centuries, might there not be some truth in them? And if so . . .

By mid-morning the memory of the vision had still not gone away, and she was beginning to be very frightened. Leoline had tried once and would try again. Perhaps even now he was fixing his thoughts on a sure way to break the barrier of her mind. Then he would come for her, not his shadow but himself, in all his unhealthy healthiness, persuading the Ellershaws that he was her rightful guardian, entitled to take her away, and she would never see Jack again – or anyone else, for long, because Leoline would kill her slowly for his own pleasure.

Mary came in and dumped a basket of white currants in her lap.

'Wilt get them picked for me? It's a fiddlin' job but there's plenty of time. What's up? Tha looks peaky.'

Impossible to tell such a wild story to the down-to-earth Mary.

'I had a rather bad night, that's all. Something disturbed me.'

'A fox, most like. They're out and about a lot these neets.'

Lilian picked away automatically at the currants, plucking off their little stems and separating them, piling them into a growing heap of pearly fruits. She was glad of the work, fiddling as it was. At least it kept her fingers occupied, if not her mind. Perhaps she could speak to Amos, in a round-about way. Anxiously she waited for him to come in for his dinner. He always looked into her room then, with a cheerful word.

When his head appeared round the door, she held out a hand to him.

'Do come in, Mr Ellershaw. I want to ask you something.'

'Ask away, lass.'

She hesitated. 'I don't know how to say it. You know so many stories about magic . . . do you know any about fighting spells – evil spells, curses and such things?'

'Nay! what a question. What dost want to know for?'

After all, it was impossible to tell him outright. 'I . . . I'm trying

188

to make up a story myself. About someone in the power of a sort of magician, someone who wants to be free.'

Amos stroked his chin. 'Well, now. There's a tale . . . aye, it comes to me. If a witch can be caught when she's turned hersen into a cat there's words can be said to howd her fast and tak' her power from her.'

'I don't think that would do. This – witch – wouldn't be caught easily. It would have to be a kind of protection the person could put round themselves. I don't know what kind – I thought you might.'

'Eh, dear. There's certain plants, like the rowan and the ash; and there's the charms o' fire and salt – and there's drawin' blood from the witch, or gettin' howd of an image of her. Any of that do, like?'

'I don't think so. You see, the witch is a long way off from the person who's being bewitched.'

'That makes it harder, then. What about sleepin' wi' a Bible under t'pillow? Yon's said to be a powerful charm.'

Lilian knew she had come to the end of her resources, and his. 'That sounds very good,' she said. 'My – heroine ought to try it. What a great many stories you know, Mr Ellershaw. Why don't you write them down and make a book of them, and call it *Tales of Yorkshire*? I'm sure people would enjoy reading them.'

'Because I can't write,' he said, simply.

The long, fine afternoon, sending a flood of sunshine into the room, ought to have dispelled night-fears. Lilian lay gazing out to the bright fields where sheep grazed peacefully, or slept, still in their thick fleeces until shearing-time, and shadows of white clouds moved over a far-off hill. Yet the heaviness would not lift from her heart. A strange, sinking feeling which she associated with childhood calamities weighed her spirits down; it could not be true, that a man in London could influence her here in this peaceful place, drawing her back to him. But she knew it was, whatever reason might say.

She thought, and thought, until it was clear at last what she must do. Mary, asked for writing-paper and envelope, produced after much searching a few small, old-looking, yellowing sheets and an unexpectedly grand envelope with a crest on it.

'I don't know where they come from – happen Burton Castle, for I found 'em in a drawer o't'press. That'll be old Countess's coat-of-arms.' Mary hovered. 'Tha'll be writin' to thi mother?'

'Yes.' Mary nodded, looking relieved, and went out swiftly.

It was not an easy letter to write.

'Dear Mamma,

I am very sorry for all the worry you must have had over me. A very great deal of trouble happened in London. I felt that if I stayed there I should become even more ill than when you saw me, and I thought it best to leave with a friend who kindly offered to bring me here. I know now that I should have come home but I was afraid you would not understand.

'I think it best if I do not bother the kind people I am staying with any more. If you feel you can forgive me, will you ask Uncle Lewis to send for me? I am much better and shall be very happy to be home again.'

It was not true, of course. She dreaded going home to endure the fire of questions and reproaches, Mamma's tears and Nelly's gibes. But at least there she would be safe; Mamma would never let Leoline take her away. Augustus would come, and perhaps she would be able to accept him, if he would still have her. Then the whole dreadful chapter would be ended.

And the Ellershaws would be safe from evil visitations.

There was the coming night to face, of course, perhaps several nights, as the letter would not go until tomorrow. She asked Mary for the family Bible, and got a sidelong, questioning look from those sharp eyes.

'I haven't read the Bible enough lately,' she said. 'When I see my clergyman cousin he'll scold me dreadfully.'

When the Bible was brought to her she flicked idly through its pages, then turned back to the flyleaf where in a large hand were written the names of the three children who had died, Thomas, William and Jane. Such short lives, the eldest only four. It was very sad, but what a lot of life's troubles they had been spared, Jack's little brothers and sister. Turning over the chapters of the New Testament, a sentence leapt out at her: 'Be not overcome

190

of evil, but overcome evil with good.' That was it: that was what she must do.

Out in the garden, at the front of the house, there was a sudden commotion: the wheels of a cart, a horse's whicker, men's voices. Then, in a moment, Amos coming in bustling with news.

'Didsta hear, lass? Jack's home.'

CHAPTER FIFTEEN

'How've you been keeping, then?' asked Jack, surveying her improved looks with the satisfaction of a farmer inspecting a prize pig.

'Very well, thank you. Or thanks to your mother and father.' She was determined not to show him how much she had missed him and longed for him to come back. Only a week, yet it had seemed months. She wished desperately that she had some other dress than the old brown one.

'Well, well. So I see. Been looking after you, have they?'

'Beautifully. I hope you had some good cricket?'

'Oh, aye. Fair.'

'You look very pleased with yourself,' she said tartly.

'I am that,' he replied, his eyes still on her. 'I got you here, didn't I, away from yon lot in London.'

'Jack.' She had not intended to tell him about the vision, or whatever it had been, now that she had written the letter which would put him and his parents out of danger from Leoline and his forces of evil. But because he was there, so strong and tall and calm, she poured out to him the story of the horrible face hanging in the air, and the words it had spoken. 'Do you think it was just a bad dream – or could there have been something in it, like your father's stories?'

'Dad's been telling you some of his tales, has he? Well, it's my opinion there's a lot to 'em. They were told before his day, and they'll be told after. Other folk believe in 'em. I do miself, until proved otherwise, like I believe in this electricity lighting they've got in America. I've never seen it, but if they say it works, it does. Well, then.'

'Oh, dear. If you believe it, then I suppose I must.'

'Aye, you'd better. "Resist the Devil and he will flee from you." '

'But how? I don't know any spells, or whatever one would need.

I borrowed your family Bible, look, and I found this text.' She pointed it out.

' "Overcome evil with good." That's sense, any road.' He was looking thoughtfully down at her, lying fully dressed on top of the bed. 'Lilian, do you trust me?'

'Of course! You asked me that once before.'

'I ask it for a reason. Do you remember that time in your garden, when I lifted you out of your chair, and your sister thought we were up to summat?'

She laughed shortly. 'Do I remember! But for that I should never have been sent to London, and none of this would ever have happened.'

Jack looked startled. 'You were *sent* ... that's not what they said when I called at your place after I'd been turned off by Sir Lewis. Some sort o' holiday, they made it sound like.'

'Oh, I suppose it was, at first, but I was certainly sent to London to get me away from you. But I never knew Uncle Lewis had dismissed you – how dreadfully unfair, not like him at all!'

'So you never got my letter.'

'No, of course not. Wouldn't I have answered, if I had?'

'Seems to me we're goin' round in circles. I wrote you and left it on the post-tray at the Hall, to be carried by hand.'

'Well, nobody did carry it by hand – or if they did, they kept it from me. How wicked! Who could have done it? Mamma, I suppose – she would.'

'Aye ...' He was remembering his bitter disappointment that day in the neglected garden, when he thought she had gone blithely to London without a word, and he had told himself he was finished with women. But now was the time that mattered.

'Never mind that, it's past and done with,' he said. 'When I asked you if you trusted me, and if you remembered the time I set you on your feet, I were going on to say – do you remember you said it didn't hurt?'

'Yes, quite well.' And the delight of being in his arms, the first embrace she had ever known.

'And at King's Cross, before – ' he allowed himself a smile – 'before I loaded you on yon trolley?'

'And I was so snappish to you. I'm sorry.' She gave him her hand, feeling the warmth and strength of his encompassing it.

193

'Lilian,' he said. 'Will you try it again – standing up? Just to see if what I think's true. Come on, easy now. I won't let you fall.'

Gently he lifted her from the bed, holding her tightly, and set her down within the circle of his arms, her feet on the ground. His eyes questioned her; she shook her head, smiling.

'It doesn't hurt at all, my back, I mean. My legs feel ridiculous – as though I hadn't got any.'

'Tha has, lass,' he said softly. 'And right pretty ones.'

'How do you know? You haven't seen them!'

'I will.' He bent his head to kiss her, a long kiss in which she forgot that she was standing, for only the third time in more than eight years; forgot everything but Jack.

His mother's outraged voice came from the doorway. 'Well! I don't know! Whativer art doin', our Jack? And Lilian, think shame on thiself!'

'Now, Mum, don't judge too hasty,' he said, laying Lilian gently down again. 'I can explain.'

'Tha'd best get on wi' it,' said his mother grimly.

He talked to the three of them that evening, gathered in the parlour, where he had made Lilian a couch of rugs and pillows on the floor by the fire, his father in the chair he had made himself, his mother upright and stern in one with no arms and an uncompromisingly straight back, like her own.

'I thought,' said Jack, 'the first time I set eyes on her, as such a bonny lass couldn't be all that ill. There's signs and tokens on a person struck down mortally, and there was none on her. And it came to me, happen they'd been wrong.'

'What did they tell thee, Lilian, when thy pony threw thee?' Amos asked.

'That my back was broken, at first. Then that it wasn't, only that there was some bad injury to it.'

'And they never tried to make thee walk?'

'Oh, no. They said it would have killed me. At least, I think so – it was so long ago.'

'Parts as don't get used rot away,' Mary put in.

'Go on, Mam, cheer us all up,' Jack said. 'Never mind that – what's to be done now? I can't tell, I know nowt of medical matters, nor does any of us, unless it's you, Mam, and I don't reckon mid-wifery'll be much help. As to doctors . . .'

Mary snorted. 'Owd Walker? Fit to dish out cough-cure, nowt else. I wouldn't ask him to a sick cat.'

Amos, who had been quietly smoking and gazing into the flames, said suddenly, 'Wat Harrison.'

'Who, Dad?'

'Son o' the Wizard of Leeds. Owd Henry Harrison, as used to tell fortunes and concoct love-potions till he got himself mixed up wi' a murder case, and niver could do right after. Wat's every bit as clever, only he won't practise, but for healin' works. I've had a few cracks wi' him.' He disregarded his wife's suspicious glance. 'He's as good as a doctor, ony day. I could get him to look in, by Tom the carrier.'

They sat in silence, Lilian darting bright glances from father to son, Mary brooding, for she had much to ponder in this new situation between Jack and the strange young woman. She was prepared for anything to happen, when Jack became set on a thing. If he wanted Lilian cured, then she would be, and it would solve a lot of problems. Reluctantly she nodded.

'Get him fetched.'

Wat Harrison was a small, weasel-like man, ginger-haired and sharp-nosed. He might have been any age or from any trade. Brought up in the shadow of his gifted, weak, villainous father, he was stripped of illusions and joyless. All that concerned him was that his claw-like hands held the power of diagnosis and healing and that he must employ them to live, without resorting to witches' tricks. Brusquely he ordered Mary to turn Lilian over and bare her back so that he could examine it. When she hesitated, he roughly moved to do it himself, until she restrained him, unbuttoning the limp green dress and pulling up the camisole under it, undoing further buttons and tapes until the long smooth-skinned back was bare to his gaze. He prodded the vertebrae one by one with sharp fingers, pressed down suddenly with both hands on the small of the back, jabbed at the coccyx. He sounded disappointed as he asked, 'Any o' that hurt you?'

'No. Only your hands are cold.'

195

With a sound of disgust, he rolled down his frayed sleeves. 'Nowt wrong wi' you. Get up.'

'*What* did you say?'

'Get up. Get on yer feet. No sense in lyin' there like a log. Get her dressed, Missis. She's got muscles like jelly that want exercise, so see to it. You're to do nowt for her, hear that? From now onwards she's on her own – should ha' been these eight years.'

In the parlour he took the money Jack proffered, ignored thanks and questions, and grumbled his way out, an uncouth, graceless angel of mercy. Jack found Lilian dressed again and dazed with Harrison's words.

'He says I'm to do everything for myself. But I can't! Not yet.'

'You can try, can't you?' Some instinct told Jack that miracles were not worked without effort, and that he must contribute to this one. 'Come on, sit up,' he said. 'Swing your legs over to t'floor. Now move 'em, one after t'other. That's right.'

Mary intervened. 'It's not decent, Jack Ellershaw! If anyone's to help Lilian it ought to be a woman.'

'You've not time, Mam, and I have, till I'm wanted elsewhere. I've got ten days.'

Ten days of torture for Lilian, of sick giddiness when she was held upright. Jack had turned into a ruthless tormentor who refused to let her rest, however she pleaded with him.

'Don't, Jack, don't! Oh, please let me alone. I can't stand any more, truly. Please, Jack!' she pleaded, as he half-dragged her on another weary round of the room. For all the good her begging did, he might have been stone-deaf. Painfully she put one foot in front of the other, each step an effort, feeling him take less and less of her weight, so that the fear of falling was added to her misery. For two days they had been doing this, Jack relentless in his determination to make her walk alone, as unsparing of her as though she had been some raw lad who had come to him for cricket coaching. His set face and pitiless voice made him seem almost an enemy. 'I hate you!' she cried out once. He answered calmly, 'Hate away.'

The only mercy she got from him was when a stabbing pain struck her side, the revenge of long-unused muscles convulsing in a stitch. Then he let her rest. She came to long for the moment when the exercises were over and he would put her back on the bed and go away. It was bliss beyond words to lie still, helpless again, free from the torture of her limbs and the dizziness in her head as the floor seemed to swing up to meet her. Unreasonably she longed to have been left undisturbed, a petted invalid. There was no petting now. If Mary felt pity for the ordeal she was undergoing, there was no sign of it. Anything she dropped on the floor she must get for herself, Mary said.

'But I can't walk yet!'

'Tha can crawl. And if tha wants t'privy in t'yard, I'll give thee an arm to it. That's all.'

Lilian wept silently into her pillow when she was left alone. She knew instinctively that Jack had no time for crying women. It was Amos who heard an irrepressible sob, and came to comfort her.

'Now then, now then. It's all for thy own good, Lilian. Our Jack knows what he's doin'.'

'He's killing me, that's what he's doing.'

'Nay, he's not, he'd not harm a hair o' thy head. He fairly dotes on thee.'

'He's a funny way of showing it,' Lilian sniffed. 'He's never even said he cares about me at all – not properly.'

'Aye, well, we don't go in much for that sort o' talk.' But Amos's voice was kind, and it was he who gently massaged her swollen ankles and put a pillow under them to keep the swelling down.

On the tenth day Lilian woke from a particularly restful sleep feeling less wretched. When Jack came in he knew at once that the worst was over.

'Come on,' he said, 'we'll try something different.' He pulled a chair across the room to within three feet of her bed. 'Now. Get up and walk to that.'

'But I can't!'

'You can if I steady you. Catch hold.' As she lowered herself off the bed he took her hand firmly. 'That's for balance. Now.'

The stretch of floor looked like an endless waste of desert. Tentatively, gripping his hand desperately, she took one step after another, expecting every second to fall, until to her own astonishment she was grasping the chair, and standing alone.

For the first time in her painful labours he smiled, and said, 'Well done, lass. Hold on.'

'I did it! I walked!'

'Didn't I tell thee? Now, the next part's easy.' Seating her on the chair, he pulled out the table from its place by the wall and moved it near to her. 'Get up and go to it. It's nobbut a step.'

She reached the table, half-falling on it but recovering herself. Then he told her to hold on to the edge and propel herself round it, as many times as she could. Slowly, laboriously, she made herself circle it four times, to his satisfaction. By the end of that day, with rests, she was walking, rather than crawling round it. Only when she attempted to get back to the bed alone she felt herself falling, then Jack's arms round her, holding her safely. She buried her face against his coat. 'I do love you, Jack,' she said. 'I love you so much.'

'And so do I thee, my good lass. Never think owt else. I know I've been a bit rough, but I had to be.'

'I know.' She clung to him until he set her gently down, saying, 'I've got to go; I'm playing at Manchester tomorrow. But I've two things to give thee, first.'

One was a stout ash-stick, to serve her as a crutch when she could trust herself on her feet without the support of the table. It would steady her, and, she realised joyfully, free her from the humiliating necessity of Mary's ungentle escort out to the yard.

The second was a small paper parcel, clumsily wrapped and tied with string. With difficulty she undid its awkward knots, and took out a tiny handkerchief, of the finest cotton, delicately embroidered with lilies of the valley.

'I bought it for thee,' Jack said shyly, 'all that time ago, after I'd left Sir Lewis. I was minded to give it to Mam, but then I thought . . . I might just see thee again. So I kept it.' He was glancing at her anxiously, wondering how she would take the humble gift.

She put it to her lips, then against her cheek. 'It's the most beautiful present I've ever had. I'll keep it always. You can bury it with me.'

'I'll try and think on,' Jack said gravely. 'Speaking of burying, did I ever ask thee to wed me?'

Lilian raised her eyebrows. 'I don't believe you did. How curious. Well, I hope you're going to ask me now, because I intend to say yes.'

He took her in his arms, and for a long time they said nothing, only kissed and held each other tightly. Then she asked, 'Would you have wanted me if I'd still been a cripple, Jack?'

'Crippled, or maimed, or blind. Aye.'

She nodded, satisfied. 'Your mother doesn't like me.'

'She'll come round. And it's me that's wedding thee, not Mam. Can you like *her*? And Dad, and the rough way we talk? It's not what a lady's used to, I know that.'

She took his hand and looked at it critically, so long-fingered and finely shaped for all its brownness and strength. 'See that? That's a gentleman's hand, if ever I saw one. You could be a duke's son, to look at you, but I'm very glad you're not. I love your Dad, and I love the way you talk, and I'll be talking like it myself before long – and I love you most of all, so don't be a fool, Jack Ellershaw.'

When he had left for the Manchester train she opened the family Bible and found the Book of Ruth. 'Whither thou goest I will go; where thou lodgest I will lodge; thy people shall be my people, and thy God my God.' It was not the sort of thing one said to Jack, for fear of embarrassing him.

She kept the little handkerchief buttoned up inside her bodice, between her camisole and her breasts, taking it out very often. When she had first seen the tiny embroidered lilies the memory had come back to her of those other lily-flowers, long, stiff, and pale, with their sweet sickening odour of undertakers' parlours; and the card attached to them, and its message, 'Liliae Liliarum'. She would not think of them or it ever again.

And the sudden realisation came to her that the vision of Bevis had not returned. She tore up the letter to her mother.

The explosion in the house in Cheyne Row which followed the discovery of Lilian's flight was the noisiest it had known in its century and a half of life. Frederica, who prided herself on her calm sophistication, frankly gave way to hysterics when she found there was nothing to be got out of Digby. Firm and intrepid he stood, saying nothing beyond, 'I'm sorry, Mamma. I don't know where she is, honestly. Yes, I could find out, but I won't because you'd only go after her and stir up trouble. I've written to Aunt Florence to put her mind at rest. Believe me, I know what's best for her, or I hope I do. Anyway, she ain't your daughter or even your ward; so what right have you to interfere?'

'We'll see what right I have. I've the right to report you to your commanding officer, and I shall.'

'Report away, Mamma.'

When Digby rejoined his brigade it was to find that she had done just that. From his C.O. he got only raised eyebrows and the comment, 'Had a busy leave, I gather?', but, to his utter horror, there came a summons to the royal presence. Brave soldier that he was, he wished himself a thousand miles away, facing the ultimate perils of war, when that summons came by the hand of a supercilious page. He had only confused ideas about what the Queen could do to him. It was not her province to order a court-martial, and in any case his supposed offence had not been a military one. The only possibility was a kind of super-wigging, the equivalent of a lecture followed by confinement to one's room on bread and water.

He kept drawing deep breaths as he waited outside the heavy oaken door of the room in Her Majesty's private suite at Windsor. From within came muffled words, followed by the opening of the door, which to Digby seemed to take at least twenty minutes.

Then he was in the room, standing on a Turkey-red patterned carpet, dimly aware of large gold-framed portraits frowning down on him, ghostly white busts, and a great many framed photographs. He was face to face with the lady he had seen so often at a respectful distance. Now she was only a few yards from him, seated in a chair of gilded wood and heavily embroidered upholstery. At close quarters she looked very tiny, as she was, less than five feet, her stoutness covered by the flowing black silk dress, heavily trimmed at the low neckline with white lace. A white lace cap after the style of Mary Queen of Scots crowned the greying hair that had once been golden. The plump fingers were loaded with rings, a miniature of her late husband was attached to a broad glittering bracelet on her wrist. All this Digby took in much as a man on the scaffold might take in the scene around him in sharp detail. Somewhere in the room a lady-in-waiting stood, correct and upright, but Digby only had eyes for the cold expressionless gaze meeting his.

'Well, Captain Stevens-Clyne?' she said. Her voice was high, almost fluting, of a youthfulness that belied her appearance. Digby bowed.

200

'Your Majesty.'

'We hear you have been concerned in an abduction.'

'I . . . not quite an abduction, Ma'am. More of a rescue operation.'
He was amazed to hear his own voice coming out clear and strong.

'Perhaps you would be so good as to explain that.'

'Er, the thing is rather involved, Ma'am. A relation of mine, a
young lady, had come under very bad influences.'

'Indeed? What kind?' Victoria sounded genuinely interested.

'A sort of corruption, Ma'am, connected with drugs and other
undesirable things. In the, er, artistic world.' How on earth could
he explain Leoline Bevis to those august ears, exposed by the lace
cap as though they intended to miss nothing?

'Ah,' she said, the prominent blue eyes now fairly sparkling with
interest, 'do you mean the new school of artists? Red hair and blue
shadows, sickly young women, that kind of thing?' Digby indicated
that he did. The Queen shook her head.

'We have never permitted any of them to paint a portrait of
ourselves or any of our family. Mr Millais has certainly improved
a great deal in his style – perhaps you admire his painting "My
First Sermon", Captain? Charming, but the unfortunate circumstances of his marriage are impossible to overlook. Things were
very different in Sir Edwin Landseer's young days. Well, continue;
your young relative was being influenced against her will by one
of these loose-living artists?'

'Yes, Ma'am. I believe he intended to marry her. My mother
favoured the match, I did not. She, my cousin, has very delicate
health and I thought he would not take proper care of her. Also,
I gathered her affections were otherwise engaged, and I . . . in short,
I helped her to run away.'

'And the young man of her choice – is he a friend of yours, a
military man?'

'No, Ma'am. He's a . . . well, he's a cricketer.'

'We don't entirely follow you, Captain.'

No, of course. Cricket to Her Majesty was something played at
country-house parties by young noblemen. 'He plays cricket pro-
fessionally, Ma'am,' he explained, 'for a living. He worked as a
gardener for a time, I believe, but his ambition was always to
succeed as a sportsman.'

The blue eyes, now that he could meet them more fearlessly,

were quite beautiful, and beaming with enthusiasm. '*Really?*' she exclaimed. 'A peasant, in fact. And Miss de Wentworth is of good family, we hear.' (So she had known about Lilian all along, the sly royal puss.) 'Well, we must say that is a most excellent thing, in our opinion. You must be aware, Captain, of the *extremely* bad relations existing in high-born families – child against father, father against child, and the *constant* struggle to maintain a large number of people who are not brought up to work for themselves. We detest what we call John Bullism, Captain, the putting-down of the poor by the rich.'

Victoria's gaze was piercing now. Young cavalry officers were high up on her list of those who ignored or were rude to servants. One of Prince Leopold's equerries had recently been dismissed the Household for offensiveness to his valet. All such unpleasant incidents were slights upon John Brown and the servants she regarded as her equals. But Captain Stevens-Clyne did not look that sort of arrogant young man at all, and he had certainly taken very commendable action on behalf of his cousin. Besides, the circumstances were extremely romantic, and the Queen had a deeply romantic heart.

'There is no greater thing in this world,' she continued, 'than the good, simple life, lived by good, simple people. We hope, we trust that your cousin will be very happy with this young peasant. Ancient blood *should* be strengthened by healthy stock. We wish it were so in our own family.'

Digby felt like a man who has marched out to meet a firing-squad and been presented with a gold medal instead. He had heard through Penelope and Lady Ponsonby of the Queen's democratic principles, but it had never struck him that they might be quite so strong or so practical. He murmured confused agreement and thanks until a diplomatic cough from the lady-in-waiting told him the audience was at an end. A tiny, fat white hand was suddenly stretched to him. He kissed it, feeling more affection and admiration for his sovereign than he had ever felt on public occasions; and not merely because he had been let off the reprimand he had expected. Bowing out of the room backwards, as custom decreed, he saw her smiling, a bright, sweet girlish smile that banished the years.

202

CHAPTER SIXTEEN

Digby's letter arrived at the Dower House with all the impact of a thunderbolt through the roof. To call it a letter of explanation would have been an overstatement; he was a man of action, not a letter-writer. All Florence learned from her first horrified scanning of the large round handwriting was that Digby freely admitted having helped Lilian to go away with the man of her choice. Then followed something rambling about his mamma not having quite realised the unsuitability of a friend of his mother's who had also offered for Lilian's hand – 'a rotter if I ever saw one'. Lilian was very well and would be writing, he was sure, and he was his dear aunt's obedient Digby.

Florence fell into paroxysms of rage and fear, alternating with sheer disbelief. Nelly, subdued for once, listened to the same exclamations and questions repeated over and over again, proffered smelling-salts, brandy and burnt feathers, while Maggie muttered in the background.

'No, I've no idea where she could be, Mamma. I didn't know she had any friends, let alone beaux. And I don't think you'll get Digby to split, he's not that kind.'

'Then your brother must go and horsewhip him!'

'Arthur? Can you *see* it?' Florence had to admit to herself on reflection that she could not see her son, now working as a rather superior bank clerk in London, standing up to Digby, or even being made to understand what the whole outcry was about.

'It's very hard on me,' Nelly grumbled, 'being bothered with all this, when I'm getting married myself in September. Lil might have had a bit more thought for me, but then she never cared about anybody but herself.'

'Married?' Her mother hooted with hysterical laughter. 'Do you suppose Albert will want a bride whose sister has disgraced herself?

Oh, no, Eleanore, you may put *that* idea out of your head. We must all suffer for Lilian's sin.'

Nelly burst into tears. 'Albert *will* marry me! He's not like you, always fussing about what's proper and what ain't, and his family aren't anything but trade, and I don't see why it should all have to come out when nobody knows where Lil's gone to.' Mopping her eyes she added maliciously, 'She might have been murdered and never turn up, you know.'

Florence gave one shriek and fell into one of her States, in which Nelly and Maggie put her to bed. The doctor was summoned, and Augustus, who was more distressed than anybody, his life's hopes turned to ashes.

'Better dead, poor girl, better dead,' he said hopelessly, when Florence wept out to him Nelly's callous speculation. 'Who knows what pit of sin she may have fallen into? She refused to take the Sacrament from me. I thought then . . . I feared . . . but nothing so bad as this. There was a man painting her, when I called at Aunt's house; I disliked the look of him very much. The whole thing seemed to me very degenerate. Do you suppose she could have fallen into his power?'

Florence shook her head helplessly. 'How should I know? Oh, Augustus, it is too, too dreadful. Of course I shall let you know if any news comes; but I have little hope.'

News came in the form of a letter from Lilian, written upon extremely odd-looking paper with a crested envelope, the sight of which briefly raised Florence's hopes until she read the contents.

'Dear Mamma, I am afraid I must have caused you great anxiety in the past weeks. I can only plead that I needed time to work out my difficulties for myself. It would have done no good to ask for your guidance. Please do not blame Digby for his part, it was done for my good.

'I find it very hard to explain on paper what my situation was and is. I think it would be best if you were to come and see me, perhaps bringing Uncle Lewis if he would agree. Please do *not* bring Nelly. You will find me at the above address and I do assure you that everything is perfectly respectable, as I am sure you would wish it to be.

'Your affectionate daughter, Lilian.'

The cool, stiff letter enraged Florence almost more than Digby's had done. The arrogance of the girl! After all her family's fears for her, to write as if . . . as if . . . *oh*! The anti-climax was harder to bear than anything that had come before it.

Sir Lewis, taking the letter from her trembling hand, raised frosty eyebrows over the address, which he recognised.

' "Stainbeck Cottages"!' Florence raged. 'Such a low address. And Barnswood, where is that?'

'Not far off Doncaster. Lot of industry growing up round there, but mostly agriculture. I bought a fine chestnut in Doncaster once – won me a nice little packet in the St Leger.'

'Never mind about horses. What can a daughter of mine be doing in such a place, Lewis?'

Sir Lewis sighed. He had a deep loathing of explanations, scenes, emotions, all that sort of women's nonsense. He wished that Florence were a horse, to be pacified with a sugar-lump, an apple, and a smart slap on the neck; but since she was not he must tackle the beastly business of telling her what he knew. 'Now sit down, Florence, and calm yourself.'

When he had finished the silence between them was volcanic. Florence's small fists were clenched; he had never seen such a glare on any woman's face.

'That *gardener*,' she said at last. 'That impudent boy who started all the trouble.'

'Yes.'

'And you *knew*. Lewis, you *knew*!'

He took up a churchwarden pipe from the rack and began to clean it, a disgusting process to which Florence would have objected had she not been carried away by outrage.

'Not so much knew – guessed,' he said. 'I know you think I'm a stupid old bore, Florence, but I can see an inch beyond my nose. That young feller's as straight as they come, dam' nice chap, dam' good cricketer. Probably get into Wisden's Almanack with a few records one of these days, when he's a bit older. Went to see him play down at Woodhouse – beautiful, beautiful. He's got a straight drive that . . . all right, you don't want to know. Well, when Digby told me the state Lilian was in, I thought it'd do no harm to bring 'em together again, seeing she'd a fancy for him.'

'So you were in the plot, not just Digby,' Florence said bleakly. 'It seems everyone is against me.'

'Oh, come now, Flo. Tell you what, I'll take you down to Barnswood and we'll see what we shall see, eh?'

'I don't want your company, thank you.'

But she accepted it in the end, and a seat in his carriage.

The sun was warm on the hillside, Stainbeck Cottages basking in it among green vegetables and fruit-trees whose blossom was turning to fruit. Amos worked, bent half double, a few yards from the door. At the clatter of the carriage's arrival he straightened up painfully and shouted to those inside the house.

Florence walked stiffly up the stony path, Sir Lewis behind her. The small gnome-like man leaning on the spade was unworthy of her notice. She looked beyond him to whoever might be ready to receive her.

'Good day, missis,' he said, without touching his cap.

'I am Mrs de Wentworth,' she said haughtily. Lewis had warned her not to put on airs, but instinct was too strong for her. The house was at least large, not the tiny hovel she had expected. 'I believe my daughter is staying here.'

'You could say that,' Amos replied thoughtfully, sizing her up. 'Go on in, you'll likely find her.' He had been told to keep out of the way.

Lifting her skirt very high, as though treading on something obnoxious, Florence stepped over the threshold, through the open door into the sitting-room, dark after the bright sunlight outside. Lilian rose from her chair and stood, holding on to the back of it. 'Well, Mamma,' she said, not allowing her voice to tremble with the nervousness she felt. Weeks of slow, painful, tiring practice had gone into the effort she was making.

Florence stared, and gasped, then looked round at Lewis to see whether he was having the same hallucination. Obviously, he was.

'Well, by heck!' he exclaimed. 'What's all this, then, Lilian?'

'Good afternoon, Uncle Lewis. I'm very pleased to see you.'

'But you're on your feet!'

'Oh yes, I'm quite strong and well now.'

'I don't believe it!' Florence shouted, banging the tip of her parasol on the floor. 'This is some sort of trick. I want the truth now, Lilian, about this and everything else, at once!'

'No trick at all, Mamma.' Lilian moved to indicate the chairs by the fireplace, not letting them see that she kept one hand on her own. 'Please sit down.'

Florence remained standing, and Sir Lewis, out of courtesy, copied her, She stared at her daughter, hardly recognising her, feeling as though she were in an unpleasant dream. Lilian seemed taller, standing, than when she had been flat on her back. Her figure appeared to have filled out, or perhaps it was the plain gingham gown she wore and the pinafore over it, like any peasant woman, and her face was rosy and thickly freckled. Her hair, which Florence had last seen spread loosely over pillows, was neatly plaited and wound round her head in a double coronet. Any resemblance to a Tennysonian princess was quite gone. Florence fished frantically in her reticule for her smelling-salts, and applied them to her nose. She would very much like to have fainted, but it was beneath her dignity to do so in that house. She did, however, at last sit down, still staring unbelievingly at Lilian.

'I've told your mother all I know about this business, Lil,' Sir Lewis said. 'About Digby and your young man. Anything else, you'd better explain yourself.'

'There isn't a great deal to explain, Uncle. Jack and his family have been wonderfully kind and helpful to me, as you can see. I'm sorry to have caused so much trouble to you and Aunt Freddy.'

'Trouble! I don't think you realise what a terrible upset you've caused, you wicked girl,' said Florence. 'Your aunt and I have been quite prostrated with shock, and your poor sister too.'

'Yes, I'm sure. But I had to get away from London, or I would probably have died, and none of you would have understood even if I'd been well enough to tell you. I was being drugged, you see, by a man Aunt Freddy trusted. It's not easy to explain –'

'I want no more explanations, thank you. Kindly collect your clothes, if you have any respectable ones. The carriage is waiting to take us home.'

'Oh, but I'm not coming with you,' Lilian said mildly. 'This is my home now. Jack and I are going to be married at the end of this month. Isn't that so, Mrs Ellershaw?'

The tall woman who emerged from the kitchen, drying her hands on her apron, nodded. A fine woman, thought Sir Lewis. 'This is my future mother-in-law,' Lilian said. 'My mother and my uncle, Sir Lewis Hambleden.'

'Pleased to meet you,' Mary said, not sounding over-pleased. She and Florence exchanged stares, Florence's icy. Sir Lewis proffered his hand and shook Mary's.

'I am not aware that my permission has been asked for any marriage,' Florence said.

'No, Mamma, because it wasn't necessary – I'm twenty-one.'

'That has nothing to do with it. I have not even seen this . . . this *person* you propose to marry – except doing menial jobs in my garden.'

'Now, Flo . . .' Sir Lewis began warningly, but Mary had already taken up the gauntlet. She folded her arms across her bosom in the age-old manner of a working woman preparing for a fight, and her eyes flashed steely sparks. 'My son's never done a menial job in his born days,' she said. 'No more have I, nor my man. I'll thank thee to keep thy tongue off him. As for our Lilian here, it's quite right that they're goin' to wed. Tha's welcome to come if tha likes, or stop away if tha likes that better. It's nowt to me and I don't reckon it's a lot to Lilian, for all she's got to thank *thee* for.'

'Oh, indeed, madam? So my daughter's been talking against me, has she? Did she tell you of the long years when I was her only nurse, almost her only companion, when I did everything for her and cherished her like a little child?' Florence stopped, choking, giving Lilian the chance to say, 'Indeed I haven't been saying anything against you, Mamma, only that nobody in my own family took the trouble to find out whether I could walk or not, so it was left to Jack, and thanks to him I'm a normal woman instead of an invalid.'

'I won't permit it,' Florence gasped, her handkerchief to her face. 'You must have gone mad. This is some sort of plot or play-acting. I don't believe you can walk at all!'

'No?' Lilian summoned all her strength and courage to make herself cross the yard or so of floor that lay between herself and Sir Lewis, quite unsupported, the first time she had done so. She was very much afraid of falling, but determination kept her upright. By his side, she took his arm and clung to it, trying not to waver at all. He gave hers a small pressure, to show that he understood.

'Well,' Florence said sulkily, 'it's all very unnatural. I'm sure our own doctor . . . and then I paid for you to go to the Wells House. Surely they would have found out if you had been curable.'

'But they didn't, and I was, Mamma,' Lilian said patiently.

Florence played her last card. 'I shall stop this marriage.'

'Oh no, tha won't,' Mary said, moving menacingly nearer to the small woman who shrank back from her. 'I wasn't that keen to have your daughter in our family when I thowt she'd be useless to Jack, just another mouth to feed. But that's not the way of it any more. Besides, she's a good lass, right handy about the house, and she'll mak' him a good wife. So put that in thi pipe an' smoke it.'

'*Really!* Well, I must agree,' Florence said spitefully, 'she looks thoroughly at home – almost as common and low as you, madam. I won't say that I hope you'll be happy, Lilian. I merely hope that in time you'll discover the folly of all this, and remember that your poor mother was right after all. Come along, Lewis.'

Lilian said, 'Mamma, won't you try to understand? You were always so romantic, and this is a very romantic situation, you must agree, quite like one of your favourite poems. And if you could only see Jack – '

'I don't want to see Jack. I have no intention of seeing Jack. I want to see none of you again. Lewis!'

Sir Lewis gently detached Lilian's arm from his, and gave her a swift embarrassed kiss. 'You'll be hearing from me,' he whispered, and followed Florence out. In the garden they heard her scolding him for not taking her part.

Lilian watched them go, a lump gathering in her throat. It had not been easy to face her mother, or to say the things which would separate them for ever.

Mary, after the slightest hesitation, put an arm round her shoulders, ostensibly for support, but Lilian knew it was meant for comfort.

'Tha's been standin' too long. Come on, we've work to do, if other folks hasn't.'

Lilian read the letter again, forcing herself to take in the distastefulness of its subject. Digby hoped she was well, in spanking condition, as he put it. He had had a bit of a front-line battle with his mamma, but she had said nothing since and he was now thank-fully back in quarters and no longer under fire.

'I felt very concerned about the fellow Bevis, and sent Penny, who has nothing better to do, along to Somerset House to delve about in the registers for anything that was to be found out about him. There was no entry of birth, which considering they began in 1837 makes him either illegit. or much older than he looks. The only entry she could discover was in Marriages, March 1858, Lionel Bevis (did Mamma not say his name was something fancier?) to Alice Hazell, sempstress, of Oxford, she being aged 21 and only able to sign with a cross for her name. Penny then searched through Deaths and found Alice Bevis, wife of Lionel, dead in November 1860 of a wasting fever. I don't know what you may make of this, cousin, but it don't seem healthy to me. Penny now tells me she will require spectacles before the age of 30.'

Jack read the letter expressionlessly, folded it and returned it to Lilian. Whatever she was going to say died on her lips. Some-times one did not ask questions. He was going south again for a match at the Surrey Oval ground.

Rain washed out play on the last day of the match, which for once left Jack unmoved by restlessness and frustration. It suited his purposes very well. He was standing outside the front door of Tudor House, Cheyne Walk. The sky was leaden grey, the river reflecting it darkly. Rain formed pools in the garden path and dripped pattering from the overgrown trees, large cold drops finding their way down Jack's collar. He thought that London was on the whole a dreary, sodden place, where rain was a different element from the clean rain of the north country. And there seemed nobody to answer the bell, though he could hear it clanging mourn-fully in the recesses of the house.

The door, swollen with damp, opened laboriously. The man who stood before him was middle-aged, shortish and shabby. His head was balding, his eyes wild and staring. This was not the person Jack was seeking.

'Yes?' the man said. 'What do you want? I don't know you, do I?'

'No.'

'Well, come in, no point in standing there dripping.'

The hall was dark, damp-feeling. The owner of the house, if it was he, was fumbling with a lamp on a table, which when lit illuminated dark walls, shadowy passages, dim pictures.

'Mr Rossetti,' Jack said, at a venture, putting together pieces of the description Lilian had given him.

'Yes. Good, you didn't ring the bell by mistake – so often they do, wanting all sorts of things, from a bed for the night to a pound of dry biscuits.' He held the lamp close to Jack. 'You're after some modelling, I take it? I'm afraid you've come to the wrong man. I don't undertake male subjects these days. You want Burne-Jones. Muscular nudes are his line, not mine.'

Jack was saved from an angry reply by the realisation that the man was quite serious. 'I'm not a model, no fear,' he said, mildly enough.

'Ah. Pity, really, you're quite a Stunner. Lorenzo, Porphyro. No Italian blood by any chance?'

'Not as I know of.'

'Roman, then.' Rossetti nodded, satisfied. 'Did you know there are pockets of pure Roman among the English? I can always recognise the breed. My father came from Vasto in the Abruzzi.' His musical voice was slurred, and Jack detected a whiff of whisky on the air. A small pale shape materialised from the shadows and moved to Rossetti's side. It was a miniature deer, lightish chestnut in colour, so far as could be seen in the dim hall, and seemed quite tame, regarding the stranger with dark lustrous eyes. 'Sabra,' Rossetti said, patting its neck, round which was an engraved collar. 'The last of my menagerie. All the others died, or ran away. I don't know why.'

Tentatively Jack stretched out a hand to the deer, expecting it to retreat or vanish. But it advanced timidly, one small hoof after the other, and tentatively licked Jack's hand. He stroked its soft ears.

'Well, blow me!' said Rossetti. 'She's never done that before. Don't like the smell of paint or cigarettes, I daresay.'

211

'She wouldn't. What she needs is fresh air. What d'you feed her on?'

'Oh . . . lettuce, cabbage leaves, that sort of thing. I thought they'd suit her. But perhaps you're right.'

Jack reflected that it was no wonder the rest of the menagerie had died or run away if they were kept in such unnatural conditions by their pathetic master. But he had not come there to give advice on pet-keeping.

'You've a man called Leoline Bevis living here, I'm told,' he said.

'Leoline.' The artist appeared to muse. 'Yes, Leoline. He keeps a studio at the back. Perhaps you're going to model for him?' he added hopefully.

'I tell you I'm not a model – sir.' Jack was growing exasperated. 'I want a few words with him, that's all. He'll not be pleased to see me, so I'd best get it over with, if you'll kindly tell me where I can find him.'

Rossetti shrugged. 'How do I know who's in the house, and who not? They come and go, all sorts of people : this is Liberty Hall, you know. We might take a look in the studio.' He led Jack down a dark corridor into a great room full of artists' clutter, the dark-papered walls showing lighter squares where pictures had hung. 'My own studio. Madox Brown took the pictures away in case they deteriorated, when I went to Kelmscott. But don't let anyone tell you I can't paint any more – I paint better than ever. Good painting is just good carpentry, just good carpentry.'

'My dad's a bit of a carpenter, but I never knew him turn his hand to painting,' Jack said, looking round with distaste. The small deer had disappeared : he didn't blame it. A woman entered, a large billowing female whose once-golden hair was now brassy with dye, and whose voluptuous features had coarsened with time and wore a look of easily-roused temper. Her dress was a bright blue loose robe with a dirty fringed shawl round the shoulders, and round her plump neck were at least six strings of beads. Long gilt earrings set with artificial gems swung from her rather large ears. Fanny Cornforth was no longer the dazzling Monna Vanna, Fiammetta, the Kissed Mouth.

'Ah, Elephant,' Rossetti said with relief. He was finding Jack's company uncomfortable. 'This young man is . . .'

'Not come for money, I 'ope?' she snapped. ' 'Cause it's run out. There ain't none in the kitty, and if you wants your supper tonight you'll 'ave to shell out, that's what.'

Rossetti sighed. 'Oh, dear Elephant, you and your economies. Look in the drawer in my bureau – I'm sure there's plenty there.'

'Not a penny. Come on, I know you've got some of the ready.'

He fished in various pockets and produced three sovereigns. 'This is all I have, truly, Fan.' She took it smartly. 'Do you know if Leo Bevis is in the house?'

'No, I don't, nor care neither, him and his bottles of wine costing I don't know 'ow much a week.' She flounced off, Rossetti looking after her with a smile of affectionate resignation. Jack followed him to the back of the house and through a door.

'This is Leo's studio.'

Inside the room Jack paused, looking, overcome by a growing sense of shock. The face of the woman in the many portraits was very nearly Lilian's face. There was a different expression, a sadness and a looking for help; yet he had seen that too, before he had rescued her.

Rossetti was watching him. 'My late wife,' he said, 'Lizzie. She was my model till her death. These are Leo's copies.'

'She reminds me of somebody,' Jack said, staring from one version of the woman to another.

'Of Alice, perhaps. Leo's wife. But that was a long time ago. You would only have been a child, surely.'

'Not Alice.'

'Poor Alice. Yes, she was quite like Lizzie. That was why Leo married her, we all knew. Poor little thing. He was quite devoted to Lizzie, but she, she . . . There was another one, too, a lovely creature he used to bring here.' He broke off suddenly. 'Why have you come here to remind me of these things? I don't want to talk about them. My friends don't remind me. You're not a police inspector, are you? There was some trouble after Alice's death, I remember, someone who wanted an inquest. You've come to persecute me, that's what it is!' His voice was rising to a shrill note. 'Go away, will you? Haven't I had enough to distract me?'

'I've no wish to bother you. Only I'm not going away till I've seen Bevis,' Jack said. Rossetti threw him a wild look and almost ran out of the studio. Left alone, Jack wandered round the pictures. They were not Lilian, yet like enough to show him how she became

213

embroiled in the fantasies that hung about Tudor House. He was disturbed, wishing himself anywhere else. But he must stay, now that he was here.

Then he saw, on an easel, a painting that stopped him dead. The subject was beyond his understanding; an open tomb or monument with a glimpse of an Italian town beyond, and within it a draped bier on which lay a dead woman, her hands crossed on her breast, her long red hair flowing loose. An angel bent over her – Jack only supposed it was an angel because it had wings and its sex was indeterminate – kissing her lips, one hand stretched backwards to clasp the hand of a sad-faced man. Two beautiful, melancholy handmaidens held a silken cloth, flower-laden, between them over the bier and its occupant. And the girl on the bier was undoubtedly Lilian. Now he saw clearly the difference between her face and the lady's in the other portraits.

'A connoisseur, I see,' said a voice behind him. He turned to see a fair plump man in a green velvet jacket regarding him quizzically. 'You admire my finest picture?'

'I don't know as I admire it,' Jack said slowly. 'I don't go in for pictures of dead folk, myself.'

'Really? But Death is the most fascinating thing in Life.' Leoline was teasing him.

'Not where I come from it isn't. It means a breadwinner or a mother or a child's gone, as can ill be spared. Nowt fascinating about that. What's it mean to you, then?' He was watching the other's face, which was becoming faintly puzzled.

'I really couldn't explain. It's all very much above your head. I don't think I know what you're doing in my studio, do I? Shouldn't you be on your way to the kitchen, or somewhere like that?'

'No, I shouldn't. It's you I came to see, Mr Bevis.'

'Oh – you're a model, I gather. I'm sure you'd do very well for a centurion, that line of work. But I'm afraid I don't paint models, so your visit has been wasted.'

'You did in that,' Jack said, indicating the picture. The other was visibly startled.

'Yes, I did – the figure at least, the rest is copied. But how could you know?'

'Because the young woman's my intended. And she's very much alive, you might be surprised to hear.'

A dark flush suffused Leoline's face. 'So you're the brute who ...
I see it now. Well, where is she? You've caused her friends and
relations untold anxiety. Don't think I shall let you go, now I've
got you here. This means a criminal charge, of course – abduction
isn't exactly smiled on in civilised quarters, you know, whatever
methods of wooing may be popular in your barbaric part of the
world.'

Jack regarded him levelly. 'Do you think you've much room to
talk about criminal charges, Mr Bevis?'

'I don't know what you mean.'

'No? And you know nowt about Alice Hazell, your late wife, and
what she died of? Nor about any other wives you've had? It looks
like you've had plenty of time to play at your little Game of Love
and Death.'

'Lilian told you.' Leoline had turned a sickly colour. 'Well, it
was a game – the sort a person like you wouldn't understand. And
there's nothing in the world you can do about it, so be off!'

'There's one thing,' Jack said thoughtfully. 'I can make sure you
don't play it again, for you'll be watched from now on. And another
thing, I want a bit of a return for what you did to my girl.' He
stripped his coat off. 'Come on, put your hands up.'

Leoline stared, then backed away. 'Fight with you? Don't be
preposterous. Get out!' Jack followed him relentlessly down the
room until his back was to the wall, then landed a smart blow to
his chin. Leoline ducked and wavered, at last attempting to strike
back at the grim face and punishing fists which seemed everywhere,
bruising his head and his body, knocking the breath out of him.
Jack let him get a few blows in, for fair play, then attacked him
seriously, until Leoline gasped and choked for mercy. In a last
attempt to defend himself he clutched wildly at Jack, throwing him
off balance. Locked together, they fell against the painting on the
easel, which went crashing to the floor under their flailing feet.
On top of his opponent Jack struck him an undercut to the jaw
which knocked him out.

He lay motionless, blood trickling from his mouth, across the
fallen picture. Jack moved him roughly aside and pulled it from
under him. The stretched canvas had cracked with the force of
their impact; a wide rift separated the kissing angel's head from
its wings.

215

Jack, breathing heavily but unmarked, gazed at the painting of his love in the power of the man he had just thrashed. It came to him that he had no wish to leave it to be gloated over in time to come. A palette-knife lay with some brushes and paint-pots on a table. Jack picked it up, and with four strong strokes in the shape of a cross quartered the picture, ruthlessly cutting across Lilian's long white throat and the copper riches of her hair. She would want that done herself. Now there was nothing left of her time with Leoline. He gave the unconscious man a quick contemptuous examination to make sure he still breathed, and left the studio, shutting the door.

Rossetti was in the hall, wild-eyed. 'What was that terrible noise? What's going on?'

Jack patted his shoulder kindly. 'Nowt to worry about, sir; just a bit of justice being done. He'll not tell you about it when he comes to, but believe me, I've given that bugger what he rightly deserved, and I'm not sorry for it. If I were you I'd chuck him out, bag and baggage. Tell that housekeeper o' yours he'll be needing some vinegar and brown paper. Good day to you.'

The artist clutched at his arm. 'Wait! Don't go for a minute. He opened a door and led out the small dear, which was trembling. 'Won't you take Sabra with you? You were right, she'll only die like the others. She needs the country, and Topsy won't have her at Kelmscott. You come from the country, don't you?'

'Aye, but . . .'

'Then take her, please! This is a wretched house for young creatures, and she's such a jolly little thing. Whatever you may have done to Leoline, I can see you're a good sort of young man. Look, she's gone to you of her own accord.' The deer was pressing itself against Jack, looking up at him with large lovely eyes, and his resolution melted. It would be extremely inconvenient to travel north with a deer, but he supposed it could be accommodated in the luggage-van. And it would be a present to Lilian; his wedding-present.

'All right,' he said. Rossetti smiled, a smile of magnetic charm and sweetness that showed Jack what he had been before tragedy changed him.

'Thank you. And you know her name,' he called after them. 'Sabra, the princess rescued by St George.'

216

Jolting towards the station in a cab, the driver of which had been hard to persuade that the animal was no bigger than a dog and would be no more trouble, Jack reflected that it seemed to be his lot to rescue maidens in distress. He wondered what St George would have said to crossing London in a cab with a deer bouncing about on his lap, and what his mother's remarks would be, and whether Lilian would like such an animal as a pet. He wondered, also, whether the dragon he had beaten that day was by now licking his wounds.

CHAPTER SEVENTEEN

'I'm not having that thing in my house. The very idea!' Mary fixed the trembling Sabra with a basilisk glare, as the small deer leaned against Jack's knee.

'It's not meant to be in the house, Mam.'

'Well, the garden, then. I can just see it, gobbling up all my young plants. Whatever got into you, fetching it all this way, our Jack?'

'I fetched it for Lilian. If she wants it.'

Lilian had said nothing during the brief battle between mother and son. Now she faced up to Mary.

'Yes, of course I want it.'

Mary snorted. 'Tha'd want a humgruffin if Jack gave it thee. I don't know, I'm sure – daft nonsense. I'll not be responsible for it, I say I'll not.'

'Nobody's asking you. It's our responsibility, mine and Lilian's. It'd be dead by now if I'd left it where it was, and I'll see it looked after. It can have a shed out in t'orchard.'

'Oh, aye? An' live off apples?'

'Does it look as if it could reach up that far, poor little runt?' Jack was growing exasperated. 'It can live off bark, and grass and windfalls. Dad'll make the shed, won't you, Dad?'

Amos nodded. He was not going to be drawn into the fight, which he was quite aware was not about the deer so much as that Jack had brought it for Lilian, not for the mother who had always had a present whenever Jack came home. The rivalry between the two women flashed across the room like sparks of electricity. If it came to a downright contest, his money would be on Lilian. She was temporising, tactfully trying not to draw Mary into open fight.

'I'm sure it will be no trouble, Mrs Ellershaw. And deer keep down the grass – my uncle's friend at Ridings Hall has a herd, and they're as good as lawn-mowers, aren't they, Jack?'

'Every bit.'

Mary knew she was beaten. She left them without a word and went into the kitchen, where in a moment they heard her furiously scrambling eggs, clattering the whisk against the sides of the mixing-bowl with the maximum of noise.

'Aye, well, I'll start on t'shed,' Amos said, bestowing a pat on Sabra as he went out. She jumped, huddling nearer to Jack, her only friend. Left alone, the lovers made up in a long embrace for the conventional kiss on the cheek Jack had given Lilian before his parents. He pulled her down to sit on his knee, and kissed her hair, her eyelids, and the tip of her nose with his customary thoroughness. She pulled away before he reached her mouth: that could take up a lot of time.

'No, Jack, give over. I want to ask you something.'

'Ask away.'

'Well, then. Where did you get her from?'

'I told you. From a place where she weren't being looked after.'

'No, you didn't tell me. Was it from – that house?'

'It was from a house, aye. No place for a wild animal, even a little 'un.'

'Don't try to put me off. It was from Mr Rossetti's, wasn't it.'

'Seeing as you know all about it – aye, it was. And as dismal a place as ever I saw.'

'What were you doing there? You must tell me. I mean it now.'

'So it seems. Well, I were going to say nowt about it, but I went to have a word with yon chap.'

Lilian did not need to ask which chap. Jack felt her shudder in his arms, and held her tighter. The angry noises from the kitchen were still going on, but he lowered his voice.

'I had a bit more nor a word, as it turned out. No, I didn't kill him, so there's no call to look so scared, but we'd a fair old scrap and he got the worst of it. He didn't look half so pretty, last I saw of him. It's my belief he won't go pestering young women to death again in a hurry.'

'Pestering to death . . . Yes, that's what he was doing to me. But why, Jack, why? What use would I have been to him dead?'

Jack made no answer for a moment or two, but stroked her hair. The word necrophilia was unknown to him: the thing, he knew of. There had been a celebrated case heard at York Assizes some years before which had caused many husbands and fathers to hide the newspaper from their womenfolk. Jack had read it and remembered the revolting details of a crime which had been punished on the gallows. For murder had been committed – in the first place. He was deeply anxious to say nothing to his love which might sicken her for honest sex, yet he must tell her something. At last he said:

'There's a lot of queer folk about. It's my guess as these artist chaps are a bit touched in their wits. Not all, just some of 'em. *His* sort, they get their fun from having power over helpless women, women as they've given drugs to and know nowt about what's being done to 'em. I reckon his wife, Alice or whatever she were called in the letter, couldn't stand it and died, poor lass.' Jack would rather have been facing the deadly left-hand bowling of old Richard Nyren in his glory than making this lame explanation, which sounded to his own ears quite unconvincing. He only hoped it would convince Lilian. To his enormous relief she raised her head from his shoulder and smiled reassuringly, hearing the strain in his voice.

'Yes, I see. I must have been very simple not to see through it, but I was so stupid from that stuff he gave me, most of the time. And I'm sure Aunt Freddy couldn't have known what was going on.' She was silent, thinking how near death had been.

Jack sensed she would say no more about it and was infinitely relieved. 'Now shift, will you, I want to get this beast outside before Mam complains.' He pushed her gently off his lap, but she lost her balance and fell. On the floor she reached out her hand for his help, but he shook his head.

'Nay. Get up thisen. It's best not to rely on other folk.'

For a moment she was hurt and resentful. Reproachful words sprang to her lips, to be bitten back. With an undignified struggle she got to her knees, then, with the help of a chair, to her feet. 'God helps those that help themselves, you were going to say next?' she enquired lightly.

'What else?' He handed her the stick she still needed. 'Now come on, Sabra.' He touched the deer, which had slumped over his feet in a half-doze, and it started to its feet, its frightened mournful brown glance going from its friend to the strange person, then back again. Lilian bent and stroked the soft quivering ears, the light pink muzzle, until the trembling lessened and she felt herself accepted. Jack picked the little creature up, cradling it in his arms; a picture from her childhood Bible flashed into Lilian's mind, and she hoped the comparison was not irreverent. There were words in her memory, too: not from the Bible, but the words of the song Janey Morris had sung. 'I'm searching for my father's sheep, His young and tender lambs, That over hill and over dale Lie hidden with their dams ... For I am thine and thou art mine, No man shall uncomfort thee; We'll join our hands in wedded bands, And married we will be.'

They were married on a Saturday in early September, a perfect day of deep blue skies and champagne air, with a golden benevolent sun risen early to shine on the bride. Such a bride as Barnswood had not seen for many and many a year, since primness and prudery came in with the late Prince Consort. Mary Ellershaw had given up the battle she could not win against the girl who had taken her son's heart, and had thrown herself grimly into a campaign to glorify the Ellershaws and shame the neighbours, not to mention her future daughter-in-law's proud-stomached relatives, should any of them condescend to appear.

For weeks she had spent almost half the money she earned at her Friday market stall on the wares of other stall-keepers. Fine nets and gauzes, lace trimmings and yards of tiny silk rosebuds, ribbons and pieces of velvet, lengths of linen and batiste, came home to Stainbeck to become Lilian's trousseau, blended with finery of an earlier time laid up in a chest with sprigs of dried lavender. Lilian looked on helpless as Mary sat stitching, stitching, cutting, pinning and gathering, with materials all round her, and Amos, feeling superfluous, pottered in the gardens or smoked his pipe in the yard.

Guilt drove her at last to ask, 'Can't I do something? It's too much to be left to you.'

Mary bit off a thread. 'Tha can't sew.'

'Not very well, no. I'm afraid I'm very clumsy. But I could do some straight hemming, or stitch on some braid... Won't you let me try?'

Mary glanced up. She approved of the offer, though her face

221

showed nothing but indifference. Tossing over a petticoat, she said, 'Get on wi' that, then. But don't spoil it.'

Stitching slowly and carefully, Lilian managed not to spoil it. Between her unskilled hands and Mary's flying fingers a pile of garments grew which, Mary observed with grim satisfaction, would make some of 'em stare. The work was still going on only days from the wedding. Then the last stitch went in, and the patchwork counterpane in the long-unused spare bedroom was covered with a fairy foam of white. Only the shoes were missing, until Jack came home for the last time before the wedding. From a box bearing the engraved name of a famous Manchester firm Lilian unwrapped a pair of white kid boots, pearl-buttoned and Louis-heeled.

'They'll fit all right,' Jack said, pleased with himself. 'I drew a pattern off your others.'

She stared at them, bland and perfect. In all the years when her feet had been useless she had never owned such boots.

'Don't you like 'em?' Jack asked, puzzled by her stony expression.

'They're beautiful. They're the most beautiful boots I've ever seen. And you shouldn't, Jack, you shouldn't!' She turned on him, storming. 'First your mother spends all that money and time making all those things upstairs, then you go and spend more money, for goodness knows what they must have cost. And all for what? A useless object like me that had to be taught to walk, like a baby, and can't do a hand's turn to help any of you, and hasn't brought you a penny for a dowry. You make me feel silly, really silly. Why did you want me, instead of someone of your own kind? You ought to have known better.'

'Have you done?' Jack asked quietly. 'Because there's a few things I could point out to you. Only I won't.' For the first time she saw him look vulnerable. Abruptly she sat down and burst into tears, her hands over her face. She heard him go out of the room and upstairs. While she still sobbed helplessly, Mary came in and stood beside her till the crying lessened.

'I heard that,' Mary said. 'I should think they heard it down i' Barnswood. Well, you're a nice one, aren't you, young madam. Talking to my lad like that, a lad that's done more for you than your own kith and kin, and worships t'ground you walk on. And it's thanks to him you *can* walk, think on. What if we have spent a bit o' brass fitting you out wi' finery? It's for us as well as you, make no mistake about that. We like to hold our heads high, and you'd best do t'same if you're taking Jack's name.'

'Better . . . cancel . . . wedding,' Lilian sobbed, fumbling for her elusive handkerchief.

'Better do nowt o' t'sort. Bride's nerves, that's what wrong wi' you, lass.' She laid a hard hand on Lilian's shoulder. 'Come on, mop up now. I won't have our Jack mithered wi' such rubbish.'

There was nettle porridge served at supper-time to calm disturbed tempers. Everybody was very quiet, Mary worn out after a day of preparations, Amos apparently lost in thought. Jack talked to him about a man called George Ulyett who was now playing for York-shire and had just made a very creditable 52, coming in at Number Four. When he remarked that he himself would have been playing at Manchester on Saturday, but for a previous engagement – his wedding – Lilian opened her mouth to enquire satirically why he didn't go in any case; then shut it again. There seemed to be nothing useful she could say.

She went to bed early and lay awake for hours torn by doubts and fears. What she had shouted at Jack on impulse was true. She would be a useless wife to him, even now she could walk. The best thing she could do would be to leave the next morning, go back to her mother and take her punishment, which would certainly last for the rest of her life.

But when morning came there seemed to be no time for any such dramatic action. Mary commandeered her as soon as breakfast was over to help in a marathon cooking of pies, puddings, brawn, pasties and cakes. Two women from the village had trudged up to lend their hands to the task, and Mrs Mossop was scuttling mouse-like from table to pan and back again. Between the four of them, even with Lilian sitting at the table to do what work she could, the kitchen was like an oven. By the end of the day they were all dog-tired, sweating and cross, and the pantry bulged with enough food to supply an army.

'But where are we going to put all the pepole?' Lilian asked. 'There's only room for a dozen or so in the parlour.'

'In t'Drill Hall. Food'll go down tomorrow. Then there'll be nowt to do but smarten up. You get that hair washed and have a bit of a rest. The worst of it's over.'

'Thank God,' murmured Amos. 'One do like this'll last my time out.'

The day before the wedding was a confusion of comings and goings, in spite of what Mary had said. A cart with a stout horse appeared from Sadler's Farm to convey the food, in the charge of Jack and Amos, down to the Drill Hall at Barnswood. They were away for hours, setting up chairs and tables and otherwise preparing for the festivities. Mary, to Lilian's surprise, went to bed in the afternoon and stayed there, keeping her feet up, as she called it. Lilian washed her hair and dried it in the sunshine of the yard. She was blazingly happy and excited, yet nervous about the wedding which was to be so different from any she had known. As a child she had been a bridesmaid at the wedding of Sir Lewis's daughter, Elsie, of which she remembered a lot of fussy ceremony and grandeur, of starting a fight with another little bridesmaid afterwards, and of being sick in the carriage going home. The wedding had been in the beautiful old church at Fellgate. Hers was to be at Barnswood Ebenezer, the Nonconformist chapel where Amos and Mary had been married and where their children had been baptised. They seldom went there now, except to tend the three small graves in the burying-ground.

How different tomorrow was going to be from Elsie's wedding: how strange that none of her own family would be there. She had dutifully written notes to her mother, to Frederica and Sir Lewis, but none of them would come, she knew. Why should they? What she minded most was there would be no father to give her away. She remembered her father at the wedding-feast at Fellgate, amused at her attack on the rival bridesmaid, mopping her up after the episode of the cream trifle. She knew now how he must have visualised the day when she would walk up the aisle on his arm, herself a bride. Tears pricked her eyes at the memory of him. She forced them back. Amos had volunteered to give her in marriage, and there was no one kinder, even though the arrangement was a little unusual.

She heard the men return with the cart, and went to meet them. Jack shut the front door behind him firmly. 'Just keep inside, will you,' he told her, 'we've got work to do out yon.'

'But why? Can't I even watch you?'

'No.'

224

'Why not?'

'Because I say so.' Jack went past her into the kitchen, where his mother was somewhat wearily stirring one of her brews. 'Your supper's ready,' she said over her shoulder.

'I've no time. I'll have a bit of bread and cheese.'

'Suit yersen. I've cooked it for nowt, then.'

'Goodness me, Lilian thought, how gracious they are. Aloud she said, 'What about your father? He'll want something, won't he?'

'Aye, maybe. I'll get him now – it's coming on dark.' He went off, again shutting the door, and Lilian said impatiently, 'What *are* they up to?'

'We'll find out if we live long enough. Tha knows what Curiosity did.'

Moodily Lilian watched Amos, who was looking oddly furtive, eat his supper, while outside sounds of hammering could be heard. She only picked at her own food. Mary said impatiently, 'I'd leave that, if I were thee. Seems Tom Sadler's pigs'll be having a wedding feast of their own off our leavings. Go and get an early night, if tha's not to look as white as a boggart tomorrow.'

Lilian obediently went to bed, or as far as the ground-floor bedroom she was to occupy for the last time. But the great harvest moon lighting up the room would not be shut out by curtains; she would never sleep in so much brightness. She pulled her dress on again and went out, into the orchard that lay behind the house, feeling her way very carefully with her stick across the rough grass, though the path was almost as clear as in daylight. She made her way towards the shed where Sabra lived. At her whisper the deer rustled in its straw, then crept out, making the small vocal noise with which it greeted friends. It put its soft muzzle into her palm, searching for the treat she sometimes brought it. Finding nothing, it bent to nibble a fallen apple, a silver globe among others that birds or insects had pecked.

Lilian knelt on the wet grass and put her arms round the soft neck.

'Sabra, Sabra. He brought us both here out of kindness, but what has it done to us, I wonder? Do you know? Do I?'

She sat back on her heels, regarding the deer. It was much plumper than it had been, and its pale gold fur, white in the moon, was sleek. It no longer jumped and cowered at the sound of a human voice. If it had been left in Chelsea it would have died; as she would.

Sabra's head shot up as a twig crackled at the orchard gate. Forgetting the apple she bounded away, a ghostly glimmering shape. Through the trees Lilian saw Jack coming towards her, the deer at his side, fawning against him, leaping up to touch his hand. They might have been figures from a Morris tapestry, a young knight and a milk-white doe against a formal screen of leaves.

'That's a daft thing to do, kneeling on wet grass,' remarked the knight, helping her to her feet. He tilted her face up to his and scanned her eyes deeply, reading the plea and the question in them. Then he kissed her gently, cool lips against cool lips, and, an arm round her shoulders, led her back through the orchard.

'It'll be reet, love,' he said. 'Never fear, it'll be reet.'

The silver moon made way for a golden sun. The bride stood attired for her marriage. From the slender waist the skirt flowed down in tier upon tier of ivory silk, each banded with tiny rose-buds, and at the back curved out over a padded 'dress improver' Mary had bought second-hand at the market. The low-cut bodice was banded with rose velvet, its long sleeves ending in delicate frills of lace; a knot of living roses was pinned at the bride's breast. Mary had disdainfully rejected the suggestion of a bonnet as being out-of-date and only for humble weddings, which this one was certainly not going to be. Instead, a band of artificial roses, cleaned with spirit until they glowed, crowned the new-washed hair, which was looped once on the neck, then allowed to fall in all its profusion down almost to the waist. Lilian had wanted to put it up, but Mary sharply retorted that a maid might as well look like a maid while she decently could. And over all, like a snowy cobweb, a veil of net clouding her in mysterious beauty.

Mary stood back. Her face was triumphant as she surveyed her handiwork.

'Now tha looks like a lady,' she said. 'I weren't sure, till now. Now it's right and proper.'

'What is?'

'Jack's wedding thee. Tha'rt fine enough for our Jack.'

Lilian put aside her veil and kissed her future mother-in-law's

226

cheek, for the first time. 'I'm glad. That's the best compliment I've ever been paid.'

'Get away with you,' said Mary, embarrassed but not displeased. Together they went down to the parlour, where Amos was waiting in the rusty black suit with the greenish tinge that was his best. He gaped at the sight of her.

'By heck! That's never our Lilian!'

'It is,' she replied. 'I can't prove it without raising this veil, and I'm forbidden to do that yet. You'll have to take me on trust.'

Almost speechless, he held out his arm to her. She must make herself do without the support of her stick on this day. Together they went out, down the sloping path between the vegetable-plots, to the swing-gate that led to the lane. Now it was Lilian's turn to gasp, for there stood the same farm-cart with the two wheels and galleried sides that had taken the provisions down to the village. The same cart, but how transformed: wreathed and banded with autumn flowers, branches of golding leaves, ribbons and knots of lace left over from the bridal dress. In the shafts was a great white farm-horse, his mane knotted with white ribbons, a cockade favour between his ears. He looked his best, and knew it.

'So *this* is what you two were up to last night, and wouldn't tell me, you close things!' Lilian pinched her future father-in-law's arm. He laughed.

'Wouldn't ha' done, would it, Mother?'

Mary, behind them, magnificent in an old-fashioned dress of steel-grey silk and a new-trimmed bonnet, agreed that it would have been unlucky, almost as bad as letting the groom see the bride on the wedding-morn. Holding the horse's head was Tom, the lad who was Jack's most frequent partner in cricket practice, grinning from ear to ear and clad in his Sunday smock with a cock's feather in his cap. He climbed into the driving seat, bride and sponsor took their places behind him, while Mary waited for the trap coming down the lane for her.

As they drew into Barnswood Lilian was aware of eyes. Eyes peering from behind lace curtains, from the interiors of shops, eyes of people in the long High Street who stopped to stare at the cortège, eyes of old men and women sitting in the sunshine at their cottage doors. And, when the cart drew up in front of the ugly red-brick chapel with Ebenezer 1821 over its door, eyes of shawled

227

women clustered on the pavement. Stepping down, moving between their ranks, she heard remarks that were not even spoken in whispers.

'Hair's as red as a scraped carrot. Fancy, wearin' it down!'

'Proud as a peacock, yo' can tell that.'

There were girls among the watchers who had hoped to capture Jack themselves. Their eyes were no kinder than their comments. 'No shame,' Lilian heard. 'Bold as brass. I were all of a tremble when I were wed,' announced a matron. Quite true, Lilian thought, she did feel bold, without a trace of the traditional fears a bride was supposed to have.

But a flush of delighted surprise rushed to her face as a man came towards her from the chapel porch. Tall, broad, magnificently whiskered and shiningly imposing in Guards' uniform of scarlet and gold, Digby Stevens-Clyne held out his arms to his cousin.

The composure of the bride broke down. 'Digby! Oh, dear Digby! I never expected . . . oh, how splendid to see you. Oh, gracious . . .'

'Now, now, old girl, keep calm. Did you think I'd stay away? Penny's here, too.' A fashionable vision in blue appeared beaming behind him. Amos interrupted the babble of conversation that was threatening to hold up the proceedings.

'Did I hear this is thy cousin, Lilian? Then he shall give thee away, not me. Nay, I'll not take no for an answer, it's nobbut right and fitting.' Mary nodded approval, and Digby, after a moment of surprise, said, 'Very kind of you, sir. Of course I will, only too pleased. Come, my dear. Let's put Jack out of his misery.'

If Jack was suffering, he gave no sign of it as he stood waiting by the front pew. The handsomest man in the church in his black suit, silk neckcloth and white buttonhole flower, he turned his head to view with apparent calm the entry of his sensational bride and her dazzling escort. What his feelings were at the sight of the lovely vision that must be his Lilian, not even his best man and team-mate, Bob Armitage, could possibly guess as bride and sponsor advanced up the aisle between the rows of pitchpine pews which were as plain and uncomfortable as everything else in the unlovely building. There were no embroidered kneelers because the congregation did not kneel, only inclined its heads on its hands; there was no stained glass in the windows because it was thought to be idolatrous, and no Wedding March because secular music was too frivolous for use. The hymn accompaniments were provided by a wheezy harmonium played by a spectacled lady schoolteacher.

The minister, the Reverend Balmforth, known by the less reverent among his flock as Holdforth, was not particularly honoured by being asked to perform the ceremony. The Ellershaws attended chapel too seldom for his liking, he had not been favourably impressed by the bride-to-be on his only meeting with her, and the bridegroom was known to have played cricket on a Sunday. He disapproved strongly of the extravagant bridal dress and veil, and of the unconcealed smirk on Mary Ellershaw's face as she sat very upright in the front pew holding Lilian's posy of flowers. Yet he was there to conduct the service, and conduct it he did, improvising loudly and at length so that the bride and groom gave only improvised replies. At one point Jack felt Lilian begin to shake, not with nervousness but with suppressed giggles, and gave her a sharp push with his elbow. The ring stuck on its way down her finger, Bob was taken with a coughing fit, someone in the congregation unaccountably began to weep audibly, and it was an immense relief when all the haranguing was over, and the worshippers rose to sing with strenuous and hearty lung-power 'All Hail the Power of Jesu's Name' to a fine rip-roaring tune, Jack and Amos contributing baritone and tenor harmonies respectively.

When the final triumphant 'Crown Him, Crown Him, CROWN HIM, Crown Him Lord of all' had rung out, they turned, arm in arm, her ringed hand in his, her veil thrown back to show her glowing face, and went with Mary, Amos and Digby to sign the register at a table. 'Lilian de Wentworth' for the last time, 'Lilian Ellershaw' for the first. As they came down through the congregation the general attention was divided between the happy couple and the towering Guardsman with a fashion-plate of beauty on his arm. Ebenezer, 1821, had never seen quite such a wedding.

Lilian's smile faded as she saw, in a back pew, who had been weeping. It was Augustus. So her wedding had been attended by more than one of her relatives, but how she wished this one had not come, for he brought a breath of unhappiness with him from another world.

She signalled Jack to pause, bent over her cousin, and whispered, 'Come to the breakfast, Gussie.'

He shook his head, but she persisted. 'Yes. For my sake. Just follow us.'

The village Drill Hall was no more beautiful than the chapel, but considerably more cheerful. Long tables were spread with white cloths and laden with all the food prepared in the Stainbeck kitchen, and with great jugs of ale and home-made wines. Mary, at her most gracious, conducted Lilian from one guest to another, introducing farmers, bailiffs, miners, their wives and children – most of the district, it seemed, so who had been the starers in the street? They were slow to warm up to the stranger bride – 'Pleased to meet you,' accompanied by a stiff smile, was the usual greeting; but when all were sat down to table and the food and drink began to circulate the climate improved rapidly, for these were northern folk who played as hard and conscientiously as they worked, and a Do was a Do. Lilian, seated at Jack's side, hardly got a word with him for answering the questions and prettily responding to the compliments that were fired at her. She listened intently to the voices, the sort of accents she had grown up hearing, and with her quick ear stored them and answered in similar ones. It got easier with practice: she could see that she was winning approval for not 'talking London'.

Further down their table Mary was winning anything but approval from the Reverend Balmforth.

'I'm very surprised and shocked, Mrs Ellershaw, I say very surprised and shocked, to see strong drink on these tables.'

'Oh, aye? I can see a good few folk as is surprised. But I don't see a lot of shock, Minister. What's wrong wi' a drop of good ale and wine at a breakfast?'

'It's against the rules of our persuasion, quite against the rules.'

'And who made t'rules, then? What about Marriage at Cana? I seem to think there was a fair bit o' liquor going round *that* day. "And Jesus saith to them, Fill the waterpots wi' water, and they filled 'em up to the brim. And He saith unto 'em, Draw out now, and bear unto the ruler of the feast. And the ruler of the feast tasted the water now become wine." Isn't that what Bible says?'

'The Devil can quote Scripture when he likes, Mrs Ellershaw.' The Reverend Balmforth sniffed. 'There's a strong smell of drink, very unpleasant, not at all nice. Have you no water?'

'There's some in t'scullery taps,' she replied indifferently, beckoning a young girl to her side. 'Fetch Reverend a big mug o' water, Dorcas, and mek sure it's not had owt nasty in it, like ale.' She winked. Mr Balmforth turned his dyspeptic face ostentatiously towards his neighbour on the other side, but noted before doing so that the bride was laughing in a very abandoned and immodest manner, and openly clasping her husband's hand on the table in the full sight of all.

Augustus saw it too, grieving. How often had he seen in his mind's eye Lilian as his bride, his sweet, pale, delicate wife, not at all like this healthy, happy, indeed somewhat hoydenish young woman. She was undeniably Lilian, the face, the wonder of hair – 'if a woman have long hair, it is a glory to her,' said St Paul, adding something to the effect that it was unlawful for her to pray with her hair unveiled. Augustus did not count the snowdrift of net as a veil, but rather as an allurement. The two at the altar might have been a nymph of the fountain celebrating the rites of Venus with a young Roman patrician, not a Christian couple. The whole service had been acutely painful to Augustus, a travesty of his own beautiful Anglican liturgy. He sat in misery through the proposing of healths. The bridegroom's mother alarmed him, and she had not cried at all, as mothers were supposed to do at weddings. The health of the happy couple was proposed by the best man and replied to by the groom in terms that were not exactly bawdy, but none too decorous either. Augustus wished very much that he had not disobeyed Aunt Florence and come so far to be made so unhappy.

Lilian had her eye on him throughout the proceedings. When the time came for the company to rise and disperse she made her way to him and sat by his side.

'Gussie, dear. It was kind of you to come, but you shouldn't. Yes, you should, because now you can see what a bad wife I'd have made you. Don't shake your head, for you know it's true. You wanted someone to hand out illuminated texts and be a perfect vicar's wife, didn't you. Well, now you see I couldn't have done that, even if I'd remained an invalid.'

'I felt it my duty to be here, Lilian. Others refused. I . . . you know what my hopes were. I shall forget them now, and I trust you'll be happy and – and fruitful. My father sent you this.' He fished in his pocket and produced an envelope with Sir Lewis's seal on it.

231

'Thank you, Gussie. And him – it was kind of him to send his good wishes, at least.' She put the envelope away in the flower-patterned reticule Mary had found for her at the market.

He shook his head again, dull-eyed. Then Jack was there, asking, with intent, 'Who's this, then?'

'My cousin. The Reverend Augustus Hambleden.'

'Glad to meet you. Kind of you to come.' Augustus gave a limp clasp to the brown hand he was offered. Jack took in the situation at a glance, and drifted away towards Penelope, who was carrying on a tremendous flirtation with a young farmer. He was, on the whole, thankful that no more of his wife's relations had attended the ceremony. He saw her drop a light kiss on the clergyman's brow, and Augustus make his way to the door. Then it was for the bridal couple to stand at the door shaking hands while the guests left, until only the table-clearers and the Ellershaws senior and junior remained, with Digby and Penelope, and the comatose Bob Armitage, considerably the worse for ale.

'Come on, Bob.' Jack kicked him affectionately. 'Look alive. I don't know about you lot, but I want some fresh air.'

'That's it – so do we all,' Digby said. 'Why not go and knock a ball about, eh, Jack, if we can find a pitch somewhere?'

The village cricket ground was across the High Street, along a narrow lane and over a stile. The party made their way there, scrutinised intensely by those inhabitants of Barnswood who had not been at the wedding, comments following them like arrows. On the rough field the coming shadows of evening lay long and dark. Jack stripped off his coat and loosened his neckcloth, Digby removed his uniform jacket ('shouldn't be wearing it on a civil occasion, but what H.M.'s eye don't see 'Er 'eart don't grieve over') and Bob found bats and balls in a shed which was supposed to be locked. The three women sat on the grass under an oak-tree among shut daisies and buttercups and watched a game which would not have edified the Yorkshire Committee at all, consisting as it did of three players, one in an advanced state of intoxication and the other two in unprofessionally high spirits.

'Darling Digby,' Penelope murmured, her bonnet on the back of her head. 'If only *we* could have been married there wouldn't have been all this trouble about my coming down here with him.

232

It was only because I promised Mamma and Papa that Chivers, that's my maid, should accompany us everywhere that they allowed it. But the dear old thing's quite a sport, only too glad to look round the shops in Doncaster. I say, Lilian, you looked simply ripping – quite a stunner.'

Lilian gave a slight shudder. 'Don't call me that, Penny – anything but that.'

'Oh, well, have it your own way. Digby calls you his Little Duck, so perhaps you prefer that. Now, didn't I tell you, the first time we ever met at Lord's, that it was quite a romance between you two? I could see it all, even with you in a bath-chair, poor girl, but Digby *would* shut me up . . .'

Lilian let her ramble on, her eyes fixed on Jack, who was doing the best he could with the wildly erratic bowling of his best man, Digby retrieving such balls as went straight to the outfield instead of to the batsman. She had taken off her wreath and veil, and sat on the grass with her arms round her knees like a village lass. Her mother-in-law sat upright against a tree, with her eyes shut, seemingly lulled by the clonk of the willow against the ball when the two occasionally made contact, and the laughter of the men. Bats squeaked overhead. In a corner of the field an inquisitive rabbit was watching, ears pricked for gunshots.

The sky was darkening rapidly. 'That's enough, Bob!' Jack shouted. 'I can't see a hand in front of my face, let alone t'ball.'

'Just a couple more. Here comes a fast 'un. Heigh! Mind thi weddin' tackle – I'd not like to disoblige thi missis.'

'Tha'd better not, lad. Nay, that'll do. Even yon coney thinks we're daft.' He threw down his bat. Digby joined him at the wicket.

'I've had quite enough exercise, myself, and the ladies must be catching their deaths of cold. Let's call a halt.' Between them they got the ball from Bob, who seemed disposed to fight them for it, and hustled him away, with a helping hand over the stile, the three spectators very properly pretending not to hear the earthy advice he shouted back to his friend concerning the coming night.

'Silly bugger,' said Jack, 'never knows when he's had a skinful. Let's get these women home. Mrs Ellershaw!'

Lilian was startled for a moment, then, smiling, reached out a

233

hand to him. Entwined they walked to the waiting cart where Amos was sleeping behind Tom, the patient driver. All five piled in upon the wilting flowers and greenery. At the village inn Digby and Penelope left them, with fond farewells and hearty wishes; they were to go to their Doncaster hotel before returning to London. The Ellershaws were driven back to Stainbeck Cottages, all silent, Lilian very close to Jack, her hand tightly holding his.

The bedroom upstairs had been unused for many years, but nobody would have known it, so swept and polished it had been, and adorned with bright rugs and an elaborate little washstand made by Amos. Lilian climbed the stairs with ease – she had not used her stick all day.

Unlike the matron outside Ebenezer, she was not all of a tremble. It seemed simply right to be here with Jack, right to be turning her back to him to have the little buttons of her dress unfastened, right to be in her chemise splashing her face at the beautiful new washstand while chatting of the ceremony and the guests. 'What a stick that minister is. Poor man, doesn't he ever laugh? I thought Penny looked charming. Why can't she and Digby get married? Is it because of the Queen or the Army, or what? She suits him perfectly, don't you think, though she *is* a perfect goose. Ugh, I've got soap in my eyes.' She clawed blindly for the towel, which Jack provided, marvelling. He had not known what to expect, even from Lilian, though he had guessed at the wedding that she would not be all blushes and protests, as brides were supposed to be.

She turned to him, damp and glowing, and flung her arms round him. 'Oh, Jack,' she said, 'I do love you so.'

'Here, here, give a chap time.' He was unfastening his neckcloth and removing the battered posy from his buttonhole, watching her as she took off her chemise and sat on the bed to pull off her white stockings, feeling his eyes on her, her own downcast and more colour in her cheeks than soap and flannel had brought to them. As she reached for her nightgown, the voluminous cotton garment Mary had made for her, elaborate with drawn threadwork and lace frills, he took it from her.

'Tha won't be needing yon thing.'

'If you say not, Jack.' She slipped between the fresh-laundered sheets and lay waiting for him, very calm, bright-eyed, her hair

234

spread over the pillow. And when he came to her she met his passion with a passion no less ardent, warm and willing, a woman starved for love, giving all of herself to him in joy. And they, who had loved long, became wedded lovers.

CHAPTER EIGHTEEN

Four silent Ellershaws sat round the breakfast table. Amos, with a headache from the beverages of the day before, drank quantities of strong tea, frequently passing his cup for a refill. Mary would like to have talked over the wedding and the guests, but knew she would get very little response from the two who sat as close as two people can be who occupy opposite sides of the table, leaning over to touch hands oftener than occasion warranted. Their eyes were fixed on each other, held together by an enchantment, searching the other's features, remembering the thrilling stranger of the night. No time would ever be so rich for them again. Jack, who was not fond of tea over-sweet, ladled spoonful after spoonful of sugar into his cup, unaware that he had put in even one, then drank the result with no sign of distaste. Lilian had drawn patterns all over her porridge with a spoon, and left most of it. Now she was cutting up her bacon into tiny pieces, eating them very slowly, with long pauses to see whether Jack were enjoying his and what his gaze was saying to her about that or anything else.

There was a visible bloom on her this morning, a glow to her skin and a shine to her eyes, as though a bud had opened in early sunshine. She had put up the flowing hair of the wedding-day, plaiting it neatly and winding it round her head to make a shining crown, for now she was a matron. And Jack, once so matter-of-fact and skilful at keeping his feelings to himself, wore a bemused look his mother had never seen before, a faint smile touching the mouth normally a shade stern. He took a token draught of rapidly-cooling tea, and then put the cup absent-mindedly down several inches from the table. It smashed on the flagged floor, showering tea over Mary's skirts and effectively wakening the newly-weds from their dream.

'There, now!' Mary said. 'Look what you've done. I'd nobbut four of that set left and now there's three. Well, if you two mean to breakfast off each other and leave my good food we might as well get afoot and start day's work. Amos, there's stuff to be brought back from Drill Hall when tha can rouse thisen. I'd wash some o' table cloths only it's Sunday – but that doesn't mean there's any call to be idle, our Lilian, so look sharp.'

'Yes, Mam.' Odd though it sounded at first Lilian had decided on this form of address. 'Mother-in-law' was much too formal, and 'Mary' much too familiar. Far easier to talk as they talked. As she got up from the table something rustled in her pocket.

'Oh! I'd quite forgotten. My cousin brought me a letter from Uncle Lewis. It quite went out of my head last night.' She blushed. 'May I read it? There might be something in it, a message for all of us, not only me.'

'Nay, if it's private...' Amos began, but she had opened the envelope, and was reading, wide-eyed. She beckoned Jack to her side, and he read it with her, his arm round her shoulders.

'Dear Niece,
    My apologies for not being with you on this happy occasion, business pressing somewhat here. Augustus at least can deputise for me. I was rejoiced to see you so restored to health on my visit to yr. new home. May I wish you and yr. spouse the best of fortune and happiness in yr. married life. I enclose something wh. may help to set you up in the beginning of it.
                    Yr. affte. Uncle, Lewis Hambleden'

They all stared as she unfolded the envelope-within-an-envelope. A banknote fluttered out, settling on the table.

'Two hundred pounds,' Jack said, awed. 'By Gow!'

None of them had ever seen so much money, even Lilian.

'Is it real?' Amos enquired, dazed.

'O' course it's real,' Mary assured him. 'He were a proper gentleman, Sir Lewis.'

'And he said I'd be hearing from him.' Lilian was still staring at the note. 'I never thought any more about it.' They had had various presents from neighbours who knew only Jack, not her: a side of ham, a cheese, an old workbox fitted up with sewing equipment from a farmer's elderly sister, a new hoe. An ancient cousin of Mary's living on the other side of Doncaster had sent

a quaint dress for Lilian, made in the style fashionable when
Queen Adelaide first came to England, of brown slubbed silk faded
with age and smelling of lavender. But Sir Lewis's present out-
classed all of these. As they looked at it in silence, the bells of the
parish church began to peal out across the quiet valley. Sabra
wandered in through the open back door, went to Jack and Lilian
in turn for caresses, then foraged in the larder for anything she
could find in the way of greenery or fruit. Mary shooed her out,
though absent-mindedly, returning to say, 'What shall you do wi'
it?'

Jack looked at Lilian, whose answering look said, 'What you will.'

'Sheep,' he said. 'I've always wanted 'em. I'll buy Low Field,
it's all of two acres. We can fence it up to take crops in one and
sheep in t'other – a dozen or twenty, say. We've enough to feed 'em
on in winter, then in spring they can move into t'other field and
leave theirs to yield hay. That'll leave us with lambs. It's a good
sheltered place, we can't lose 'em in snow, and the slope drains it.
If I buy a score and each throws twins, that's forty profit.'

A horrid fear of what might attach to the status of farmer's wife
overcame Lilian. 'We won't have to kill them, will we? The lambs?'

Jack patted her shoulder. 'That we won't. What d'you take me
for? I'll not make a murderer of thee, or any of us. Lambs'll be
sold at sheep fairs for breeding, not to butchers – I wouldn't fancy
that.'

'You'll need a herd,' Amos said. 'A lad, and a dog.'

'There's plenty of lads wants work. And Burton at Howclere
breeds dogs.'

'Happen Lilian might like a bit of yon to go for her dowry,' Mary
suggested, eyeing the fateful note.

'She's her own dowry.' Jack touched the coronal of hair as
though it were gold indeed. 'But she must do as she wants. It's only
my idea.'

'You know I want what you do. It's ours, not mine. We'll buy
your sheep, and I'll be shepherdess, if you like.'

'Wi' a little straw hat and a crook and ribbons, like the old
pictures? It's nowt like that, love.'

Lilian was surprised, as she was increasingly to be by Jack. She
knew about the Arcadian shepherdess costumes so popular for
fancy dress occasions, but when had Jack seen them? He never

missed an opportunity of looking inside any book that came his way, so perhaps he had found a picture of one of these Little Bo Peeps there. Her husband, she decided, was not only gentle, tender, exciting and beautiful (she was studying the strong curving line of his throat, rising from the open shirt-neck) but remarkably wise as well. He astonished her further by saying, 'There's this Married Women's Property Act now. That means I can't take all that's thine, so pick summat that can be *all* thine.'

You, her eyes told him, you are all mine and I want nothing else. But to please his pride she said, 'I'll take ten pounds, and choose.' She had already chosen: a new bat for him, to stand as substitute for his old beloved one, which must give out some day.

'Tha' might like a pianner,' Amos suggested helpfully. Lilian laughed.

'I can't even play one, Dad. They tried to teach me but it went in at one ear and out at the other. No, I don't want anything like that. I haven't any fancy tastes. Let's get on with the work and leave you and Jack to add up figures.'

As she and Mary bustled about, aproned, Amos and Jack sat at the cleared table with paper, pen and ink. The women heard snatches of conversation. 'If rent's twenty-seven shilling a month, then a fair price'd be . . .' 'Twining's Billy wants work. He's simple, but he'd be honest enough.'

'We could keep hens, too,' Lilian suggested over the washing-up. Mary shook her head. 'Too much bother. All the feeding and hatching. Too many chicks die, and hens lay abroad. It can take hours to collect eggs of a morning. We kept 'em when Jack was little, but I couldn't be mithered wi' 'em now.'

'You've got me. I could collect the eggs, and feed the hens. We could have one cockerel . . .' She was remembering Old Howard's long-dead wife, and her own childhood excursions to the gardener's cottage to help in the scattering of grain and the gathering in her basket of eggs maliciously deposited in the most remote and un-likely corners, a challenge to sharp young eyes and nimble young hands. There had been a splendid cock, a fine fellow of golden browns and sheeny peacock blues, strutting among his humble wives and waking the day with a shout shrill enough to carry to the Dower House. Yes, they would have one just like him. Mary inter-rupted her visions.

'Can tha kill chickens?'

Lilian was startled. 'Kill them?'

'Aye. Wring their necks. It's got to be done if we're to eat. Nay, never look so down, lass, for I'm smart enough at it.' She looked complacently at her large strong hands, work-lined, short-nailed. 'It's none so bad as pigs, if that's any comfort to thee.' Lilian shuddered and filled a bowl of potatoes for peeling. She failed to notice that Mary left her the bulk of the dinner preparation, even to the face-flushing basting of the meat in the oven. It was the first meal of her married life, for breakfast hardly counted, and she might as well get used to it. In her haste to get from one place to another, pantry to table, table to pan and oven, Mary noticed that her hesitancy in walking almost disappeared; she no longer held on to the edges of furniture. Mary nodded, satisfied. Work was the cure for almost everything, barring love. By the look of this bridal pair, that would take a long time; a lifetime, if they were lucky.

And so the hens came to Stainbeck, soon after the decision had been made. It was a pouring wet day when they arrived, trussed bundles of wet flattened feathers in a cart, huddled miserably together in silence, but for an occasional frightened cluck or squawk, even the proud cock quiet, throwing his eye here and there for a sight of the danger he feared for himself and his six wives. Jack and Lilian lifted them out gently, smoothing the small wet heads, untrussed their feet, and ushered them into the fowl-house Amos had made for them.

He was very proud of it, 'fit for t'Queen', was his description, though it was doubtful whether Her Majesty's bulk would have fitted inside, roomy though it was, this weather-tight house of wood (for bricks would have been too damp and porous) facing south so that the fowls could enjoy the early sun, well lit with real glass windows, approached by a neat door with a lock on it, for fear of foxes, and floored with a mixture of lime, cinders and gravel. Its walls were whitewashed for cleanliness, against the dreaded vermin which cling to poultry.

Once inside, the drenched travellers began to recover, fluffing out their feathers and beginning to cluck more hopefully. Lilian had supplied their feeding-trough with grain, though Mary grumbled that it would spoil them to find food laid out except at

240

one of their three daily feeding-times. They made their way to it and began to peck, turning as they were satisfied to the earthenware water-pan with a smaller bowl upturned inside it, so that they might stand within and drink without getting their feet wet.

'They *like* it,' Lilian said. 'They're quite at home already.'

'Aye, and I'd like it, too, if I was to come in out o' t'wet and find thee and a good spread waiting.' Jack squeezed her waist and received a damp-faced kiss for the compliment. The hens were already finding the perches they fancied, scratching among the straw on the floor, and generally behaving as though the trying journey from market had never happened. The cock assumed a theatrical attitude, not condescending to scratch about, fixing the humans with a challenging eye.

'Henry,' Lilian said.

'What?'

'We shall have to call him Henry. Because he has six wives, you see. I don't know much history but I do remember Henry the Eighth.'

Amos had joined them. 'Aye,' he said. 'He turned out monks and friars and priors an' all, did owd Harry, from Kirkstall and Fountains and Jervaux, and t'other abbeys. He were a right bad man. Did I ever tell thee, Jack, how the Abbot of Byland came to lead his monks to Jervaux? Well, it seems they were lost i' the hills round Byland, when Abbot turned a corner and met wi' a bonny lass in a blue robe and a babby in her arms, and t'babby pulled down a winter branch in its little hand, and branch bursted out in flower. Then Abbot knew who he'd met, and he says, "Fair and tender lass, what dost wi' Thy Son in this desert place? I beg Thee to lead me and my brethren out of the wilderness to our new monastery, for we are of Byland." And she said, "Ye were late of Byland, but are now of Jervaux. Sweet Son, be their leader, for I'm wanted elsewhere." And t'babby went before 'em through the air, the blossomy branch in his hand, and led 'em to Jervaux.'

'Nay, I didn't know that,' Jack said. 'Come on in now, our Lilian's getting wet.' He locked the fowl-house on Henry, three Catherines, two Annes and a Jane. It was to be hoped they would get on better than their human counterparts.

The little gold-spangled Dutch fowl were happily settled, and laying well, when the sheep came. Farmer Sadler had driven them back from market with some he had bought himself, to save the inexperienced Jack and the slightly simple Billy Twining from what might have been a fearsome journey. Lilian saw them coming over the low hill that ended in Sadler's land, a straggle of grey forms running confusedly in all directions, the great broad-shouldered hulk of John Sadler behind them, waving a stick and shouting, his black and white wall-eyed dog at its work of herding.

Between dog and man they were got into the field that was to be theirs, newly fenced off, and into their pen, where they huddled together, baaing. Lilian made her way to it over the slushy ground, and stretched out a hand to the nearest one. She was pulled back roughly before she could touch it

'Let it alone!' Jack said angrily. 'Don't you know better than touch sheep's wool? It can give you summat nasty, that can. Never let me see you do that again.'

Lilian bridled, hurt at his tone. 'Oh, my apologies, I'm sure. I was only trying to comfort the poor thing – it's not much more than a lamb.'

'Lamb or not, let it be.'

'What about the shearers? Do they all get something nasty?'

'That's different.' Jack went to talk to John Sadler. She sensed that it was not merely fear for her that was making him edgy, but the new responsibility that came with the sheep, the extra work and the extra knowledge he would need. Her own annoyance melted. Her money had bought the sheep, she must make it as easy as she could for him to look after them. They were both sure it had been right to buy the sheep. As John Sadler said over a pint of ale by their fire that night, it was true enough that no ram, no lamb; no sheep, no wool; no wool, no spinner; no spinner, no weaver; no weaver, no cloth; no cloth, no clothes . . . and so the litany of Yorkshire went on.

But nothing was very easy, that winter, when snow and ice kept away but continuous rain fell and fog came down in depressing blankets. The Cheviot sheep cropped well on the lush grass and clover of their field and wolfed the plentiful crop of turnips Jack provided, but they obviously hated the rain and damp, crowding in a corner of the field in an attempt to keep dry. Jack took advice. Nothing drastic was likely to happen to the little flock, but for their comfort and the best lambing results he was advised to build a shelter for them. The sheep-house that resulted from his labours, combined with those of Amos and Billy, was constructed of wood from two felled trees and a lattice roof of woven hay and twigs, with more hay to provide a sort of carpet. Lilian was reminded of the tale of Rumpelstiltskin, which must somehow have slipped into her childhood ears among the Arthurian legends, and the girl who was set to weave straw into gold, for so it felt, making some sort of substantial roof from bits of material which seemed to want little to do with each other. But the ewes seemed to like it, and grew great in lamb, crowded in their curious house with their small tractable ram, the very opposite of the arrogant Henry in disposition.

They needed daily feeding from their trough, whatever the weather, and the poultry demanded it three times a day, starting at first light, when they made a noise out of all proportion to their numbers as Lilian went out to throw their food. They lived up to their reputation by laying well, every-day layers in winter as well as summer, supplying enough eggs for the family and some over for the market or for preserving in lime and water; so well that none of them was doomed for the pot, to Lilian's relief. She was not yet prepared to face their slaughter, even at Mary's hands and out of sight.

Early rising, swift dressing, cursory washing in cold water, a non-stop day's work in the kitchen and the fields, early supper and early bed were now Lilian's life. She felt and saw herself change, her white lady's hands grow red and cracked, her careful arrangement of hair piled into a practical cap, her feet encased in heavy boots which defied cleaning. There was nothing she could do about it but to keep rubbing goose-grease into her hands, and to wash her hair with essence prepared from dried rosemary. At least it stopped her smelling of the hen-house. She thought of the days when she had reclined in Lilian's Bower, trimming and polishing her nails into shining filberts, rubbing Mamma's scented cream into her hands. Yet she would not have those days back; so long as Jack thought no less of her.

But their short, precious nights were as ardent as ever, and by day they only met over hasty meals. It was Mary who snapped at her once, surprisingly, 'Tha doesn't look much like a lady these

243

days. Can't tha take a bit more trouble? When I were a young wench I'd see to it I did miself justice.'

Goaded, Lilian answered sharply, 'I thought you wanted me to be a help to Jack and take my place in the household. Do you expect me to be a fashion-plate as well? Because I'm afraid it's not possible.'

Mary looked taken aback, if not ashamed. 'I meant it's a pity for a handsome lass to let hersen go. Happen it's my fault – I ought to do more. I've been leaning on thee too much.'

'No, of course you haven't, Mam. What rubbish. You couldn't do more if there were twice as many hours in the day. There's all the extra dirt coming into the house from the Low Field, what with the new crops and Billy tramping in for his dinner, and one of us has to go to market on Fridays – not to speak of the cooking and the brewing, and Dad not being fit to do much outside . . .' She paused for breath. 'It strikes me you and I have both got more than enough to do without me wasting time prinking in front of a mirror.'

'Nay, nay. I want thee to be a credit to Jack, that's all.'

'A credit to Jack? Do you suppose he's the time to sit admiring me? Never you fear, when spring comes and we've made enough money I'll go to Doncaster and set myself up in finery like the Queen of Sheba. You won't know me, I'll be such a dream of beauty.'

She was laughing as she went back to her work, but Mary sighed, looking after her. She had never seen anyone change as much as her daughter-in-law, and though it was good and right that she should have turned from a poor helpless creature into a tough practical housewife Mary regretted the picture-book delicacy she had once owned.

At least one faint line on Lilian's brow had come there because of her worry over Jack. He was working harder than he had ever worked before, and now it mattered that he should not ruin his health and fitness in the perpetual damp and chill of the fields. The shadow of rheumatism lay over all farmers, ready to cripple their limbs and agonise their muscles. Amos had it already. Since Lilian had first come to Stainbeck his shoulders had become more stooped and his hands more contorted. Though he smiled often, the sudden pain he felt could not always be hidden. Jack *must* not

244

go the same way. A professional cricketer could not be less than physically perfect; and if Jack's chosen career were ruined, then his life would be ruined too.

Lilian watched him furtively in the evenings, when the day's work was at last done, and he sat by the fire, stretching his legs to ease their aching, his head heavy with weariness. She knew what he saw in the flames. Green pitches in summer sunshine, fellow-players of his own mettle, crowds eager to watch the play, himself defending and conquering wickets. Sometimes he talked of the fixtures for next year. It was rumoured that the Prince of Wales was to patronise Lord's with a bevy of fashionable friends, so perhaps Jack would have the chance of playing before royalty. With these dreams Jack tried to shorten the winter, and his family supported him nobly, guessing at the scores he might make and the records he might beat.

But Lilian grieved over the tired look on his face, the tightness of the skin over the fine bones, and the stiffness with which he moved his shoulders. She had taught herself, with difficulty, to knit, so that she could make him a thick woollen jersey to wear under his sheepskin jacket. It was of a strange and baggy shape, with sleeves markedly different in length, but Jack kissed her for it and said she'd have him as nesh as an old woman with her coddling of him.

At first, in these dark nights of December, the deer Sabra would snuffle at the door to be let in and lie by the fire at their feet. She had grown no bigger, though her look of fragility was no more. Mary complained that the warmth of the fire brought out a reek from the fur.

'Deer don't reek, only goats,' said Amos.

'This one does.' But she let it stay, because at heart she was fond of its gentle ways. Then, one day, Sabra discovered the sheep. Butting her way through a gap in the orchard fence, she found herself in Low Field, amongst strange creatures whose wool steamed in the damp air. At first they ran from her as though she had been the sheepdog puppy who was their guardian and slept in an outhouse; then one, venturing nearer, found her out to be harmless, and the other ewes approached too, eyeing her timidly then settling down to graze, reassured. Only the ram put down his head and ran at her, but her flight told him that she was not something which would turn round and bark; thereafter he let her alone.

Jack found her cropping unconcernedly with the flock, and was astonished. They had all thought her a lone, exotic being who enjoyed her orchard solitude. Evidently it was not so. 'If she thinks she's a sheep, let her,' Lilian said.

So Christmas came, and with it a sudden lightening of the gloom, mild weather and sunshine and a general feeling of gladness. Between them Mary and Lilian baked an oven-full of Yorkshire pork pies, very fine and delicate, and gathered the best of the winter greens, reserving a gift from one of their wedding guests at Barnswood, a handsome goose, for Christmas Day itself.

'We'd best go to Chapel,' Mary said glumly, so they went. But the Reverend Balmforth was too hidebound in his tradition of Puritanism to pay any regard to a festival he and his predecessors had thought of as largely pagan. A brief prayer, no decorations, no special hymns. The Ellershaws were used to it and would have thought little of it, but Lilian's annoyance was impossible to ignore. She fumed audibly, with heavy sighs and impatient standings and sittings. After all, but for the quirk of fate she might have been an Anglican clergyman's wife. Jack shot amused looks at her as she glared at Mr Balmforth and ostentatiously knelt when everybody else was sitting uncomfortably forward with faces bowed over hands. When all filed out of the chapel, to a normally dismal improvisation on the harmonium, she clutched his arm and began to sing, in a high true untrained soprano that rang out in the still air.

'Angels, from the realms of glory,
    Wing your flight o'er all the earth!
Ye who sang creation's story
    Now proclaim Messiah's birth!
        Come and worship –
    Worship Christ, the new-born King!'

Utter silence fell among the gossipers. Then the fat wife of a tradesman joined in, and her husband's bass boomed in below her treble line. Slowly others who knew the old Yorkshire hymn added their voices.

'Shepherds in the fields abiding,
  Watching o'er your flocks by night,
God is now with man residing,
  Yonder shines the Infant-light,
    Come and worship –
  Worship Christ, the new-born King!'

What the Reverend Balmforth thought, glowering in the porch, nobody bothered to enquire, except perhaps his shocked wife. Jack shook his head.

'You'll be in *Yorkshire Post* tomorrow. That'll read like a fair old tale.'

She hung on to his arm. 'I don't care. Time somebody made a cheerful noise in this place, and it might as well be us. Whatever made your people go over to Chapel?'

'How do I know? I weren't born. Some row or other, I daresay.'

Amos was still wiping tears of mirth from his eyes, and Mary struggling between conventional affront and unwilling approval. 'That were a terrible thing to do,' she told Lilian, unsmiling, 'carrying on like a ballad-wench at a fair.'

'I know. But everybody enjoyed it, didn't they? Don't worry, Mam, I feel a lot better now; let's go home and have our Christmas dinner.'

Twining's Billy was basting the goose, for which task he would receive an extra sixpence and a share of it. Potatoes, roasted turnips, the hearts of greens, surrounded it on a huge blue china dish. To follow there was a plum pudding with brandy in it, made a month earlier and kept maturing in the larder. They drank milk-punch, growing first merry, then quiet. Amos and Mary nodded off by the fire; Jack and Lilian disappeared upstairs. The young sheepdog gnawed bones and scraps in the outhouse; Sabra, lolling on straw in the sheep-shelter, toyed with a piece of young Swedish turnip.

Boxing Day dawned fair, and the days after that. Daring snow-drops appeared in the garden, farm-boys whistled and birds sang unseasonable songs. On New Year's Eve John Sadler, his big deaf silent wife and two big silent sons, with their sister whose cheeks were like red plush pincushions, came to Stainbeck for a cup and a crack, as the farmer put it.

The conversation was comfortable and intermittent.

'That were a good song tha gave us after Chapel, Mrs Jack,'
Sadler said. 'Happen it took a few by surprise, but it were a joyful
noise unto the Lord, as they say. Weren't it, Martha?'

'I saw a primmyrose this morning,' his wife replied, not having
heard a word. 'That's a rare bad sign.'

'First I've heard of it,' Mary said. 'Good sign, more like. I can
smell fortune i' the air.' Four Ellershaw heads had been bent over
sheets of facts and figures the night before, with great satisfaction.
Given good luck for the lambing season, and continued good laying
from the hens, Lilian's dowry looked like gaining interest. All of
them knew it was not wise to count chickens before they were
hatched, but this was literally what they were doing, having in-
vested in another dozen hens with the intention of allowing a
number of eggs to hatch and selling the resultant birds. Lilian was
fascinated to know that it was possible to know which eggs would
produce males and which females; hens tended to come from
round-shaped eggs, cocks from the oval ones, and if in doubt the
air-cell at the base of the egg would settle the question, for in
female-producing eggs the cell would lie a little to the side. She
never tired of holding the fragile globes up to the light and
prophesying the sex that would emerge.

'In Paris,' said Mrs Sadler through a mouthful of hot-pot, 'folk
was etting rats and mice while t'Siege were on.'

Jack put down his knife and fork hastily, and John Sadler said
loudly, 'We want to know nowt about that, Martha, thank you
kindly. That's a rare nice picture you've getten, Mrs Ellershaw.
I've not seen it before.'

'That's our Lilian's. Jack give it her for Christmas.' It was a
brightly-coloured print showing a small May Queen crowned with
flowers and surrounded by her little attendants. He had found it
in Doncaster and thought instantly that Lilian would like it, so
cheerfully different from the pictures they both remembered at the
house in Chelsea. 'She got a book, too,' Mary said proudly. Lilian
was invited to display it, a handsome copy of *Through the Looking-
Glass* by the mysterious 'Lewis Carroll' who was said to be a famous
professor of mathematics but amused himself and a great many
other people by writing nonsense books. Jack, who longed to be
educated, tried to fathom it, particularly as he remembered Lilian
making a joke about flamingoes which was out of Mr Carroll's

earlier book. But its fantasy and weird logic defeated him, though he liked to hear Lilian reading aloud from it of an evening in her pretty clear voice, stuff about walruses and carpenters and oysters and kettles of fish. Jack urged her to read a little of it now for the edification of the company. Three of the Sadlers listened in polite if stunned silence, while Martha, blissfully removed from it by her deafness, consumed bread and cheese and tea.

Somehow the time had gone long past the usual hour for bed. 'Listen!' said Mary, holding up her finger. Far away the parish church bells of Barnswood were ringing a peal. It was midnight, the Old Year gone.

'Well, God bless us,' Amos said. He bestowed a kiss each on Mary and Lilian, a hearty handshake on the guests, who after a health to the New Year drunk in Mary's home-brew, departed homewards by the light of lanterns.

In bed, too sleepy for loving, Lilian and Jack kissed each other a solemn good-night. 'May it be our year, love,' he said, 'the best of our lives.'

They slept late, waking at full light to the insistent crowing of Henry.

'Good gracious!' Lilian leapt out of bed, dragging on her woollen bed-gown and slipping her feet into the first shoes she could find. 'The hens! You take your time, I'll put the kettle on when I come back in. Mam and Dad can't be up yet, with Henry making all that din.'

She hurried downstairs and through the passage to the kitchen, noticing with surprise that the kitchen door stood open – it was always closed at night to keep the warmth in. Then she stopped, transfixed. Mary lay on the floor, face downwards, one arm flung out and the other bent under her.

'Mam! Oh, what is it?' She dropped on her knees and turned Mary half over. She was breathing, but with an unnatural heaviness, and her face was darkly flushed. The hand Lilian raised fell limp as soon as she released it. Terrified, she ran to the bottom of the stairs and shouted for Jack.

CHAPTER NINETEEN

But why? Amos asked the doctor repeatedly, too distracted to know how often he had asked before. Why, when his wife had never had a day's illness in her life, should she be the one to be struck down? It seemed against all sense and reason that she, so active one day, should lie inert the next, just from a fall on the kitchen floor.

'It was not the fall,' the doctor answered patiently. 'These seizures cause a collapse, not the other way round. And as to why they afflict some people but not others, there's no telling. Mrs Ellershaw's over sixty and a fine big woman – if she were younger and slimmer I'd be more surprised than I am. Keep her in bed, give her liquids and some food if she feels like it, but not too much.'

'She's in a lot of pain,' Jack said. 'What's to be done about that?'

'I'll make up some pills for her containing digitalis. They'll help, and the pain will gradually lessen in any case. If you come down this evening I'll have them ready.'

'But you'll visit her again?'

'Not this week, unless you send word that she's worse. There's a lot of illness in Barnswood, despite the fine weather – you know the proverb, "a green Christmas makes a fat churchyard".' Unconscious that he had said something profoundly tactless, he left. They heard his trap rattle off down the lane, as though horse and driver were glad to get away from the house.

'It's a wonder he wasn't whistling,' Jack said bitterly. 'Frisky as a dog wi' two tails. That's no way to be in a house of sickness.'

'He sees a lot of sickness, Jack,' Lilian said. 'And much worse than Mam is. In fact it's a good sign that he didn't seem very concerned about her. Let's look on the bright side.'

But she spoke more hopefully than she felt. It was so frighteningly unlike Mary to lie still, moaning sometimes, answering Lilian's gentle questions in an inaudible mutter. Her face seemed to have fallen in, and the flush that had been on it had given way to a

250

deadly paleness. Lilian spent all the time she could spare at the bedside, talking of trivial things, any bits of news she had been able to gather, urging the sick woman to take gruel or hot milk, sometimes rubbing her chest and shoulder, where the pain seemed to be.

What she omitted to tell her was the dismaying story that Jack brought two days after Mary's seizure. He had insisted that he should take over the feeding of the poultry while Lilian did the nursing. As the weather continued fine, the hens were laying abroad, sometimes in the nests prepared for them about the yard, sometimes in cunningly remote places. Jack searched all the spots, knowing before he started that something untoward had happened in the night to upset the clucking, restless hens. It was only too true.

'Nowt but empty shells. And not as many of them as there might be. A rat's been in, or happen a weasel. One of the young 'uns is dead, and summat's had a go at it. That's this week's profits gone, the eggs and the chicks for hatching. Well, it'll not happen again, I'll see to that.' He and his father set about the work of filling in any possible gap in the walls through which the lissom body of a rat or weasel could have made a way. The hard labour they put in was, as things turned out, wasted, for on Twelfth Night the weather turned. Steady rain was coming down when Jack went out with the chicken-feed. He shut the fowls in after feeding, for it did them no good to wander about in the wet. The second of Farmer Sadler's sons, Hugh, heard the story from Jack at the border of Low Field, where the Ellershaw men were strengthening the fence to prevent the ewes straying and dropping their lambs in remote places.

'Wormwood and rue,' Hugh said, 'that's what you ought to be sowing round t'nests, anywhere they're like to lay.'

'But they can't be sown till spring,' Jack pointed out.

'Aye, that's true. There's stoats about, too, and I've seen 'em get up a high wall before now.' He surveyed the flock. 'Them ewes wants to be under better cover than yon.' He indicated the roofed shelter under which some of them were huddled. 'They'll get the foot-rot poddling about i' this downpour.'

'We can't build on to it now,' said Amos. 'We've no help but Billy, and he's as much use as a stuffed dummy. They'll have to tak' their chance.'

'Aye, well. Give 'em plenty o' Swedish turnips. Mangel's no good for lambin'-time.'

'I never heard yon lad utter so much,' Amos reflected, when Hugh had gone. 'Pity it weren't more uplifting. He's a proper Jonah, he is.'

As it proved, Hugh's gloomy words were borne out. The rains went on as though the skies had permanently opened and would never close again, every day as grey as the last, Low Field a swamp. Jack caught a heavy cold, becoming so feverish that Lilian announced he would stay indoors if she had to lock the doors to keep him in. So Amos went painfully out to see to the flock; and, after a long time, came home and let himself in very quietly.

'Lilian.' She came out of the kitchen, wiping floury hands on her apron.

'Where's Jack?' Amos asked her.

'Gone to bed. He was so bad I made him go.'

'He'll be worse when he hears this.' The old man's face told her what the news would be. 'There's three of 'em dead – the ewes. One's dropped her lamb premature, and that's dead too. Stone dead. And not a sign on 'em of what might be wrong.'

'Oh, Dad! Oh, poor things. And poor Jack. I don't know how I'm going to tell him.'

'He'll ha' to know. As if we'd not enough badly, wi'out this. Lil, don't tell Mother.'

'As if I would! Especially now she's a bit better and taking food. I kept it from her about the eggs, too.'

When Jack came downstairs they told him. He put his head down on his arms, sprawling across the table, and there was nothing they could say to comfort him.

'I shouldn't ha' risked it,' he said, muffled. 'I shouldn't ha' risked the money on summat I don't know about. I'd best give up – go and work on t'railroad. I'd make a better navvy nor a farmer.'

'Don't you dare say such a thing!' Lilian flared. 'We've had bad luck, the devil's own luck, since Christmas, but it's not your fault. Sheep die of all sorts of things – I've been reading the book Mr Sadler lent you. We'll just have to look after the ones that are left, and if you think you're going out there yourself, you're very mistaken, Jack Ellershaw. Dad and I and Billy will do what's to be done. Now then!'

He knew she was not to be defied, and he was too broken in spirit to try. Very near weeping, he watched them go down to Low Field, his wife with a thick wool shawl over her head and an old frieze cloak round her shoulders, Amos a bundled-up little figure, hobbling with a stick, and Billy, walking with loose un-coordinated steps and staring up at the sky. He was carrying a spade. Lilian had worked out from the text-book on sheep rearing that the ewes had probably died from braxy or the black disease, and if they had others had probably caught it. In any case the bodies must be buried at once.

As though Heaven had relented, propitiated by the sacrifice, the rain began to slacken off not long after the graves had been filled in. Watery sunshine filtered through the clouds, even its mild warmth sending steam up from the sodden fields. And the lambing began.

Jack was well enough now to go out of doors, which was for-tunate, for every hand was needed to help the ewes, all first-time bearers. Jack had attended at lambing-time on farms where he had worked; but Lilian had never seen anything born before. When the first lamb slid out, bloody and unrecognisable for what it was, she jumped back with a stifled scream. Jack heard it, saw from the corner of his eye her reaction, and knew from the closeness between them what she was feeling; but there was no time to spend on sentiment. He let her watch, doing what he had to do by the light of a flickering old horn-lantern.

So this was birth, this ugly distressing process more like the carnage of a battle-field than the beautifully idealised giving of life which was the image fed to girl-children. This was what women had to go through, not only ewes. Sickened and shocked, she looked in spite of herself as Amos dealt with another struggling animal, and at last said, 'What can I do?'

'Catch howd. That's it. Now pull, help her.'

Jack held up a tiny limp form. 'This 'un's dead.' Lilian, bloodied to the elbows but getting over her first sick revulsion, took the slimy object from him and tried to clean it. A dark eye flickered up at her and a foot twitched. 'It's not, it's not!' she cried. 'It was half-smothered. What shall I do with it?'

'Get it out of here,' Jack called back across his shoulder. He had twins on his hands, tiny things, one following hard upon the

253

other, the ewe distressed. Lilian ran back across the field to the house, not knowing what she should do or how; yet once indoors knew enough by instinct to clear off what clung to the newly-born and dry it, to put it before the fire wrapped in an old cloth, then to warm milk and feed it, drop by drop, from the spout of a teapot into the gaping mouth. At first the lamb had shivered and jumped convulsively; now it was quiet, sucking the milk from time to time, staring blindly at the glow of the fire. She saw the drying wool form into curls, the transparent ears emerge, the tiny hoofs, and realised that what she had on her lap was a baby like any other. Until then she had wished desperately that Mary could be by her side, telling her what to do. Now she knew that for herself.

They saved eight lambs that night, losing two and their mothers, leaving the safely delivered ones under shelter with the lambs by them, scenting and recognising one another, so that the next day mother would feed child and call to it and no rejection would ensue. The men were exhausted, cold, barely able to speak. Lilian got their top clothing and their boots off and a hot drink made with rum and milk into them. Then she dragged in from the yard the old bath Amos had used in his pit days, still brought into service on a Saturday night, and filled it with kettle after kettle of hot water.

'Get your clothes off, both of you, and into that. I shan't watch but I'll scrub your backs if you want me to. Quick, now.' It was not the first time she had insisted on their having hot baths and massaged aching muscles into pliancy. Something had remained with her from the days at Fellgate Wells House, even the dissolving of Epsom salts in the water. Jack let his father take the first turn. He knew his own would be the more enjoyable.

Afterwards they lay together on the bright rug in front of the smouldering fire, wrapped in one blanket, happy and sleepy.

'I was awful,' Lilian murmured. 'I was frightened, you know. Next time I won't be.' Beside them, in a cocoon of cloth, the lamb slept.

Mary was told the good news, not the bad. She smiled, saying, 'Well done,' not wanting to know what had been the hazards or how they had been faced. She who had always been dauntless must now save herself for the sake of the others for whom she could do nothing. She knew that Lilian's back ached constantly from the strain of going up and downstairs as well as the extra work she had to do, that Amos worried himself sleepless, and that Jack seemed to have aged two years since Christmas. But her own pain had grown less; it would be foolhardy to risk a relapse by trying to go downstairs and take her turn. She lay in her bed, day in and day out, reading newspapers, knitting, receiving – once – the Reverend Balmforth, to whom she had nothing particular to say, nor he to her, discussing recipes with Lilian, who had become a surprisingly good cook now that she was no longer supervised.

'You've heard nowt more of your folk, then.'

Lilian shook her head. 'Not since the shawl from Digby, at Christmas. It's far too fine to wear. Poor man, he doesn't know how things are up here.'

'He's not wed yet?'

'I don't suppose so. The Army doesn't encourage it at his age, and Penelope's very young too.'

'And Sir Lewis hasn't written?'

'I wrote to thank him for the wonderful present, and told him what we were going to do with it, and he wrote back and said he was glad but we were to be careful and take good advice. About the sheep.'

Mary studied the downbent auburn head, so pretty on its lily-stalk of a neck, and the roughened hands busy on the turning of a sheet sides-to-middle. She had a fair idea that not enough advice had been taken about the sheep, and that more had happened at lambing-time than she had been told. But it was best not to know for sure, not to set her heart beating wildly and start the shooting-pains in her arm and chest. Instead she talked idly to Lilian about her child-hood, the Hall and the Dower House, her uncle's sporting company and her mother's ladylike friends, showing an interest which sur-prised her daughter-in-law.

'I saw a bit of life in service when I were young,' she said defensively. 'It's nice to be reminded. Takes one's mind off things. Read us a bit of the *Post*, will you. No, don't bother. Just tell us some news.'

Lilian scanned the pages. 'Well, Princess Louise is soon to marry the Marquess of Lorne. The Queen wore ermine and a new crown to open Parliament. Sir Henry Ponsonby has said something quite publicly contradicting the scandalous rumours about the Queen's servant, John Brown. He's the godfather of Digby's Penelope – Sir

255

Henry, I mean. She stays with them at their house in Mayfair – I think it's in Mayfair – and hears all kinds of bits and pieces from the Court.' She saw Mary smile and nod, and thought how odd it was that when she had worked so hard to turn herself into a country-woman her mother-in-law should have taken to relishing snippets of fashionable news. Well, it was probably all a part of her illness. And Mary, like the weather, was improving. Lilian no longer needed to lift her, so heavy and helpless, until her back threatened to break in two and she had dark visions of what would happen to them all if she became a useless invalid again.

Her fear of that disaster receded now that Mary was coming downstairs in the evenings, supported by her two men, shown the new life beginning in the garden, entertained with stories of the sheep and hens that had survived, kept in the dark about those that had not. The hand-reared lamb was well and back in the Low Field, adopted by a healthy ewe, for its own mother had died, and the others were doing well on the special feed Hugh Sadler had prescribed for them. Four ewes of the original twelve were dead, but eight lambs had been added to the flock, and the little ram had survived the winter well. Silly Billy was proud of his own accomplishment, the remembering of the old sheep-counts that come from far back beyond the Dark Ages and the Romans. As the sheep were penned, one after another, his harsh high voice could be heard above the bleating of mothers and the tremulous cries of their young. 'Yain, tain, eddero, peddero, pitts': that meant five sheep were counted. Then 'Tayter, later, overro, coverro disc, yain disc', and so on, making up the seventeen animals.

As the sweet spring air came into the house, blowing away the winter stuffiness, and curtains and bed-linen were taken down to be washed and dried on clothes-lines in the yard, flapping wildly in the breeze like tethered prisoners struggling to escape, an exhilaration came to Lilian that was like nothing she had ever felt before. For the first time she was fully aware of herself, of her new health and strength and maturity, of joy in the living, grow-ing things around her. It was as though her existence before coming to Stainbeck had been a dreary, meaningless prologue to the real play. Pride: how strange never to have felt that before, pride in the slow recovery of Mary under her care, pride in the cherishing of Jack through a time that threatened him, pride in the lamb that pranced and butted in the meadow because she had nursed it back from death; pride in clean house-linen and scrubbed floors.

Yet pride, as ever, went before a fall. On a March morning Jack came in to breakfast with a face that told his wife there was trouble.

'Go on,' she said, turning bacon in the frying-pan. 'What is it?'

'Sabra's gone.'

'Oh, no!' She turned, aghast. The deer had been removed from Low Field when lambing began, and confined to her old home in the orchard. Gradually she had forgotten about being a sheep, and often appeared at the orchard gate hopeful to catch the eye of anybody who would take her in to the familiar smells and warmth of the kitchen. Once there, her ambition was to climb up on Jack's knee and demand his full attention. As she was now the size of an Airedale dog and growing distinctly plump, there were problems attached to this, but it was not in Jack to refuse affection, and Lilian sometimes declared herself jealous: she also liked to sit on Jack's knee.

'She can't have gone,' Lilian said. 'She couldn't have got through the fence.'

'She has, though. Nibbled through a place that was a bit worn away. She must have ate enough bark to choke her, little devil.'

'Perhaps she's with the sheep.'

'She's not – that was the first place I looked. And she's not in the gardens eating the young stuff, where you might expect. I don't know where to try next.' He looked so dejected that she went to him and gently propelled him towards his own chair.

'Sit down and have your breakfast. It'll do no good going without.' They tried to pretend to themselves and Amos that they were not worried. But the food was tasteless in their mouths, and the strong tea went cold in the cups. As soon as they had finished Jack went out. Lilian saw that he took his gun with him.

He should have been planting that morning, instead of walking abroad. Amos took on the work for him, so that it should not fall behind, laboriously digging and sowing, while Lilian went about the household tasks, with a heavy apprehensive feeling round her heart. When Jack came in, just before noon, she dreaded to hear what he would say, for she knew the burden of it already. The gun was still under his arm, and he carried nothing else.

'Well? Did you . . . find her?'

He shook his head, and sat down heavily at the table to tell her. He had gone through all the territory, likely and unlikely, hoping to find Sabra browsing in some remote corner, then back into Low Field in case she had made her way back to the sheep, thinking once that he had found her – but the sleeping creature by the hedge was a lamb. Then he had gone back through the market garden where the spring greens, broccoli and new cabbages grew, seeing that some of them had been recently nibbled on each side of a path which ended at the copse of no-man's land, where old Widow Adkins was allowed to gather firewood, though gipsies were strictly warned off. On the lowest rung of the fence that bordered it his sharp eyes saw tufts of blond fur, as though something had burrowed underneath. He walked through the copse, seeing here and there a strip of bark torn off very lightly, where something had stood up on small hind legs and delicately peeled it.

And then, further into the trees, he found the patch of spilled blood, soaking the earth and reddening the rough grass patches and early flowers of the celandine. He saw that it had gushed out, as if from the severing of an artery, and that the victim had lain there alive and bleeding. The trail of blood led further, along a path beaten between trees and scrub, and the foliage was flattened by an object having been dragged along it. At last the trail gave out, and only the marks of a human's passage along the narrow path remained, leaving snapped twigs and flattened herbage.

'A poacher. Aye. Not that this is poaching country, but there's no keepers to stop 'em potting small game. I reckon whoever it was was after rabbits – and he got a deer instead.' Jack laughed, without mirth. 'Must have thought it was his birthday and Christmas all in one. What irks me is that he didn't kill her right out, just wounded her bad and dragged her off. By God, I wish I had him here, the swine, I'd make him sorry he was born.'

'You're sure it was ... Sabra?'

'There were too many signs for it not to be. It was no rabbit, nor no hare. Oh, love, don't cry. You'll have me at it if you do, and there's no sense in being soft. She had a good life, even if it weren't very long, and a quick death once the ...' He patted Lilian's shoulder roughly and went swiftly out. When he was gone she gave way to tears. It was her first loss. They had never kept a

258

pet at home, her mother disliking dogs and regarding cats as kitchen things little better than rodents.

Sabra, the little rescued princess, Jack's wedding gift, escaped from the dark gloom of Rossetti's house to end in a poacher's gipsy-pot slung over the fire to make venison stew. There was an earthenware bowl Lilian had kept for Sabra's food, a brown dish with a green line round it. She took it up from the floor and put it into the bin kept for rubbish other than pig-food. She never wanted to see it again.

Life had to go on, even with a shadow over the brightness of the day before. She knew that Jack was growing restless as the spring advanced, longing for the start of the season and the end of his bondage to the small-holding. To please him, she got out his prized flannels, washed, dried and pressed them, made him two new neckcloths of silk, tenderly hemmed in her large irregular stitches. There were other things she could not supply. Summoning her courage to meet his pride, she chose an evening when they were alone downstairs, Mary resting and Amos out in the shed making a table for a man in Barnswood. Jack had lit his pipe and drawn a mug of beer; he was relaxed and amenable. Lilian produced from her pocket an envelope, and from the envelope twelve gold sovereigns. She counted them one by one into her lap, as he watched in surprise, then reached for his hand and placed them in it, with a tentative smile.

'Here! What's this?'

'What I kept back – from Uncle Lewis's present. You said I was to keep some.'

'Aye. Well, what are going to do with it?' He counted. 'And there's twelve here – you said you'd keep back ten.'

'I saved the extra two – from the eggs. The goldies have been laying so well, I thought it might be all right to . . .' Her eyes dropped before the piercing blue gaze. She was trying hard to make him understand without having to say it, but he would not.

'To what?' She could not guess what was going through his mind.

'To give it to you for what you need,' she said in a rush. 'A new bat and gloves and pads. They shouldn't cost more than that, should they, even the best ones, and I do want you to have the best.'

His expression was a blend of emotions, alarming her. She was not afraid of him, only of upsetting him by seeming to belong

259

to another world where money was more plentiful and men accepted gifts without being insulted at receiving something they had not worked for. It was so important that all differences between them should be levelled out, that he should take from her what she wished to give without embarrassment or anger.

But Jack was not, thank Heaven, angry. He pulled her to her feet and into his arms, looking down at her with love and wonder, though his words were harsh. 'I never met such a slithery, round-about baggage in all my born days. Aren't you ashamed, Mrs Ellershaw? Robbing poor fowls to buy cricket gear?'

'It wasn't the fowls, it was the housekeeping money – that I robbed, I mean. Only . . . oh Jack, do please take it. I don't want anything for myself. I can sew now, well, in a fashion, and I've plenty of stuff put aside to make up. Oh darling, do take it!'

Jack had never been used to being addressed as darling. He found he liked it very much; almost as much as he admired his unusual wife, who was clinging round his neck exactly as though she had been any submissive female with no will of her own. He struggled to express some of this, failed, and gave her a long and passionate kiss instead, which seemed to do just as well. It led to a spell of love-making such as the old parlour had seldom seen in its long life, and certainly not at that early hour of the evening. Then, rather breathless, he said, 'About the money! It's a good job I'm a trustworthy chap. Do you know how much such things cost?'

'Well, of course I don't,' Lilian said, twisting up her hair by her reflection in the glass of a picture. 'Pounds and pounds, I expect.'

'I could get a Lillywhite's Superior bat for ten bob. Buckskin leg-guards for one bob. Gloves for . . . oh, say about three. So a chap less honest than me could have put your twelve pounds in his pocket and gone for a trip round t'world.'

'Yes, well, men know about such things,' said Lilian airily. 'At least I wasn't silly enough to make a guy of myself trying to buy them, without consulting you. And what *are* you going to do with the rest of the money, if I may ask, Mr Ellershaw, since you're so upright and trustworthy? If you're thinking of seeing the world on it, you can give it to me back here and now – I'm not having you meeting lovely ladies all over Paris and Rome and . . . and Constantinople, in case you fancy going there, with tropic moons

260

and gondoliers serenading you, and all that sort of spoony nonsense.' The thought of Jack in such exotic surroundings was suddenly too much for her; she collapsed on to a chair in fits of laughter, mopping her eyes, unable to speak. He began to laugh himself. They were able to set each other off like this, like a pair of schoolchildren let out of the classroom. Amos was drawn to the door by the sound of their laughter. He stood watching his once solemn, impassive son, and was happy for him, and yet a little wistful; for himself, perhaps. It was best not to think too much. He went back to his carpentry shed. He had just decided to add a drawer to the table and put a nice brass handle on it.

In bed Jack said, 'I'll tell thee what I'm going to buy wi' that extra money.'

'What?' Lilian hoped he was not going to suggest another little deer, even if such a thing were available in South Yorkshire. Sabra was gone, it was best to put her out of mind.

'A grand new dress, as you can wear when I'm playing at home, and make t'other ladies green wi' envy. And I don't want to hear about running it up yourself. We'll have no economy on this one. I'll not be argued with, mind.'

Lilian gave in meekly. They set off in good time for Doncaster, after rising early and doing as much work as they could get through, Mary insisting that Amos could look after her with the aid of a spirit-kettle in the bedroom to make tea. The day was brilliant, late March sunshine and wind, the stalls in the Market Hall bright with goods, among them sheaves of new daffodils. Lilian wanted to linger, but Jack pulled her on. 'We'll buy in proper shops today.'

They found the proper shops in a handsome street near the Bridge, where the Don flowed high with spring rains and small boys fished on its banks. The sportswear shop offered all Jack needed for the coming season, though costing rather more than he had expected. Lilian sat watching as he tried bat after bat, buckled on pads and took them off again, compared the varying advantages of white buck batting gloves trimmed with grey rubber against elastic slip ones trimmed with red. He chose the white. Lilian thought he looked impressively handsome even in his ordinary clothes, decked up in these. She was more concerned with his purchases, but interest in her own present flared when they entered the double-fronted shop with the proprietor's name up in curly letters of black and gold, proudly offering, by a pinned-up notice in elegant handwriting, a Spring Sale of winter stock, including silk costumes and skirts, ball and evening dresses, petticoats, shawls, mantles, opera cloaks, lace and fancy goods, together with exclusive French millinery.

'Come on,' Jack said. 'They'll not eat us.'

The lady assistant who swam forward to serve them was obviously charmed by Lilian's voice, which raised high hopes of lavish purchases suitable to a lady's wardrobe, though her escort's tone did not match. But there was an air of authority in the way he sat, arms folded reviewing critically the garments she produced for inspection. Lilian cast a glance of despair at him, after rejecting several. 'I'm afraid they're all too – too like evening dresses,' she said. 'What I really need is something for daytime, in summer.'

'Well, madam, that makes it difficult. This being our Spring Sale the garments are mainly winter stock we're selling off.' The assistant shrugged. 'Madam should really wait until the summer goods come in – we shall have a delightful selection.'

Jack suddenly said, 'That.' He was pointing to a gown of grey-blue taffeta, the colour of a pigeon's plumage, striped with cherry. Panniers billowed out at the back, the front of the skirt was draped with a swathe of the same material, but plain, like a very elegant apron. The sleeves were long, squared shoulders covered with a wide shawl collar trimmed with lace, falling down the back of the bodice in a point.

'Oh,' Lilian said. 'Oh, no, Jack. It's too fancy.'

The assistant, scenting her last hope of a sale, put in hastily, 'Not for summer outdoor wear, madam. I assure you, it's just what the ladies will be wearing for summer occasions. The style's hardly changed since last year.' Somehow Lilian found herself being led into a small room with discreet curtains before it, and expertly helped into the dress. It fitted perfectly. When she came out, moving with careful grace because the swishing, rustling material demanded dignity, Jack looked her up and down. 'How much?'

'Two guineas, sir. It has been four – it's a Paris style. The material alone is four and sixpence a yard.'

'We'll have it.'

'But Jack . . .' Lilian began.

'I said we'll have it. And some fandangles to go wi' it.'

Lilian left the shop with the dress, a tiny straw bonnet covered with silk flowers, and a pair of white kid gloves, all packed in a beautiful box which Jack carried as though it weighed less than an ounce. High-flown with euphoria, they lunched in splendour at the Angel and Royal Hotel, served by waiters and surrounded by elegant people. Lilian was secretly surprised and proud of the way her husband behaved, ordering the meal with a lordly air and surveying the company as though he were used to better and thought them on the whole rather poor quality. When he failed to understand something on the menu-card he asked bluntly about it, thereby earning the waiters' respect. They despised a nervous, hesitant diner. Lilian, toying with a fiddle-patterned dessert-spoon, found her hand covered by his. He raised and inspected it, letting the light catch the still-bright wedding ring.

'Don't,' said Lilian, meaning nothing of the kind. 'They'll think we're honeymooners.'

'We are.'

'Oh, you! You say the most delightful things as if you were quoting the price of – of fish.'

'There's worse things nor fish.'

'We're not discussing fish. I mean, you never pay proper compliments.'

'Compliments? How much a pound are compliments?'

'Well, then.' She faced him, elbows on table. 'What colour are my eyes?' The eyes were firmly shut.

'Green. Wi' a touch of blue. Another of grey. Like broken glass.'

'There! You see what I mean. You ought to have said jewels. Broken glass, indeed!'

'If you want jewels,' said Jack evenly, 'you'll have to wait. I'll buy you them one day, somehow or other.'

'I don't want jewels. I don't want anything but you.'

Two hands were tightly clasped across the table; the waiter hovered with treacle pudding for dessert, and decided he would leave the honeymooners alone for the moment.

There was springtime in the air, and happiness, and even money, Lilian thought as they jogged home in the borrowed trap. They could have bought a trap of their own with the money they had spent that day. But never mind, it would come in good time. Now was what mattered.

Amos came downstairs as fast as his weak legs could carry him. 'Mother's bad,' he said, trembling, 'you'd best come.'

Mary was lying rigidly on her back, grimacing with pain, trying not to moan, one arm across her chest. Lilian flew to her and began to massage chest and shoulder, as she had done in the first attack, while the men stood awed by the door. After a few minutes the stiffened body relaxed, though the frown of pain remained and the breath came short and difficult. Amos went for the digitalin pills, which Mary managed to swallow, with Lilian supporting her head. The room was very quiet. Outside, early swallows twittered and the occasional bleat of a sheep disturbed the silence. All those in the room knew that some kind of crisis-time had come.

Mary opened her eyes at last. 'That's better,' she said. 'I thought . . . I didn't expect any more o' this. But it's come.'

'I'll make some tea, Mam,' Lilian volunteered.

'Nay. Nay. I've summat I want to say to thee and Jack . . . while there's time. Amos knows.'

The laboured breathing went on, interrupted sometimes by a twinge of pain. Mary's eyes were shut as she said, 'Lilian. I've not done right by thee.'

'What do you mean, Mam?'

'I . . . didn't like thee, at t'first. I thought tha'd be a hindrance to Jack.'

Lilian took her hand. 'Of course you did. And I would have been, but for you all helping me.'

'Nay. I didn't help much. Not enough. I were jealous, that's t'truth of it. Jealous, that my lad had getten a sweetheart.' She tried to laugh. 'What a daft old woman I was, to be sure!'

'Hush, hush. It was nothing. I understand.' Lilian saw Jack turn away and go to the window, so that nobody would see his face.

'I'm . . . that sorry,' the dying woman went on. 'Happen we're a bit too dowly wi' each other, in this part o' t'world. I've never towd thee I were fond of thee, Lil.'

The words would not come out that should answer her. Lilian kissed the furrowed brow, stroking the cold hands continuously. The faint voice struggled on.

'I want thee to have a few bits ... I shouldn't 'a kept them so long. In t'owd press ... top left hand cupboard, there's a bit o' carving ...'

'Yes, yes. Oh, Mam, it doesn't matter!'

'An acorn. Betwixt leaves. You press it, and then ... there's a drawer ...' Mary seemed to sleep suddenly for a minute or two. Amos looked wildly at Lilian, but she shook her head at him. The tired eyes opened again.

'Jack, love,' she whispered, and he came to her side, taking her other hand.

'I'm here, Mam.'

'Tha ... tha'll do well. One of the great ones. I can see it. Never mind about sheep, if they fail or they don't. It's t'game as matters ...' The voice changed suddenly. 'Dad! Is dinner ready?'

'Aye, love.'

'Then I'll get up and ... lay t'table ...'

After a moment Amos said in a flat voice not at all like his own, 'Draw t'blinds. There's none to see, but draw 'em.'

CHAPTER TWENTY

The secret spring in the old press was not difficult to find. Lilian took out the shallow drawer behind it and laid out the contents, one by one. A little necklace of coloured beads, childishly pretty. A gipsy ring, gold with four tiny colourless stones inset. A flaxen curl, so fine that it must have come from a baby's head – could Jack's hair ever have been so fair? A pressed flower, brown with age. An unframed silhouette of a little boy's profile, taken at some fairground, the tilt of chin and the way the hair sprang from the brow unmistakably Jack's. A pair of bright blue flower-patterned earrings, that had once complemented the colour of eyes as blue; discarded when the eyes paled and age made the wearing of such gauds unseemly.

Lilian put the gipsy ring on her finger. She would wear it for Mary's sake, but the other treasures must be put away, so that Jack should not be upset. Mary, with all her strength, was gone now and her daughter-in-law must find strength of her own to carry on.

The spell of May was over the land, bringing fair days and winds that carried sweet scents with them. The tidy rows of vegetables in the market gardens were a delight to the eye: the sharp green spears of spring onions, the tender lacy frills of young carrots, the lines of plump cabbages, like large blue-green roses. The apple orchard was afoam with pink and white blossom, and thrushes sang there until dark fell, and nightingales took their place, filling the air with poignant music.

Lilian stood at her door, looking down to the roofs of Barnswood, softened in a light veil of spring rain, then up to the hills clad in green velvet turf beyond the clustering trees. She breathed deeply of the rich air, feeling life coursing through her as it had never done before; wave on wave of joy in youth and health broke over her. Down in the meadow by the Low Field she could see Jack, batting to the bowling of Jim Easton, a lad who came from the village every day to help with the planting and picking, now that Amos was so crippled. The ball was flying over Jim's head, soaring across the field so that he had to go chasing after it over the uneven ground, while Jack practised graceful strokes, using the new bat she had bought him with her own money.

Soon he would be going away; her heart contracted at the thought. At this sweet season, when they should be together. Sometimes he would come home, then leave again, the misery of parting repeated every time.

Why should it have to be? The lambing was safely over, thanks to the mild winter and the lambing-shed that had been built, the flock doubled. They could have a pleasant summer, working not over-hard, taking some time to make excursions to country or town, perhaps even the sea. They might come to know other young farmers and their wives and enjoy some social life. The pleasant prospects were boundless – if only Jack were not ruled by the tyranny of cricket.

The treachery of the thought dismayed her; yet the fact was there, she resented bitterly, at this moment, the career that came between them. The glamour of it was undeniable, of course. Yet she had fallen in love with Jack when he was only a gardener. Surely that love could survive, if he were to be only a glorified gardener again?

She had stood at the door so long in silence that Amos came out to join her. Bent, old and wise, he peered up into a young face set in lines of discontent that told him much. He glanced down at the players in the meadow.

'Getting in a bit o' practice, I see, is Jack.'

'Yes.'

'Well, he'll be off any day now. First fixture's Saturday.'

'I know.' There was a faint tremble in Lilian's voice.

'And tha doesn't like it, eh?'

She was startled. 'How did you guess, Dad? I haven't said . . . I mean I wasn't going to . . .'

'Weren't you? I wonder, now. I wonder if tha weren't meditating on making it just a bit hard for him. A sigh here, an' a sob there, and a pair o' bonny arms clinging round his neck when he's all set to go . . . so that next time he'll stop a bit longer, and time after that happen he won't go at all. Is that it, what was going through thy mind?'

She laughed. 'You're a wicked old warlock. Why don't you set up in business like the Wizard of Leeds? You'd make a fortune.'

'Owd Henry Harrison? Aye, I might. But look where he fetched up. I were right, weren't I?'

Suddenly impatient with him and herself, she said sharply, 'It doesn't matter. If I thought anything like that I've forgotten it. I must go and get Jack's supper now.'

Amos ignored her. 'It reminds me of a tale . . .'

'Not Potter Thompson?'

'Not Potter Thompson. There were this young princess – oh, a long time ago, after the Romans went. She were as bonny as could be, and a many suitors came after her. But she fancied none of 'em and gave out she'd never wed, but go and be a priestess in one o' them heathen temples. Then, one night, she were sitting in her tower, rocking and sighing like a furnace (for she weren't inclined by nature to be single), when in through the window, all silver in the moonlight, flew in a fine young prince as was one o' the Other People. "I've watched thee for a long time," says he, "and I'll be thine if thou'lt tak' me." Well, what could she say but Aye, gladly, and they two were happy as t'night was long. Before he flew out again he says, "Only one thing. When t'time comes for me to go of a morning (and you'll know it by cockcrow) never try to howd me back, or you'll lose me." She promised she wouldn't, and she didn't, until one morn when she couldn't abide to see him go: and she took him fast in her arms and said, "Stay this once, love." Next thing she knew, her arms was empty, and he were flying out through t'window, into t'dawn. An' after he went she knew no mortal man would ever suit her, so she went off to temple an' took the veil and was miserable as sin ever after.'

Lilian surveyed her father-in-law long and hard. 'And I suppose all this happened in Yorkshire?'

His gaze was blandly innocent. 'Oh, aye. Up near Northallerton. Somewhere between there an' Kirkby Moorside.'

She began to laugh. 'All right, you wicked old man. Get on in with you.'

The day Jack left, Lilian had secretly bathed her face in butter-milk the seventh time that week, softening and freshening the skin, though it had to be wiped off completely if she were not to smell like a dairy in bed. Her hands, too, were as smooth as she could make them by wearing a pair of Mary's old gloves about the house and gardens; they were intensely irritating to her fingers, but the important thing was to make Jack see that she could be a working housewife and still look like a fine lady. He was very fine himself, in his best suit and a new corduroy cap, his precious gear packed neatly into new canvas cases. Tom, the young drover who had taken them to their wedding, was to convey Jack to the train in his master's trap; he was proud to be driving a real professional and good-naturedly envious of the beautiful bat and pads. The bat, he said, was as grand a bit of willow as ever came from the workshop of Harry Hayley at Wakefield. He waited in the trap, whistling, as Jack and Lilian said goodbye.

'It won't be long. Let's get first match or two over, then you can come and watch. It'll be a chance to wear all that finery. I'll be proud of thee, lass.'

'And I'll be proud of thee, lad.' They held hands tightly, not wanting to separate. Then Jack, with a most unusual gesture for that part of the world, bent and kissed each of her hands. 'White as lilies again.'

'Oh, you noticed! Of course they are. Go on now, you'll be late.'

Waving and smiling, she watched him go down the path and get into the trap. When it was out of sight she went back into the house, still smiling. Amos looked depressed.

'We'll miss him,' he said. 'I don't know how we'll manage, that I don't.'

'We'll manage,' said Lilian. 'Cheer up, Dad. We'll do very well.'

So they did, better even than they had expected. The weather stayed mild and sunny. Because of the lack of rain little mud got trampled into the house, so that Mrs Mossop was free to embark on a spring-cleaning foray. The hens laid well; three replacements for Jane, Anne Boleyn and Katherine Parr proved better layers than their predecessors (long since roast chicken) and new strong fencing kept the sheep out of the vegetables. Amos, now useless for outdoor tasks, thankfully accepted what Lilian offered him indoors.

'You can keep the furniture polished, if you like, Dad, and sweep the floors. That means I shall have all the less to do, and it won't tire you too much.'

'Aye, I'd like that.' Every morning he went round the pieces in the parlour, lovingly anointing with beeswax polish the articles he had made, wiping off the film with vigorous rubs to leave a bright sheen, his thoughts far away.

'I wonder how he's doing?' he would say, more times a day than he knew, and Lilian would reply, 'Splendidly, of course – what else would you expect?'

'Then why don't we hear owt?'

'You wouldn't expect Jack to tell us himself, would you? He's far too modest – besides, he hasn't all that time for writing. No, we'll read something in the papers one day, and then I'll tell you all about it.'

The first report, when it came, was in the *Yorkshire Post*. Lilian scanned it eagerly before running to Amos with it.

'Here you are! I told you it would come. He's playing at Lord's.' She spared a sigh and a smile for the memory of Lord's and the may tree. ' "Mr W. G. Grace once again astonished spectators with the magnificent total of 187 on a pitch which had clearly benefited from the new custom of covering before the commencement of a match. In answer to the determined slogging of Yorkshire bowlers, Mr Grace gave a brilliant display ..." Oh, never mind about *him*. Where does it say about Jack? Oh, here it is. "J. Ellershaw of Yorkshire glorified our county's reputation with perhaps the most elegant batting performance he has yet given us. Easeful and deliberate, with a natural elegance and style, he curbs his long-limbed strength with admirable control, producing without apparent effort an unending series of what we might describe as copy-book shots, from the measured forward push to the powerful soaring drive and the beautiful sweep which characterises this young batsman. His worst failing is perhaps his readiness to be tempted into the hook shot, and thereby into a pair of eagerly waiting hands. Cool, graceful and unhurried as ever, his 102 runs reduced bowlers to despair and drew the hearty plaudits of a large crowd." ' She paused for breath. 'There, Dad, isn't that what you were waiting for?'

' "Elegant, beautiful, grace and style",' Amos murmured. 'Fancy saying them things about a professional. Mostly they gets saved for the Gentlemen. Our Jack must have struck 'em all of a heap.'

'Are you surprised? I'm not. If it were me writing, I'd do a lot better than that, and spread it over a lot more of the page. Mr Grace, indeed!'

'Well now,' said Amos slyly, 'writer's not sweet on our Jack, nor yet wed to him.'

'I should hope not! Oh dear, *when* can we go and see him play?'

But three weeks went by, bringing May into its fullness of blossom and scent, and reducing Lilian to a state of restlessness and longing for Jack that drove her into a frenzy of physical work. Poor Amos's dusters were put aside as she took over the polishing, washed the flagged floors, beat rugs on a line strung between two trees, re-lined the hens' nests and picked the entire crop of red currants to be made into jelly. She had a boundless store of energy, 'skittering about like a mouse on wheels', as Amos put it, without any need for rest. It astonished and gladdened her; to be idle would be unendurable. She had never felt such lightness and strength. At night, even in the wide bed where Jack should have been, she slept dreamlessly and woke with the first light.

Then the summons came, by the mailcart with the slow old brown mare in the shafts. A letter from Jack, enclosing a well-worn, carefully folded five-pound note, telling her that he was to play the following Saturday at a ground on the borders of Yorkshire and Nottinghamshire, in a village called Ashinghall, only an hour's ride by train from Doncaster. It was to be no great match, only a two-day affair beside a picked Yorkshire eleven and one selected from the Gentlemen of Northern and Midland counties. But it would be a chance for them to meet. 'I could come home after. Tell Dad to perk up for Saturday.'

But Amos, who shared Lilian's excitement and washed his best neckerchief for the day, was stricken with acute pains in his limbs the very day before. Shivering and twitching, he took to his bed. 'Tha'll ha' to go baht me,' he told Lilian.

'I won't, and that's flat.' She banged down the water-ewer on the dressing stand so hard that a frailer vessel would have smashed, her heart full of disappointment and anger with Fate, even a shameful unreasonable anger with poor Amos for being a drag on her. From his eyes she could see that he guessed it and understood, and his understanding was hard to bear. She went downstairs and ironed a batch of washing, thrusting the iron into the coals to re-heat with savage enjoyment, pressing the linen with such vehemence that she burnt one of her best petticoats in two places. Next time she went up to Amos he was lying on his side, the sheet drawn up to his face, one sharp eye peering assessingly at her.

'I've made up mi mind what I'll do,' he said. 'I can crawl, if I canna walk, and crawl I will, down to t'gate, and get me a lift in a cart to Doncaster. Some kind body can put me on a train, and that way I'll get to Ashinghall and see Jack play. O' course,' he added thoughtfully, 'there'll be plenty more times I can see him, when I'm not badly, and it'll put me to a lot o' pain, but never mind.'

'Oh, Dad!' Lilian was half-laughing, all exasperated. 'You're the stubbornest old party I ever met in my life. You're not going, and I'm not going, and that's all there is to it, so drink up your bread-and-milk and go to sleep.'

But in the end Amos got his way and she went by herself. Billy, who now slept in an outhouse near the kitchen door, memorised with difficulty the tasks he had to take on that day, and repeated them many times to Lilian, who also got Dorcas Sadler, youngest and handiest of the farmer's daughters, to come over and look after Amos. 'She owes me a favour for that hen and chicks I let her have,' said Lilian with satisfaction. She was up half the night making preparations, so that nothing should go wrong in her absence and cover her with guilt when she returned.

It was strange and embarrassing to travel alone, dressed as she was in her Doncaster finery. On the train she managed to secure a Ladies Only carriage to herself, but the stares of guards, porters and passengers at each end of the journey brought a permanent colour to her cheeks. Only when, at Retford station, she was able to hire a cab for the short journey to Ashinghall and hide behind its dirty windows did she feel safe. She wished fervently that Amos were with her, or that she had worn a plain dress, or never wasted money on this one at all. Especially as it was uncomfortably tight round the waist and bosom.

But at the cricket field everything was quite different. A brilliant sun shone down on ladies dressed as showily as herself: only a few of them, but enough to make her feel like one bright bird in a flock of others of her kind. The pitch was well-mown green velvet, wild daffodils bloomed in the long grass beyond the boundary, a marquee of white canvas, scalloped like a kingly tent on the Field of the Cloth of God, presided over one end of the meadow. Other humbler tents, were obviously the headquarters of the teams. She moved towards them, remembering not to hurry in a hoydenish manner. There seemed to be a great many very well-dressed players, airing themselves in the sunshine, a few smoking expensive-smelling cheroots. Jack was not to be seen, or anyone who might have been playing with him. There was activity round the score-board, which was operated by a young boy with a step-ladder and an old man in a flannel smock. It read PLAYER ONE 0 b. 0 c. 0, and so on, a whole nestful of duck-eggs, Lilian thought. So play hadn't yet started, and it had been worth getting up at dawn. Feeling daring, she strolled towards the lesser tents. Some of the gentlemanly characters swept off their caps and hats to her. She smiled in what she hoped was a dignified manner.

'Well, I never,' said a voice beside her. She swung round to see Jack, a sporting vision in immaculate white shirt dotted with pale blue, perfectly pressed white trousers and a cap which sat jauntily on his curls. He looked not a whit different from any of the gallants who had saluted her, only more handsome. She knew he would not kiss her in public, and he did not, only patted her arm lightly.

'You're looking bonny. Where's Dad?'

'Not well. He's sorry he couldn't get here. He sends you his love and hopes you'll have a good day of it. Jack, do I look too fancy?'

'Not a bit. Just right, like yon woman said you would. Look at them over there, it's a wonder there aren't bees perching on 'em.'

'Well . . . I felt awkward on the train.' She was looking round. There were no quietly-dressed women in sight. 'Where are the other wives?' she asked.

'The what?' He was studying the wicket. 'Oh, I doubt there are any. They've most got too much on their plates to come laking wi' the men.'

And I haven't, I suppose, she thought. If you'd seen how I had to work to leave that place in order this morning . . . Other players were appearing at the door of the Yorkshire tent. Jack pointed them out. 'There's some of our chaps. Big Joe Rowbotham, he's skipper. George Freeman. Yon little tyke took eight for seven last week, young Andrew Greenwood, new last season. You'd never think it, would you. It's not size that counts.'

'I suppose not. Oh dear, they're going to start.'

'Aye, I've got to go now. Enjoy yourself, love.'

He left her. The captains were coming out to spin the coin. Enjoy herself? She hesitated, feeling conspicuous, the only woman in what would obviously be the path of the fielders as they took their places. There seemed nothing for it but to go across to where the ladies had congregated in a colourful bevy in front of the marquee, and to arrange herself in a folding chair with as much unconcern as she could. A few polite smiles came her way. She was gratified to find that her nearest neighbour was wearing a gown of vivid cyclamen trimmed with crimson, giving her the appearance of an enormous fuchsia and reducing Lilian's colours to those of the modest clover-flower.

The Yorkshire eleven won the toss. Jack appeared from the tent, partnered by a youngish fair man, strolling on as though he had all the time in the world. At the wicket he continued to give the same impression, adjusting his pads in turn, taking a glove off and putting it on again, tapping the wicket critically with the tip of his bat, before condescending to receive the first ball, which he hit gently to cover point, who picked it up and returned it to the bowler. Four further balls he treated in this courteous way, before driving the fifth unerringly past mid-on to a place where no fielder was, so that it sped bullet-like to bury itself in the long grass. A ripple of applause from the spectators greeted this, the first boundary of the match. From then onwards Jack played cat and mouse with the bowlers, letting the ball go just so far in one stroke, smiting it in the next, so that his score went up in twos and fours until it reached forty-three, at which point, with a beautiful forward drive, he sent the hapless ball over the heads of the fielders, over the old man in the smock and the small boy on the step-ladder scoring with chalk and blackboard, out of the field into the adjoining one, and so earned himself six runs.

In the long search for the ball that ensued Lilian caught his eye. He gave not the flicker of a sign that he had seen her; she knew his mind was completely fixed on the game. He had made fifty-two by the time the umpire gave the signal for the luncheon-break.

Luncheon? Lilian had given no thought to it. The other ladies, some joined by the fielders, were moving into the marquee, where a lot of bustle was going on. She hovered nervously, wishing Jack would come out and tell her what she was to do. A large young man with flaming red hair approached her, with an unmistakable gleam of admiration in his eye, doffing his cap.

'Do I take it you're alone, ma'am?' He hardly waited for her reply. 'If so, may I have the great pleasure of giving you luncheon?' He extended his arm to her. Hardly knowing what she did, she took it. His voice was loud and authoritative, like Uncle Lewis's. 'If I may introduce myself, Frank Wolferstan of Tamworth. Couldn't help noticing how keenly you watched the game, ma'am. Unusual to find a lady so keen.' They were almost at the marquee, in which she could see long tables on to which the contents of picnic-baskets were being unloaded. She could see dishes of chicken, piles of sandwiches, legs of breaded ham, and she was suddenly ravenous. 'By George, what a nice little spread,' exclaimed Mr Wolferstan. 'That's my man over there, unpacking the turkey. Plenty for both of us, eh? Oh, there's Mamma.' He waved to a lady built on the same lines as himself.

Lilian, feeling extremely silly, pulled away from the large arm clamping hers to his side. 'It's very kind of you, but I'm afraid I couldn't take luncheon without my husband.' Her escort's look of disappointment was unmistakable, but he banished it gallantly.

'Oh, sorry – didn't gather you had one with you. Where is the lucky fellow?'

Lilian looked desperately round, but there was no sign of Jack. 'I'm Mrs Jack Ellershaw,' she said. Mr Wolferstan appeared momentarily baffled; then realisation dawned, and wrote on his wide pink face a mixture of distaste, surprise, and downright unbelief, in that order.

'You mean, the . . . the Yorkshire player?'

'That's right.' Her arm was relinquished without a struggle.

'Oh,' said Mr Wolferstan lamely. 'In that case . . . how extraordinary.' He was rescued from further floundering by the arrival of his mother, a billowing figure in saffron and brown, with a positive work of art on her head composed of real birds and unreal flowers.

'Frank dear, how clever of you to have found a lady for yourself.'

275

She beamed on Lilian. 'Coming to join us, are you? That's right. I can't wait for champagne, myself.' Her voice was warmly Lancashire, and Lilian liked her instantly, and was sorry for her son, by now almost choking with embarrassment. 'The fact is, Mamma,' he was saying, 'the fact is, this lady's husband is a – well, a Player.'

'How nice for you, dear,' said his mother to Lilian. 'Is he by any chance that handsome dark lad who was doing so well just now? I saw you looking at him very hard. How proud you must be!'

'Oh, I am,' Lilian said. Mr Wolferstan struggled on.

'When I say a Player, Mamma, I mean a Player, not a Gentleman. Only Gentlemen are allowed in the luncheon tent, so I'm afraid . . .'

'That's quite all right,' Lilian said sweetly. 'I'll sit outside and wait for him. Someone might throw us a bun, who knows?' Some devil of challenging temper awoke in her, and she added, 'It seems disgraceful to me that *any* player shouldn't be as entitled to luncheon as much as any so-called Gentleman. I thought cricket was a sporting game but I see now that it's not. Whatever silly old men made such a rule ought to try going without luncheon themselves – I'd like to see them do it. My husband's too much of a sport to tell me about the sort of thing that goes on, and I'm very glad to have found out for myself.'

She knew her cheeks were almost as red as young Wolferstan's, and she felt a curious disposition to cry; that would be the ultimate disgrace in this company. But the Wolferstans' eyes were fixed not on her, but on something over her shoulder. She turned swiftly, to find Jack standing behind her.

From fever-heat she froze into apprehensive stillness. How long had he been there, and how much had he heard? He would be very, very angry, of that she was sure. But his expression was much as usual as he said, 'I saw you over here. Do you want to sit down, or go for a walk?'

Agonised, Lilian said, 'Er. This is Mrs and Mr Wolferstan, Jack. They, er . . .'

Jack touched his cap. 'Pleased to meet you.'

Frank Wolferstan murmured something, obviously as embarrassed as she was, but his mother sailed forward, extending a plump gloved hand.

'Delighted, Mr Ellershaw. I meet some of Frank's team-mates

but hardly any other cricketers at all, and I must say I'm particularly pleased to be introduced to you, after all that lovely batting you gave us this morning, didn't he, Frank. We were just saying to your charming wife . . .' Her small snapping brown eyes took in the whole picture, the distressed girl who so obviously adored her man enough to make a fool of herself for him, the young man whose pride must not be hurt. Rapidly deciding on a tactful course, she went on, 'Well, now, this is nice. Why shouldn't we all have luncheon out here in the sunshine? I must say I don't feel at all like sitting in that stuffy tent. Go and tell Thomas to bring it all out here, Frank, and to find a little table for us, one of the folding sort, oh, and a cloth.'

The silence that followed was only a second's length, but seemed to Lilian to last the best part of an hour. Would Jack refuse to accept a privilege his fellow Players couldn't share? She saw him glance towards the Yorkshire tent, then, to her infinite relief, he said, 'That's very kind of you. Aye, we'd like to.'

The thought of refusal had crossed his mind. But luncheon, to most of his mates, meant little more than a butty tied in a clean handkerchief, and more ale than he himself cared to drink during a match in the beer-tent. Some of the Yorkshire lads had an unfortunate reputation for unsteady play in the afternoon. Then, too, he knew himself to be a little different from them : a different sort of wife, different ambitions. There were ways of getting to the top besides dedication and hard work. So, for Lilian's sake and a little for his own, he accepted.

The food was delicious, bringing back memories to Lilian of Digby's picnic at Lord's. Jack ate moderately and drank only one glass of champagne, but drank it as carelessly as though he had it every day for breakfast. Lilian ate ravenously, from real hunger and immense relief at the way the situation had turned out. For Jack and Frank Wolferstan were talking cricket: the science of stroke-play, the setting of a field, the vagaries of umpires, the strange laws of luck and chance that rule a player's fate. Lilian decided that Frank was a much nicer person than he had appeared at first, and that Jack was still a mystery to her, as she listened to him talking in men's company with a clarity and a depth of knowledge of his beloved game surpassing mere zest for playing or physical skill. He was a man with cricket in his head and heart as well as in his muscles; it seemed dreadful, listening to him, that he should have to do anything else, ever, tending fowls or growing cabbages or delivering lambs. Someday, somehow ...

'You're a great expert, Mr Ellershaw,' their hostess was saying. 'A lot of the lads Frank plays with just enjoy knocking a ball about, as they call it – at least that's how it seems to me, though I'm very ignorant. I expect you're quite a match for this young Grace they all talk of so much – aren't you, now?'

'I wouldn't say that. He were first batsman to get two thousand runs in a season, last year. I can't match that yet.'

'Goodness!' said Mrs Wolferstan, forgetting to be tactful. 'He ought to turn professional, oughtn't he – wouldn't it pay a lot better than doctoring?'

'He's not a doctor yet,' Jack said, 'and he'll never be a professional, as I see it. The time's not come for a Gent to turn into a Player. But he gets paid, does young Grace, and very nicely too. So you see, things are changing. I happened to hear a bit of what you were saying before,' he added, causing Lilian to choke on a crumb and Frank Wolferstan to look sheepish, 'and I know what Lilian here meant. It may not seem fair and right now that lads should eat in one place and chaps like your son in another. But it'll come to one table for all, one day; happen not in my time, but one day. Cricket'll do it.'

'Well! Cricket seems to be your God, young man.'

'Aye, it is,' Jack said.

He reached a superb 127 that afternoon. He had to, for not only was Lilian there to be impressed, but the entire camp-following of the Midland and Northern Gents watched him with eagle eyes, this young man with the face of a Roman emperor and the lithe grace which was supposed only to come from a public school education. He looked altogether romantic, and the pretty wife was obviously a lady. A particularly daring miss, very much deploring the wedding-ring on Lilian's hand, suggested to her brother that Papa might like to see Mr Ellershaw play, and couldn't they invite him over for a social weekend and a friendly match, quite soon? Her brother, failing to see through Alice's wiles, agreed in all sincerity that this would be a good notion. (And when they got home that night put the notion to his Papa, who was amused and intrigued by his children's accounts of this Yorkshire divinity, and agreed to send out the invitation. Which was duly accepted; and so began Jack Ellershaw's ascent up the social ladder.)

At last, on 127, feeling equal to batting all day and all night, he was out to a cunning ball which he should not have touched. Lilian was glad it was all over, for she was feeling slightly sick with excitement, sunshine, champagne and lobster salad. When play ended for the day, Yorkshire with a respectable total, it seemed to take hours for Jack to change into his ordinary clothes, pack his gear, and take leave of his mates. As if they wouldn't all be seeing each other again the next morning; men were obviously as bad as women for gossiping. At last he emerged, accompanied by the little wicket-keeper who fancied himself as the wag of the team and was now in the middle of one of his stories.

'. . . and I says to Mr Tinsley, I says, tha wants a reet big score, Mr Tinsley, I'll tell thee what to do. An hour before t'match, send out for a quart o' t'best and a good fat woman. Well, time come, out he walks, and he stops and he stops and he hits 'em all over t'bloody field, till he's made enough to beat t'other side baht anybody else battin'. And I goes up to him and claps him on t'back, and I says: Were she good and fat, Mr Tinsley? Were she good and fat?'

At this point the story-teller caught Lilian's eye and broke off in mid-guffaw. 'Don't mind him,' Jack said, leading Lilian away.

'Oh, I don't. Just so long as you don't follow his advice.'

The sweetness of the weekend was spoiled because he must go away again so soon. Lilian heard herself snapping at him, as though it were his fault, then was ashamed. She remembered the pretty girl in the fetching bonnet who had spoken to him afterwards, flirting with him openly, and the undisguised admiration in the gaze of Mrs Wolferstan, old enough to be his mother, and how he had agreed that Cricket was his God. What was she, Lilian, then? a sort of under-priestess? Yet she must not hold him back or let him see that she was jealous. When he left for Cambridge she kept her farewell cheerful, even casual. But Amos sent her spirits down when he said, 'He's different. Happen it's changed him, going up in t'world.'

'Nonsense, Dad. He's just the same Jack. He always will be.

Don't be so gloomy about everything. Now I've no time to waste, I've stuff to get ready for market.' Only by bustling about, keeping herself continually occupied, could she fend off the niggling worries which kept invading her mind like swarms of ants, and one in particular.

That week, she knew for certain that she was pregnant.

CHAPTER TWENTY-ONE

It was not astonishing: how could it be? Yet Lilian had never given any thought to children. Of course they occurred in a marriage. But hers was so young and new. Only a few months ago she had been a bride, and now was to be a mother without the slightest desire for motherhood.

If only she were wrong about it. But she knew she was not, though nobody in all her life had ever enlightened her about such things. Mamma would have died rather than utter a word on such a matter, except to hint at horrors connected with the birth of her children, especially Lilian. Mating was a different thing – it was not difficult to work that process out, brought up in the country. But birth and its beginnings must remain a mystery to the unmarried young lady. Yet she could not be mistaken in the changes of her body, the newly full blue-veined breasts and strange discomforts, the unnatural energy which had driven her to scrub and sweep and polish; though that had died away now, leaving her languid. There was no other possible explanation.

And she was frightened. It was impossible not to remember seeing the lamb born, a repulsive bloody object. Would her baby be like that, at first, and would she have to be helped, as Jack had helped the sheep? She longed to ask somebody, somebody wise who would reassure and comfort her, but there was nobody, no family of her own to turn to, no friend, up here in the wilderness, only a few farming acquaintances scattered here and there, people whom she knew just well enough to pass the time of day with. Amos was kind and good, but it was impossible to imagine having such an intimate conversation with him, especially since he had become a little vague and wandering in his manner. One day, perhaps very soon, he would be an elderly child to be soothed and humoured along with the baby that was coming.

Then there was Jack. When she told him, it would be a worry

that might take his concentration off his play. And if he lost his place in the team, why, that would mean the loss of the good money he earned, £80 or so in a season and £1 bonus for each match won. A tide of worries swept over her, keeping her awake at nights and fretting her temper.

On Manchester's home-ground it was no happier a day for Jack. The match had been an unsatisfactory one, Lancashire's first innings a steady accumulation of runs which should not have been. The number of extras grew alarmingly as sloppy fielding and bowling gave away run after run through byes and misfields. Jack looked often at Joe Rowbotham, hoping for a bit of stern captaincy; but Joe had very recently taken over from the experienced Iddison, and, senior player though he was, seemed unable to stop the rot by occasional discreet words to the offenders. Two somewhat mere Lancashire batsmen stayed together interminably, scoring far more runs than their form deserved. 'For ever and ever, Amen,' Jack muttered under his breath, and swore when a catch he had run for went to another man and was unforgivably dropped. It would have got rid of one of the stoppers-and-stayers who had settled down at the wicket like a nesting hen. When play ended for the day Jack's temper was not sunny.

He had been put on to bowl early that hot afternoon, and kept on for too many overs without the satisfaction of taking a wicket. The main cause of his displeasure was one Massie, a young apprentice butcher from Rotherham, playing only his second match. It was not Jack's way to air grievances, but this one refused to be suppressed. He strolled over to Massie, who was lacing his boots.

'What were up wi' thee, letting ball get by every time it come anywhere near thee? We could have got rid of yon nancy-lad in a couple of overs, wi' proper fielding.'

Massie looked up. 'Eh?'

'I'll say it again. A chap as fields second slip can stop what t'keeper lets past him, more often than not. I never saw thee stop owt, and tha'd every chance. Fours and twos running away like rabbits, and the batting not much cop, so I reckon fielding were at fault.'

Massie stood up. He was a large youth, already running to fat, with a face the colour of prime beef and jutting black eyebrows.

'That's for captain to say.'

'Well, he's not said it, so I am. It were my average that suffered. Any road, I reckon he were no sharper at seeing t'ball than thee.'

'What's that mean?'

Jack's temper rose. 'It means too much supping ale, that's what it means. I say nowt about Joe, seeing the game's his responsibility, but I'm damned if I'll bowl my heart out to chaps as reek like a brewery – aye, even now.' He sniffed contemptuously. He knew very well that it was not his place, as Massie had said, to criticise another player, but in his wrath he pushed the knowledge aside. Massie was even redder in the face now, and growling. Several of the other men had drawn close, hearing the altercation.

'What's it to do wi' thee, tha cheeky bugger?' Massie asked ominously, waving a ham-fist. 'Happen tha thinks tha's Lord God Almighty, too good for t'likes of us poor worms. Thee and thy cocky airs, as if rest of us weren't good enough to spit on. Who were thy feyther, then – Prince o' Wales, or Duke o' Doncaster? Thy mother were no better nor she should be, I'll bet . . .'

Jack's fist shot out to collide with Massie's jaw, causing him to grunt and shake his head like an angered bull before throwing a heavy punch to Jack's ribs. They fought, obeying no sporting rules, hitting in anger, without science, while the others watched amazed. The captain, who should have intervened, had gone, too uneasily conscious of a bad day's play to want an inquest on it. One of Jack's blows struck the butcher's cheekbone; in retaliation he lashed out with his great right foot, the boot landing in the middle of Jack's shin with agonising impact, causing him to step back and disengage from his opponent.

'Had enough, hasta?' Massie asked jeeringly. 'That's what cocky bantams get for crowing too loud. Happen it'll teach thee better another time.' He turned on his heel, while the other men crowded round Jack, little Pinder, the wicket-keeper tut-tutting over his friend.

'Eh, lad, tha shouldn't ha' talked to him like that. He's a fair old temper, has yon. Has he damaged thee much?'

Jack limped to a bench, and rolled up his trouser-leg. A long graze over the shin-bone was already beginning to bruise. Another ounce more of weight behind the kick, and he would have had a broken leg. Wincing, he covered the bruise again. There was the taste of blood in his mouth, the knuckles of his right hand were raw and bleeding. He sat, staring in front of him, not answering the well-meant advice that was being showered upon him. He was furious with himself, furious with Massie. He would certainly not be able to play tomorrow or perhaps for days. He had done no good, and had made an enemy.

Sitting gloomily in the hot, dirty train bearing him eastwards, he decided that he would not tell Lilian. Bad enough to have made a fool of himself without diminishing his image in her eyes. She would have to know about the injury, but he would lie about it, a difficult feat for him. And he was taking very little money home – a reduced match-fee, and possibly a fine to follow.

It was washing-day at Stainbeck. The yard was full of garments on clothes-lines, the kitchen of unpleasant dampness. Lilian, in a swamping pinafore, her steam-frizzed hair piled into a cap, was surprised and not over-pleased to see him.

'What on earth are you doing here? I didn't expect you back till Friday.'

He gave her a brief account of an imaginary incident in which he had fallen and bruised his leg on the handle of a roller. She exclaimed at the sight of the wound, but not over-solicitously, as though she thought that it was somehow his fault and just another thing to try her. Jack saw for the first time that she could look plain, with her face unusually pale, the freckles standing out on it like pennies, her eyes dark-shadowed. He heard her snapping at Mrs Mossop, and thought that he was in for a cheerless few days.

They were going over the accounts together when the storm broke. Jack, in pain from his leg and his conscience, pointed out a discrepancy between the debit and credit columns, the result of Lilian's careless adding-up.

'That was a pretty silly mistake to make. Mistakes cost money.'

She turned on him. 'And is it any wonder if I make mistakes, with all I've got to do? Every bit of work round here gets done by me, all day and every day, and when I sit down to do the books at night I can hardly see for tiredness. Oh, I suppose it doesn't look like that to you, joy-riding all over the place with nothing to do but play cricket and look smart. I don't know what you think I'm made of, I'm sure.'

'Lilian, Lilian! It's not like you to go on at me.'

'No.' She burst into tears, great gulping sobs that shook her, flinging herself down beside Jack's chair, her head on his knees, a shower of red plaits and hairpins falling about in confusion. His leg was painfully jarred, but he bit his lip and kept silent, stroking her hair, knowing she would tell him what was wrong in her own time. When she did, her words were so muffled that he heard nothing but a tearful murmur.

'What, love?'

'I'm going – to have a baby. Oh, Jack . . .'

He raised her and comforted her, talking to her softly as to a frightened animal, wiping her tears away with his own handkerchief, pretending that her news had not shaken him. To be told this now, with his career in jeopardy and his reputation tarnished. He was afraid for her, for himself, for the coming child; yet he must show nothing of his fear. At least she was calmer.

'I'm sorry, my darling. I was a beast to you and you ought to hate me. But I feel so rotten . . . and I don't know how I'm going to manage. I didn't mean to tell you, at least not yet, but somehow . . . I'm not myself at all and I lose my temper so. Jack, what are we going to do?'

They talked all evening and for some of the night. As soon as he was fit, he said, he would go down to Barnswood and find her a strong young woman prepared to live in and help the failing Mrs Mossop with the rough work. Another of the Twining boys might come to deal with the garden work; they were none of them too bright but at least they were honest and willing. And in autumn, long before the baby was due, Jack would be home himself.

Lying in bed, Lilian's head on his shoulder, he watched the stars in the dark blue summer sky, and wondered where the money was to come from to pay for the extra help; and what was to become of him if his leg failed to mend quickly. In his time he had taken plenty of knocks and bruises, but never one that looked as ugly as this. There were terrible things, tumours of the bone, injuries that spread . . .

All night the stars looked down on a young man who slept only fitfully, being, for the first time in his life, very frightened.

The morning brought some kind of cheerfulness to Stainbeck, with the brilliant sunshine of a spell of hot weather, and the comforting scents of breakfast. Amos, this being one of his better days, sat at the table with them. Inquisitively he peered from one to the other.

'What's up, then? Let's have it, if it's owt I should know.'

Jack buttered a slice of bread with artistic symmetry. 'You might say that, Dad. We're going to have a bairn, Lilian and I.'

'Nay! Well, that's grand news.' He had half-suspected it, seeing Lilian's haggard face and hearing her shrewish tones, remembering vividly Mary's four pregnancies. But least said soonest mended; now he was all happy surprise. 'Tha's a deep one for secrets, our Lilian. When's it to be?'

'December, sometime. I think.' Lilian bent her head over her plate.

'Will it be a lad or a lass, I wonder?' Amos mused.

'Bit soon to tell, Dad,' Jack said. 'I don't mind, so it's like its mother. What about you, love?'

'I've not really thought about it.' Lilian was surprised to find that she had not. Up to now the baby had been no more than a threatening stranger, but of course it was a person, something of them both, created by their loving, a creature in whom the strong peasant blood of the Ellershaws mingled with the in-between blood of the de Wentworths. Jack caught her thoughts. 'It'll be a funny mixture, poor little tyke,' he said. Lilian laughed. She was beginning to feel ordinary again, less menaced by the unknown.

Amos shook his head at the unpleasant appearance of Jack's leg, by now a vivid blend of colours. 'That's nasty, that is. Fell over a roller? Not like thee, to be clumsy. Art sure that's how it was?' Jack, not meeting his father's eye, said that he hoped his memory hadn't gone yet. It was not quite a lie. Pleased to be busy, Amos got Mary's receipt-books out of the cupboard where they had lain untouched since she died. Yes, there it was, the rough drawing of a bone against five lines of writing. 'There,' he said triumphantly, 'that tells how to cure rheumatics. Look and see if there's one against knocks. Eh, I do wish I could read.'

Jack found the cure his mother's book recommended for bruises, sprains and damages in general. It said nothing about kicks. He was not encouraged to pursue it, since it consisted of gathering snails at dawn and boiling them in cider. Snails were certainly the enemies of vegetables, but he preferred to leave it to thrushes and

286

blackbirds to keep down their numbers; and Lilian would never provide a pan for such a purpose. Amos sighed: there was nothing like Mary's remedies, if only people would follow them. But he remembered one, a good all-purpose one, out of his head. It was to find a well-shaped stone, name it after the saint on whose day the injured person was born, immerse it all night in a stream, then apply it to the wound, which would immediately be cured.

'But,' said Lilian when he came in with a piece of limestone, 'how do you know who Jack's name-saint is – if he has one?'

'Barnabas.' Amos seemed surprised at the question. 'June eleven. That's a grand day to be born, that is, for Barnabas was a good man, and full of the Holy Ghost and of faith, and much people was added to the Lord by him.'

'I thought you were Chapel.'

'Oh, aye, we are now. We were Church once, but summat were said wrong, and Mary would have it we should go over t'road.' Lovingly he put the stone in his pocket and went out, hobbling along field-paths to the little beck that snaked its way down a hillside. There, in a pool, he anchored the stone, wrapped in a clean handkerchief. Next morning he retrieved it, cool and glistening, and in that state applied it to the wound, disregarding Jack's sceptical comments. And sure enough, the bruise began to pale from that hour, the dreaded inflammation and fever failed to appear. 'There, it's worked, I told thee.' Lilian touched the little stone with an involuntary shiver. She had begun to believe in Amos's stories. He saw it, and pressed his advantage.

'It's my belief we've vexed a hob. A hobgoblin, that is,' he explained, seeing her puzzled look. 'Some call 'em lobs.' He went on to tell her how the Hob, a friendly household fairy, liked its own chair by the kitchen fire and a saucer of cream put down every night. Given those, it would tidy up, sweep and dust during the dark hours, but if it were offended, the housewife would be plagued with afflictions.

'Then why haven't you told me before about it?' Lilian asked, half-amused, half-believing him. 'The poor thing's had no special chair and certainly no cream.'

Amos looked vague. 'Mary didn't think it were reet.'

'Oh.' Lilian thought she understood. Thereafter, wondering if she were a little mad, she pulled a chair out from the table every

287

night and set it invitingly by the kitchen hearth. The saucer of top-of-the-milk she set outside, by the step. Sure enough, it was gone every morning, possibly by the agency of one of the visiting cats or hedgehogs. She told Jack, expecting him to laugh. Instead he said, 'It may not make much sense, but it does no harm.'

'Well . . . I don't know. I suppose some people would blame the baby on our Hob, but I don't think I regard *it* as an affliction – not now. As for your accident . . .'

'No accident.' He told her exactly how it had been, sparing himself nothing. When she had heard him out she said, 'I think you were wrong. He needed telling – but not quite like that. If you say things in anger you'll get an angry answer. You ought to have asked him to have a drink with you after the match, and said it then, as though it had only just occurred to you. Next time it happens, if it does, count up to twenty before you turn round and say anything. That's what a governess of mine used to tell me, and I believe it did work, only I forgot about it as I grew older.'

'So what should I do next time I see Massie?'

She thought. 'Don't say anything. Offer to shake hands with him. He won't want to bear a grudge after that.' If only that advice would prove good! Massie might be a born grudge-bearer, or Jack unable to make peace with him. She was relieved when Jack said, as though he meant it, 'I'll think on.'

Within a few days the bruise had almost faded. Lilian refused to let him go into Barnswood in search of help. 'There's no haste, I can work for a long time yet. Goodness knows, there must be plenty of girls wanting work. You rest while you can.' It was true, she had felt better and stronger since Jack came home, as if his presence made all the difference to that of the baby. Excitement was rising in her at the thought of the new life. Watching Jack, as he packed his flannels and shirt with meticulous care, she felt a tenderness towards him which had not been there before. The hero with a flaw, the perfect grace marred by a wound, brought out in her a new motherliness, as though the helplessness of the child within her reflected itself in its father. She touched him, wanting to keep the memory of him in her fingers, the crisp ringlets of hair, the sun-browned brow and cheek and long elegant hands that might never have known spade or trowel.

'I read in the paper that they're calling you the North Star,' she said.

'Oh, aye? Daft sort of name.' But she knew he was pleased.

'No, it isn't. There's only one North Star in the sky, and only one Jack Ellershaw in cricket.'

'Happen there'll be two before long.'

He glanced at her waist, just thickening into matronliness; and she knew without being told that he was gladder and more proud than he had let her see.

When he was gone the house seemed deadly quiet. The lambs had ceased to bleat for their mothers as they had done in spring, and the late thrush no longer sang till dusk in his apple-tree whose branches brushed the house-eaves. Amos had gone to bed, weary in his bones. Lilian went upstairs to the cupboard where Mary had stored linen, garments too good to throw out, anything that might be made into something else. The wedding-dress had come from there, in part. Perhaps the useful cupboard could provide baby-clothes.

There was a substantial roll of flannel, cream with age, but none the worse for that, and a large square of knitted blanket which could be cut up for cot-clothes, and several generously-cut petticoats of linen and cotton that would yield plenty of small garments; if only one knew how to make them. Lilian picked ineffectually with a pair of pocket scissors at gathers only too well sewn and hems whose strong thread resisted her feeble attempts.

She sat back on her heels, sighing. Simple cooking had not been too difficult to master, but sewing had always been beyond her, even the silly embroidery in which the clumsy sempstress could cheat with lazy stitching and ugly knots at the back where they didn't show. And what would the baby need in the way of a layette? She realised that she had not the faintest idea. A few minutes before, the memory of Mariana in the Moated Grange had flitted through her mind, as she glimpsed the new moon through the apple-branches.

> . . . And ever when the moon was low
>> And the shrill winds were up and away,
> In the white curtain, to and fro,
>> She saw the gusty shadow sway.

What would Alfred, Lord Tennyson say to a Mariana languishing in her moated grange in front of a pile of cloth she was quite incapable of sewing for the baby already rounding her out? Such a situation would alter the words considerably. Perhaps there would be more sense in getting down *Alice's Adventures in Wonderland* and looking carefully at the pictures of the Duchess's baby, the one which turned into a pig, poor little thing.

Curled up in Amos's chair, before the small fire that always burned in the parlour grate, Lilian was startled out of her study of the pig-baby's robes by the crunching of footsteps on the garden path, followed by the sound of voices and an authoritative knock.

She dropped the book and jumped up. It was not yet dark, but very late for callers. Amos liked to chill the blood with a story of a traveller assaulted and murdered by highwaymen on a moorland stretch not two miles away, the bones being discovered a summer later when the river ran almost dry, revealing them among its rocks. Twining's Billy would not knock; he always came in by the yard gate and the back door.

Her heart beating rapidly, Lilian sidled to the window and peered round the curtain. Whoever was at the door was hidden by the porch. But surely there was a woman's voice? Very gingerly she drew the bolts, top and bottom, and loosened the heavy chain enough to open the door a few inches.

'It's the right place!' exclaimed a hearty female voice. 'I knew as soon as I saw that hair. Well, Lilian, aren't you going to let us in?'

'Aunt Freddy!'

'Well, of course. Thank you, dear girl.' Frederica stepped confidently inside, throwing brisk glances about her, and beckoning to the person behind her. 'Come along, child, no one's going to eat you.' The person advanced and bobbed a curtsey, smiling nervously. Thinner, better-dressed and more ladylike in appearance than she had once been, she was unmistakably Millie.

Lilian was lost for words. 'I . . . good gracious. I never expected . . . how did you know where to find me?' (And what do you want with me, was her unspoken question.) Apprehensively she watched her aunt select as the most comfortable chair the one Lilian had been sitting in, while Millie slipped into the background shadows. Frederica looked every inch the wealthy countrywoman, in expensive tweeds of a mannish cut, a small feathered hat reminiscent of Robin Hood crowning her massed hair, her gloves and boots of superb leather. Above her crossed ankles her skirt was distinctly shorter than fashion dictated, and her hip-length jacket was fastened all the way down with formidably large buttons, like crown pieces.

'Well, this *is* pleasant,' said Frederica. 'Can we have a little more fuel on the fire, do you think? I find these evenings very cold in this part of the world, and we were positively frozen in the trap. By the way, the man is waiting by the gate – will you send someone to take him round to the stables?'

'We haven't any stables, Aunt. And there's no one to send. My father-in-law has gone to bed.'

'Oh.' Frederica looked round as though expecting a horde of retainers to scuttle out of the skirting-boards. 'How odd. I should have thought . . . well, never mind. Millie, run down and tell him to come back tomorrow. What time do you take luncheon, Lilian?'

'Luncheon?' Lilian was beginning to feel like a parrot. 'We don't exactly have *luncheon*. I get a meal for us about noon.'

'Rather early, but I expect we can make do. In that case tell him to return about two, Millie. Now, Lilian, I really must take a good look at you.'

Lilian felt a blush creeping up as the look raked her figure.

'H'm. Yes. Your father-in-law, you said. Then you *are* married.'

'I should hope so! Digby came to our wedding.'

'Oh, I know that – wearing his uniform strictly against Regulations, naughty boy – but I thought there might have been something a little out of order about the ceremony, as it was conducted in one of these chapels . . .'

Lilian bit back a retort. Obviously Aunt would have preferred her to be unmarried, even in her present condition, but the important thing was to find out why she had come to Stainbeck at all. At least her voice and expression were amiable, not those of an avenging Fury.

'Aunt, please tell me how you knew I was here. It's a little disconcerting when people turn up so suddenly, especially at night.'

'Oh, that was easy. I got it out of Digby, when he was quite sure I didn't intend to tear you into small pieces. Oh, you expected that, I'm sure, and indeed I was very angry over your escapade last year.

But that's all in the past now. I think I should like some tea, if your girl is about.'

'We haven't a "girl", Aunt. I thought I explained – my father-in-law and I look after everything, with a woman who cleans and a boy who does the rough work in the garden, but they don't sleep here. I'll make you some tea myself.'

Preparing it in the kitchen, Lilian was annoyed to find her hands trembling. She had been very afraid of Aunt Freddy once, and fear does not wear off easily. Obviously she had been forgiven for her elopement, and the wretched Millie too; but it was disturbing to see a person from the past walk into one's home. At least it would take her mind off Mariana and the pig-baby.

Without her hunting-hat and the jacket with the alarming buttons, Frederica looked easy and relaxed. Millie, sipping her tea, smiled shyly over the rim. Lilian remarked that she had grown and was quite changed.

'Aye. And so've you, Miss Lilian.'

'Yes. But I'm not Miss Lilian any more, you know. I'm Mrs Ellershaw now. Thanks partly to you, Millie,' said Lilian defiantly. She found that she was sitting with her arms folded protectively over the place where her baby lay.

'Yes, miss – madam.'

Frederica looked dreamily into the fire. 'Dear me, what a business that was. I do believe Digby thought I would kill him. It was such a terrible risk to take with your life, and not at all what I expected of him – or you. But all worked out for the best, I suppose, especially as you now have your health.'

Oh, so you did notice, thought Lilian.

'Really remarkable,' Frederica went on. 'Florence told me. She seemed not to believe her own eyes – thought there'd been some trick played on her. However, I see it's perfectly true. Do tell me how it all happened.'

'I would rather not, if you don't mind, Aunt. It's a long story – but it was mainly due to Jack's good sense. And of course if it had not been for you taking me to London it would never have happened. Life is so much stranger than fiction, isn't it. How are your friends? Mrs Morris and – Mr Rossetti?'

Frederica lit a cigarette, puffed it, and waved the smoke away

292

languidly. What had happened to the old ban on smoking in the house? 'Oh, I don't see anything of *them*. Quite démodé. Gabriel has gone completely to the dogs, drink, drugs, Heaven knows what – and is living very scandalously at Kelmscott with Jane, upsetting poor Topsy by shutting all the windows to keep out the fresh air and sitting about the house all day taking medicine. Nobody knows him any more. As for Jane, I'm quite disgusted with her. Such a useless life. No, I've given up Art. You wouldn't know my house, dear. Do come and see how different it is.'

'Thank you,' Lilian said, resolved to do nothing of the kind. She braced herself for the next question. 'Do you see anything of Mr Bevis?'

'Good heavens, no. Didn't you read about it?' Lilian shook her head. 'Well, there was a court case. It seems the nasty creature picked up some servant-girl or other, and kept her in his rooms and starved her; and very unluckily for him she died and the police were called in and found evidence of poison. I never should have believed it if anyone had told me, but it was all there in the papers.'

'Then where is he now?'

'In prison, of course. For a good many years, and lucky it wasn't the gallows. No, I never should have believed it: such nice manners.'

Lilian hoped her sigh of relief was not audible. It was, in any case, overlaid by a huge, uncontrollable yawn from Millie, who was leaning sideways in her uncomfortable chair.

'Poor thing, she's worn out,' Frederica said casually. 'No stamina. I suppose you've a bed for her somewhere? And for me, I hope?'

Lilian remembered the downstairs back room she had slept in when she first came to Stainbeck, and another at the end of the passage upstairs, beyond her bedroom. The sheets would need airing. Assuring her aunt that accommodation could be managed, she asked Millie to go upstairs with her and fetch them down. As they sorted the linen, she glanced curiously at her one-time maid. For all the improvement there was something else: was it a look of hopelessness? She turned the girl round to face her.

'What is it, Millie? Are you unhappy? I know you're very tired, but try to tell me.'

'Oh, miss. Missis. I mean madam. I don't like to say.' The

roughness had gone from Millie's voice. Lilian guessed that it had been coached out of her.

'Come on,' she said gently. 'You can tell me.'

'I were so feart of her, miss. It's none so bad now, but . . .' her voice trailed off into a weary slur, and she seemed about to collapse on the pile of sheets.

'Never mind now. We'll talk about it tomorrow. Just carry those down for me and we'll put them round the fire, and while they're airing you can lie down on your bed and rest.' The girl was only too glad to obey, falling like a sack of coal on the mattress. Lilian took off her bonnet and loosened her collar, then laid a blanket over her. Before leaving the room she paused.

'Just tell me one thing. Do you want to stay with my aunt – in whatever position you serve her?'

The answer was clear, for all the onset of sleep. 'No, Miss.'

Seated by the fire, the spread linen at her feet, Lilian said, 'I think you should tell me about Millie, Aunt. She seems very changed, and not very happy.'

'Has she been talking to you?'

'No.'

'Very well. There was a good deal of domestic trouble after your abrupt departure, as you might guess. Digby and I had strong words, and he went off to his Club. And I'm afraid Millie got her share of scolding, since she seemed to have had a hand in it, and the silly girl ran away. It was quite some time before she came back, or rather Digby brought her back; it seemed she had actually found out the address of his Club from that man of his, and had gone to it asking for money, or help, or something.' Lilian sensed that a lot was being left unsaid. 'I took her back, of course, and looked after her. I think she may be a help to us, in her way.'

'Us?'

'I am a follower of the Women's Movement, Lilian. Well? Don't look so blank, girl. Surely you've heard of us, even in this forsaken spot.'

'I've heard Mamma talking about it to friends – and Uncle Lewis, sometimes. They were both very, er, disapproving.'

Frederica snorted. 'They would be. People like that who should know better are holding us back. Well, since you seem fairly ignorant, let me tell you something about the Movement.' Straight-backed, upright, radiating enthusiasm, Frederica launched into what would have served nicely for a public speech. Lilian heard how the tide of civilised thought had turned against the subjection of Woman to Man : Woman, the superior creature, more physically complex, more beautiful, more intelligent, enslaved to the coarse male by age-old custom, bearing his children at the expense of her own health, subject to his gross desires, deprived of equality with him in every sphere of life. America was leading the way, with better education for girls, freer speech, splendid lady leaders whose fire reached across the Atlantic to kindle the torches of such as Emily Davies, founder of the first woman's college, and Elizabeth Garrett, who had opened a dispensary for women and set herself to be a practising doctor in spite of the jeers and hoots of male opponents. 'Yes, they jeer at us – because they're afraid. Afraid for their precious pride and their dominance and their lusts. Why should women not become doctors, lawyers, politicians, clerks? Why should they be tied to hearth and home, to waiting on a man or arranging flowers for Mamma? Why, Lilian?'

'I don't know, Aunt. I've no idea. It seems to be the way things are at the moment.'

'But you must agree that we should take an equal place in the world with men.'

Lilian considered. 'Now you mention it, I suppose we could do a lot more than we do. We're cleverer and much stronger than men suppose us. But . . . who would bring up the children and look after the house?'

Frederica made a sweeping gesture. 'There are people to do these things. Come, Lilian, don't quibble. You *are* on our side, aren't you? You must acknowledge the superiority of women to men.'

'I don't acknowledge it at all. I think men are beautiful.' (At least, Jack is, she thought.) 'If it comes to that, I don't really know many women, only a farmer's wife or two round here.'

'I can imagine the life they lead, poor serfs. But would you not like to know other women, happier women, to have them as your intimates, feel the pure flame of their affections warming you to life? Believe me, men are poor things compared with us. How I wish I could have had a daughter instead of wretched, ungrateful

Digby, a girl who would have been friend and companion to me – as *you* might be . . .'

Lilian wondered whether the late Timothy Stevens-Clyne had been a poor thing, and if that was the reason Frederica had no daughter, or any other children besides Digby, and how much all this was responsible for the present phase she was going through. Aloud she said, 'Aunt, are you sure you really feel these things? When you first came to visit Uncle Lewis and Mamma I thought of you as a very sensible person. Then you suddenly turned into an enthusiast for Art, and now that's over and you're all for Women's Rights. Don't you think these are all ways of trying to find what you really want?' She knew she was being prosy, probably talking nonsense; she was dreadfully tired and rather nervous of her visitor, but there was no point in showing weakness. 'As for liking women, I'm not all that keen on them, I hope my child will be a son.'

Frederica's eyes were on her, brooding, considering. At last she said, 'You've just shown me what a good mind you have. You may think you mean what you say so very prettily and sincerely. But search your heart, and you'll find deep truths there.' She stretched her hands towards Lilian, pleading. 'Whatever attitudes I may have struck in the past – and I despise them now – this is truly me, Frederica. (Won't you call me Frederica, or perhaps Freddy? "Aunt" is so ageing.) You must see that I'm entirely serious. That's why I've rescued this poor creature, Millie, because she is good material. I've taught her a little, brought her out – she's not as stupid as Flo always thought her. And I mean to rescue *you*, my child.'

Lilian stood up. 'Well, *Aunt*, I don't need to be rescued and I don't want to be. And now I really must go to bed. As you can see, I need plenty of rest at the moment. I'm sure you're tired too. I'll make up your bed.'

When she came back Frederica was still sitting as she had been. The flickering fire made caves of her eye-sockets and the hollows under her cheek-bones, picked out details of her dress in vivid highlights. A cauldron and a toad were all the picture needed to complete it, Lilian thought.

'Would you like some more tea before you go to bed? I can easily make some.'

'No. No. Just give me a candle and show me the way.'

Lilian was only too glad to obey. Leaving Frederica at her door, with a cheerful good-night, she looked in on Millie. The girl was too heavily asleep to hear the door open, or feel the extra bedclothes placed over her.

'Oh dear,' Lilian said to herself, safe in her own room. 'Oh dear, oh dear.' The coming of Aunt Freddy had meant trouble before; she hoped it didn't mean trouble now.

Frederica came down to breakfast heavy-eyed. She had not slept well, she said. The room had been very cold and some strange unsettling noises had been going on outside, a high-pitched screaming for one thing.

'That would be a fox,' Lilian said. 'They had one of our lambs last month.'

'Ugh. Don't the hunt keep them down? No, not in these parts, I suppose. Oh, how chilly it is, even downstairs. Do you always breakfast in your kitchen? How strange. Well, never mind, a pot of good coffee will put everything right.'

Lilian said that there was none in the house, as nobody took it. Frederica sipped unenthusiastically at the tea provided, only picking at the toast which was all she would accept to eat. But Millie, who had obviously slept very well, sat down at table as one dedicated to eating, disposing in alarming fashion of the eggs fresh-gathered from the goldies' nests and the rich streaky bacon, and chatting animatedly between mouthfuls with Amos, whom she seemed to take to on sight. Frederica barely acknowledged him. When he had finished he left the kitchen swiftly and silently, throwing Lilian an appealing glance. She shrugged, as if to say, 'I know. But it can't be helped.'

Millie looked up. 'Eeh, miss. It's like a dream, being back. I'd forgotten there were owt like this. You know, the milk in London were like water, dirty water at that. And butter, well, it's no better'n soap, and we never had . . .' She stopped, seeing Frederica's frowning face.

'What does it matter how you breakfasted?' that lady said chillingly. 'Better at my house than before, I expect. And is your food all-important to you?'

'No, ma'am. Sorry, ma'am.'

297

'Dreams can be deceptive, you know.'

'Yes, ma'am.'

There were the hens to see to, and Billy's breakfast, the pea-picking and the household tasks. Millie took to all of them as a duck to water, while Frederica sat in the parlour, reading old newspapers in which not a line about her consuming passion appeared. Half-way through the morning Lilian, laden with baskets of tender young pea-pods, paused at her side, unwilling to raise the subject of last night's discussion, yet knowing it must be settled.

'Would you like some more tea, Aunt? I'm afraid it's all we've got to offer. Are you quite comfortable there? You could have a chair outside, if you like. The sun's very strong – it might be pleasant, after London.'

'Lilian. My dear. No, put those baskets down and listen to me. I tried to talk to you last night but I know you were tired. Lilian, this place is not worthy of you. The cold, and the discomfort! You must feel it. I had hardly any water to wash in this morning. And no proper company for you – that poor old man, almost too lame to walk – oh, I know he's your father-in-law, but these things mean little to people like that. Sit down, don't hover. Standing is not good for you in your condition, poor dear. I pity you from the bottom of my heart. These cruel things happen to women because we *are* women, but they can be overcome.'

'I don't want to overcome my child, Aunt, thank you.'

'I'd give you a good life,' Frederica said. 'Money, leisure. You could have the child and then forget about it.'

Lilian pulled herself away from the clutching hand, and went out of the room. Millie was peeling potatoes in the kitchen, humming tunelessly. As Lilian entered she looked up, brightly, a different girl from the frightened slavey of Chelsea, and the dull underservant of the Dower House.

'Miss, they're lovely, these little taties, too good to peel – I've scraped 'em and picked a bit o' mint to put wi' 'em. If peas are ready I'll pod 'em next.'

'Yes, they are, but never mind them for the moment. Millie, do you understand Mrs Stevens-Clyne's attachment to the Feminist Movement? Do you know what it's about?'

'Not rightly, miss. I've got an idea, but that's all.'

'Do you want to go on with it? I asked you last night, and you said no, so I ask you again, when you're awake and able to answer properly.'

Suddenly Millie broke, like a clear pool scattered by a hail of stones. Her face crumpled as tears sprang out of her eyes and spilled down on to the table-top. Lilian had never seen such tears, or hands clasped so pitifully.

'Please, miss, don't let me go with her, oh don't! She fair frights me, I tell you. I know she's been very kind and taught me things. But I can't seem to like it at all, and it's not natural, and I'm not clever enough . . .'

Lilian's mind was made up. She patted Millie's shoulder briskly.

'Now, Millie, nothing to go on so about. I shall speak to Mrs Stevens-Clyne about you.'

Frederica stood stiffly outside the front door, looking about her, down to the lane, across to where a gentle line of hills was punctuated by the black skeletal shapes of coal-mines. A fresh wind was blowing from the gardens; on the climbing rose that entwined the porch a great butterfly, coloured deep red and brown, perched lightly, its proboscis buried in a flower. Lilian touched Frederica's cold hand.

'Aunt.'

'Well?'

'I can't come with you. But will you leave Millie with me – please? That would be more useful than anything. I do so much need a strong young woman about the place, and she and I know each other so well. And – she would be no use to you. I'm sure you know that, really. One day she'll get married and lead her own life, and it won't be yours.'

The butterfly flew away. The wind blew another soft gust before Frederica said, 'Very well. I was wrong to come. I shall leave directly after luncheon.'

Everything seemed very peaceful when Frederica had gone. Lilian went to bed, telling Millie to do the same. But when she rose all evidence of luncheon had been washed and tidied away, the peas were picked, the parlour grate cleaned and re-laid, Frederica's bed stripped and the sheets washed.

'Yon was a funny woman,' Amos said. 'Thy auntie? Well, it's a wise niece as knows its own aunt. But this lass, Millie, she's grand.

I reckon we could do a good job here, the three of us, if we can keep her, for she's an appetite like a horse.'

'Oh, I think we can do that, Dad!' Four clean five-pound notes had been put into Millie's hand before Frederica left; a fortune, coldly given. Lilian stored it away in a drawer of the press. One day it might be needed more than it was now.

CHAPTER TWENTY-THREE

Millie bloomed as the days went by and Frederica's shadow receded. She would never be pretty, but as the gauntness left her face and she began to smile often a comeliness emerged which Lilian did not remember from the days when Millie was a put-upon maid, treated as little more than a half-wit. But then she had never given Millie much thought as a person, let alone as a potential angel sent to minister to the household at Stainbeck. For what needed to be done there Millie could do. The eldest of a family of eight, she had been deputy mother in her parents' cottage at Risedale, sewing, cooking, nursing, tending fowls and a pig. No job was too lowly for her, no skill beyond her powers of learning. Strong and sensible and calm, she took the weight of the work off Lilian by day, and sat stitching by night. In her hands the baffling rolls of cloth from the upstairs cupboard turned to tiny vests, napkins and pilches, bibs, nightgowns, long dresses beautifully embroidered with drawn threadwork, cot sheets and blankets. There was even a cloak of fine cream flannel with lace appliqués, fine enough for a grandchild of the Queen.

'Gracious,' Lilian exclaimed, 'you'll turn its head. How do you think we're going to go on dressing it in this style?'

'No bairn was ever the worse for a good start,' replied Millie, bending her neat head again over her work. Yet for all her obvious content, something still lurked behind her eyes, a remembered distress. She was not given to undue conversation. It took Lilian a full month to get out of her the truth of what had happened to her in London after the elopement, and the truth was not at all like Frederica's account.

Millie had not run away from the house in Cheyne Row. She had been turned out remorselessly, the only object on which Frederica could expend her wrath; and it was done after Digby and Stokes had left. With a week's wages in her pocket and her small bundle of possessions in her hand, Millie was put into the street, knowing no more of Chelsea than she did of London itself.

Yes, she had been very frightened, she said. She had spent most of the first night sitting on a seat by the river, until a policeman had moved her on, directing her to an address in the mean streets round Millbank Prison. There, after hours of asking, she had been taken in by a slut of a woman and given a dirty basement room, parting with half her money for it. The worst of it had been that the people didn't seem able to understand her northern speech, so that she felt stupid, like a foreigner.

Then a man had spoken to her civilly, offering to find her a better lodging. She went with him to what he called his rooms. There were only two, at the top of a rickety old house almost in the river. After asking her some questions, he had gone out, returning with another man. Millie would not say what had happened then, but began to shake. Lilian drew her own conclusions; there had been an attempt at rape, and a struggle. She would never, probably, get out of Millie what the result had been. All she would say was that the first man had been very angry, and had beaten her, and that she had run out of the house.

Only one person came into her mind as a possible saviour. Millbank was a military prison, soldiers coming and going from it all the time. She had summoned up enough courage to speak to one, while others jeered, giving him Captain Stevens-Clyne's name and the information that the Captain was something to do with guarding the Queen. The soldier was kind-hearted and intelligent enough to give her sixpence and the address of the Army and Navy Club, to which, after a day's wandering, she found her way. The people at the Club were not pleased to see her. She would have been out in the street again had not an officer overheard Digby's name and volunteered to take a message to him at some Palace: the Guards' quarters at St James's, of course.

And Digby had come as soon as he could, to where she waited miserably in the Club's kitchen. 'He were that *kind*, Miss Lilian. I never knew a gentleman as kind as him.' They had gone in a cab to Chelsea, where, while she waited outside, Digby talked with his mother. Then she had been asked in, and found the mistress quite changed, very pleasant and concerned for her. 'She'd had a proper telling-off from the Captain, you could see that.'

Lilian asked no more questions. She knew enough by now of the experiences that had etched lines across Millie's square brow and at each side of her mouth.

'I'll make it up to you, Millie,' she said.

'Aye. You and t'bairn.'

Jack's spirits were high. He was delighted by the changes in his home, which had never been so cheerful. Millie and he got on splendidly, she was charmed by his handsomeness and the reputation Lilian had given him as a romantic hero. It was explained to her that she had, in fact, seen him before, working as a gardener at the Dower House, but she seemed either not to take this in or not to believe it. He noted with amusement that Lilian showed not the least jealousy at his friendliness with the girl, for he suspected that things might have been very different had Millie been a ravishing beauty with a come-hither eye. He was pleased to see Amos in less pain, now that the summer weather was at its height. He was able, even, to drive the second-hand trap they had bought to market and, in the evening, carve, with delicate skill, a cradle. It was of fine oak, the best he could get, the rockers so perfectly shaped that it moved at a touch. On the hood he had drawn a picture with the red-hot point of a narrow poker: it was copied from a print of Shakespeare's church at Stratford-on-Avon, and was considered by all who saw it to be a remarkable work of art.

Most of all Jack was pleased with his wife. She blossomed with pregnancy into mature beauty and acquired an unassailable calm which helped him through the time when his career seemed in jeopardy.

His first match after his injury healed was Iddison's benefit, against Gloucestershire, the county which drew the biggest crowds. At Bramall Lane turnstiles had been fitted to stop the infiltration of people who were more anxious to see the match than to pay for that privilege. George Freeman, who had virtually retired from cricket to attend to his business, returned for his friend Iddison's benefit, his amiable face, still boyish and chubby at 28, warmly welcomed by his team-mates. Massie had been dropped, to the relief of others besides Jack, and a comparative newcomer, young Allen Hill, had aroused great expectations by his bowling in a Surrey match.

303

The late summer sun shone, the crowd was a capacity one, excitement ran high : for not only was the legendary W. G. Grace playing, but his two formidable brothers, Edward and Fred. Larger than ever, diabolically beaming, the six feet and two inches of him magnified by the sparkling white of his flannels, he made his majestic way to the wicket, towering over T. G. Matthews, his regular opening partner. They exchanged a friendly word, took up their positions : and remained at them for the whole of Gloucester's first innings, an entire day. Yorkshire bowled their hearts out, vainly. Jack disposed of E. M. Grace for an undistinguished 11, and G.F. for an even less distinguished 3, but their terrible brother batted implacably, piling up the runs and giving never a chance to the bowlers, contributing largely to a massive 238, at which point the brothers Luke and Andrew Greenwood took W.G. jointly, Luke bowling and Andrew making a magnificent catch, leaping into the air for it like a rising salmon, to the accompaniment of deafening cheers.

But Gloucestershire had a total of 294 runs. Walking back to the Pavilion, the wicket-keeper George Pinder remarked to Jack, 'I think I'll chuck it up and keep fowls.' 'Don't,' Jack replied gloomily, 'I do, and they're a bloody nuisance.'

'At least tha can wring their necks. I'd fancy a go at *his* if I could get mi hands round it.' He surveyed them, enormous in padded gloves, and shook his head resignedly.

Next day dawned even brighter, one of those harvest-gold days with a hint of coolness in the air that surpass any weather England can provide. Jack walked to the wicket to begin Yorkshire's first innings partnered unexpectedly by Allen Hill, who was primarily a bowler, but had given such a display of run-getting the week before that Rowbotham had been tempted to experiment by moving him up the order to Number Two. Some of the other players, Jack included, were not sure this was a good idea. Joe was as fine a batsman as ever, even after twenty years' service, but was his judgment as a captain wholly reliable, they wondered? Allen at least looked confident.

'How d'you feel?' Jack asked him before they took up their opposite ends.

'Grand. Full of runs.'

Jack nodded. 'That's the stuff.'

Taking his stance, a curious feeling came over him. It was as though he stood outside himself, seeing himself as clearly as he saw Allen at the other end. Now, the present moment, held him in a shining bubble of suspended time; just as long as it took him to survey the quiet expectant crowd and to tread down an uneven piece of turf. He was twenty-three. He had fulfilled the ambition that had been with him all his life, to become a professional earning his living by cricket. His batting average was 29·88, the highest in the County, his bowling average for the season 19·12, more than respectable. Without vanity, he knew that there was something in his make-up which would take him out of the league of his fellow-players, into the ranks of All England, into the future when cricket would have moved far beyond the game these men had known in their boyhood. He knew that he even looked different from these men, stocky, thickset in the main : elegant and graceful were the words most often used to describe him by the sports writers. And he was beginning even to sound different, whether he intended to or not, influenced by his wife's speech and vocabulary.

He knew, too, that these qualities would take him into places he had never dreamed of, some of them perilous. Out there, in a basket chair in front of the pavilion, reclined one of his perils, for these days he seldom played without feeling the dark eyes of Lady Celia Masham following his every movement. She was the daughter of an ex-Lord Lieutenant of the County; she had a will of her own that had seldom been crossed, and that will was set on him. If he escaped her toils, as he fully intended, there would be other bright eyes beckoning, other invitations to other manor-houses and even castles; not only desire would follow him, but envy, hatred and jealousy. He was going to need all the strength he had to deal with these things; and he was not afraid.

Suddenly the bubble burst. He was back at Bramall Lane in the sunshine, with drops of moisture from overnight rain winking from the pitch. There might be something in it for the bowlers. C. L. Townsend, loping gently down towards him, appeared to think there was, by the hopeful smile on his face.

The umpire signalled a wide. Jack returned Townsend's smile. Some of the radiance of the bubble remained with him, and he could do nothing wrong. After a quiet start he began to collect runs, a few singles, then a four that brought cheers from the crowd.

Obligingly he treated them to an exhibition of virtuosity: the smooth glide, the lovely balletic sweep, the square off-drive that was his speciality. The bowling changed. The ball was hurtling down at him, breaking sharply and sometimes leaping up in menace. Hill, receiving similar treatment, went out to a ball he should have left alone, and was bowled, passing on his forlorn way back to the pavilion the incoming batsman, Andrew Greenwood. To Hill's one run Greenwood added a humiliating duck, out before he had even scored. Jack batted on, as smoothly as though an angel's hands were on the bat above his. In record time his fifty was in sight, when he swung round to send a ball flying to the boundary between third man and deep fine leg, and saw it fly into a pair of eager hands. He had made 47. Sympathetic groans followed his walk back, but he smiled and tilted his cap cheerfully. It would teach him not to rely on euphoria. Yet he still felt unusually light-hearted.

And so he remained, through the second Gloucestershire innings and another daunting exhibition by the greatest of the Three Graces. For hours, it seemed (and was, indeed, almost two) the monolith stood at the wicket, sometimes lumbering across with surprising speed for one of his weight, defying the efforts of Hill, Andrew Greenwood, his brother Luke, and George Freeman. Jack took over. The afternoon shadows fell black on the grass, the sky was cerulean blue, pearled with white clouds, the spectators a dazzle of colour, for many Yorkshire and Gloucestershire ladies were there in support of their men. Jack, still euphoric (though he knew it was dangerous) sent a friendly half-toss down. With a contemptuous swipe the ball was killed. Jack tried bowling at Grace's wicket, and outside it. He sent balls down temptingly short, to lure the monster out of its den. Grace let two pass, then got behind the third one with a magnificent blow that sent it soaring up beyond the circling pigeons, high over the covers, across the boundary and into the crowd. Another six.

Jack caught Grace's glance, twinkling under the bushy brows. At once baleful and benevolent, it was just the goad the bowler needed. His next run showed an extra turn of speed, and the ball left his hand like a bird released, flying straight to the off-stump. At the sound of the impact Grace spun round on his heel, stared at the fallen stump and scattered bails, hunched his mighty shoulders and began the walk back, to resounding cheers. The six had brought up 150 for him, and he departed in glory.

Whatever happened to him afterwards, Jack reflected, he would never forget that moment, the culmination of what had been for him a magic match. It had not won the game for Yorkshire, that deadly ball, for Gloucester beat them by 56 runs, but it had been well worth bowling.

When stumps were drawn and the fielding side returned to the pavilion Jack found himself waylaid by a vision in deep pink that set off enchantingly the dark ringlets and white skin of Lady Celia.

'Superb, as usual, North Star,' she said. 'You must be exhausted, poor thing.'

'Not a bit of it, Lady Celia. It's been a very good day out there.'

'Well, at least you must be dying for a cup of tea. Won't you join us? Papa couldn't come – it's just myself and Miss Ainslie, my chaperon, you know. Oh, *do*.' She made a bewitching face at him and laid a small, predatory, rosy-gloved hand on his arm.

'I've got to get cleaned up. I'm not fit to eat with ladies.'

'We'll wait for you, then.'

'As a matter of fact, I'll have to go as soon as I'm changed. I've an errand to do – for my wife.'

'Oh.' The hand was withdrawn. 'What a pity. Next time, perhaps.' The dark slumbrous eyes followed him until he disappeared into the pavilion. He had not dared look back, for she was very lovely.

It was true that he had an errand, though Lilian was quite unaware of it. When he came home in the evening he wore the look of a man with a secret which half-elates, half-alarms him. Lilian read it in his face.

'What have you been doing now?' she enquired sternly.

'Me?'

'Who else? *I* know. Come on now, what is it?' He thought wryly that he might well have come home with a guilty face if he had been doing what Lady Celia would have liked him to do. 'It's your birthday,' he said.

'It isn't! Well, not until Wednesday. Oh dear, you haven't been spending money again? There isn't anything I need, really.'

Amos looked up over his spectacles. 'The Lord loveth a gracious

307

taker as well as a gracious giver, daughter. Wait and see what it is before you throw it back.'

'You may not like it,' Jack said, 'but I can't help that.'

'Perhaps if I could see it I should know better.' She waited for him to produce whatever it was from his pockets, but he moved to the door. 'It's out here.' Lilian, with a suspicious glance at him, followed, Amos behind her. There was a beautiful sunset light on the gardens, the distant prospect of village and valley; and on the animal which stood, head drooping, on the path outside the door.

'Jack? What . . . a horse?'

'Nay, a pony.'

'Out o' pits,' said Amos. 'I know t'look they get.'

'It's had a bad time.' Jack patted the pony's neck, and indicated marks on its body where the hair was worn away and gouts of blood had dried. 'Them's the places where the belly-band's been kept too tight, and the collar's not been searched for bits as get wedged and tear the skin. He's had a bad master, he has. There's some teeth broken with forcing the bit in, and . . . and I don't know what.' His voice shook with anger, though he had grown accustomed to the sight of the injuries since he had collected the animal. Amos looked closely at them, shaking his head.

'How come he's not been put down? They don't often keep 'em when they're as bad as this.'

'Oh, he was due for it, all right. I heard from one of our Colts (you know, Lilian, the club's young hopefuls) whose brother's a pony driver down your old pit, Dad. This was his nag, but he got taken off it because they reckoned he were too soft and wouldn't work it enough. You know what it's like down on t'roads – time's money. He got all sorts of nasty tricks played on him by other chaps, and at last word got to the deputy, and he were taken off ponies. It near broke his heart when he saw what happened to Tommy here afterwards. Last night he went crying to his brother and said Tommy'd been laid off and was to be put down – not worth retiring, they said. The old ones get put out to grass if they last that long.'

'This un's not old,' Amos said. 'What is he – ten?'

'Seven. Only seen fourteen weeks of daylight, two a year. Not much, is it.' He stroked the pony's nose gently; it turned its heavy head towards him, with a faint whicker. 'So I thought I'd go and see about it. Tom brought us up in the waggon. Stable-keeper said he weren't worth buying, but I reckon he is, with rest and food, and some of your cures, Dad – I'll bet you've plenty of horse doctoring in your head.'

'That I have! We'll get him fixed up in no time, you wait and see.'

'I thought,' said Jack, still apologetic, 'when he got fit again we could buy a little pony-trap – it'd be like feathers for him to pull, after all them tons of steel and coal. You could get out a bit in that, Dad, and – and the little 'un could learn to ride, when he was big enough. Eh, Lilian?'

'If you let him off cricket practice long enough,' Lilian said, then burst into tears and flung her arms round her husband. 'Oh, Jack, you're so good, so very good.'

'Here, here, now, now, don't get upset.' He held and soothed her, while Amos talked softly to the pony.

'I don't care what you paid,' she sobbed. 'If it was – a hundred pounds – it wouldn't have been too much. And I know you meant it to make up for . . .'

'For Sabra? Aye, well, partly. And because you used to ride, before you came that cropper. But for its own sake, too, poor beast. Now you go and get it a bit o' cake or some raisins, anything sweet they like, then I'll take it to the lambing shed and settle it down for the night. It'll look different tomorrow, you'll see.'

Sure enough, with the instinct of its kind the pony sensed freedom and kindness. The next day its eyes were brighter, and it walked staggeringly in the meadow where Jack hoped it would soon gallop and roll as joyful ponies do. Very soon it began to eat well; new hair grew over the bare wounded spots, thanks, Amos said, to his doctoring. The young lad Dave who had been its driver came up to see Tommy, beside himself with happiness at the pony's restoration, and was recognised instantly, with a glad little sound and a lowering of the head to Dave's pocket.

'He's lookin' for mi snap-tin.' Dave was almost weeping with joy. 'I used to give him sweets out of it, every mornin'. Here, see, lad, I've brought you the ones you like. Oh, Mr Ellershaw, can I stay wi' him?'

'As long as you like, whenever you like. And before you go, you come up and tell my wife how he likes to be handled, and that she's not to get too near his hind legs. We don't want any accidents.'

The harvest moon shone and waned, the leaves dropped and were swirled about in wild winds as winter came to Stainbeck. It was very snug in the old parlour, with a fire that never went out, constantly refuelled with logs kept drying in the hearth. The family had somehow acquired cats now; three strays who had heard by the mysterious communication system cats have that a hearthrug, food, and unlimited mice were to be had for the asking. The third arrival was heavy with kitten. Lilian said 'Oh, no!' but then decided that she could hardly turn it away in a condition similar to her own. There they were, three Ellershaws and a fourth not far off, very comfortable and compared with last year very prosperous.

Snow blanketed the fallow fields and a full moon shone down as the three of them came home one night, up the hill from Barnswood, in the big trap, with a stout borrowed horse in the shafts. They had been to hear the Choral Society performing the *Messiah*. The two men had known Handel's great work all their lives; it was a tradition as strong as Christmas itself in Yorkshire. To Lilian, in her present dreamy state, it was a glorious discovery. The moon turned the blue shawl that shrouded her head and shoulders to silver, her face to a pale oval with a soft blurred mouth and shadowy pools for eyes, an Impressionist's Madonna, dreaming of Heaven's music. She was still wrapt in its wonder as they travelled uphill, slowly because of half-frozen snow under hoof and wheel.

'Sing it again,' she commanded. 'Go on, as much as you remember.'

'That'd be the lot,' Amos said, but broke into song in a tenor still sweet and true. ' "And the government shall be upon his shoulder, and his name shall be called" – ' Jack joined in.

' "Wonderful! Counsellor!

The mighty God, the everlasting Father, the Prince of Peace." '

They were more than half-way home, still singing, when Lilian asked, 'How long will it take from here, Dad?'

Something in her voice made Jack look at her sharply. She smiled. 'Oh, there's nothing wrong. It's only . . . I've a pain in my back.'

'I thought so. Ten minutes, Dad?'

310

'Aye, give or take a bit. We're nigh to t'turn.'

Briskly encouraged, the stout horse made good time. Millie heard the trap's approach and opened the door, sending a stream of lamp-light down the path. As soon as she saw them, Jack supporting Lilian and her face turned up to him, she ran down to meet them.

'To think it should be on Christmas Eve – well, fancy! Now don't get mithered, you men, I've got all ready as should be. Come, on, Miss Lilian, upstairs.'

'Hardly Miss Lilian at the moment,' murmured the expectant mother. 'I never felt less like a Miss anything, in fact. Wish me luck, darling Jack, if I don't see you again for an hour or two.'

'Oh, you can look in now and again if I say so, Jack,' Millie said. 'Nowt to be feart of, and a lot of rubbish talked about it, owd wives' tales and such. I've seen six of my ma's into t'world and I never thought owt much to it. Come on, love.'

On this cheering note Amos and Jack settled down by the fire with their pipes and a quantity of home-brewed ale. They discussed cricket, music, the possible advantages of keeping a cow, the likelihood of Gladstone's ministry falling and the interesting news that Prince Alfred was to marry a Russian princess in St Petersburg. Far away, they heard the Christmas bells ring over the silent countryside.

'Good job moon were full, driving back, considering what's happened – happening,' said Amos.

'It's always full moon when the Choral Society meets. So they can get home easy, afterwards.' Amos, who knew this perfectly well, nodded. Jack's gaze went frequently to the ceiling. In that stoutly-built stone house they could hear nothing, and Millie did not come down. Old wives' tales that had come to his ears beset Jack, whatever Millie said. He drank more ale than usual, though it seemed curiously tasteless.

Their vigil was not prolonged. Christmas Day was nowhere near its dawn when Millie appeared. 'You can come up now. Only four hours i' labour, what about that? And first time, too. You'll get a whole eleven at this rate, Jack. Oh, and it's a lad.'

'Thank God,' said Amos. ' "Unto us a son is given." '

Lilian was sitting up in bed, very pink in the face and brilliant-eyed. Her hair was all about her shoulders, brushed out of its tangles though still curling damply on her brow; some of it covered the downy head of John Ellershaw, Junior, who seemed resigned to

311

his situation after a somewhat sudden entry into the world. Jack kissed his wife, and the amazingly soft cheek of the baby, unable to speak. Lilian put the tiny hand in his, where it was quite swallowed up. The fingers curled into a flower-like fist.

'There, you see,' she said. 'He wants a bat to hold.'

'Happen he'll be a left-hander,' said Jack, rather indistinctly. 'They make a lot more trouble for t'other side.'

None of them guessed, that Christmas morning, how splendid a christening John would have. Lilian wrote to Digby, wanting him to share their happiness, and Digby, overjoyed, wrote to his uncle Sir Lewis and his cousin Augustus. Astonishingly, a letter from Scarbrick Hall to the new parents expressed Sir Lewis's pleasure at the birth of a son into the family, and enquired whether they would like the christening to be held at the Hall, and conducted by Augustus, who had been approached and was most willing.

'*Well!*' said Lilian. 'How amazing. I never thought Uncle Lewis would unbend like that, or want a baby about the place, even for a day or two. How odd people are; but why not, Jack? Why shouldn't we accept? It would be a lot jollier than the Ebenezer.'

'And that wouldn't be difficult . . . Aye, we'll accept. Give the lad a proper start in life.'

Lilian was so gratified that Jack had raised no objections on the grounds of pride and the disgrace of accepting favours that she sat down immediately to write her letter.

Amos and Millie steadfastly refused to go. Amos pointed out that it was almost lambing-time and he wanted to be on the spot to see that Billy didn't make a mess of things. Millie said it would fluster her to go anywhere near Scarbrick Hall, and that was that. She would stay at home and keep the fire warm.

The drawing-room of Scarbrick Hall had not been used since Sir Lewis had been reluctantly persuaded to give his younger daughter a coming-out party. Since then dust-sheets had covered the furniture, drawn blinds had kept light from the room. Sir Lewis's orders to uncover, clean and illuminate everything astonished his servants, whose duties were on the whole monotonous and uninteresting. His housekeeper, Mrs Akroyd, was delighted. She sent for extra help from Fellgate and donned a pinafore herself to assist with the work. A week of scrubbing, dusting, washing and polishing, carpet-beating and dangerous operations up ladders brought back life to the beautiful room so long neglected. Only the rich brocade curtains at the long windows could not be cleaned in time, even if they would stand cleaning at all.

'I warrant those have been up since the time of old King George,' Mrs Akroyd told the maids. 'My grandmother was a sewing-woman here when she was a girl, and she admired them then. We could try, but as like as not they'd fall in pieces. Best leave them alone.'

She surveyed the drawing-room with pride. The classical plaster mouldings of the ceilings looked down in their faded pastel tints, arabesques framing a central painting of some Grecian feat of horsemanship. The floorboards had been waxed to a high shine, setting off the Axminster carpet of deep crimson, patterned in blues and creams; twin settees of carved and gilded wood and elaborate Hepplewhite chairs displayed silk upholstery as bright as when it was woven; 'too good to sit on' thought the maids. The china display cabinet and occasional tables were of satinwood, the porcelain behind the glass delicate Meissen and Bow, brought to the house by a southern-born lady a hundred years before. In the centre of the carpet a round table draped in a lace cloth bore as its centre-piece a large bowl of Italian marble, round whose rim marble doves perched, rested and dipped. It was, Sir Lewis considered, hideous, but it would do for the purpose.

Now all was ready, and just in time, for the most important person in the ceremony had arrived, and could be heard screaming as he was removed from the carriage Sir Lewis had sent to meet the train.

'Oh, dear,' Lilian said, kissing her uncle dutifully. 'I'm afraid he's very noisy just now, but he was good in the train and slept all the way, so I suppose that's why.'

'No matter, no matter. Good God.' He surveyed his niece's healthy bloom and matronly figure displayed in an elegantly tight jacket and mermaid's-tail skirt. 'Thought you much improved last time I saw you at that place, what's-its-name, but nothing to this. And Ellershaw.' Not knowing quite how to greet his erstwhile gardener, Sir Lewis held out his hand, which was firmly shaken. 'How are you, sir. Good of you to have us,' Jack said, as one used to visiting stately homes every weekend. Sir Lewis hardly recognised the boy he had known in the man Jack was now – surely taller, if that were possible, and with a square-cut authoritative look to him. For a second the thought flashed across his mind: good blood there? It was possible.

'Well, well, come in. What about the, er?' He indicated John, now calmer as his mother bounced him up and down and staring interestedly at the bright brass gong from India which stood in a corner of the hall.

'Oh, he'll be all right, unless you've company, Uncle, and would rather I took him upstairs.'

'Not a bit of it. Company, aye, we've got company, but not our Elsie and our Louie, if that's what you're thinking. Can't stand those swarms of brats, no offence, young man.' He advanced a large hand to pat John's bonneted head, then thought better of it. A hovering maid curtseyed and opened the door of the morning-room, a comfortable parlour used by the daughters of the house while on visits. Four people who had been sitting round the fire rose and came forward. Digby and Penny, all laughter and open arms and exclamations of joy, Augustus, benevolently smiling. And, from a corner, Lilian's mother, somehow grown small and mouselike, tentatively smiling but ready to weep at a word. Penny hugged Lilian.

'Darling Lilian – and your Jack, oh my goodness, how handsome! And what a love of a baby! I declare I must kiss it at once, I never saw such a pet.' John dribbled contentedly on Penny's silken shoulder, watching his mother being clasped to a large, luxuriantly moustached gentleman in mufti, while a short black-clad one looked on wistfully and his father gallantly made conversation with him and the little elderly lady. There were a good many people to get used to, but before long it would be time for his feed and they would all become unimportant.

Lilian's greeting to her mother was slightly awkward. So much had been said when they last met that could never be forgotten, so much had happened since. It was not in her nature to bear rancour, even if she had not been so happy. 'Mamma,' she said, 'how nice to see you,' brushing her mother's cheek lightly with her mouth. Once she would have been instantly enfolded in a clinging embrace and wept over. The case was altered now;

314

Florence withdrew after the first contact, and Lilian sensed that she was just a little frightened of this new, startling daughter.

She looked on at the babbling, kissing, exclaiming young people, wondering within herself. It had all turned out so strangely different from her imagining: Lilian healthy, even robust with a hint of stoutness to come, the despised gardener transformed to some sort of professional man who seemed to be respected by all, and was certainly quite as handsome as the late Prince Consort, with such beautiful side-whiskers. And the baby, who had not ruined his mother's health; and poor Augustus, looking pale and ineffectual beside Lilian's tall brown-complexioned husband.

'We're going to be married in spring,' Digby told them, 'and a good thing, judging by you two.'

'Such a delicious baby. I shall have four, or five, or possibly six,' Penny promised him.

The ceremony of Private Baptism of Children in Houses was carried out in the drawing-room, the marble bowl serving as a font. Digby and Sir Lewis stood as godfathers, Sir Lewis refusing to give the child his own Christian name as a second one because J. L. Ellershaw would sound daft in the Yorkshire team-order. Penny, the godmother, presented John with a silver goblet; she had brought the family christening robe he wore, a delicate confection of ivory silk and lace. When Augustus held up the Cross, the baby's blue eyes became fixed on it, and the intermittent whimpering he had kept up died away.

'He's going to be a good child,' Florence sobbed. 'I'm so glad, he's going to be good.' Lilian patted her hand. She was quite determined that her mother was not to be allowed to get ideas about turning John into a young Sir Galahad. Over the sherry and biscuits that followed they chatted amicably, while Jack and Sir Lewis talked over Yorkshire's prospects for the coming season, and Augustus showed Penny, who was nursing John quite like an experienced matron, the miniature he carried of a sweet-faced maiden with brown hair and a pensive look. She was, he revealed, a church worker in his new parish, charming, accomplished and devout, who had promised to be his bride when a suitable companion for her invalid mother could be found. Lilian knew that she herself had been no more to him than a dream.

'I say,' Penny exclaimed, when she had done admiring the

miniature, 'I knew there was something odd about all this. You two were married in a chapel, and now you've had John christened as an Anglican. Does that mean you'll have to be married all over again, to match him, if you know what I mean? Perhaps that funny cross-looking clergyman wasn't really in Orders, and you aren't married at all.'

'We'd better be,' Jack said grimly. 'I'm not parting with her now.'

Two months of John's life grew to two years, and three. A baby sister joined him, christened Mary after her grandmother but called May by everyone, as John pronounced it so. They were a startlingly handsome pair, with dark red hair and with their father's deep blue eyes. Both regarded the world as their kingdom. Only the firm rule of Millie and their mother prevented them from turning into young tyrants, especially as John handled a miniature cricket bat with expertise almost as soon as he could walk, and was quite aware of his precocious gift.

Lilian loved them only second to Jack, who would always be first in her heart. Yet it was a relief to be free of them for a few days, to be alone with Jack, in London for the first time since she could walk, exploring the shops and the sights. A heavy rain-shower drove her into an art gallery on one of these pleasant expeditions. She wandered idly from room to room, then stopped, transfixed, before a huge painting. A woman, perhaps a goddess, green-robed, the draperies falling away to reveal a naked shoulder and strong, even brawny arms. The figure was almost monstrous, badly painted. But the face above the thick column of neck was the face of Janey Morris, older and sadder, despair in her eyes beneath the rippling brown locks which should surely have been grey, to match the haggard face. Two torch-bearing acolytes looked skyward, one on each side of her, their faces echoes of hers but more youthful.

Within a blazon on the frame was the title *Astarte Syriaca*, the Syrian goddess of Love, and beneath it a fragment of verse.

> Torch-bearing, her sweet ministers compel
> All thrones of light beyond the sea and sky
> The witness of beauty's face to be.

316

The painting had been kindly loaned, said a card on the wall, by its owner, who had commissioned it from Mr Dante Gabriel Rossetti.

Beauty's face, thought Lilian; tragedy's face, more like. So this was Janey now, her life spoiled as Rossetti's was spoiled, and Lizzie's in her Highgate grave: all spent in futility. When the last of them had gone, only beauty on canvas would remain as memorial to them, remembrance sadly earned. Yet, her eyes drawn irresistibly to the mournful painted eyes of Astarte-Janey, Lilian was conscious of a faint, unreasonable regret that she herself would never make one of the gallery of loved ladies immortalised by their lovers, to be looked on with wonder for centuries to come, symbols of sweet decadence and high romance. She glanced down at her bosom, swelling matronly under frills, and her sensible little boots; touched her plump cheek and the saucy Dolly Varden hat tilted over her curls. Rossetti, wherever he might be, would never look twice at her now.

She shook herself out of the idle dream. If I'd stayed with them, she thought, I might have been famous by now – or stupid with drugs – or dead. Leoline's chilling description of Lizzie, crumbling bones among glorious hair, leapt into her mind. Suddenly the Astarte was frightening. She turned and hurried out of the gallery, startling an attendant with the haste of her passing. Outside the rain still fell, but the air was sweet to breathe, even flavoured as it was with London smoke and soot. She hailed a cab and gave the address of her hotel. It was urgent to see Jack and touch him, to assure herself that he, her love and her life, was real, that fantasy was past and done with.

And they would be together only another day. Tomorrow she would see his ship sail from Tilbury Docks, watching till it was lost to her sight. When spring came again to the prospering farm, ten thousand miles of ocean would lie between them. In a season to come, if his luck held and he was recalled to the team, she would go with him. But not this year: not until he had ventured first into the unknown far-off country, to play for England in the first Test Match against Australia.